#12 JUDGEMENT DAY

WARBOTS

G. HARRY STINE

I0627632

Imholt Press

Originally published by Pinnacle Books

Copyright © 1992 by G. Harry Stine

Currently Published by Imholt Press, LLC

ISBN: **978-1-951810-05-4**

For more information contact **tim@timothyimholt.com**

MOUNTAIN SKY ATTACK

"Grey Head, Harrier Leader here! Take cover! Take cover! You're under tacair assault! Pakistani *Vulturs* are laying ordnance on the main building!"

Colonel Curt Carson knew he should probably take cover if the Pak aerodynes were firing at him. He didn't know whether they had smart people-seeking killers or just dumb iron bombs designed to flatten the area. He didn't know and he didn't care. He wanted those Vulturs off his back.

"Harrier Leader, this is Grey Head! Intercept those damn *Vulturs* and give us some breathing-"

Another Pakistani bomb struck the barracks to the south of Curt's position. Casualty reports began to clog the circuits.

"Harrier Leader, this is Grey Head. Blow the shorts off the bastards!"

"Acknowledged, Grey Head. Harrier Leader, out!" The sky lit up with an explosion. The remains of one Pak aerodyne spiraled down onto the plains several kilometers away.

"Got him! Got him! Got the sonofabitch!" came the excited cry from the Harrier pilot.

TO:

Peter Manly, former captain, USAF

"When you lead in battle you are leading people, human beings. I have seen competent leaders who stood in front of a platoon and all they saw was a platoon. But great leaders stand in front of a platoon and see it as forty-four individuals, each of whom has aspirations, each of whom wants to live, each of whom wants to do good."

- General H. Norman Schwarzkopf
  Address to the Corps of Cades
  United States Military Academy, May 1991

"I have eaten your bread and salt,
I have drunk your water and wine,
The deaths ye died I have watched beside,
And the lives that ye led were mine.
Was there aught that I did not share
In vigil or toil or ease-
One joy or woe that I did not know.
Dear hearts across the seas?

I have written the tale of our life
For a sheltered people's mirth.
In jesting guise-but ye are wise,
And ye know what the jest is worth."

- Rudyard Kipling

Forward

In this final installment of Warbots, G. Harry Stine takes us further into the world of robotic warfare that G. Harry saw as the future, we see it as the present. The technology we use for this task improves every day. G. Harry reminds us that no good weapon or tactic development program goes unnoticed.

Some things seem to change at an ever-increasing pace, while other things stay the same. It has been a long road to get here. We have lost friends; we have followed careers. This is the end of the original series, and as such ties up a few loose ends and introduces new dangers.

Are warbots safe? Can they even be utilized or has the enemy found a way to render them useless?

Only in this final book can we see those answers, and potentially the future that G. Harry Stine had envisioned will become our future, sooner than any of us think.

Timothy Imholt PhD

Chapter One

"I'm losing it! I'm losing it! Why? This shouldn't happen! Goddammit, get the hell out of my way! I've gotta get back to the linkage van!"

Captain Dyani Motega, the chief scout and S-2 of the 3rd Robot Infantry (Special Combat) Regiment, had been monitoring the verbal channel of her recce platoon's remotely controlled bird robot operators. When she suddenly heard this abrupt break from normal birdbot operational protocol, she came immediately to the full alert.

Something was going badly wrong with Sergeant Bill Hull's mind-to-robot neuroelectronic linkage. Hull was controlling a huge bird warbot shaped like a western red-tailed hawk.

The field exercise against the 27th Robot Infantry (Special Combat) Regiment, the "Wolfhounds," had been non-lethal up to this point. Dyani was trying to coordinate the incoming data stream from her birdbot operators with the on-the-ground reports pouring in from Lieutenant Harlan Saunders's scouting platoon on the ground. The human "calibrated eyeball" with its "head-mounted computer" was often a better intelligence source than the visual sensors on the bird robots. But both were valuable on the twenty-first century battlefield. Intelligence and recce data were vitally important to winning any battle in any period of history. This was especially true at this point when the opponent was another Special Combat or "Sierra Charlie" regiment with the same equipment and training in a field exercise.

Dyani didn't panic. She took immediate action. She punched up Hull's bio readouts on her monitor screen. Thinking her message into the neuroelectronic tacomm communicator's circuitry through the skin-mounted sensor pads of her battle helmet, she thought-messaged, *Mustang Medic, this is Mustang Leader! Al, get on Bill Hull's case ASAP! He's got trouble! I don't know what it is!*

Sergeant Al Williams was a bio-tech with a P.N., one of the first Army bio-techs to re-learn how to treat human wounded on a battlefield. He was also was an expert in the biological and psychological problems of warbot brainies, who operated with their minds in neuroelectronic linkage with the computerized brains of war robots. So, he could see the danger signs portrayed on Hull's monitor. His thought message came back through the tacomm circuitry and sounded in Dyani's head, *Mustang Medic is on it, Mustang Leader! Dammit, another one! What the hell is going on?*

Hull was now in real trouble. His verbal thoughts were translated into audible sounds by the circuitry of the birdbot platoon's nanocomputer mounted behind the panel in the bot control van. "Dammit, I'm gonna crash! I'm gonna crash! I'm not going to hit the recovery net! I'm going into the side of the van!"

His final words were those of thousands of airplane pilots, soldiers, and others who'd tried their best to avoid disaster up to the last instant and failed: "*Oh, shit!*"

The birdbot linkage van where the warbot brainies of Brown's Black Hawks controlled their bird robots was the size of a sixteen-wheeler semi-truck trailer. Inside were the couches on which the birdbot controllers lay while they were in intimate linkage with their machines. It was camouflaged and stealthed. But it didn't have much armor.

When the heavy birdbot hit the side, the impact rocked the van. The warbot brainies inside were fortunate. They wouldn't be injured unless the birdbot penetrated and actually hit them. However, the birdbot didn't broach the thin vehicle skin. That would have caused major damage to the intricate twenty-first-century computer equipment inside. If that had happened, the mind-machine linkage electronics would have been damaged. Then the other six people lying on their linkage couches remotely controlling birdbots soaring over the battlefield on reconnaissance missions would be in trouble.

Instant disruption of the perceived or virtual reality of a person who was mentally "inside" a robot was traumatic. It meant the immediate shifting of reality. It was worse than coming out of a bad dream. And such rapid de-linkage usually threw the warbot brainy into shock. If the trauma was violent enough, it could cause catatonia. If the nanocomputers got the message in time, the rapid de-linkage programming would be activated to reduce the shock.

Sergeant Bill Hull was lucky. The linkage nanocomputer's artificial intelligence circuitry detected the inevitable break in the mind-warbot link a few microseconds before the birdbot hit the van. It didn't dump Hull's program. It activated the rapid de-linkage program. It was the only factor that saved Hull from being KIA - Killed in Action. And that was the worst physical harm that could come to a warbot brainy on the modern twenty-first-century battlefield.

This sort of threat separated the warbot brainies of the warbot-based U.S. Army from the Sierra Charlies of the 3rd Robot Infantry (Special Combat) Regiment, the Washington Greys. Warbot fighting doctrines had been unable to handle anything more than guard duties and the massive armored infantry assaults for which they'd been developed. So, the Greys had been the first unit to relearn the trade of the "poor bloody infantry." The Sierra Charlies of the "Third Herd" put their pink bodies back on the battlefield alongside voice-commanded warbots having lots of artificial intelligence.

But like any military system, the warbots were still valuable in such roles as recce and patrol. That was why the Washington Greys still had a birdbot recce platoon staffed by warbot brainies. Everyone else, including Captain Dyani Motega, was a twenty-first-century infantry soldier who also had warbot training. The Sierra Charlies were different from the johnnies, doughboys, GIs, and grunts only in the education and training needed to operate modern military technology.

Because the Sierra Charlies were all trained warbot brainies, they had far better mental stability than most people. They'd undergone the intensive mental training required to run warbots by direct neuroelectronic linkage. As a result, they were intensely sane. They knew who they were. They had overcome their psychological quirks and fears. Most warbot brainies were also mentally disciplined. But the Sierra Charlies put their bodies on the battlefield; the warbot brainies didn't. The Sierra Charlies were unique in the world.

Dyani messaged to her battalion commander, Major Kitsy Clinton. *Cougar Leader, this is Mustang Leader! I'm taking down birdbots! We're running into the unknown interference factor again. Hull just lost a birdbot, and I almost lost Hull in the process.* Dyani was a cool customer. She rarely lost her composure in a fight.

Major Kitsy Clinton was more mercurial. *Dammit, Mustang Leader, that will knock out our recce capability!*

Affirmative. I'll restore it with Saunders' Scouts.

Aren't they already out there?

Affirmative. But I'll reconfigure. Don't forget: If we're having linkage interference problems, so are the Wolfhounds. Their birdbots are likely to be in trouble too.

Kitsy didn't like that, but there was little she could do about it. They were in the midst of a field exercise against the Wolfhounds on the broad pampas of southern Arizona west of Fort Huachuca, the home base of the 17th Iron Fist Division. At West Point and during many campaigns since, Kitsy had learned the hard way that a commander has to be versatile in combat. Furthermore, said commander has to teach subordinates to do the same. Linear command structure never worked for the United States Army - or for any other army in the world when it came up against Americans, Brits, and other Europeans.

The U.S. Army had learned the truth of George S. Patton's admonition; "Never tell your soldiers *how* to do something. Tell them *what* to do, and you will be surprised by their ingenuity."

Kitsy, therefore, knew that Dyani would handle the matter. Captain Dyani Motega was a true Army mustang; she'd made it up from the NCO ranks the hard way. Furthermore, her Crow Indian ancestors had proudly served the United States Army since the Indian Wars on the Great Plains during the nineteenth century. Dyani was a professional; she was completely reliable.

So Kitsy flashed a tacomm message to her regimental commander. *Grey Head, this is Cougar Leader. We've lost our birdbot recce capability.*

Mustang Leader reports another outbreak of linkage interference. We're covering with the scouting platoon.

Colonel Curt Carson also reacted in a professional manner. He could do little else. In the first place, this wasn't a balls-out combat situation, only a war game. He also knew that if his Washington Greys were having birdbot linkage problems from an unknown source, so were those of Colonel Rick Salley's Wolfhounds. Curt had lost exercises to Rick Salley before; it cost him only a couple of drinks and a little pride. But losing people to the rapid de-linkage of KIA was a different matter.

Roger, Cougar Leader. Thanks for reporting the linkage interference. I'll pass the warning word. Do you want any help in the form of more warm bodies and calibrated eye-balls out on recce? About time I got Wade Hampton's service battalion personnel out of the rear area and gave them a little practice. Curt followed an old tradition of the Washington Greys: Everyone fights when necessary.

No, sir, but it might help if the AIRBATT would lay on a little more recce with the Harpies, Kitsy suggested. The Regiment's Air Battalion was made up of both Chippewa airliners and Harpy attack aerodynes. A Chippie was a huge aircraft, but a Harpy was smaller. Both types were larger targets than a birdbot disguised like an indigenous bird. However, Cal Worsham was an aggressive AIRBATT commander. When he couldn't "strafe the town and kill the people," he and his pilots were happy to go out and snoop just to be flying.

Goddammit, Clinton, we're trying! came the unmistakable tacomm voice of Lieutenant Colonel Cal Worsham. He didn't mince words. He overused them. He was about as foul-mouthed as any in the Greys. This served only to encourage the ladies of the Greys to shock the hell out of him on social occasions with their own knowledge of vulgar scatological terms. *Some of my Harpy drivers are having trouble with their direct linkage to the aerodynes. And they've got their pink bodies strapped into them! I've got about forty percent of my attack group on the ground with headaches or an inability to control their ships! This is the shits! When is the fucking Army going to give us some new equipment so we can quit patching this old crap?*

Worsham was also one of the prime hitchers, snivelers, and

moaners in the Third Herd. However, nearly every other Grey was running him a close second. The Washington Greys had suffered heavy losses in both personnel and warbots during Operation Bloodbath in Senegambia. Two years later, the regiment still wasn't up to strength.

Part of the problem was Playland on the Potomac and Fort Fumble - the Pentagon - across the river.

The resignation of the pacifist President had been forced by public attacks by both congressional hawks and doves. Vice President Henrietta Hamlin had moved into the Oval Office. This had eased the previous President's anti-military policies somewhat. She'd had to do something. The East World - India, Southeast Asia, and China backed covertly by the industrial might of Japan - was raising hell around the world. Hamlin had recognized this. She'd done her best during her months in office, but she couldn't get rid of the doves in the Executive Branch fast enough. She'd managed to turn on some of the supply spigots. But the production lines for many warbot types, aerodynes, and vehicles had been shut down by then, and the tooling sold off surplus at pennies per pound. It would take time for the next generation of warbots and equipment to go through RDT&E - Research, Development, Testing, and Evaluation.

Hamlin had lost her bid for election to the Presidency, but that was no great loss to the armed services. The new President, former General and Congressman Jacob O. Carlisle, tried to speed up the process. But as he pointed out in his usual blunt terms; "Just because a woman can have a baby in nine months doesn't mean that it's possible to get a baby in one month by putting nine women on the job." He caught hell from the women's lib groups for that statement but stood by it as an appropriate simile.

Curt broke in at this point. *Warhawk Leader, Grey Head! FIDO! TACAMO! Soldier, shut up and soldier!*

Worsham fired back in such a way that Curt could tell the man was still pissed in spite of the tendency of neuroelectronic tacomm to eliminate voice nuances. *Yes-sir, Colonel! I'm pedaling as hard as I can, Colonel!*

Easy, Cal! You're now a colonel too! Curt advised him. At least the make sheets had been good to the Greys.

Only a light one! Okay, we'll fly by the seat of our pants, Grey Head! But you'll get your air cover! Worsham was willing to have his pilots disconnect as much of their neuroelectronic equipment as possible and fly their unstable aerodynes with only the minimum of computer flight control. It would be good practice for the aerodyne drivers, anyway.

But the war game was going to worms even as Curt and his officers tried to salvage what was left.

Grey Head, Cougar Leader again! I'm grateful for the air support, but we've got a heap of trouble out here! Kitsy reported again. *The Panthers' Mary Anns just went Tango Uniform! So, to add to my woes, Hassan the Assassin just told Puma Leader to go piss up a rope because Lew ordered him not to conduct an assault without Mary Ann support, which Hassan just lost too. Dammit, why won't people follow orders all of a sudden?*

At that point, Curt realized that something was coming unbonded in a catastrophic manner. He didn't know what it was. It was unusual to have so many old, patched-up Mobile Assault Warbots - Mary Anns - going inop all at once with no pattern to the failures. And the birdbots were suddenly going ape shit too. In addition, he sensed that his Greys were somehow being affected by an unknown agency. They were irritated, short-tempered, and rebellious. *That* was indeed unusual because all of them, even the new ones, were serious pros.

In an attempt to find out what the problem was, he turned to his regimental technical sergeant. Edie Sampson was in the OCV with him, so he didn't use NE tacomm but asked her directly, "Sergeant, can you get a make on *anything* that might be interfering with our warbot comm links? Any ECM?"

Edie looked harried and replied in an uncharacteristic sharp voice, "Goddammit, Colonel, I don't see a god-damned glitch anywhere in the spectrum that could be interfering with our command and control links. Nothing! It shouldn't be happening! But it is! And dammit, it irritates the shit out of me that I can't find it!"

Yes, something was. wrong. Edie Sampson had a red-head's temper. She normally kept it well under control. Curt knew that it was just about to break through Edie's professional facade. He hadn't seen her this close to toggling over except in extremely intensive and stressful combat situations where the Greys were losing badly.

"Patch me in to Colonel Salley!" Curt snapped. It was time to bring this sheep screw to a roaring halt before something worse went wrong.

"Yessir! Channel open!"

"Rick? Curt!"

"What the hell's the matter with your forces, Curt?" came the reply from Colonel Frederick H. Salley, the Wolfhounds' CO.

"Same thing that's probably wrong with yours!"

"Oh. You noticed."

"No, I guessed," Curt admitted. "Our NE links started going Tango Uniform. My chief techie couldn't find any ECM. So, I figured something had happened that would affect both of us."

"Strange. I was about to call you about this very problem."

"Rick, I may have lost some of my birdbot people to spasm mode. My Sierra Charlies are acting strangely. If your troops are experiencing similar problems, I recommend we knock off this sheep screw right now before someone gets hurt real bad," Curt told him bluntly. He knew Salley well. And they weren't enemies, just opponents.

"Agreed! No winner. No loser. Call it a draw. Except we *were* winning, after all."

"Oh, hell, I'll go you two falls out of three in the gym for the honor of prevailing in this furball!" Curt told him testily.

Salley replied cautiously using formal protocol. "Uh, Colonel, may I point out that you are exhibiting some of the irritability that my Wolfhounds are struggling with at the moment?"

"Sorry, Rick! I didn't realize it was getting to me too. Apologies."

"Accepted. We stand down now?"

"Roger that!"

"But I'm damned if I'm just going to sit here wondering what the fuck happened to us and the warbots," Salley came back, his voice suddenly edgy. "If someone is trying to screw the Robot Infantry of the United States Army, I think we'd better report this and start running some real serious diagnostics! Damned if I want to put the Wolfhounds back in the field under these conditions! Even with jelly rounds chambered!"

"Colonel, whatever the irritation factor is, it looks like it's got you too!" Curt observed.

"If that's the case, let's get the hell home and start looking for the cause! Got any ideas?"

Curt thought about this for a moment. "Yeah, Rick, I do. I know just who to call, and we'll do it together when we get back to Fort Huachuca!"

Chapter Two

"You think *you've* got problems?"

The response from Dr. Willa Lovell at McCarthy Proving Ground told Curt that he'd somehow stepped in it.

The retired colonel who was one of the Army's top warbot scientists looked drawn and tired. However, her holographic image in the tank didn't hide the fact that she was an extremely attractive woman. Ever since the Zahedan hostage operation more than twelve years ago, she'd looked to Curt Carson for a special kind of relationship. Totally devoted to her professional work, she found in Curt a way she could relax and let free the scared little girl who was inside her. She had all her neurons lined up straight. As a neuroelectronics expert, that was a necessity, just as it was with a warbot brainy.

Willa Lovell could have had her star. But she'd opted for twenty-and-out. Being a general officer would have tied her to a desk in administrative work. She was a scientist, a researcher, and totally devoted to her work in military neuroelectronics. Dr. Willa Lovell was known and respected around the world for her work. So she'd retired from her military career rather than give up her professional work.

Of course, she'd immediately substituted the civil service rank of GS-14 for her O-6 military pay grade...with more than forty percent more money. As a retired officer, she still enjoyed numerous military perks. She now had a light colonel working for *her* to handle the administrative side, and she kept right on doing the same job she'd done as an officer.

But it was obvious to Curt that she wasn't enjoying that job at the moment. So, he backed off. "Willa," he said gently to her, no longer using her military title and trying to be pleasant in spite of feeling tired and irritable himself, "we do have problems. Serious ones. I reported them to General Hettrick. She's taking it up the line to Fort Fumble. But she also approved my request to talk with you. You're the neuroelectronic robot expert. If anyone has the answers to our problems, it's you. If you don't, it's Owen Pendleton or one of your people at McCarthy. We believe we have some serious problems that you would want to know about. Want a sit-rep on our heartburn here?"

"I told you: You think *you've* got problems? And speak English, please! I hear too much Army slang and not enough scientific terminology around here as it is," Lovell fired back sharply. Then she ran her long hand through her heavy auburn hair and tried to bring herself under control. She was partly successful. "Sorry, Curt. I'm not feeling up to par this morning. And as for your problems, you're not alone. Or the first. Is this a secure line?"

"If it wasn't, would I be talking to you about matters that threaten to reduce the effectiveness of military equipment and personnel? Or maybe eliminate them? Or kill the people? I hope to God you'll listen, Willa! Or has being a civilian changed you that much?" Curt felt like he'd gone four nights with very little sleep. He was becoming edgy and sharp.

Lovell sighed. "I should know better. I've unloaded my problems on you a hundred times in the past, and you've always listened. I guess it's my turn to listen. I need more data about this phenomenon in any event. You may supply the missing point on the curve."

"Well, if it's of any help to you, nothing here seems to make sense! We can find nothing wrong! Nothing! Yet things are going toes-up right and left!" Curt bitched.

Lovell sighed again. She was a few years older than Curt. And for the first time since Curt knew her, she looked it. "Damned right nothing makes sense!" she shot back in a manner totally uncharacteristic of her image as a dispassionate scientist - which Curt knew she wasn't in spite of the facade. "If it will make you feel any better, here at McCarthy you think the answers exist, but everything is coming unbonded! I've got a hundred people and a hundred comm messages screaming for my attention. I don't have many answers, Curt. I accepted your call because of who you are and what you are to me. And because you've never lied to me. When you've got problems with your warbots in the Washington Greys, I'd damned well better listen! I need the data anyway. So, what's bothering the Iron Fist at Huachuca?"

"Sounds like more of the same sheep screw that's going on at Hood. And in your shop. Our warbots are going inop. Especially the birdbots that are operated in full NE linkage. Some of our birdbot operators have lost linkage control and nearly gone KIA. Our medics and the rapid de-linkage programs saved our warbot brainies. But our voice-commanded Mary Anns are acting up too. They were going irrational. We had to shut them down and tow them back from a field exercise. Now the Greys are starting to act like they've undergone serious personality changes. Same for Rick Salley's Wolfhounds and Maxie Cashier's Cottonbalers." Curt paused, having recited the litany of troubles faced by the regiments of the 17th Iron Fist Division.

The robotics expert thought about this for a moment, then asked, "Did Sergeant Sampson make a spectrum sweep for interference with the warbot linkage channels?" Lovell also knew the Number One techie of the Greys very well. She respected Edie's hands-on expertise and thoroughness; they'd been held hostage together in Zahedan those many years ago.

"Affirmative!"

"I should have known better than to waste time asking. What did she find?"

"Nothing."

"*Nothing?* What did she sweep?"

"The usual. Ten kilohertz up through the low infrared."

"How about the unusual?" Lovell wanted to know.

"The unusual? What do you mean?"

"Lasers. Infrared to ultraviolet."

"I don't think so. Probably not. This doesn't act like pinpointed laser stuff. It's epidemic. Broadcast. It hit the Greys and the Wolfhounds both. Our units were-scattered over a hundred square kilometers of Sonoran Desert," Curt explained. "And how would that sort of thing cause apparent personality changes in my personnel?"

"One question at a time. Each earth-shaking threat to the freedom of the Free World taken only in order as they come," Willa said wearily. "I don't know how. Or even if it's connected. I'm searching for answers myself. But if I don't ask questions, I don't get answers. So I'm going to ask you some questions."

"Okay. I understand. 'There are no dumb questions, only dumb answers.' I'll try not to give you dumb answers to anything you ask me, Willa," Curt promised.

"Any answer could turn out to be not-dumb in this situation. I'm operating right now with the philosophy of 'When in ignorance, try anything and become less ignorant,'" Willa admitted. It was apparent that she really didn't like to operate this way. She was methodical. Come up with an observation. Create a hypothesis. Design an experiment to test the hypothesis. Determine if the hypothesis was real by learning if it predicted something unanticipated. Check to make sure that it didn't violate any existing hard data. And so forth through the rigorous protocol of the Scientific Method. "I don't know what relationship exists between warbots going inop, warbot operators losing linkage control, and people suddenly acting strangely." She shrugged. "Maybe no relationship at all. Maybe different phenomena involved."

"Whatever it is, it looks like it got you too," Curt observed.

"It does?"

"Yes. I've never seen you so upset about what seems to be a scientific puzzle," Curt confided in her, hopeful that he wouldn't trigger some hostility lying just below the surface as he'd done with some of his Washington Greys.

He didn't. Lovell was a pro in her own field. "Okay, let's start with the obvious subjects. I can get better data from you right now than from your warbots. Sometimes a warbot's self-diagnostics get screwed up. But people have the same problem too. So, we start at

Square One. How do you feel, Curt?"

"Like I'd been in extended combat. Like I hadn't slept for a week. Like I'd been awakened every fifteen minutes the night before a fight by some dumb-john second lieutenant who's going to suddenly be transferred elsewhere in the morning. Hungry when I shouldn't be. Sleepy when I shouldn't be. All out of synch with everything. Oh, hell, I guess I'm generally pissed off at the world. Ruth Gydesen still has some of her sense of humor left. She told me I was probably suffering from optorectalitis."

"I'm too busy for jokes, Curt! But I'm curious. What is that?"

"Ruth claims my optic nerve got connected to my anal sphincter nerve. Gives me a shitty outlook on life!"

Willa laughed. It gave Curt a good feeling to have made her laugh a little. It might restore a little of her perspective on the problem. Will Lovell was an intense, intellectual person except when she chose to relax with Curt. This was not the time for that, of course. But Curt felt he had to relieve a little of the tension Willa was obviously laboring under. "Thank you, Curt. I'll use that one on some of my medical types."

Curt figured he'd try to get her to open up a little too. From the way she was acting, she was probably suffering from the same symptoms he was. "So how do you feel, Willa?"

Willa Lovell thought about that for a moment because she hadn't bothered to think about herself lately. The problems of others had occupied her attention. "Uh, like I'd just returned from a biotechnology conference in Brunei. Jet-lagged out. Hungry when I shouldn't be hungry. Wanting to sleep when I should be at work. Come to think of it, my symptoms are very much like those of circadian asynchronization."

"I like it when you use those big scientific words. And you were complaining about my Army slang!"

Her eyes suddenly ceased being dark holes in her beautiful face. They flashed. "Curt, *that's* it! Something might be interfering with our biological clocks!" Willa Lovell acted like she'd just discovered the Law of Gravity. She came alert, bright and insightful again. The lines of weariness and fatigue disappeared from her face.

"Something? What the hell could...?"

"Something. I don't know yet. But I think we can find out. And easily too." Willa was now animated and excited.

Curt found himself excited too. Over his bone-weariness and out-of-sorts outlook, he suddenly felt the endocrine rush that occurred after intensive combat. Why the hell was he experiencing that now he wondered. He knew a lot more about that now than he had when he'd first gotten shot at, survived, and wanted to screw any woman he could find. He knew why it happened.

Willa's own research into the physiological and psychological reactions of combat soldiers had clearly identified what went on when a human being fought. The "flee or fight" syndrome exhibited by all animals triggered a massive endocrine "storm" in the fighter.

Everyone who has ever been in a fight or seen animals threatened knows the consequences of this. But few understand what happens.

Eons of evolution have produced survivors in whom a physical threat causes a massive response from the pineal gland at the base of the brain. This gland dumps endocrine chemical triggers into the body. These in turn cause massive releases of adrenaline from the adrenal glands over the kidneys. Adrenaline acts like a turbo. It also causes some animals (and people) to urinate and defecate in a spasm, ridding the body of excess waste and weight and allowing the kidneys and bowels to accommodate the excessive amount of waste products produced quickly by a "turbocharged" system.

The massive endocrine "storm" created by the "flee or fight" reaction also triggers other endorphins and endocrines like testosterone and estrogen. Combat stress and hyperactivity stress seem no different to the body than sexual stress.

One of the pleasant features of the American mixed-gender military and naval forces in the twenty-first century was the fact that people of both sexes had the ability to relieve this sexual stress in a natural way. It was part of the reason for the existence of the infamous

Army Regulation 601-10, "Rule Ten," prohibiting physical contact between personnel of opposite sex while on duty. And the reason why wise commanders lifted Rule Ten as often as possible. The problems with unwanted pregnancy encountered by mixed military and naval personnel in the early mixed forces of the twentieth century were largely overcome by the advanced biotechnology of the twenty-first. So, there was no human reason to prevent people from doing what they were going to do anyway since they were together in the first place.

The troops weren't about to screw up a good deal like that. And those who did were promptly disciplined in both official and unofficial ways. Furthermore, a man does not easily rape a woman who is skilled in personal combat without suffering severe physical disablement. The women weren't quite so forceful; they used skill instead of brawn; In any case, a disciplined military force composed of warriors operates in all matters with a great deal of mutual consent.

Some civilian prudes often complained about the military services encouraging unabashed orgies at taxpayer expense. But they couldn't complain about the fact that those same military and naval people not only performed better than any in history but had a much lower birth rate per thousand people than the general population.

Women had served aboard ships of the British Royal Navy until 1846. And American military history contains many incidents of women serving alongside men in battle. Troops from India, Kurdistan, and other countries had boasted women combat soldiers for centuries. To American women, it was the ultimate expression of freedom and equality.

With candor, Curt asked, "Then why, my dear, do I have the overpowering urge to climb into this holo tank with you right now?"

Willa looked at him strangely. "I don't know. But the feeling is very, very mutual, Curt. Another datum point. Sorry, but I'm supposed to be a scientist!" She took a deep breath and then went on forcefully. "Colonel, I need solid data from your people as quickly as I can get it! Get Edie Sampson in your office ASAP! And Major Gydesen, your medical officer. I'll hold here until you do!"

"That won't take long, Willa," he told her as he passed his hand over the intercom switches on his terminal desk.

Sergeant Major Edwina A. Sampson was right across the hall in her cubicle and was there practically at once. While the two ladies exchanged the pleasantries of friends - Willa Lovell never paid much attention to rank when she was on active duty, although she tended to mix more with general officers than NCOs - Major Ruth Gydesen showed up from the sick bay in a nearby building.

"First of all, Major," Willa told the chief biotech of the Greys, "because of the symptoms exhibited by most of your people, do you think it would be a good idea to run some biochemical workups on a random sampling of about twenty of the Greys? Look for the sort of imbalances you'd expect to see as a result of circadian asynchronization?"

"I thought that's what it felt like to me," Doctor Ruth admitted. "Yes, Colonel, right away. Results in about four hours, ma'am."

Willa touched her collar tabs. "No more silver eagles, Major. Let's keep this on a professional basis."

"Yes, Doctor. Will do. I think your suggestion is a good idea," Ruth replied in a professional tone. "Since we're in Level Three right now, I'm going to put the worst cases in quarters. No work. See if they can somehow get resynched."

"I'd appreciate knowing what you find out."

"Of course."

"Edie, the colonel tells me you swept the EM spectrum down to about ten kilohertz," Willa went on, addressing the chief techie NCO of the Washington Greys.

"Yes, ma'am. I did. Nothing there but the usual. Nothing I could identify as any sort of interference signal with warbot channels," Edie snapped back with confidence.

"Can you have a look between five and fifteen hertz?"

That stopped Edie Sampson. "Did I hear you right, Doctor? *Five to fifteen?*"

"You heard me right."

Edie hesitated for a moment. "Hell, I've got nothing that will work that low. But I guess I could cobble-up something by using some frequency dividers and…Uh, yes, ma'am, I can. But what the hell do I look for?"

"I don't know. We're looking too."

"I'll do it right away, ma'am!"

"Good! Colonel, when you get your data, I would like to have you, Major Gydesen, Sergeant Sampson, and whoever else you think might provide valuable data to grab an aircraft and get over here to McCarthy," Willa went on. "I'm bringing in some of the people from Fort Hood too. We need to get our heads together on this."

Curt nodded. "I'd like to request that Owen Pendleton be in on this!"

Pendleton was the best artificial intelligence mentor and warbot programmer Curt had ever known. The man was a pure techie. Curt had once arranged for Pendleton to achieve a dream: serving in the Army as a warbot researcher.

"You mean Colonel Pendleton?" Willa asked with a smile.

Curt's eyebrows went up. "Well! I guess you people climb the greasy pole of promotion a little faster in the science specialty branches!"

"When you're a certified genius, you do," Willa admitted.

"Doctor, I'm curious. Where the hell did this idea of mucking around in the basement with five to fifteen hertz come from?" Edie asked.

"From the best neuroelectronics expert to join us here in quite some time. You and the colonel both know her: Doctor Rosha Taisha."

Chapter Three

"I've never been given a direct order that's so difficult to obey," Captain Dyani Motega said privately to Curt in a voice that could be heard only by him over the roar of the Chippewa aerodyne knifing through the sky toward Las Vegas and McCarthy Proving Ground.

"Rosha Taisha isn't my most favorite person either, Captain," he admitted to her. They were on duty. They treated one another with protocol only slightly less structured than when they were off duty together. The two of them had learned that in a close personal relationship formal courtesy between them was far more important than for-mal military courtesy. This kept them from taking one another for granted. "It surprised the hell out of me that she's on Doctor Lovell's staff. But you're the only officer in the Greys who's in charge of actual NE linkage warbots and warbot brainies."

Dyani didn't sigh, but Curt could tell from the slight change in her otherwise passive expression that she accepted that rationale even though she didn't like it. "You're right. I couldn't just tell Dale to go all by himself. Colonel, when one is an NCO, it's sometimes difficult to realize that an officer never asks subordinates to do anything the officer wouldn't do." Dyani was a "mustang"; she'd come up through the ranks from an NCO because of a field commission in Iraq.

"And it doesn't get any better or easier as we climb the greasy pole of promotion, Captain," Curt reminded her, then added, "Besides, Taisha specifically requested that you come along with us. And Hettrick approved."

"Why? I had to destroy Taisha once because she tried to destroy me. So why does she specifically want to see me?" Dyani shook her head slowly in confusion.

"I don't know. I wasn't told. As for Taisha's habit of destroying people by trying to use neuroelectronics to control them, I've got a little bit of seniority over you in this matter, Captain," Curt told her bluntly. "Taisha tried to destroy me in Zahedan twelve years ago."

"The woman is evil personified. I've been inside her mind. I know," Dyani said firmly. The Eurasian neuroelectronics expert had once tried to brainwash Curt during the hostage rescue screwup in eastern Iran. Then she'd shown up with the religious cult in Nevada, where she'd tried the same process on Dyani, who had ambushed Taisha during a mental probe. Dyani had better control over her mind and had merely unleashed the demons inside Taisha's head.

"People can change," Curt reminded her.

"Not really. Not deep inside their spirit."

"Oh? Haven't I changed since we first met?"

Dyani hesitated, then finally replied, "With some help from me."

"And I thank you for that. But how about you? Captain, you've changed too. You're not the nineteen-year-old recruit I first met either."

"That's because of you."

"Not entirely. Give some credit to about seven really deadly campaigns where you got shot at and sometimes hit. And to our colleagues in the Washington Greys. I can claim only a small part of the credit. After some twenty years in this man's Army, I've discovered we change because of both internal and external stimuli. That's growth. You've grown. You're far more formidable now. Even more than you were at Battle Mountain. So, what are you worried about? You once proved you could withstand the worst that Taisha could do to you. And you beat her on her home court." Curt had decided to try to get right to the center of Dyani's concern.

"No one could beat down the devils I saw in her mind. They were her own. They went long and deep. They controlled her life." She waved her hands before her in an action of frustration. "They were part of her spirit. I can't explain it. I only *know* it."

"Let's give her the benefit of the doubt. And keep our powder dry while doing so. After all, you scrambled her neurons at Battle Mountain. The government sent her to the Army's neuroelectronics reprogramming hospital at Fort Benning," Curt explained. "The biotechnicians there know how to handle recruits who dive into their belly buttons in early warbot training because they can't face who they really are. They're also specialists in handling warbot brainies who've gone KIA. Even the Mayo and Menninger clinics send them no-hope civilian patients whose brains have been scrambled by drugs or neuroelectronic misuse."

"We'll find out soon enough," Dyani remarked, looking at her watch. "Colonel, I just want you to know that I'm likely to be a bit bitchy with her. I can't help it. Once she tried to hurt me. I had to do things to her I didn't want to because I don't like messing with other people's spirits. I'm not afraid of her; I could kill her with no regrets if I had to. However, I shall try to behave like a lady and an officer. There must be a reason for General Hettrick to issue a direct order to me," Dyani concluded, a bit mystified by all of this.

"Captain, something in the equation has changed and we don't know about it yet," Curt advised her. "According to Doctor Lovell, Taisha is playing a critical role in this present sheep screw. How or why, I don't know. Nor do I understand why Taisha is suddenly the golden girl of American warbotry. I'm a bit defensive about this meeting myself. I've tangled with her twice as a deadly enemy. But maybe third time's a charm or something. Maybe what you did to her allowed the head-handlers at Benning to put her neurons back together in a row for a change."

Dyani shrugged, then gave a little smile. "At least I won't be sitting in quarters back at Huachuca worrying about what Taisha might do to you this time."

"I took care of myself before. I knew a whole hell of a lot less about myself then. You needn't worry. I'm a big boy now." Curt tried to inject a little humor into a very intense situation. He understood Dyani's mixed feelings. She was worried about herself and about him. Dr. Rosha Taisha had been a formidable enemy in the past. Now the Eurasian scientist appeared to be wearing a white hat.

Things had obviously changed.

Curt wasn't precisely certain what had happened when Dyani had tangled with Taisha. Dyani had tried to explain it to him. Her father had passed along to her the generations of Crow Indian thinking processes that were in some ways alien to Curt's European heritage. He thought he understood how she'd conquered the twisted mind of Rosha Taisha. He wouldn't have been able to comprehend it if Dyani hadn't taught him a lot about her heritage. This had come about during their personal problem-solving sessions "getting the priorities straight," as Dyani put it.

"Yes, Colonel, and I am reminded of that fact quite often. For which I am also pleased and delighted, sir!" She did lighten up a bit, but she maintained her rigid discipline. Both of them were on duty and on official business. When the fetters of duty and discipline came off, Dyani was almost another person. At the moment inside the Chippie, she was an officer, a warrior, and a scout who was "the truth-bearer of the tribe."

Major Ruth Gydesen slipped into the net-covered seat next to Curt. "Just wanted to check. You look a lot better this morning, Colonel. Obviously, you took the sleeping pill I sent over to your quarters."

Curt shook his head. "No, Major, I didn't need it."

"Dammit, I wish I could chew out my regimental commander for failing to follow a medical directive! Colonel circadian asynchronization isn't something to ignore, especially when it appears to be chronic," the regimental medical officer pointed out. She guessed why Curt hadn't followed her orders, but she asked Dyani anyway, "How about you, Captain?"

"I didn't need it, Major."

"I told you to take it."

"I don't like to take chemicals to help me," the Crow Indian woman said, repeating what she'd told Gydesen many times. "I took care of myself. But I had some help."

Gydesen shook her head sadly. "Dammit, you I can chew out. But I won't. Sometimes. your medicine is more powerful than mine.

31

Maybe I ought to get you to introduce me to one of your medicine men, Dyani. I might learn something."

"I don't know any Crow medicine men, Major. I've never been on the reservation. I was born at Fort Riley. I grew up as an Army brat all over the world. What I know I learned from my father."

"Then maybe I should talk to him."

"He's not a medicine man. He's a retired captain, a former warbot brainy in the Greys," Dyani explained.

"I know. I've read your One-Oh-One," Gydesen admitted. "Well, what can I say? You've both got your heads up and locked. A favor, however: Just let me know when you decide to make it legal, will you?"

"It already is," Dyani said firmly.

This surprised Curt. The two of them had agreed they wouldn't get married until both of them were no longer in duty assignments Where they might be killed in combat. But, as everyone in the Washington Greys knew, that would be only a formality. And the Greys respected it as they did all the other close relationships formed by other personnel of the Washington Greys. Life could be short in a Sierra Charlie outfit. Combat could ruin the best of plans. Rule Ten was a blessing often cursed. But both warbot brainies and Sierra Charlies didn't bitch too hard about Rule Ten. They could and did live with it. The Army easily could think up some other way to draw a line in the sand between love and war.

The neuroelectronic voice of Lieutenant Nancy Roberts, the pilot, sounded throughout the cargo bay over the noise of the Chippie. "Hear me, pax! Return to your waffle-makers. Snap your straps and assume the landing position! We're on approach to Lost Wages and Warbot Paradise!" Nancy was feeling good today. The threat of disruption of the neuroelectronic linkage between her and the Chippie had forced her to fly the huge aerodyne manually, letting the flight control computer system maintain only the stability of the ship. She liked that. Most of the pilots in Worsham's Warhawks did. It reminded them of the "olden days" when pilots actually flew aircraft. It also took them back to their early flying careers where they actually controlled the whole airplane with no computers in the loop at all. As any non-NE pilot knows, that sort of direct control contributes greatly to the inexplicable high experienced by pilots.

"Ah, yes, these damned webbed seats! They do indeed imprint one's buttocks like a waffle iron!" Ruth remarked. "But at least they don't restrict circulation! See you on the ground!"

The "ground" was Indian Springs Army Aviation Field. Except for different buildings and the surrounding mountains, it looked just like Libby AAF at Fort Huachuca.

"One of the comforting factors of military life," Captain Dale Brown commented as they debouched from the Chippie, "is the world of Surprise, Surprise. Military people love to spring surprises on each other. But there's never any surprise in the facilities. They're the same everywhere."

Captain Helen Devlin looked around in distaste. "Yeah, century-old buildings held together with composite fibers and bonding agents."

"We've seen worse," Ruth Gydesen reminded her.

"Like Fort Huachuca the day we rolled in and reactivated it," Major Russ Frazier remarked, looking around. "But it should be some comfort to know that some things never change. Like this place. It looks the same today as it did ten years ago."

"Probably just like it looked a hundred years ago," Major Ed Otis added.

Three Army sedans moved across the ramp toward them. The lead car stopped in front of the Chippie and two people got out.

Curt knew them both.

Colonel Owen Pendleton had come a long way since he'd been one of the hostages rescued by Curt and the Greys from the eastern Iranian town of Zahedan years ago. No longer the quiet, embarrassed techie nerd who had longed for a military career working with warbots, Pendleton had matured into a man who had achieved his dream and was now in charge of Warbotics

Development at the U.S. Army's Number One warbot development and testing center. Pendleton had come up fast among the ranks of the high-tech military scientists, much faster than Curt. But Pendleton was still junior to Curt, although both wore silver eagles. Pendleton not only knew it but knew who had championed him after Zahedan. So, he threw the first salute to Curt.

"Welcome to McCarthy Proving Ground! Good to see you, Curt!" Pendleton remarked informally. Although he'd observed military protocol with the salute, he was less formal with an old friend. Formality didn't cut much ice in the technical side of the Army, where people weren't shot at and therefore operated with less military discipline.

Curt returned the salute and reached out his hand. As Pendleton took it in a firm grip, Curt replied, "Happy to be here, but not happy about the circumstances, Owen! I hope you've got some answers for us!"

"We think we do." Dr. Willa Lovell stepped up and didn't salute. She didn't have to. She'd never saluted Curt even when she wore silver eagles. Willa Lovell shared a lot with Curt. In fact, she shared something with Curt and Edie Sampson that Pendleton also rated: All four of them had been Zahedan hostages. She took Curt's hand in both of hers. "We'll find out when we begin to compare notes and data! I'm glad you could come and bring your warbot tech people. Hello, Edie!" She turned and greeted Sergeant Major Edwina Sampson with only a little less warmth.

Greetings were exchanged by all other six Greys, all of whom knew Lovell and Pendleton. The Army is really a small and select corps of people in spite of the hundreds of thousands of personnel in service. Over the years, everyone develops deep friendships with others with whom they've been shot at and survived. Because of this, military people are really very sentimental at their cores. It's only partly reflected in military protocol and ceremonies.

Curt was curious, so he asked Pendleton, "Where is Doctor Taisha?"

"Back at the lab," Pendleton explained. "For two reasons. First, we're short of vehicles, just like you are."

"Damned penny-pinching Congress!" Willa Lovell erupted. "A world always on the edge of war, and they think we can beat our swords into plowshares." The former colonel could speak that way now since she no longer held her commission. Curt also sensed that she was considerably more political now than she had been in the past. Maybe that was part of shucking the uniform. He'd seen that in the case of former General Jacob O. Carlisle, who had become so political that he now sat in the Oval Office. Curt noticed, however, that Lovell didn't criticize the President; among the military, Carlisle was not only the Commander in Chief, he was one of them.

Pendleton ignored Lovell's remark and went on. "So, it will be a little cozy riding to the lab, but we'll get there in time for a short briefing before lunch."

"What's the second reason why Doctor Taisha isn't here?" Curt asked.

Lovell looked directly at him and told him, "She stumbled onto something about two hours ago and wanted to run it down."

Scientists were often like that. Even Willa Lovell sometimes seemed distracted when she was with Curt in more personal circumstances. Curt always figured that it was "work in progress upstairs." Even his own technical people exhibited this total distraction when working on a problem with the bots. When it was a problem that required a creative approach, this was even more intense to the point of compulsion. But Curt went on to ask anyway, "Does she have some new insight on this warbot linkage problem?"

Willa Lovell nodded. "I can't explain it. So, I'll let her do that. With her Chinese background, she looks at things somewhat differently than the rest of us. Remember that wadi mine you discovered in Yemen?"

"The one that whanged Bob Vickers?"

"Yes. And by the way, your loss was my gain," Lovell admitted. "His medical discharge allowed me to get him, and he's one of the best civilian warbot development techs we've got."

"What's the wadi mine got to do with this, Doctor?" Edie Sampson wanted to know. The Greys had encountered this East World booby trap in Yemen. It had a mystifying triggering and fusing mechanism. Edie had originally identified it as being a consequence of Chinese acupuncture technology combined with the new physics of scalar fields. But she didn't know much more about it. The wadi mine's fuse was triggered when it detected the nearby presence of the scalar electric field around a human being.

"Remember what you figured out about the fuse, Edie?"

"Yeah, but I still don't understand it."

"Neither do we, but Rosha thinks she's made a breakthrough because of your discovery in Yemen," Lovell explained. "I'll let her bring you all up to the same level of ignorance and confusion that Owen and I enjoy at the moment. But suffice to say, she thinks the East Worlders have expanded that technology so that they can disrupt the linkage between warbot brainies and their warbots. Furthermore, like their ability to raise hell with our biological clocks, they're apparently doing this from halfway around the world!"

Chapter Four

"Curt Carson, so nice to see you again! And Dyani Motega! And Edie Sampson!"

Dr. Rosha Taisha was a shock to Curt. He'd steeled himself to expect a radical change in the former renegade neuroelectronics scientist, but nothing like that which confronted him in the laboratory at McCarthy Proving Ground.

When Curt had first met Taisha in Iran long years ago, she'd been an exotic young woman. He'd rated her a twelve on a scale of ten. She'd been a real "crasher" who would have caused him to total a car if he'd seen her while driving down the street. When he'd encountered her again at Battle Mountain, she'd become a withered crone because of the stress of the intervening years. Taisha had always had a dangerous look in her large almond-shaped eyes, a look that reminded Curt of a leopard.

Now she was again a beautiful woman, older but nonetheless very attractive. The lines were gone from her Eurasian features. She no longer showed inner tension with a tight-lipped look.

She'd shaved her head like a warbot brainy.

The predatory look was gone from her eyes. It had been replaced by an inquisitive, questioning gaze.

Curt had seen that sort of a detached expression before in the eyes of Doctor Willa Lovell, the penultimate researcher, when some scientific question or problem was occupying her mind.

Thus, when Taisha extended her small hand to Curt, he not only took it but kissed it in the European fashion. "I see changes, Doctor. And they seem to be for the good."

"I think so," she replied, and turned to Dyani. She extended her hand. With a smile, she remarked, "And I want to thank you, Dyani."

If Dyani was caught off guard, she didn't show it. Instead, she took Taisha's hand. "Why?" Dyani's tone of voice told Curt she was still wary of this woman.

"You brought me face to face with my devils," Taisha told her bluntly. "You forced me to deal with them. I feel not only close to you but a strange bond with you. We know each other. We've been in each other's minds. But I still don't understand you."

This was a remarkably candid statement on Taisha's part. Usually, people don't want to discuss such deeply personal matters, much less admit them.

"Few people do," was Dyani's brief reply.

Taisha turned to Edie Sampson, who'd really been thrown off balance by the change. "And Sergeant Edie Sampson, the first woman warrior I ever met! And one who could have killed me instantly with a knife at my throat."

"But I didn't. That's always a warrior's choice," Edie reminded her, and said no more. She decided she'd wait and see if this apparent change in Taisha was real.

Curt introduced the rest of the contingent from the Washington Greys that had accompanied him. Then Taisha's demeanor changed. She remained pleasant but became all intellect and business.

Willa Lovell noticed this and said, "You found something this morning, Rosha?"

Taisha nodded and her eyes flashed with excitement. But Curt saw that it was intellectual excitement, not physical. "Yes! But if it's to make sense to these people from the Washington Greys, we'd better proceed with the initial in-brief as planned."

Curt was surprised at Taisha's use of current governmental slang. Maybe she was becoming integrated with serious, accepted neuroelectronics research.

Pendleton motioned for everyone to take a seat in a part of the lab that had been set up as a briefing and discussion center. "Okay, everyone take your seats for the dog and pony show," Pendleton said lightly as he stepped up to the podium. Curt was always mystified by the sea change that Pendleton had undergone since they'd first met. Once he was a tongue-tied, stammering, introverted techie nerd whose only interest and concern were mentoring artificial intelligence equipment. Owen Pendleton had metamorphosed since being commissioned in the Army. This was something he'd aspired to but hadn't been able to achieve until Curt and Hettrick had interceded after Zahedan. He was assigned to work at what he dearly loved and wanted to do: warbot design and mentoring.

Once everyone was seated, Pendleton began with confidence and aplomb. "All of you from Fort Huachuca discovered these phenomena at the same time we did here at McCarthy. Actually, two phenomena have surfaced in the past two days. They may be linked. They may not. We don't know yet. We think we have a countermeasure for one of them, but we're still working on the other. We have some WAGs - wildly assumed guesses - and some working hypotheses. But nothing has really checked out yet. We haven't had time. The purpose of this conference is for those of us here in the brain bin at McCarthy to compare notes, experiences, and data with those of you who've taken it in the shorts down at Huachuca. I learned the hard way at Kerguelen Island that what we do in the lab is a hell of a lot different from the way it is when someone's shooting at you."

"Owen, if this current sheep screw has anything to do with the Kerguelen matter, that whole operation is still under wraps. Eyes only, suicide before reading, that sort of thing," Curt reminded him gently. Sometimes these techie types didn't bother with security. Many of them still believed that "science knows no country."

"We're all cleared for Secret, and this room is clean," Pendleton pointed out.

"As I said, that affair is pegged higher than Top Secret. A lot higher," Curt added, glancing at Dr. Rosha Taisha. He wasn't certain she'd been cleared higher than her job required at McCarthy. Changes or not, Curt still wasn't about to completely trust Taisha.

He didn't know the details of her mind scrubbing at Fort Benning's NE hospital. He probably wouldn't have understood everything anyway; that wasn't his area of expertise. And he didn't have his walking, talking encyclopedia, Captain Hassan Mahmud, along on this trip. So Curt was wary. He knew this might have been caused by what he'd learned from Dyani. "The only reason some of us know about it at all is because we were there."

"Well, I don't think this matter has any connection," Pendleton explained. "Let me bring you up to the same level of ignorance and confusion that we enjoy. We asked you to take certain data yesterday. That was very helpful. We think there may be some real significance in the data Sergeant Sampson has squirted up to us. But we want to make certain. The two factors we're up against are, one, externally induced circadian asynchronization and, two, interference with human-warbot linkage, especially with direct NE linkage. Yes, I know you had some Mod Seven-Eleven Mary Anns and Jeeps go tracks-up at Huachuca. We had something similar happen here with our advanced prototypes. But in all respects, it was worse here. Some of our experienced high-level warbot brainies went KIA yesterday."

That news surprised Curt.

Captain Dale Brown, the only warbot brainy commander in the Greys because his platoon ran the birdbots, echoed Curt's reaction. "Colonel Pendleton, we ran up against that too. But our rapid delink therapeutic programs took care of it without trouble. I damned near went KIA myself yesterday, but I ended up with just a bad headache caused by a bit of cranial hypertension."

"You had a bit more than that going on in your jelly-ware, Dale," added Helen Devlin, the chief nurse in Ruth Gydesen's bio-tech unit. "You were out of it for a while."

"Really? I wondered where the afternoon went."

"It went while some of us were putting your neurons hack in step with reality," Devlin explained.

"Maybe we should have had you over here, Captain," Pendleton told her. He knew she was one shit-hot neuroclectronic bio-tech.

Helen had once ministered to real warbots brainies when the Greys were still operating as a full Robot Infantry regiment. "I've got three top-grade experimental warbot operators down for six weeks of rehab."

"I'm sure you have therapeutic delink protocols standing by when you've got people strung out in experimental warbots," Major Ruth Gydesen interjected, turning a question into an observation. If the brain bin at McCarthy was slacking off on its precautionary safety measures, she wanted to get some information on that. Having warbot brainies go KIA shouldn't happen if proper safety measures were in place. Ruth had both the power and the responsibility to shortcut the chain of command and forward a medical squawk to the Army's Surgeon General. It was the sort of thing one did only if absolutely necessary. But in the past Ruth had had to repair damage done to the Greys by the forgetfulness of the techies at McCarthy. She wanted to protect her wards.

"We do. But they didn't function normally. That's one of the interesting data points, Major," Willa Lovell put in. "It's another one of the significant - we think - differences between what happened here and what took place at Huachuca."

"How come the Second Warbot Armored Division at Fort Hood didn't report problems?" Major Russ Frazier wanted to know.

"We don't know for certain, but we have a hypothesis," Pendleton put in. He wasn't used to this free-thinking exchange of non-scientific questions and answers. When he conferred with his warbot researchers at McCarthy Proving Ground, a more stringent protocol ruled. They were scientists and technicians. They were trained to listen to another person's complete presentation of information and data before lapsing into a free exchange of comment, critique, and criticism. These combat officers in a non-combat environment seemed to believe they were all entitled - nay, expected - to make direct contributions to the idea flow. Pendleton had been shot at in combat himself, so he reflected that this might be at the root of the disparity in briefing protocol. A bond of equality existed between these Sierra Charlies; that bond was the fact that they'd all been shot at and lived to talk about it.

So, Pendleton tried to attack the protocol problem. "The Second Warbot Armored did have some problems, but they weren't severe. If you'll give me the courtesy of your attention, I'll explain to you what's been going on and what we think is happening. We also have some countermeasures that you should know about. Then I would gladly welcome your inputs."

"Owen, I've trained my people to ask questions when they don't understand something," Curt explained. "If it sounds like disrespectful interruption, it isn't. They're used to asking questions. Their lives and those of their colleagues may be on the line as a result of a briefing. Expect us to ask dumb questions."

Pendleton smiled and decided it was time to forge a contract with these combat people. Curt had told him about "the contract," an agreement far more binding than mere friendship. "There are no dumb questions, Curt. Only stupid and incorrect answers if someone is trying to hide behind ignorance. Okay, I'll expect questions dealing with clarification. But if someone asks a question, I don't have the answer for, I won't give you a dumb answer. I won't give you any answer at all. And I'll tell you I don't know."

"You've been talking to General Hettrick," Willa Lovell remarked.

"How could you tell?"

"I've dealt with her before."

"Why isn't she here? I extended the invitation to her because it's her division that's affected," Pendleton wondered.

"She's got the Seventeenth Iron Fist Division to run, and she's beginning to line up her ducks against retirement in a year or so," Curt explained.

"So, who's the heir apparent?" Pendleton asked.

Curt shrugged. He knew he was in the running. But he wasn't sure he was ready or even that he wanted it. "Rumor Control Headquarters is rife with speculation."

"Okay, back to business," Pendleton snapped, aware that he'd let things wander afield from' the business of the conference. He went back to his agenda. "Two associated phenomena are taking place: circadian asynchronization and NE linkage interference. It hit us hard at McCarthy. It hit you less severely at Huachuca. And it barely touched Fort Hood. However, we've asked DCSOPS in the Pentagon to order a quiet stand-down of all warbot operations except those in the Gulf, Sakhalin, Senegambia, and other active overseas commands where warbot patrols are absolutely essential. Even at that, we've recommended as much hands-on warbot command as possible, sort of semi-Sierra Charlie operational doctrine. You all can feel smug about that because you wrote the Sierra Charlie book. Turns out that under these circumstances it may be the salvation of the Free World. But that's nothing new to you Washington Greys in any event.

"First, the external disruption of our circadian rhythms. Doctor Lovell has been concentrating on that. Doctor?"

As Pendleton sat down, Willa Lovell took the podium. "We saw it first and asked Sergeant Sampson to confirm it. She did. I want to thank the sergeant because it wasn't an easy phenomenon to detect, much less measure. The background is rather deep and goes back to the work of Tesla. But I'm no electricity expert, so I won't dwell on that. If anyone is interested in deep research, I'll point them to the proper sources."

Lovell paused for effect and to catch her breath, then went on pedantically as if she was teaching a class, which she was. "The planet Earth has a layer of charged particles in the part of the high atmosphere called the ionosphere. It acts like a mirror to reflect certain electromagnetic frequencies. Basically, it turns the planet into a huge electromagnetic resonance chamber. It's called the Schuman Resonance after the scientist who discovered that the Earth's magnetic field oscillates at eight to twelve hertz in resonance with this spherical cavity. Back in the last century, Doctor Siegnot Lang in Germany discovered that this change in the Earth's electromagnetic field is sensed by our nervous systems. It sets our natural body rhythms. He called it the 'Zeitgeber' or 'time-giver.' So, our bodies like the ten-hertz signals because it works similar to the crystal timing base in a warbot computer or a clock. It paces us. Our nervous systems are tuned to it.

"I noticed we were becoming disoriented, losing a sense of time, and experiencing disruptions of our sleeping and digestion rhythms. We were out of balance. Our acupuncture meridians were skewed. Other data from our neuroelectronic warbot experiments here suggested that something was stressing our nervous systems. So, we went looking.

"We've been exposed to 'electrical smog' ever since we began living with the very weak signals generated by alternating electrical current. We're radiated by the sixty-hertz frequency from low-voltage wiring all around us. It isn't strong enough to overcome the ten-hertz signal we're used to and which our bodies prefer."

Willa Lovell activated a control on the lectern, and an oscilloscope trace appeared in the display tank behind her. It showed the typical ten-hertz signal of Schuman Resonance. "The ten-hertz natural field was still there. But it was being overwhelmed by another one at six-hertz."

She superimposed another waveform over the first. It was of lower frequency and longer wavelength, but it was almost a square wave. It didn't look natural. "This is what it looks like. When we got your problem call, I asked Sampson to look for the six-hertz field at Huachuca. It was there, but its intensity was lower."

A third trace appeared in the tank. It had a lower peak-lo-peak amplitude and a lot more distortion to the waveform. "It also showed analog degradation of what appeared to us here to be a digital signal. This sort of degradation is expected off a resonance point in a cavity resonator."

Lovell looked at each of them. "We believe this six-hertz signal is causing the sort of personality changes we've observed here and that you've seen down at Fort Huachuca. It was strong enough to overwhelm the ten-hertz Schuman Resonance here and just barely strong enough to cause problems for you at Fort Huachuca. We are beginning to get data in from other army units in the ZI as well as overseas. The data is interesting. Colonel Pendleton has made some additional observations and can report some startling hypotheses.

Colonel?"

Pendleton stood up and took the podium. He flashed yet another visual in the tank. It was a map of the world, a circular projection with Fort McCarthy at the center. "Knowing the frequency, we could determine the wavelength quite easily. It's about twelve thousand kilometers."

A circle twelve thousand kilometers in radius came into view. Since it wrapped nearly around the world, it appeared as a small circle centered near the top of the subcontinent of India.

"Centered in the East World!" Curt muttered.

"Yes, but we can't tell where from just this analysis," Pendleton observed. "However, as all of you know, the art of radio direction-finding is old and well established. With three data points, we could triangulate a source for the signal. The three points we had available are very close together on a global scale, so we haven't pinpointed the source very well yet. However, it looks like it's coming from an area in northern India or even Tibet. Ladies and gentlemen, something out there is broadcasting a disrupting extremely low frequency electromagnetic signal. It appears to be targeted on Fort McCarthy. We'll have a better idea of the location of the transmitter as quickly as more direction-finding data come in. And then we can look for it with reconnaissance satellites.

"But it comes down to this: Someone, maybe East Worlders, is attempting to jam our nervous systems. Call it 'neuroelectronic warfare.' It could render our whole warbot military establishment ineffective!"

Chapter Five

"It could render our whole warbot military establishment ineffective!"

"Oh, come on, Al!" was the objection from Jeffrey G. Pickens, the National Security Advisor. "You and I both know that the warbot linkage technology is highly classified! And extremely complex! The Russkies tried to crack it for years. They couldn't do it even after they captured some of our old warbots. And the East World warbots we got from Yemen and Senegambia showed no sign that our linkage technology had been-copied!"

Al Murray, the chief of the National Intelligence Agency, had information that Pickens didn't know squat about the Department of Defense's most guarded military secret. Pickens was an old warbot brainy. Like other warbot brainies who engaged in combat where he might be captured, he'd never been told how the duplex link worked between a human being and a warbot. He didn't have to know. Even as National Security Advisor, Pickens didn't have to know.

Murray did know how it worked. That was part of his job. When he was on active duty as an Aerospace Force general officer, he hadn't been told either. But as head of NIA, he'd found out. Of all the people in the Oval Office that morning-and inside the Washington Beltway - Murray was the one person who would never compromise any of the information he had. And he had a lot of it.

So, Murray knew Pickens was full of shit, but he didn't tell him that. Fran Kellogg, the Secretary of State, was also in the Oval Office. Murray had never been a vulgar-mouthed person, even when he'd been driving hypersonic fighter-bombers for the Aerospace Force. He'd known plenty of women who could swear better than the men around them. But Fran Kellogg was a lady who never swore. So, Murray maintained a high level of decorum. Besides, this was the Oval Office. A lot of high-level swearing had gone on there in the past, but the current President wasn't contributing to history in that manner.

"Jeff, nobody here but just us chickens," Murray advised him, looking around the room. He went on in a confidential tone as if everyone else didn't know that he knew. "So, I'll have to admit that I know. Don't ask me how because I won't tell you."

"Why is it that you know so much about it?" the white-haired, black-bearded man in rumpled tweed remarked with a slight accent. No one really knew where Dr. Mark Hankamer, the Presidential Science Advisor, had picked up that obscure European accent. Murray knew; the man was a stuffed shirt and affected the fake accent. Hankamer had nothing else to distinguish himself, including brains. He was a "political" scientist. The President had appointed him as a sop to the academic world.

"Doctor, it's my job," Murray reminded him with a sigh of frustration. Every new Administration required that he educate a new bunch of staffers, managers, administrators, bureaucrats, and political hacks. "Let's just say that I got it by 'national technical means.' "

"That's always been a convenient excuse, General," Hankamer replied, deliberately using Murray's retired military rank. Hankamer didn't like the military. The science advisor was forced to overlook the fact that the President was a retired military officer. After all, the President was Hankamer's boss. Without the President, Hankamer wouldn't have a White House office and be in on most of the inner workings of the Administration. When his tour was over, he was guaranteed an outstanding position at some university or academic research center.

"If I could tell you, Doctor, I would. If the President orders me to tell you, I will," Murray snapped. It was obvious to the others in the room that the two men didn't like one another very much. But then few people in the room liked the science advisor anyway. "If I don't know these things and know them in advance, I'd be asked to resign. If I tell anyone how I know what I know, I'd be asked to resign. So, I just report what I know. Never mind how I know. You probably wouldn't want to know anyway. When this signal came on the air about forty-eight hours ago, I knew it was coming. And I knew what it was intended to do."

"Then you know more than most of the best scientific minds in America," Hankamer said petulantly.

The President had let this exchange go on as long as he intended. He had always allowed his subordinates the opportunity to exchange information, comments, observations, criticism, and even jibes. But this exchange had rapidly become a pissing contest. He knew that Murray would win.

He wished that someone more qualified than Jeff Pickens was available to serve as his security advisor. But in spite of being a stuffed shirt, Pickens did know and understand more about national security than anyone the President knew. Pickens had served with honor in the Army around the world. He knew that people out there hated one another with an intensity not understood by most Americans. Twenty-first-century military technology was capable of permitting these people and their leaders to wipe out their hated neighbors. Thus, most of it was highly classified. But even twentieth-century technology was capable of doing that. It was impossible to keep a security cap on technology that old. What is impossible to one generation of engineers is only difficult to the next, and commonplace to the third.

The only factor that kept genocide in check and violence reduced was the cop on the beat. That was the United States of America. It was a role Americans didn't cherish. Most of them wanted to be left alone to trade around the world, to make money, to live the good life. They were always ready and willing to protect their families and homes. And they could and did sally forth to protect the unfortunate against aggression. It had taken decades for Americans to accept the fact that it was a nasty job, but someone had to do it. Maintaining a police force anywhere is an expensive proposition. The bigger the force and the larger its area of jurisdiction, the more expensive it is. But taxpayers had reluctantly accepted the price as one of the costs of doing business. Without the U.S.A. as the cop on the beat around the world, international trade would become too risky. Far too many countries were big, strong, wealthy, and covetous. The world had bullies. The U.S. Department of Defense stood ready, to clobber them.

It was the succinct presentation of this "cop on the beat" philosophy in everyday terms that had won former General Jacob O. Carlisle the Presidency over an opponent who'd held nearly all the political cards. But the opposition hadn't been willing to commit U.S. military forces to what was termed in a well-played sound bite as "power projection that would make America itself the bully in the world."

The United States and its North American economic union were rich. Europe was rich. Japan, Brunei, Singapore, and the other Pacific Rim economies were rich. Together, they were pulling the rest of the lazy and rapacious world out of historic poverty, famine, and violence by its bootstraps.

The most difficult problem faced by the peoples of the world was not how to keep from blowing themselves up.

It was learning how to be rich.

In a world like that, the American military establishment had taken on a new goal, a new doctrine, a new sense of being needed for a very specific purpose. Not conquest. Not colonization. Not domination. But true peacekeeping, which meant swatting down the bullies.

The biggest one around right then was East World.

East World thought little of individual human life.

Life was plentiful and cheap in East World.

East World had lots of. hands and feet. Thus, they also had lots of cannon fodder. They didn't particularly care if a couple of million of their people died. People were cheap. Life was cheap.

East World had too many people.

And it was apparent from what Murray had reported that this new threat to the cop on the beat was coming from East World.

The President was willing to commit American military forces to police actions. So were the members of the National Security

Council. Except Hankamer. Again, the President wished that Hankamer hadn't been forced on him by the Big Science people.

So, the President held up his hand for silence. He got what he wanted. Then he said quietly, "Let me make sure that I understand what's going on. If I don't understand it, the nation's in trouble. And some of you will go back to your offices and work like hell to come up with a briefing that will permit me to understand it. Al Murray has sources; don't question them because they're good. So's his analysis."

"Mister President, the Defense Intelligence Agency-" the Secretary of Defense began.

The President looked sharply at his Secretary of Defense and pointed out, "Dave, if your DIA people want to pick nits with Al's people, the two of you set up the spook meeting and fight it out between you."

David P. Henshaw spread his hands. "Mister President, have I voiced any questions or doubts? Not at all. DIA confirms NIA data. No argument, sir."

"Jeff, you sounded like you had doubts," the President observed.

When put on the spot, Pickens retreated. "Let me explain my position, sir. I've learned to question Gee-Two. Sometimes the basic assumptions are incorrect. I've had intelligence staffers inflate or degrade intelligence data to conform to their preconceived notions."

"We aren't running a division or a theater command," the President reminded him. The President had done both in his career. "If you have doubts about the integrity of Al's information, contact Al privately."

"Sir, it just seemed to me that Al's statement was a bit sweeping in its generalization," Pickens tried to explain. "It's my job to spot such things, draw your attention to them, and ask questions."

"You're a good staff man, Jeff," the President said, soothing him. "But a good staff man also knows when to quit. I don't require that everyone agree with me. That's not my style. Let me restate what I've told all of you publicly and privately. I don't care how smart a person is. I expect and demand only one thing: loyalty. If a person doesn't have that, good-bye. That doesn't mean I want a lot of 'yes men' around me - with apologies to the Secretary of State for using a gender-specific cliché. I'll give any of you an adequate opportunity to state your case on any major issue. But you'd better be able to state it concisely and succinctly without beating around the bush. Yes, I like people who are smart. But they'd also better have the attribute of wisdom as well as intelligence. I want to see initiative. And I like aggressive people. Which is why I let you go at one another during these NSC meetings."

The National Security Council sat silent now. So, the President went on. "Back to my agenda. Let's see if I understand the situation. Extremely low frequency electromagnetic pulses with a rep rate of six-hertz began bombarding the western part of the United States about forty-eight hours ago. This began to affect the biological clocks of many people. The effect was most pronounced at McCarthy Proving Ground. Other effects were felt at Fort Huachuca, and Fort Carson. Right, Al? Correct, Dave? Have I got it right, Jeff?"

The persons mentioned nodded.

The President went on. "Dave, you reported that McCarthy has a personal electronic antidote that will negate these effects."

"Yes, sir, but I don't have the details yet," the Secretary of Defense replied. "I'm told by Colonel Pendleton that it's very simple. The first units developed by Doctor Lovell are about twenty millimeters on a side, a little larger than a ten-gigabyte memory cube. The biggest component is the battery. Pendleton says it could be quickly reduced to a size that could be implanted. That would eliminate this time-bending problem they used to call jet lag."

"But if I understand it," the President went on, "the identification of the six-hertz circadian asynchronization phenomenon doesn't explain the interference with our warbot linkage systems. Mark, you've told me that no one in the neuroelectronic sciences has an answer for that one yet."

"Mister President, I passed the information along to my colleagues at several universities late yesterday afternoon," the Presidential Science Advisor explained pedantically. "Some of them worked all night in their labs. Only the NE Research Center at the University of Nevada Las Vegas reported detection of the six-hertz signal. Doctor Butterworth has no idea why this signal is cross-interfering with robot linkage, even in some industrial robots. By the way, he's cleared for NE warbot linkage technology because he does so much work with McCarthy. Other university labs have attempted to duplicate the six-hertz signal and duplicate any NE interference. But they haven't succeeded yet."

"When can we expect some answers?" the President wanted to know.

"Sir, I wish I could give you a firm schedule, but I can't," Hankamer replied rather lamely. "This is a typical situation in scientific research. Science isn't done by the numbers. Or on schedule. It's likely to require months, perhaps even years, to properly investigate this and come up with a hypothesis."

"Your recommendations?" The President already suspected what these might be.

"I'll look at the funding situation after this meeting, sir. I'll try to find funds to provide grants for some additional research," the science advisor commented. "I'll then put out a request for grant proposals. I'll also look into extension of some existing R-and-D contracts."

The President repeated his earlier question, "When can we expect some answers?"

"Well, it will take six weeks to three months on the grant awards. Perhaps we can get the extensions rammed through the contracts people in thirty to forty-five days. Depending on the funding level and a lot of good luck in the breaks, I suspect we might have some answers in a couple of years..."

The President said nothing in reply to his science advisor. He'd expected that answer. But he'd had to allow the man to give it. So, he turned to his National Security Advisor and asked, "Jeff, how long can we risk having our entire warbot military establishment in this toes-up situation before something comes unbonded somewhere in the world?"

Pickens replied without hesitation. "If this phenomenon has its source in East World, we could be in trouble within weeks. It will take East World intelligence that long to assess the damage and determine whether or not this neuroelectronic warfare weapon works. They won't move until they're certain they have us knocked out. Then I'd estimate they'll initiate some low-level probes around their periphery and in their satellite states."

It was obvious to everyone in the room except the science advisor that the groves of academe couldn't be counted upon to pull the rabbit out of the hat and save the Free World.

The President asked his Secretary of Defense, "Dave, what are your recommendations?"

The Secretary of Defense was the former CEO of a Fortune 500 corporation that had done a lot of military contracting in the warbotic field. He was a no-nonsense person who cut right to the heart of problems. "Mister President, I'll accelerate R-and-D in my department immediately. I've got some discretionary funds. But in the meantime, we have to cover our minus-x. The Aerospace Force will be tasked to find the source of this signal. We'll use existing surveillance sats. And hypersonic overflights if we can. Then you'll have to authorize some hypersonic assault aircraft to go in and take out the facility with kinetic kill weapons."

The Secretary of State spoke up. "Mister President, that's an act of war!"

"I agree," added Dr. Mark Hankamer.

"And irradiating the United States with a neuroelectronic weapon isn't?" the Defense Secretary countered.

"I advise against such draconian measures at this time," replied the Honorable Frances Kellogg. "I may change my position as more information becomes available. Or if East World aggression results."

"'Perhaps it is draconian," Henshaw admitted, "but it was a quick reply off the top of my head. I haven't had the opportunity to run this past the Joint Chiefs and get their assessment. They're meeting right now in the Pentagon. I can have several scenario war plans on your desk this afternoon, sir."

"It seems to me," the President mused, recalling his own military service and the campaigns in which he'd participated - especially on Kerguelen Island, "that this might call for a non-NE warbot response. Fortunately, we've got just such an outfit. Dave, you might want to put the Seventeenth Iron Fist Division at Fort Huachuca on yellow alert and get some airlift in place. The Sierra Charlies could probably handle this in a very surgical manner once we know where to send them."

"Mister President, I know where to send them. I just don't know the precise location yet." Al Murray's statement took everyone by, surprise, although it should not have done so. Everyone knew the man had a lot more information than he normally revealed.

"Then why the hell didn't you say that before?" the President snapped.

"Because I didn't get to that part of my briefing and because no one asked me after I got cut short," Murray explained without rancor.

"Where do we send the Sierra Charlies and what do they break up when they get there?"

"We send them somewhere high in the Himalayan Mountains in that part of Kashmir known as Hunza Province," the intelligence chief said. "We'll pinpoint the exact location as soon as radio direction finding activities give us a better fix. That will be in a few hours at most. Then we'll look with high-res satellites. If we go looking with sats first, we'll spend weeks peering at every peasant's hut on half-meter resolution photos."

"What's the timeline on this?"

"Within twelve hours."

"Good," the Secretary of State remarked with some relief. She wasn't a peacenik. No member of the Cabinet was. But she was sensitized to the foreign policy ramifications of what was happening.

"It isn't just a matter of blowing up whatever we find, ladies and gentlemen," Al Murray went on. "We're going to extract the brainpower behind this weapon. I didn't get the chance to report that my agency was contacted by East World scientists a few hours ago. These people don't like the idea of their work being used as the basis of a deadly weapon that could destroy the minds of people around the world. Fran, you'd better get your people ready to issue visas for these East Worlders, because I have no doubt that we'll get them out. Mister President, you'll have to send in the Sierra Charlies!"

Chapter Six

"You mentioned a countermeasure for the circadian asynchronization," Colonel Curt Carson reminded Dr. Willa Lovell.

The neuroelectronics scientist held up a small grey cube about thirty millimeters on a side. On one face, a dim red LED blinked rapidly. "This is a Schuman Resonator, also known as an Earth Resonance Generator. The battery is the largest component in it. Sorry our techs couldn't make it any smaller. After all, we threw it together in less than twenty-four hours. As you know, that's impossible to do in a government lab, but...We built it from existing modules so we could get enough to equip most of you. The next version, Mod One, will be mote professionally done."

"Doctor, I don't give a damn how professional it looks as long as it works," Henry Kester, the regimental sergeant major, remarked.

"It works. But it's sloppy design work."

Kester shrugged. "An adequate working gadget in hand is far better than a perfect gizmo that might be issued next week."

Lovell put a small cardboard box on the table and began extracting resonators. She handed them around the table. "We'll have more by the time you leave. Actually, one resonator per five or six people is enough because each has a range of about a hundred meters."

Edie Sampson looked at the one that had been given to her. "What the hell is in it, Doctor?" Edie would be the one to ask that question, of course.

It was Colonel Owen Pendleton who replied. "As Doctor Lovell pointed out, it's mostly the power source, a four-point-eight-volt power cell good for about six weeks."

"Draws lots of current!" was Henry Kester's observation.

"Mod Zero does, yes," Pendleton explained. "When we get the nanochip fully designed and grown, we'll probably be able to implant it. However, as it is, it can be carried easily."

Edie repeated her question, "What's in it, Colonel?"

"A ten-hertz sine-wave oscillator, the LED indicator that shows it's working, and a Mobius strip antenna," Pendleton told her. "The radiated output waveform closely matches that of the Earth's magnetic field pulses."

"Glad to see that McCarthy Proving Ground is hot on the stick when it comes to quick and dirty inventions," Curt observed.

"We didn't invent this," Willa Lovell admitted. "We stumbled on it in some twentieth-century scientific literature as we were researching the biophysiological effects of extremely low frequency electromagnetic fields." When she saw that this new area of bioelectronics was causing Edie to look somewhat perplexed, and that even Major Ruth Gydesen had an inquiring expression on her face, she explained. "When the human nervous system is given the choice between a ten-hertz field and another of nearly equal intensity, it chooses the ten-hertz field. It likes it better. It's most comfortable with that because it's the Earth's own frequency."

"That makes sense," Ruth said as she nodded.

Major Russ Frazier spoke up for the first time. Curt thought that all this advanced neuroelectronic technology might be somewhat alien to the man because he wasn't known as a techie type but a hard-fighting, aggressive combat officer. Russ surprised him. "If this six-hertz East World field is also screwing up our warbot linkage, can we cobble-up a quick fix to the NE gear to put this ten-hertz signal into it as well?"

"Major, I don't want to screw around with the NE circuitry of my birdbots or in the RCV," Captain Dale Brown said with concern in his voice.

That concern was well founded. Warbot brainies such as Brown - commander of the only true NE warbot unit in the Washington Greys – didn't go screwing around with the circuitry. In the first place, they knew they didn't know what they were doing. Second, they also knew better than to mess around with any gadgetry that allowed NE signals to get into their minds and their own NE commands to get out to their warbots.

"I'll happily volunteer as a guinea pig working with the McCarthy people on checking it out," Dale went on. "But it's a definite negatory to go messing around with the NE warbot circuitry."

"Yeah, we were all trained to use it, not to mess with it," Russ said. "I remember the scare stories about people hotting-up the circuitry to run faster or pick up more sensitive thoughts. Genius creators, they thought they were. Blew their mental fuses in most cases, we were told...although I never met anyone that had it happen to them. So that's probably just brainwashing from your training days."

Brown shook his shaved head. "With all due respects, sir, no, sir! Not after this most recent sheep screw where I damned near lost four of my birdbotters! Everything in the NE circuitry checked out tickety-boo. We didn't see one damned thing wrong until we started to go KIA. As for figuring out the circuitry so we might alter it, I need to point out that it takes all the neurons we've got just to work warbots. You know that, Major. You were a warbot brainy yourself before the Greys went Sierra Charlie. I don't have to be a space scientist to know that the NE linkage circuitry is well beyond my feeble comprehension. And I haven't got time to learn it, even if I was cleared for it."

"I won't touch it either," was Flight Lieutenant Nancy Robert's input. "Dale and his people have their pink bods on the ground, but I'm up there with nothing between me and the rocks but a thin Chippie!"

"The captain and the lieutenant are both correct!" Dr. Rosha Taisha stated, ending her silence, which had lasted up till now. "Colonel, I need to explain to you what I discovered this morning!"

"Go ahead, Rosha! The floor is yours," Pendleton told her, resuming his seat.

Taisha rustled some hard copy in her folder, then stepped up to the tank projector. She put up the trace of the terrestrial magnetic field fluctuation first. "This is the normal field. It's almost sinusoidal. Yes, a few higher frequency overtones exist in this natural signal, but nothing we haven't known about for decades. The overtones have very low amplitude. However, in some neurological conditions they will occasionally interfere with normal nerve trunk messages, weak as they are. I suspected this while working for the Immam Abdul Mojid Rahman, but I couldn't get the equipment necessary to measure this. I got the facilities at Battle Mountain because Doctor Clarke Jeremy Mathis supported me at a higher funding level and I was closer to the supply."

She paused, then went on. "But I wasn't looking for what I found today. I was, uh, trying to do something else then. I once wanted to find a way to control people using neuroelectronic technology. Now I know why I was doing it. I don't have that motivation any longer. Those 'devils' were 'exorcised' down at Fort Benning."

Curt decided that maybe Taisha was indeed a different person, that perhaps she'd been changed by her therapy at Fort Benning's neuroelectronics hospital. There was no denial on her part. She seemed ready and eager to talk about it, especially with those in the Washington Greys whom she knew remembered her as she had been. Or perhaps this had been just a catharsis on Taisha's part. Curt decided to continue reserving judgment, but he was more inclined to believe the Fort Benning people had done a nearly impossible job.

Taisha went on. "But I remember all too well the path of research I was on. That's why this morning I suddenly realized what was going on. Someone in East World was actually doing what I'd been trying to do! The six-hertz signal is only part of it! The insidious technology is hidden in the main six-hertz signal!"

Curt was fascinated by the woman's brilliant insights. He's always known she was a genius when it came to neuroelectronics; she'd proved that before. However, until now she had shown herself to be a truly mad genius who wanted to use NE technology to make people do what she wanted. Naturally, her insights into the problem would allow her to identify someone else's attempt to do what she'd been working on!

The wave trace of the six-hertz signal appeared in the display tank overlaying the ten-hertz earth signal.

"Notice please that the East World signal is not sinusoidal!" Taisha continued, highlighting what she was discussing by causing the East World signal to be displayed more brightly. "I don't know enough about atmospheric propagation of electromagnetic waves, but this East World signal looks like it has many overtones to it."

"It's a distorted square wave," Edie told her. "That's what usually happens to a square wave when it's been transmitted over long distances. Knocks the higher harmonics out. We don't give a damn about that anymore because we're working digital signals, not analog."

"Thank you." Taisha seemed genuinely grateful for Edie's input. "I didn't know that. However, I put the signal through a spectrum analyzer. It's absolutely full of harmonics that match certain neurological event potentials or signals."

Taisha did something to the projection, and a spectrum sweep appeared. Following the high spike of the six-hertz East World main signal were a series of lesser signals of low power and increasing frequency or repetition rate. "Here's the auditory nerve band. And this is the visual band. And here's the kinesthetic band. All of these have specific coding associated with them. However, I haven't had time yet to begin deciphering the codes. I'm sure that Doctor Lovell will be able to help here because this is her area of expertise."

"But those signals are very weak compared to the main signal," Pendleton pointed out.

"Sir, as you may know, the main sinusoidal component of the terrestrial magnetic field is *nine orders of magnitude* more powerful than a nerve impulse," Taisha reminded him.

"Owen, that's why it took so long to develop neuroelectronics," Willa Lovell told him. "We had to wait until we had SQUIDS and Super-SQUIDS. Otherwise, the terrestrial field overcomes what we're trying to look at. We needed instrumentation capable of filtering the ambient field and pulling nerve impulses out of the noise."

Pendleton was a super AI mentor. No one was better than he when it came to developing the operating commands and rationales for AI units, something several levels above what old-time computer programmers did. But he was no neuroelectronics expert.

Willa Lovell and Rosha Taisha were. But on the other hand, they weren't good AI mentors. That took a special way of thinking about the interface between humans and machines. It was different from that used in straightforward neuroelectronics.

And Taisha was obviously looking at the problem from a unique Asian perspective. She'd grown up in China; she knew how East World people thought.

So did Curt because he read, wrote, spoke, and understood Mandarin Chinese. He was well aware that Asians had a completely different worldview. Their thinking processes, as reflected in the content and structure of their languages, was the key to this. It had been one reason Curt had studied Mandarin Chinese as his second language at West Point; the other reason had been a highly attractive Chinese-American female cadet.

"So what are the consequences of what you've discovered, Doctor Taisha?" Pendleton wanted to know. The rehabbed Eurasian NE scientist fascinated him. She was brilliant in a strange sort of way. She looked at the world differently from the other NE scientists at McCarthy. As a result, she was becoming an important part of the proving ground's research staff.

"The harmonic components of the main East World signal probably aren't getting into the warbot NE circuitry," Taisha guessed. "I don't know enough about the circuitry to make a more definitive guess than that. But I suspect that the East World harmonics are somehow getting into the neuroelectronic system. This may be as a result of an NE warbot operator being more highly sensitized as a result of working in linkage. Or because the harmonic signals amount to something like a super-subliminal set of commands."

Pendleton was sobered by this finding. "Uh, yes, and I can see that we're maybe in real deep slime here. And why you were so adamant about rigging up the NE linkage circuitry with a gross countermeasure to the East World six-hertz signal. That could make it even worse!"

"We've got a *lot* of work to do!" Willa Lovell said as she realized the magnitude of the problem.

"And maybe very little time in which do to it," Pendleton added. "Where did the East Worlders get the basic information on warbot neuroelectronics that allowed them to come up with this weapon?"

"You were there, Owen," Curt reminded him. "We left a lot of old warbots on Kerguelen's Cook Glacier about ten years ago. We know that some of those warbots ended up in Moscow. And others were carefully studied in Beijing. We should have anticipated that this might happen someday. Looks like it did."

"Uh, yeah, I remember," Pendleton mused. "But I can't figure out how they reverse-engineered the NE linkage technology. Hell, that's *complicated!*"

"Colonel," Taisha told him quietly, "please do not forget that the Chinese, the Hindus, and other Asian peoples have developed many biotechnological applications. It has been only in the past hundred years that these have been recognized in the Western world as having any validity whatsoever. I'm thinking of acupuncture and all its ramifications, including the concept of acupuncture meridians and balances. Or 'humor balance.' Or the techniques of both colloidal and crystalline life-power technology."

"Doctor, many of the effects of those can be attributed to the placebo syndrome. It works because people believe it does." Pendleton was extremely rational and therefore Western in his response.

Taisha shook her shaved head. "The fact that it works at all even part of the time in unskilled and untrained hands is reason enough to look into it. I have."

"But it's *unscientific!*"

"Owen, the application of something in technology usually leads to scientific investigation," Curt added. He was no expert in this area, but he worked with high technology every day. And he knew something about it. Many had been the times when the Washington Greys had come up with some new technical wrinkle in their high-tech equipment. They'd then called in the scientists to explain what was going on. Often, their answers made little sense to the Sierra Charlies. Or the explanation didn't matter. And too many times the scientists had foisted some new gadgetry on the Greys that hadn't worked worth a damn in the real world of combat.

"Owen," Lovell reminded him gently, "we don't even know how a simple electrical transformer really works. Or how and why a neuron behaves the way it does. Certainly, we have some theories, but..."

"We do not yet understand acupuncture, humor medicine, and other Oriental medicine. They involve technologies we do not yet fully grasp because we don't know where to start measuring and for what," Taisha went on.

Pendleton sighed. "Yeah, I guess that in every century, interest has been renewed in these 'non-scientific' technologies."

"Some of them end up being the technology of the next century," Willa Lovell reminded him. "After all, electricity itself was once only a parlor game. Some of 'new age science' was truly that. Some wasn't. We must accept the fact that the East World researchers have developed a technology that may be based upon something we'd consider fantasy. That makes it very difficult for us to discover what they've done because we *know* it isn't so. In the meantime, they cripple our world with it."

Everyone was silent for a moment.

Curt and the others from the Washington Greys knew the consequences of this might be that all the NE warbot technology of the United States Army was now ineffective.

And this meant that the United States would have to depend upon the Sierra Charlies, who operated only by "soft linkage" with their warbots. Their helmet sensors would pick up their thought commands and transmit them to the Mary Anns and Saucy Cans. There was no downlink from the warbots to the Sierra Charlies other than as verbal messages.

Curt wasn't certain at this point whether this East World NE weapon would make such soft linkage impossible as well.

He and everyone in the room knew that perhaps this meant the end of the warbots.

As a result of this East World development, perhaps the most powerful of all weapons yet developed for waging war might now be totally obsolete.

That meant that people would have to go back to fighting without the help of the robotic machines.

If so, given the state of modern weaponry, that would be very lethal indeed.

And East World certainly had lots of people who could be expended as soldiers.

"I think," Colonel Curt Carson suddenly said, "that we'd better shag our tails-back to Fort Hucahuca. General Hettrick will want a full briefing on this. And you people here at McCarthy need to get us out of your hair. You've got a lot of work to do. I guess we'll be your guinea pigs in the field."

Curt rose to his feet and continued. "But I don't think we'll have a lot of time for that. My guess is that we'll be on yellow alert later today. And then we'll have to go out and save the Free World again. Looks like we're the only ones who can do it!"

Chapter Seven

"It just doesn't make sense!"

The President looked at the satellite images in the holo tank of the Oval Office. The three-D image - made up of two frames taken by the same high-resolution recon satellite a short time apart - showed a cluster of one-story buildings grouped together in a high mountain valley.

"Jeff, sometimes the world doesn't make sense," the President admitted. "At least four times every day I think I've fallen down the rabbit hole again."

"Excuse me, Mister President?" The National Security Advisor wasn't known for his sense of humor, and he often reacted this way to the dry humor of his boss.

The President looked at him but didn't explain. "Maybe Lewis Carroll was right about the world after all. Go read *Alice in Wonderland* again. And don't make the mistake of thinking it's a children's story. Now, what makes you think this doesn't make sense? Does it have to?"

"Yes, sir. It should. When I look at this picture and make a typical War College analysis of what I see, it can't be what we think it is," Jeff Pickens announced.

"Why do you say that, Jeff?" asked NIA chief Al Murray.

"If that's the place transmitting an ELF signal powerful enough to overwhelm the Earth's magnetic field, it isn't big enough," the former general pointed out. "Compare it to the Navy's ELF facilities!"

"Mark, do you have any indication of how powerful that signal has to be to do what it's done in Nevada?" the Chief Executive asked his science advisor.

Dr. Mark Hankamer didn't know. So, he waffled. "I can't give you a quick and easy answer to that question, Mister President. Extremely low frequency transmissions require a lot of power because they achieve their range by ground signal, not by bouncing the signal off the ionosphere."

Everyone in the room -no one had left since early morning because this was shaping up to be a major security crisis - stifled a laugh. Hankamer wasn't known for his scientific brilliance. But he did have one thing going for him: He knew where to get the answers. So, he went on. "Let me check with Doctor Hunyadi out at the University of Colorado-"

"No soap, Doctor!" Al Murray interrupted. "That guy is known for his internationalist leanings. Not only isn't he cleared but he can't keep a confidence."

"General Murray," Hankamer replied sharply, deliberately using the intelligence chiefs retired rank, "the scientific community cannot operate without open discussion and exchange of information! That's part of the scientific process! 'Science knows no country.'"

"Yes, I've heard that's sometimes the case," Murray told him bluntly. "Not a good idea when someone else wants to take that scientific data, turn it into technology, and use it against you as a weapon."

"You're my science advisor," the President snapped at Hankamer. "I don't expect you to know every fact in the universe. But I do expect you to know who to go to to find the answer. If this Hunyadi isn't cleared or reliable, get someone else. I don't expect an answer correct to nine decimals, Doctor, but I do need to get some idea of the magnitude of the power requirements."

"If you want a guess, Mister President," Hankamer rejoindered, "I can do that. But I want it understood that it's a guess. Based on the Navy's experience, that Himalayan signal has to be at least half a million watts at the transmitter!"

"Which means several million watts energy input if losses are considered," Murray added.

"Mister President, that's why I remarked that it doesn't make sense," Pickens put in. He stood up and moved to the holo tank. Sticking his hand and arm into the image, he indicated the surrounding area as he went on. "I see no indication of an electric transmission line coming into this place. I discount the use of a small nuclear power source because I see no way to get rid of the waste heat. And I see no evidence of wind-power or even solar-power facilities. Therefore, they don't have the power resources to transmit a five-hundred-kilowatt signal! What we do see are buildings - maybe barracks here, a small motor pool over here with several trucks visible, an unimproved mountain road leading into the facility. And some evidence of digging as indicated by those dirt piles in the vicinity."

"Geothermal power?" asked the Secretary of State.

"No, Fran, there's practically zero volcanic activity in the Himalayas," Hankamer pointed out. He did know a few things.

"I was thinking about the chance that hot spots could exist where the Arabian tectonic plate is slamming into the Asian plate," Frances Kellogg said quietly. "I'm an amateur geologist, in case you didn't know. Comes from growing up in Colorado."

The President had the fleeting thought that perhaps he had the wrong person as his science advisor. But Hankamer had been a political appointee. The President wasn't a malicious man. He knew that Hankamer would someday stumble badly, providing the excuse necessary to ask gracefully for his resignation in a way that wouldn't enrage the academic community. In the meantime, the President knew that one of his responsibilities was to detect when his science advisor was giving poor or dangerous advice. If he thought that was happening, he'd act in such a way that this bad advice didn't become dangerous to the health and well-being of the nation or the world.

"Interesting," was Hankamer's brief comment. Insofar as he was concerned, amateur scientists were uneducated, uninformed, over-enthusiastic meddlers. He believed that science should be left to the professionals. "However, I see no power source at this location that would allow a transmission of this magnitude to be created. The two active volcanoes are too far away. And we have no record of any hot spots in Kashmir."

"Have we considered that something like a trigger effect may be involved here?" Secretary of Defense David Henshaw asked, his brow furrowed in concentration and deep thought.

"What do you mean, Dave?" the Chief Executive wanted to know.

"Doesn't take much energy to cause a bell to ring because the bell sounds off at its resonant frequency. Someone - I think it was you, Al - pointed out earlier today that this six-hertz signal could resonate with the natural frequency of the Earth and its ionosphere. Provided that we were in the right season of the year, the solar activity was right, and the phases of the moon were proper..."

"Sounds like you've been reading too much science fiction, David," Hankamer told him. "Or listening to those technological forecasters you have over there in the Pentagon." Hankamer didn't like the people Henshaw had hired and put to work trying to determine where science and technology were going in twenty to fifty years. Hankamer knew some of them and considered them to be far-out visionaries who didn't have their feet firmly planted in the reality of the present. It would have been just as effective, Hankamer believed, if Henshaw had taken a couple of generals and ordered crystal balls for them.

"Those think-tankers are doing a pretty good job of forcing new paradigms and unstuffing stuffed shirts, Doctor," Henshaw replied coolly.

The President decided that it was time to call for action. Otherwise, this discussion and argument could go on for days. There was so little information upon which to base a solid conclusion that he felt it was time to break out and see what might happen. "Very well, we don't know what's causing the six-hertz East World signal or how they're generating it. Fran, this East World site looks like it's in that part of Kashmir that's disputed between Pakistan, India, and China."

"Yes, Mister President, it's in that part of Kashmir known as Hunza Province," the Secretary of State replied. "That's supposed to be under the administrative control of Pakistan."

"Will you please meet with the Pakistani ambassador and see if they'll support us in sending a 'scientific expedition' up there to have a look?"

She nodded with a smile. She liked the way this President operated. "I think they will, and they may want some of their people to go along."

"I'll get with the National Science Foundation and have them talk to their counterparts in Islamabad," Hankamer added.

The President shook his head. "Please don't take me literally, Mark. This expedition has nothing to do with science. It's a covert military operation. We must find out what's going on up there in supposedly friendly territory. And we have to stop it."

"But Mister President, science is certainly involved! If that transmission is indeed coming from there, it may be powered by some new energy source! We need to know!"

"I'll concede that, Doctor. Some scientific observers should be attached to the expedition. Want to go?"

"Sir, my job is here!"

"Then who do you recommend we send?"

"Can I get back to you on this, Mister President?"

"Of course. But remember that this is being conducted under the tightest possible security restrictions. The effectiveness of our military and naval forces is at stake. Otherwise, this ELF transmission from Kashmir would be nothing more than a scientific oddity that I would gladly turn over to the NSF for an explanation...when they got around to giving one."

The door behind the President opened and his secretary, Kim Blythe, came quietly into the room. She stepped up behind the Chief Executive and handed him a note on orange paper.

Normally, the President didn't like to be disturbed in NSC meetings such as this. But this one had gone on all day, and he still had other duties and responsibilities to take care of. The orange note told him immediately that it was important. He sighed. If it wasn't important

Kim would not have come in. Kim Blythe had been with him for a long time as an aide-de-camp. He trusted her.

When the President read the message, he said, "Thank you, Kim. Al, you've got a scrambled telephone call from Pyramid. And Doctor Hankamer, you've also got one from someone who calls himself Stegosaurus." It didn't surprise him that the NIA chief would receive a call from a code. On the other hand, it was unusual for Hankamer to have such a call.

And it was unusual for two such calls to come in simultaneously.

"You can take those calls here or in the offices down the hall," Kim Blythe remarked.

Murray didn't want anyone to see or even know about the decryption device he had in his pocket that would clip to the telephone. "I'll take it in private, Kim."

The President wasn't surprised about that either. His intelligence chief had been in charge of the NIA for a long time. Al Murray had never broken a confidence or blown the cover on one of his people. He worked very quietly and very efficiently. "I should have presumed that, but I know better now than to presume anything in your case, Al. Doctor, how about you?"

"I have nothing to hide, Mister President. I'll take the call here, if that's amenable to you."

"It is." The President arose. "Ten-minute break to stretch and visit the latrine."

But he didn't leave the room. He remained standing, looking out the windows at the White House grounds.

The Secretary of State joined him. "Kim Blythe has been with you for a long time, hasn't she?"

The President nodded. "She was my first ADC when I got my star. She's very good at what she does."

"And she does a very good job of being a surrogate First Lady."

"Fran, that's not a subject for discussion or even idle conversation," the President said, not taking his eyes off the scene outside. "As we know, there's been far too much scandalous behavior in this mansion over the past several decades. I do not intend to perpetuate it. That wouldn't be professional of me."

Rumors had abounded in Washington, a city that runs on rumors and leaks. And an occasional scandal when it's politically beneficial. The President had made it known through what he called "calibrated leaks" that just because he'd never married didn't mean he was AC-DC, multi-polarized, or even a neutral particle. With tact, he'd explained that life with a combat officer in today's military world with a super-lethal battlefield would, in his belief, not be fair to a wife or a family. Like many other military people, he'd remained unmarried. And he still was.

"Sorry," Frances Kellogg apologized, and changed the subject tactfully. "I've noticed that you spend a lot of time looking out the window."

He nodded. "I've never really been an office type or a city boy. And this place can create the damnedest closed-in feeling. It has a tendency to warp one's judgment, to make a person feel that this is the whole world. Well, it isn't. So, I try to look out the window as much as I can to remind myself that there's still a world out there."

"You should get away to Camp David more often."

"Even Camp David seems hemmed in," the President observed. "That's why I'm spending a little of my own money fixing up my hideaway out at Diamond Point, Arizona."

"You aren't the first President to have a western retreat," she pointed out.

Although the President had been engaged in this idle social chatter with his Secretary of State, another part of his mind had been listening to Doctor Hankamer's voice speaking into the telephone nearby. Trained as a warbot brainy, the President had the ability to work his mind on several levels at once. He didn't want to be totally surprised by what Hankamer reported to him. And he was certain that it was a matter that Hankamer would indeed make a report about. Kim would have otherwise filtered the call in a graceful manner, or Hankamer would have asked her to take a message for a call-back. The telephone call was apparently something Hankamer believed would enhance his status as Presidential Science Advisor.

But hearing one side of the conversation was like receiving incomplete G-2 reports, the President decided. Hankamer was curt and brusque. He also used some strange terminology that the President didn't recognize as being scientific jargon; therefore, it had to be code terminology.

But before Hankamer hung up, Al Murray came back into the room. The intelligence chief had a broad smile on his face. When Hankamer saw that, he quickly brought his conversation to a close with a promise to call back as soon as the meeting was over.

Murray shot a quick look at his boss. It was obvious from the signal that Murray had something hot to report. So, the President stepped back from the window, returned his mind to the confines of the room, and announced that the NSC meeting was being reconvened.

The President then remarked, "Al, you look like you just won the lottery. What's up? Report, please!"

"Better than that. The Devil decided to move Hell to Texas and has given me the option to do the job." Murray was indeed happy or he wouldn't have joked in that manner. "Seriously, we just had our first break in the East World warbot countermeasures affair. That telephone call was from one of my people. Please don't ask who and where. We've been contacted by an East World neuroelectronics scientist who wants to defect with most of his staff to West World. Preferably the United States."

"Interesting," Doctor Mark Hankamer observed. "I was just called by one of my colleagues - again, name and affiliation don't matter at this point. Some members of the scientific community involved in the international neuroelectronics conferences have been contacted as well. Specifically, by a representative speaking for Doctor Wen Ling Dongzhu. He's the top NE researcher in the People's Republic of China at Beijing."

"My contact has spoken with Doctor Dongzhu directly," Murray reported. "He's not at the People's Institute of Intelligent Machinery Development at the moment. He's in charge of something called the

Deosai Research Establishment. And he doesn't like what he and his staff are being forced to do. In fact, he's lost some of his people as a result of the hazards involved in this work. It killed them, as a matter of fact. Dongzhu isn't happy that his work has been turned into a weapon."

Hankamer nodded. "It's my understanding from my recent telephone conversation that Doctor Dongzhu has been forced to leave Beijing and to interrupt what he considers important work in neuroelectronic research. He and his staff want to defect to gain the freedom of thought and action that scientists require." Hankamer was pedantic in his attempt to upstage Murray.

But that was a difficult thing to do, even for the Presidential Science Advisor. Murray had more information. But he remained silent. The President asked, "Doctor, where is this Deosai Research Establishment?"

"I don't know, Mister President. Probably an annex to the Institute of Intelligent Machinery Development."

Murray switched on the holograph tank and the three-D satellite image of the buildings in Kashmir built up again. "We're looking at it," the intelligence chief remarked. "This facility is located on the Deosai Plains about five thousand meters up in the Karakorams. That's why I said this is a breakthrough. Dongzhu and his people are apparently behind the technology here."

"If so, is this Doctor Dongzhu's request for asylum real?" the President asked.

"Of course!" Hankamer replied quickly.

Murray was more cautious. "I have to check it out, Mister President. It sounds real. But it could be yet another tactical move in this undeclared war with East World. I won't recommend we do anything until I feel certain of the validity of Doctor Dongzhu's request."

"Mister President! A respected international colleague and his staff have asked for asylum!" Hankamer objected.

"Well, he's asking for more than that," Murray added. "He can't get out of Deosai. He not only wants asylum. He wants us to come and get him out of there before he and his staff are killed by the backlash of this weapon!"

Chapter Eight

"I've never been late for a Stand-To before," Colonel Curt Carson complained as he stepped up to the bar with his chief of staff. He told the robot bartender, "Make and serve me my usual. Except make it a double."

"One double vodka and tonic for Colonel Carson," the bartender announced in a voice that was too loud. Curt thought that everyone in the Club could probably hear that their colonel was stressed out and hitting the juice heavily as a result.

"Well, the Greys have never been put on yellow alert while their CO was in the air either," Lieutenant Colonel Joan Ward reminded him. "And how often have you traveled more than seven hundred kilometers to a meeting and returned the same day? Damned long commute."

"Especially under the circumstances. Do you feel any better now that we brought the Schuman Resonators back from McCarthy?" Curt asked his chief of staff.

Joan shrugged. "Hard to say. I've been working pretty damned steadily all day. I'm bushed as a result."

"So am I." Curt picked up the tall glass full of clear liquid and ice that the robot bartender offered him. "Excuse me, I've got to make the rounds."

It was incumbent upon the regimental commander to circulate through the Club and try to say something to everyone. The Washington Greys wasn't just a regiment to Curt, although he knew it would remain an entity long after he was gone. The regiment was 137 people, all of whom were individuals. They were adult professionals, and the Army was a career for them. They were the most competent, well-balanced people imaginable because they had all been through NE warbot training at Fort Benning.

This training had made them unique among the soldiers of history.

To extend yourself and your nervous system out into a warbot by means of neuroelectronic linkage meant that you had to be extremely well-balanced without any serious psychological hang-ups. You had to have your neurons all in a line, as the saying went. You had to have faced your personal devils and put them in their proper place. In short, you had to know yourself, to like yourself, and to be able to live with yourself. The result was that you liked other people too. Especially the ones who had gone through the same rigorous training.

Some of the more sensationalistic, anti-technology, anti-military media types (most of whom did not have their neurons all in a line) preached the gospel that warbot soldiers were brainless, dehumanized killer automatons no more emotional and caring than the warbots they controlled. One evening with the Washington Greys in their Club would have showed how wrong their assessment was.

Gone were the days of the Officers' Club and the NCO Club. The Club was the Club. If you were or ever had been a Washington Grey, you were more than welcome on an equal footing with everyone else. Everyone there had been shot at and survived. That was an exclusive club!

Curt often longed for the days when he could just come to the Club and relax. Sometimes - like tonight, when he was fatigued from a hard day - he wished he could just retire to his quarters and relax. Or come to the Club as he had when he was still a junior officer. But now he had responsibilities he'd never had as a junior officer. Now he was the regimental commander, and his first thoughts were for the Washington Greys.

True, there was a certain amount of prestige attached to the command of the 3rd Robot Infantry (Special Combat) Regiment, the Washington Greys. It was still the top Sierra Charlie outfit in the Army, and not because it was the first or the oldest. The Wolfhounds and the Cottonbalers were good. Competition with them kept Curt and his officers working hard to maintain the regiment's honor of being Number One. It wasn't easy.

As he went around the room, chatting informally with people, it occurred to him how much he missed some of the old Washington Greys – the ones who had paid the ultimate premium on their unlimited liability contract, the ones who had opted for resignation or retirement, or the ones who had gone on to other positions in the military service.

However, their places had been occupied by newcomers, and these new Greys were slowly carving their own niches in the old regiment. In the years to come, they'd be the ones who earned the battle streamers and other awards that hung from the regimental colors.

Curt kept this in mind as he chatted with them. Lieutenant Dan Power was impressive like several officers he'd known in the past; he was a comer. And Lieutenant Matsu Mikawa, the little Japanese-American samurai, had become a hardened combat veteran, although she looked like a fragile doll leading her Marauders. Captain Larry Hall's artillery company had some new NCOs, but Hall, Jay Taire, and Ted "Tiger" Kyger had all been blooded in Yemen and Senegambia.

The lead NCOs at battalion, company, and platoon levels were also old Greys.

Curt hadn't yet had time to assess those who were yet green to combat - Lieutenants Willard G. Stone and Steven M. Zugg, both West Pointers. They seemed aggressive and competent, although very young and very green.

He wondered if he had really been like them once. He concluded that it was probably so.

Most Greys wore the ribbon of the Purple Heart medal earned by being wounded in combat. This was in addition to their other awards for bravery and valor in combat. (And Curt encouraged the Greys to wear their ribbons; they were badges of honor, and he told them they should be proud of them.) Among the Greys, the Purple Heart was a real badge of honor. Warbot brainies who fought from the comfort of their couches in control vans to the rear of the FEBA were rarely wounded in combat. On the other hand, the Greys had exposed their pink bodies to incoming metal jackets and shrapnel.

They all had the Warbot Combat Badge, but that was only because Fort Fumble hadn't yet come up with a unique badge for the Sierra Charlies.

The last table at which he stopped was occupied by his closest comrades in arms. There he stopped table-hopping and quietly took the vacant chair that was always there. He was grateful to be with close friends, although everyone in the Greys was his friend.

"So where are we off to this time, Colonel?" Major Kitsy Clinton asked brightly.

"Who said we were off to somewhere?" Curt responded, leaning forward and putting his elbows on the tablecloth as he cradled his glass between his palms.

"Rumor Control has been buzzing," Pappy Gratton explained.

"Well, let's consider what's been happening," Kitsy went on. "One: Our warbots start going pan-up. Two: We're hit with some sort of NE weapon. Three: You rush off to McCarthy for a conference and come back he same day. Four: Fort Fumble puts us on yellow alert while you're in the air on the way home. Ergo: Something has hit the impeller, and we've got to go out and pee on a brushfire somewhere."

"I haven't been told where we're going," Curt told her truthfully. He was aware that Rumor Control Headquarters was running with a full cube of guesses. "Maybe we go. Maybe we don't. Maybe Fort Fumble just wants to keep us on our toes. But I confirm that East World has an NE weapon. But we don't know exactly how it works yet. Or where the control and transmission points are. Or what can be done about it."

"Oh, we'll go, Colonel!" Russ Frazier growled. "We're on yellow alert until the State Department fogs around with diplomacy and tries to get East World to shut the damned thing off under the international rules relating to electromagnetic radiation and spectrum allocation." Russ was showing himself to be more and more savvy beyond just being aggressive. "East World will either tell us to go piss up a rope or play innocent. Either way, we'll have to go out and bust up something somewhere in one of the garden spots of the world. Like the Gobi Desert maybe. Sort of like Kerguelen."

"Kerguelen was awful!" Kitsy recalled with distaste. "And I couldn't spell it."

"Can you spell Kashmir, Kitsy?" Joan Ward asked rhetorically.

"Was Kashmir mentioned in the yellow alert order?" Henry Kester asked. "I sure as hell didn't see it."

"Your eyes are giving out," Sampson told him.

"Probably. If so, it's the only thing thus far."

"Henry, you're like the Wunnerful One Hoss Shay," Nick Gerard kidded him.

"Mebbe, but I ain't got to a hundred years and a day yet. I gotta tell you that some of our warbots are gettin' close, however. Colonel, when are we gonna get enough new ones to replace what we smashed up in Dakar? We're still about fifty percent short in the bot department."

"Probably not until someone figures out what the hell is causing warbots to go pan-up," Captain Hassan Ben Mahmud guessed. "If some warbot countermeasures weapon from East World is screwing up the Mod Seven-Eleven units, you can bet we can't look forward to getting any more Mary Anns or Jeeps until McCarthy finds the problem and puts the fix in."

"Then why did they put us on yellow alert? Fort Fumble knows we're short-botted," Russ Frazier pointed out.

Dyani spoke up in her quiet voice. "Maybe we're going to have to go somewhere and do something about that warbot countermeasure weapon without the help of our warbots."

Russ sat straight up at that. "Jeez, Dyani! That would turn us back into pure grunt infantry!"

Dyani looked at him and smiled. "Russ, we work that way in the recon company. The warbots are there just to provide fire support."

"Could we fight without warbots?" Kitsy wondered.

"Yes, ma'am, we could," Henry said. "And we have. And we will probably have to in the future. People fight. Warbots don't. Warbots just do what we tell them."

"Sometimes," Edie Sampson added.

"It's part of your job to see that they do," he reminded her.

"Fighting without warbots..." Pappy Gratton shook his head. He was the regimental adjutant, one who wouldn't normally fight with or without warbots. But everyone in the Greys was expected to fight if necessary. It had often been necessary. Pappy wore the blue and white ribbon of the Purple Heart. "I've been through a lot of sheep screws with this outfit. But being without a warbot to hose jackets into the jerks bothers me. That might turn me into a genuine pacifist."

"Major, with all due respect, there ain't no greater pacifist than a combat veteran," Henry Kester observed.

"Do you think we're going to be sent to destroy this weapon, Colonel?" Hassan asked, getting directly to the matter of concern to everyone there that evening.

Curt thought about that for a moment before he answered. "If the previous Administration was still in office, my answer would be a resounding no. But with this one, I expect it. We know the Commander in Chief personally. We've served under him before. I don't know what rationale he'll use, but I'll bet he's told Foggy Bottom to figure out some sort of reason. I don't know what we'll be tasked to do, but I also suspect that he's told Fort Fumble to trot out a war plan. I imagine that General Bellamack is earning his pay as Army COS tonight. When they're all ready and everything is lined up in a column of ducks, we'll get the word."

"In the meantime, here we sit," Battalion Sergeant Major Gerard complained.

"What are you sniveling about, Nick?" Edie asked him. "So here we sit on yellow alert, ready to move out on twenty-four hours' notice. We're ready to do that anyway at any time! So, relax. It's just been made official, that's all."

"Well, no passes. No leaves," Gerard reminded her.

"So maybe you're nervous in the service? So, we stay here at Fort Hootchy-Cootch and wait. Why do you need to go into town? The food isn't bad; it's not gourmet cuisine, but Army food rarely is. The Club has plenty of Class Six supplies, and it's cheap here. So, what's your snivel, buddy?" Edie suddenly brightened and went on. "Aha! Got a hot honey in Sierra Vista maybe? If so, some of the ladies could get a bit upset about *that*," Edie pointed out.

"I think I understand Nick's problem," Dyani remarked. "We know we're probably going to go. But we don't know when. Or where. Or what we're going to have to do when we get there. Only that we'll have to do something deadly when the time comes."

"And maybe it won't."

"Sort of hikes you up, doesn't it?" Pappy Gratton said. "The thought that maybe you'll eat the big one this time, and all that. So, you make the best of it while you've got it." Pappy had touched on a subject few Greys really wanted to talk about although it was nagging them.

"Pappy, I never used to worry about that. Especially when I was younger and immortal," Curt admitted. Then he added, "I still don't. Much, that is."

"Well, Dy, at least we're here under yellow alert, which means Rule Ten isn't in effect while we wait," Kitsy observed.

"Damned well better not be!" Russ muttered.

"Aha! Then Rumor Control was right!" Joan Ward piped up in her small voice, which was so much out of character coming from such a Valkyrie.

"I beg your pardon?" Russ said innocently.

"Then you deny there was a woman in your quarters last night?" Joan was kidding him.

Russ riposted well. "A woman? Ma'am, you underestimate me!"

She looked askance at him. "You're starting to sound like Hassan. Maybe I should check out that rumor, seeing as how I'm chief of

80

staff with certain responsibilities and all that."

"Check away," Russ replied brightly.

The group known loosely as the Third Herd Sextet began to sing somewhere in the Club. This wasn't a formal concert, but apparently someone had come up with a new Stand-To ditty. They weren't all together on it, but under the circumstances that wasn't necessary. Everyone understood what was being sung anyway and could join in when appropriate. As the song progressed, more and more Greys joined in the chorus.

"In peacetime the Army is happy.
They'll eagerly fight practice frays.
But just let them get into trouble.
And they send in the Washington Greys!"

Someone yelled, "After all, warbots are too expensive to send into combat!"

The chorus followed each verse:

"Send in, send in,
Send in the Washington Greys, the Greys!
Send in, send in,
Send in the Washington Greys!

"So here's to the Regular Army,
They have such a wonderful plan:
They send in the Sierra Charlies
Whenever the crap hits the fan!"

"Warbots have firepower, but this operation calls for mobility!" said another raucous voice just before the chorus sounded again.

"They ignore the butt weary brainies,

They forget the eager young rates;
They send in the poor Greys to do battle
While warbots group stay in the States!

"Warbots have to stay ready for the Big War!" The shout preceded the chorus rendition. Everyone was bellowing the chorus now.

"So here's to the Regular Army,
With their medals and warbots galore;
If it weren't for the Sierra Charlies,
Their ass would be dragging the floor!"

"So, what makes you Sierra Charlies think you're special?" someone shouted.

The last chorus was deafening.

Curt found himself laughing. He noticed that Dyani was laughing too. She was always pleasant and smiling, but she had rarely laughed in public, before. Now she was revealing her emotions in public, though she usually would only in private. Curt reflected that Dyani was changing, mostly for the better. A lot of it was due to the big-sister accommodation between Dyani and Joan Ward. Curt understood why Joan could be a "big sister." She'd served in that role with him since their days together as cadets.

But he didn't understand what was going on between Dyani and Kitsy. They were now very close friends, and the reasons eluded Curt. He knew that Kitsy had tried to compete with Dyani for Curt's attentions. But Dyani had been maddeningly confident in herself. Perhaps Kitsy had become aware that Dyani wasn't super-possessive. And Kitsy had always played the field with joyful abandon. She still did so and took every opportunity she could to be with Curt. But Curt knew she enjoyed the company of Russ and Hassan and probably several others as well. When the confrontation between Kitsy and Dyani over Curt had occurred in Yemen, it had turned out to be a wet-firecracker war.

Maybe all of them were maturing.

Or "growing old," Curt corrected himself.

He didn't like to think of it that way, of course.

Dyani touched him on the arm. "You're exhausted," she observed.

He shook his head. "No, I'm hungry."

"So am I. But we haven't eaten yet." Sometimes a Dyani statement had double meaning.

"Manny has cooked up some good chili rellenos," Curt noted. One of his supply sergeants was a frustrated cook and delighted in obtaining edible Class 6 supplies so he could prepare local dishes that the Army didn't list in their meal menus.

"Let's go to quarters," Dyani suggested. "We can cook up our own wants."

"What have you got?"

"Come see."

Chapter Nine

"It's real, Mister President."

No one was trusting the telephone lines on this subject. Knowledge that East World had indeed threatened the entire warbot army of the United States with its NE radiation weaponry wasn't something that the Commander in Chief wanted to broadcast to the world. So, he'd scheduled a breakfast meeting, but it wasn't held in the White House. Too many meetings of the National Security Council would tip off someone that something was happening. It had been hard enough the day before to cover up the fact that the NSC had met nearly all day save for a few breaks. The President had had to step out from time to time to take care of several "cornerstone-laying" appointments, the sort of activity that's part of his job and no one really knows about.

This morning, the NSC met in an obscure high-rise office building near the White House. It could be reached by underground access. The meeting-room floor in the building could be accessed only by a secure elevator; other elevators skipped the floor because it didn't exist. The President liked this meeting room. It had large one-way window walls that overlooked the city. The morning sun streamed in through the bulletproof windows. The sunlight lent an air of pleasantry to a meeting that wasn't about a very pleasant topic.

Dr. Mark Hankamer was very positive and adamant in his statement. So, the President asked him, "Mark, how do you know?"

"Doctor Cook at the University of Arizona's robotic laboratory in Tucson analyzed the East World signal last night," Hankamer explained. "He found subcarriers on the pulses. Most of these were at frequencies that matched NE patterns for human sensory nerve signals. However, he also discovered a digital signal that turned out to be ASCII code. It's a message from Doctor Dongzhu that confirms what General Murray and I learned from our contacts yesterday afternoon."

"Is Doctor Cook cleared?" Murray wanted to know.

"Of course! He's doing some work for McCarthy Proving Ground on the Project Wizard Mod Thirteen AI modules. And yes, he reported it to Colonel Pendleton at McCarthy this morning."

The President turned to his intelligence chief. "Al, do your 'national technical means' confirm this?"

Before Murray could answer, Hankamer handed the NIA boss a memory module. "General, here's a copy of the memory unit that Doctor Cook expressed to me overnight. I suspect your people will want to analyze it."

Murray didn't reveal that his techies had also discovered the same subcarrier signal. The NIA's covert Pyramid Corporation laboratory in Las Vegas had sent an online copy of their reception as quickly as they'd gotten it around midnight. Murray and his people didn't mess around with commercial express outfits; they had faster means. But, maintaining. his cover, Murray reached out and took the memory module from Hankamer. "Thank you, Doctor. I appreciate this. Mister President, I'm not as sanguine as Doctor Hankamer, but I'd say Doctor Dongzhu's request for extraction and asylum is ninety-nine and nine-nines clean."

"What's bothering you about it, Al?" When the President's intelligence chief wasn't one-hundred-percent certain, the President wasn't either. He'd worked with Murray on similar operations in the past.

"Multiple message channels," Murray admitted. "Usually, requests of this sort come through a single covert channel. It's almost as if Dongzhu wants to be absolutely, positively certain that we get his message. Furthermore, it may be that he's using redundancy to convince us that the message is legitimate."

The President nodded. "I understand. You think perhaps he protests too much, to mangle a Shakespearean quote."

"Yes, sir."

The President looked around at the members of the National Security Council and asked, "Does anyone else have any new information this morning?"

Secretary of Defense David Henshaw raised his hand. "Mister President, McCarthy Proving Ground has also analyzed the signal. So has DIA. At McCarthy, one of the NE scientists there believes the message is sincere because she says she knows Doctor Dongzhu."

"Who's the McCarthy scientist?" Hankamer asked.

"Doctor Rosha Taisha."

The name was familiar to General Jeffrey Pickens, the National Security Advisor, so he asked, "Isn't she the crazy renegade NE scientist we rehabilitated at Fort Benning after the Battle Mountain episode?"

"I believe so. I was at Battle Mountain when the Washington Greys recovered her. She was catatonic at the time," the President replied. "And I remember her from the Zahedan hostage rescue mission."

"Mister President, I wouldn't trust her," Hankamer warned his boss.

"Why?"

"She's been a renegade obsessed with using NE technology for controlling people instead of developing it for people to control robots. I'm not comfortable with her in her present position at McCarthy." Actually, Hankamer didn't like Taisha because she'd never been an accepted and respected member of the Big Science Club in the United States. She had no record of peer-reviewed scientific papers. She hadn't been to scientific conferences to exchange information and let other scientists get to know her. She'd operated outside The System. Hankamer couldn't condone such "non-professional" behavior.

Henshaw spoke up. "Doctor, I personally reviewed her case when Colonel Pendleton and Doctor Lovell requested that she be hired at McCarthy. At that time, the specialists at Fort Benning began to believe they'd been successful in reprogramming her." The Secretary of Defense didn't like Big Science trying to dictate to him when it came to military research. "I even asked for comparisons between her therapy and recovery and those of warbot operators who'd undergone similar trauma. I approved Doctor Taisha's appointment at McCarthy because the Fort Benning report was very positive."

"We're getting afield here," the President pointed out, and got down to business. "As a result of our discussions, I see three alternatives. One: We can ignore this and hope it goes away. This choice possibly leaves Doctor Dongzhu and his researchers in a very untenable position. Two: We can press the governments of the People's Republic of China and India - to name but two - to cease and desist transmitting a signal in this wavelength because it's interfering with our industrial robots. This won't necessarily reveal that the signal is disrupting our warbot operations, and it again leaves Dongzhu out in the cold. Three: We can pursue the necessary diplomatic initiatives to permit us to send a strike and rescue force into Kashmir through Pakistan. I would like to have your recommendations, ladies and gentlemen."

"Now, sir?" Hankamer asked.

"Now, Doctor. If you have some reservations or want to establish a position as the Loyal Opposition, I'll accept such reports in writing when you've completed them. But this act on the part of East World is overtly threatening. I believe we must respond now. We should be ready to activate whatever operation we decide upon. Or to change it as new information is forthcoming. But it's time to act. We may not have the time to study it to death." The President knew from his distinguished military career that a good plan executed well today is better than a perfect plan next week. So, he leaned back in his chair and began going around the room to get recommendations.

They were as he suspected. But he knew the recommendations of the NSC didn't relieve him of the responsibility for making the final decision and issuing orders to implement it. Which he did.

***

More than three thousand kilometers to the west, the sun was just rising over the Mule Mountains to the east of Fort Huachuca. In Colonel Curt Carson's quarters, Dyani was already up while Curt lay groggily abed, still exhausted.

There are more tired commanders than there are tired commands, he reflected.

Dyani came back in carrying two steaming mugs of coffee. Had Curt not seen her movement, he wouldn't have known she was there. Dyani walked silently, almost catlike, in her bare feet. The only sound she made was the nearly inaudible swish of her suede leather robe. She liked wearing primitive attire that, on her, became sensual by the way she wore it.

As she sat down on the edge of the bed and handed one of the mugs to Curt, she said something in Arabic.

"And what did you just tell me in some obscure foreign language?" Curt asked as he sipped from the coffee.

"It's Arabic:

" *'Awake: for Morning in the Bowl of Night*

Has flung the Stone that puts the Stars to Flight..."

"It loses in the translation, I'm told."

"You've been spending too much time with Hassan," Curt grumbled, although the grumble was only because he hadn't come totally awake yet. Since he wasn't in a combat situation where he had to be alert, he relished the opportunity to stay groggy.

"Perhaps not enough. After all, you've spent time with Kitsy. And Willa Lovell." There was no jealousy in Dyani's voice. Long ago they'd agreed that, in the absence of a formal marriage, variety was the spice of life. They spent as much time with one another as possible, but it wasn't always possible. It had taken Curt some time to realize that in a world of growing abundance, love wasn't something scarce that had to be rationed. He knew he loved many people, but he loved one more than all the rest.

"So? Do you want to make this permanent?" he asked.

"It's not yet time, Kida."

"Okay, do you want to move in here permanently?"

"No, Kida, it wouldn't look right, in spite of the fact that everyone knows," Dyani said, although her eyes said something else.

"Ah, hypocrisy remains with us, even in the modern Army!" Curt sighed.

"Protocol, my Colonel."

"Screw the protocol!"

"No, I'd rather you reserved that for something else. But not at the moment. We're under yellow alert, and the red flag could go up at any time."

Curt sighed. He knew that Dyani was getting strung out by the tension. As a result of the meeting at McCarthy Proving Ground yesterday, they'd both agreed they'd probably be sent out to destroy whatever facility was generating the disrupting NE signals. "Likely. Other similar operations have taken place in the past. And you were right yesterday: We can probably operate without our warbots if we have to. But so could the Wolfhounds and the Cottonbalers."

"They'll call on the Washington Greys," Dyani said simply.

"Why do you say that?" Curt was interested in her insight because she always looked at the world from a slightly different perspective than he did. It was part of her heritage as a Crow Indian, a tribe that had proudly served in and with the United States Army for more than 200 years.

"We're both Washington Greys. We will be forever. So is the Commander in Chief, the Army Chief of Staff, and the division commander," Dyani reminded him. She thought about this for a moment, then observed in an unusually loquacious manner, "When they want to make certain that something is done right the first time, they'll call on an outfit they trust. They certainly won't give the job to an outfit they don't really know, no matter how good the unit is. You do the same in the regiment. I've watched you. You've called on me when you needed someone to move around behind an enemy position for scouting or tactics. You've called on Russ or Kitsy when you needed the sort of aggressive offense each of them can mount in their different ways. You prefer to have Nancy fly the 'dyne in which you're riding. When you want tacair fast and surgical without a lot of Worsham's blustering aggressiveness, you call on Paul. In the past, you've called on other trusted colleagues and subordinates who are no longer with us. Kida, people who've been Washington Greys will behave in the same manner as the present regimental commander because the Washington Greys have shaped them in the same mold."

"You're probably right," he told her somberly.

"I hope I'm not. I have the feeling that this one will be very dangerous."

As if on signal, the comm unit chimed.

Dyani looked askance at Curt.

Curt returned the look.

"Whoever it is, they had the good grace to call after dawn," Curt muttered.

"It usually comes at a worse time," Dyani observed.

"Are you psychic or something?"

Dyani shrugged. "This early in the morning, it's either the OOD with a major problem, or someone from the Pentagon who's forgotten the three-hour time difference. Either way, it's important."

"It had better be, or someone will be patrolling the south boundary for the next sixty days!" Curt promised, and got up. When he got to the comm terminal, he didn't activate the visual pickup. "Colonel Carson speaking!"

The image of General William D. Bellamack took shape on the screen. "Good morning, Curt! Hope I didn't disturb you."

"No, sir, it's only oh-six-ten here."

"Damn! No wonder you haven't turned on your video! I wouldn't want people to see me just after I rolled out of the sack either! And I forgot that Arizona doesn't go on daylight time!"

"A lot of people forget," Curt reminded him. People in Arizona - which was well west in its time zone anyway – didn't *want* to have the desert sun stay up another hour in the summertime. "Well, what's up, General? You wouldn't have called me this early unless it had something to do with the yellow alert and the reasons behind it."

"I know the Greys are short-botted," Bellamack began. "No one in the Iron Fist has come up to a full T-O-and-E since Senegambia. Hopefully, that will change once the warbot production lines begin to run full time in a few months."

"If we don't get this current countermeasures matter squared away, General, we may wait longer than that for new warbots," Curt observed.

"There's that, yes. But in the meantime, I notice that the Greys are up to strength personnel-wise."

"Yes, sir."

"How's your readiness level, as if I had to ask?"

"Hot to trot and good to go, General."

"Okay, there's an operation coming up. It's not going to be easy. You're in line for it. But the Washington Greys have been going out to piss on every little brushfire in the world for years. I was on some of them with you. But it's possible to wear out a good outfit by overuse. That's why I called. We could specify the Wolfhounds or the Cottonbalers with the Greys in reserve. I want to give you the unofficial chance to turn down this one." Bellamack was candid with Curt and always had been. But this was a highly unusual move on Bellamack's part.

"It's not my decision to make, General. If we get orders, we march."

"You haven't got orders, so you aren't rejecting them," Bellamack pointed out.

"As I told you, General, if we get orders, we march."

"Dammit, Curt, you and the Greys have been marching to every drumroll for over a decade! I just want to know if you and your people are up to undertaking probably the most dangerous fire-pissing operation yet!"

"Yes, sir. The Washington Greys are ready, sir."

"You may be, but what do the rest of the Greys say?"

"If we get orders, we go. We always have."

Bellamack sighed. "Will you take an informal survey of the Greys on this one?"

"Only if ordered to do so, General." Curt had wondered why Wild Bill Bellamack had called him directly, cutting division commander Belinda Hettrick out of the loop. This was an intensely personal and highly unofficial conversation. "Look, I appreciate the fact that you had us in mind and that you called me unofficially about it. But you know the only answers I can give you are the ones I already have. The Army doesn't run permissively by asking commanders if they'll accept orders."

"We don't elect our own officers either," Bellamack said, "but any commander who doesn't have a silent vote of confidence from his subordinates won't be able to lead them."

"I do my best, sir. You and General Hettrick taught me a lot."

"Hell, you taught me more than I ever managed to teach you, Curt!" Bellamack had gotten the answers he really wanted anyway, although Curt hadn't given him a direct response on any of the questions. The Washington Greys hadn't changed since Bellamack had commanded them, the Army's Chief of Staff decided. He grimaced, then said, "Here's an unofficial heads-up. It looks like Zahedan and Kerguelen again. But different. This time with tassels on it. And maybe no warbots. Minimal warbots in any event. Can the Greys hack it, Curt? Can you carry out a destroy and retrieval mission without warbots? With nothing but Sierra Charlies?"

Curt had thought a lot about that possibility in the last twenty-four hours. He didn't like it. He told the Army Chief of Staff, "I don't like it, Bill. But if the Greys have to do it that way, we'll do it. I hate to say this, but we may require a larger issue of body bags as a result."

"If you're ordered to go, Curt, and you have to do it without warbots, what else do you need?" Formal military protocol had blown away between the two men at this point. They were old comrades in arms. They knew they'd be giving lethal orders that would send their friends and colleagues into a very deadly situation. They were dealing with one another then in a very basic manner. Lives were at stake.

Curt Carson answered without hesitation. "A damned good ops plan with lots of options in it, Bill. And a damned good reason to go do whatever we have to do! As you know, the Washington Greys will follow orders because that's what we've all agreed to do to protect the United States and the Free World. But sometimes that isn't enough, Bill. The Washington Greys will fight and survive much better if there's a damned good reason why they should lay their lives on the line."

"There is, and everyone will be given the full story, Curt. You may not like it, but I think you'll agree with the reasons. If we don't pull this thing off, it's the end of the warbots."

Chapter Ten

"You heard correctly!" Colonel Curt Carson told the assembled Washington Greys. The briefing room or "snake pit" had become filled with excited mutterings and exclamations. "Assume at this moment that we no longer have neuroelectronic capabilities. Assume that they've gone away. Assume that we have to reconfigure our operations in such a way that we work without any NE whatsoever. Assume that any use of NE communications or linkage will backfire. It will either kill you or kill someone in the Greys."

"Colonel, is this just another war game, or are you talking real world stuff here?" Major Russ Frazier wanted to know.

"It's the real world," Curt admitted. He sat on the edge of the table on the low stage located at the focus of the raised rows of seats in the snake pit. The briefing center for a Sierra Charlie regiment wasn't like the snake pit of a Robot Infantry unit, where everyone lay around in linkage couches, getting briefed directly into their minds by neuroelectronic techniques. This was more like an old collegiate lecture hall except for the holo tank behind the stage.

Curt put the long wooden pointer, the surrogate sword of command, across his knees and went on. "In domestic industry, it's called the 'Green Field Approach.' Companies use it to solve apparently insoluble problems. You start with the assumption that everything you have no longer exists or doesn't work. Then you figure out how you'd do something if you had to start with a green field. The field has nothing on it that you have to save. You start from nothing. You start thinking about how you'd do something without techniques you take for granted but with everything you know. Well, we're in a similar green field situation.

"We went to Fort McCarthy yesterday morning. No one was sworn to secrecy within the regiment, so I know the word has gotten around by now. Let me reconfirm it. But let me also tell you that what you hear today is highly classified. Not quite to the level of Destroy before Reading, Suicide First. But don't talk about it to anyone or anything, including your friendly warbot."

He activated a switch on the lectern. A map of the world came up in the holo tank behind him. Whatever the East World signal was doing, it wasn't affecting the regimental computer, "Grady," named by the ladies of the Greys after the Kipling poetic reference to "the colonel's lady and Judy O'Grady." They'd shortened it to "Grady" and made it masculine.

"Someone in East World is beaming a six-hertz electromagnetic signal at McCarthy Proving Ground. We were in the splatter or overshoot. But the signal was strong enough to disrupt our biological clocks, which apparently are synchronized to the ten-hertz pulse of the Earth's magnetic field. That's why we were feeling so lousy yesterday at this time. The whizzos at McCarthy came up with these little grey cubes they call Schuman Resonators." Curt held up the one he'd been given by Dr. Willa Lovell. "They generate a more powerful ten-hertz signal that blanks out the East World signal. We passed around some of these when we got back. Did everyone sleep better last night? Show of hands, please."

Every hand in the snake pit went up.

"Good! We were told by Colonel Pendleton at McCarthy that the signal from these Schuman Resonators has enough power and range that a few of them would do the job for the whole regiment. It seems he was right.

"Colonel, will we be getting more of these?" Major Harriet Dearborn, logistics chief, asked.

"I'm told everyone will have one," Curt reassured her. "McCarthy is working around the clock to fabricate handmade prototypes of them. You should receive a shipment today."

"Who in the regiment has them already? And how do I account for and keep track of these gadgets?"

"Harriet, pass around a sign-up sheet. Everyone who has a Resonator should put down their names. You can build a data base from that. As for keeping track of them by normal Army methods, forget it!" Curt insisted. "Officially, they don't exist. They have no serial numbers. And they sure as hell don't have any Log One component identifiers. They're experimental units. Let McCarthy worry about the accounting.

"But this was the easy part of countering the East World signal," Curt went on. "McCarthy believes that somehow the signal is an NE warbot counter-weapon. But it apparently doesn't work against the warbots themselves. It works against us as we direct the warbots. It somehow affects the neuroelectronic signals picked up by our helmet sensors and Dale Brown's birdbot command couch sensors. And it screws up the NE signals fed back into our heads by the warbots. Some of the bird-botters nearly went KIA day before yesterday. Captain Brown, how are they today?"

"We're all here, Colonel! Good to go!" the birdbot platoon commander fired back brightly.

"Okay, but you're not going anywhere. At least not with NE linkage," Curt told him. "The same goes for everyone else. This is a direct order: Until McCarthy figures out what's going on with this East World signal, no one - I repeat, no one - will use or operate any equipment by neuroelectronic means. We will henceforth operate without it until I rescind this order."

"Colonel, that puts us on the ground!" Dale Brown objected.

"Same for us!" Lieutenant Colonel Calvin J. Worsham of the Air Battalion growled.

"FIDO! That's the way it's going to be! I don't want anyone to go KIA as a result of this East World weapon!" Curt snapped firmly. He turned back to the world map in the holo tank. Using his pointer, he indicated the subcontinent of India as he spoke. "We're on yellow alert. This means the fairy godmother in Fort Fumble has touched us with her magic wand and we aren't supposed to go anywhere off post. It also means to me that we're undoubtedly going to have to go out there and take care of this threat to our warbot forces. We may do it with the Wolfhounds and Cottonbalers. It may be a Seventeenth Iron Fist Division operation.

They may be behind us in reserve. However, it may be a super-quiet operation involving only the Greys. That would preserve security. The Greys are only a hundred thirty-seven people, a little over a hundred vehicles, eighty-four warbots, and sixteen aerodynes. We come and go around Huachuca irregularly on war games and maneuvers. No one will notice us. If the whole damned Iron Fist Division goes somewhere, no matter how tight the security, it will make the newspapers in Sierra Vista and probably Tucson too.

"So, it's likely to be just the Greys. I'm reasonably certain we'll be tasked with this operation because we're the most experienced Sierra Charlie outfit in the world. If we have to go in and do a job on whatever is transmitting this signal, we'll have to do it without NE warbots.

"As a matter of fact, I'm sure of all this. I got a call this morning. Not exactly at oh-dark-thirty, but damned close to it," he continued. "It was an old friend of ours, General Wild Bill Bellamack. He gave me a heads-up and a lot of information. And I'm passing it along to all of you so you can start thinking and reconfiguring.

"First of all, certain 'national technical means' have located what may be the transmitter for this ELF signal." No one asked what those "national technical means" were. They knew they could include satellites, high-flying hypersonic recon spaceplanes, or espionage agents.

America had not let down her guard over the years, although it had grown soft and weak occasionally. Threats were everywhere out there. The world was a very dangerous place in the twenty-first century. Weaponry had become very sophisticated and deadly. And the number of deadly, vicious, and covetous people hadn't decreased.

The Greys knew that was why the armed forces of the United States existed and why they still had jobs.

Curt's fingers played with the lectern controls. The map zoomed in on Pakistan, then enlarged that segment known as Kashmir in the north of that country. Bellamack had agreed with Curt's assessment that the Greys should have all the information possible. So, Curt had the latest info from Army Intelligence and DIA. It had been squirted down to Fort Huachuca, where it went into Georgie, the divisional computer, and the Greys' own regimental computer. Thus, Grady continued to zoom the image until a series of buildings came into view. "Something new is going on in a place called the Plains of Deosai five thousand meters up in the Himalayas. Deosai is in an area that's been contested by Pakistan, India, and China for nearly a hundred years. However, it's always been considered worthless mountain territory and not much worth killing a lot of soldiers. Until maybe recently. But no one seems to know why this transmitter is located there."

Curt paused. "So if and when the slime hits the impeller, this is where we'll go. And we'll undoubtedly be tasked with finding out what those buildings are. And probably destroying them."

"*Five thousand meters?*" Cal Worsham growled. "Goddammit all to hell, that's *above* the fucking service ceiling of a *loaded* Chippie! And *damned near* above the fucking service ceiling for a Harpy *unless we off-load some ordnance!*" Worsham always spoke in highly vulgar and strongly emphasized phrases. It was just his. manner of talking, and everyone had gotten used to it. The ladies of the Greys had determined that a lot of Cal Worsham was bluster. According to Rumor Control, his bark was far worse than his bite.

"I suspected that would be one of your problems, Cal," Curt told him. "So, figure out what to do about these problems. If we call for airlift or tacair up there, I want to know how much you can lift in each Chippie. I want to know how much ordnance each Harpy can haul."

"Where do we base? Where's our fuel supply?"

"I guess it's somewhere in Pakistan proper. I don't know where yet. That's up to the people in Foggy Bottom and Fort Fumble who work the Pakistani military support mission. We'll be told what the logistical support elements are. Fort Fumble is aware of the air support problems. After all, American warbot troops have supported the Pakistanis up in Kashmir before," Curt pointed out. "Cal, you tell me what you can do, then be prepared to do that plus one hundred percent more."

"Shit, so what else is new?" Worsham grumbled. "Damned right! You call, we haul."

"Major Frazier, as backup, figure out how we might be able to do it only on the ground," Curt told his operations staffer.

"Yes, sir!" Russ knew why Curt had said that.

And Worsham reacted accordingly. "Colonel, you'll get what you asked for."

"You and your Warhawks always come through, Cal," Curt told him, stroking the man's ego the way a good commander should. He turned to the whole regiment. "Now, to keep the rest of you from going stir-crazy under yellow alert, I want you to get busy, start thinking, and figure out how to do what we normally do. That's easy. You've done that many times before. But this time it's different. This time, figure out how to do it *without* neuroelectronic support of any kind."

Silence fell over the snake pit as the impact of these words sunk in.

"Well, the first thing we should do is rip the NE equipment out of our helmets," Edie Sampson suggested. "That will remove the temptation to use NE tacomm when the world goes to slime. We can all carry verbose tacomm bricks. Major Dearborn, how many voice tacomm bricks do you have available in stores?"

"Not enough to supply everyone in the regiment with one," the S-4 logistics officer replied. "If I have enough time, I can get enough bricks. How much time do I have, Colonel?"

"Harriet, you know how the Army works," Joan Ward put in. "If we needed those tacomm bricks tomorrow, the request would hit your terminal screen at quitting time tomorrow."

Dearborn sighed. "That's what I thought! We've got nearly fifty out there in the regiment now. But what with the need for spares and all, hell, I don't know where I can find about a hundred additional bricks!"

"Why not ask Colonel Kleperis at Division G-4?" Ward suggested.

"Because if this NE prohibition covers the whole Army, we're all going to be using smoke signals instead of tacomm bricks."

"So you'd better get on it, Harriet."

"As soon as this Papa brief is over," she promised. "I'll start out working dicker swaps. What have we got lots of that we aren't going to need?"

"Birdbots," Captain Dale Brown groused.

"Right, but no one else will be able to use them either," Curt advised him.

"So, we swap them out before anyone else knows," Dearborn decided.

This made Captain Dale Brown unhappy as hell. "Goddammit, Colonel, we've got to have birdbots for recce!"

"No birdbots," Curt confirmed.

"So there goes our real-time aerial recon capability."

"Not necessarily," Dyani put in.

"With all due respect, Captain, I don't think it's a wise thing to ask my birdbot brainies to pick up Novias and get down and dirty with your ground scouts in Harlie Saunders' platoon," Brown complained.

"I know. It's a dirty job – literally - but someone has to do it. My normal scouts will continue to work on the ground and be shot at if they're seen. I wouldn't ask you to get down and dirty with us, Dale. I don't have time to train you," Dyani admitted. Then she seemed to have a bright idea, and she asked him, "Can your bird-botters use binoculars?"

"Use our uncalibrated naked-type Mark One eyeballs? Sure!"

"Colonel Worsham, you won't be able to use the NE circuitry hooked to the recce sensors in your Harpies either," Dyani pointed out. "Suppose we put the bird-botters in the spare seats up under the canopies, let your Harpy drivers do the flying, and let Dale's people be the recce eyes. What do you think? Can you hack it?"

Cal thought about this for a moment. Finally he admitted, "It *might* work because my 'dyne drivers are going to be *very* busy flying their ships *without* even soft linkage into the *autopilots*. Matter of *fact*, we're going to have to *disable* the NE pilot controls and go back to letting the *autopilots* have *direct control*. The pilots' jobs will be to *visually monitor* the instruments and give *verbal and physical* commands to the autopilot. That's going to keep us all *goddamned* busy up there! Flying a 'dyne *without* linkage isn't *easy!* So if you *want* to put a pair of *calibrated eyeballs* in the cockpit with us to look outside, I'll *welcome* it. It will relieve *pilot* workload. Same goes for *anyone* in GUNCO. Larry, if we can't *lift* your Saucy Cans into the area, I'd *appreciate it* all to hell if you could put *some* of the gunny people in my Harpies as *weapons systems directors*."

"I can do that," Captain Larry Hall of GUNCO replied without hesitation. "Okay, we're used to squattiug on the ground and digging in if we start taking too much incoming. In the air, it's going to be a different drill. I don't know how my gunners will feel. They're not used to having their asses bare to the world up there in the air. But we'll work it out!"

"Aw, we'll give 'em a *manhole cover* to sit on," Worsham promised. "Or a spare suit of *body armor* to use as an armored *seat cushion*."

"That ought to work reasonably well. We can go try it this afternoon," Captain Paul Hands, commander of the tacair flight, suggested.

"Hands, not until *all* your 'dyne drivers get a *couple of hours'* practice flying those frisbees *by hand* with your naked mind!" Worsham corrected him loudly. The flyers in the regiment were somewhat looser in their discipline and more direct in their leadership tact. "I don't *mind* if you *want* to risk your *own* pink asses, but *damned* if I'm going to let you haul a *back-seater* and risk *them* too! The *same* goes for any *passengers* or *cargo!* Listen up, 'dyne drivers! Orders of the day: *Every* 'dyne driver logs *four hours* today, including *four* night landings! *All* without *linkage* to the autopilot! And tomorrow. And the next day. And the day after that, if we're still here!"

"What the hell, Colonel! We're not supermen!" came the complaint from Jay Kennedy.

"The *hell* you're *not!* You're *'dyne drivers,* aren't you?" Worsham retorted. "You *did it* in training, *didn't you?* What's the matter? *Forgotten* how to be a *real* pilot?"

"Everyone in the regiment is going to go out in the field this afternoon and learn how to do things without neuroelectronics," Curt told the Greys.

"Colonel, it's going to take us a day or so to reconfigure the Mary Anns and Jeeps for total verbose mode," Major Elwood Otis of the warbot technical company pointed out. He was in charge of all warbot repair and maintenance.

"With all due respect, Major," Edie Sampson said, "how long does it take to pull the connectors on the NE modules? Two twists with a screwdriver and a yank with a Mexican speed wrench. Out come the NE modules. Slicker than hell!"

"Sergeant, that kind of a modification is a Level Two matter," Otis reminded her. "Maybe you and some of the others get away with such things in combat, but the regulations are very specific about modifying warbots. Pulling the NE circuits from a warbot means making it partly deaf and dumb. That could create a very dangerous rogue warbot if it isn't done right. That's why the Army doesn't want warbot operators doing that sort of thing."

"Elwood, this isn't a leisurely sort of mod that can be done at Level Four status in garrison," Curt told him quietly. "We're on yellow alert. The ops orders to move out can come at any time. Under emergency conditions, the Sierra Charlies can pull those bot modules because you and BOTECO don't have the time or the manpower. Yellow alert implies semi-emergency conditions that could turn into red alert full emergency panicsville fifteen seconds from now."

"Colonel, I'm the guy who will catch hell if the modified bots go pan-up. And maybe I'll gel blamed if some Greys get killed or wounded us a result," Otis reminded his commanding officer. "That's not an easy thing to be forced to live with."

"I agree. Warbot maintenance is indeed your responsibility. I won't relieve you of that responsibility for our hardware and software any more than I would relieve Major Gydesen of her responsibilities for the health of our jellyware," Curt told him easily. Then he suggested, "Suppose you and your people were to make a quick check of each bot once the mod has been carried out by that warbot's mentor."

"I'd feel better about it."

"So would I, Colonel. Sometimes people get over enthusiastic or over cautious," Henry Kester advised his CO.

Lieutenant Colonel Wade Hampton, service batt chief, spoke up. "Elwood, everyone will cover you. I suggest that your people tell everyone what warbot modules can be removed or disabled by the warbot operators. Most of the Sierra Charlies know the insides of their warbots pretty well. Once told what to do, the cognizant Sierra Charlie will carry out the mod. Your people can then pull an inspection to make sure it was done right."

"I think I'd want an operational test as well," Otis added, moving to an even more conservative position.

"You'll get that," Colonel Curt Carson told everyone in general. "Yellow alert doesn't mean we have to sit on our asses here waiting for the red one to go up the pole. So, we're going out on maneuvers at eighteen hundred hours today. That should give everyone enough time to make the emergency mods to the warbots. We'll take the warbots along, but we may not operate with them all the time we're out in the boonies. How long are we staying out? Figure on the full tactical logistics duration: one hundred hours. We've *got* to learn how to fight with verbose-control warbots. And we've also *got* to learn how to fight without warbots at all. Just like the infantry of old. Sampson, make sure I've got a good comm patch in case someone finally throws the panic switch and we really have to go out and save the Free World again."

Chapter Eleven

"Mister President, Pakistan says yes, but with conditions."

The President sighed. "What are the conditions?" He knew his Secretary of State was an outstanding diplomat, negotiator, and foreign affairs expert. He knew she'd do her best. But in this case, he expected the worst.

He guessed it would include a "request" - i.e., a pay-off - for several billion dollars in foreign aid or military assistance. Pakistan was a modern Muslim nation in a critical position on the Indian subcontinent. However, the country had too many people, a runaway public health problem, and enemies facing it across ill-defined borders. These enemies didn't share the Muslim faith of Pakistan. Across the plains and deserts of the subcontinent was Hindu India. Up in the high mountains was yet another enemy: Tao-Communist China.

The President knew it hadn't been easy for Pakistan to defend itself and its resources, given its chronically poor economy. American warbot troops had been stationed near Islamabad from time to time in order to "assist Pakistan by patrolling critical economic reserves." This freed troops of the Pakistan Army to handle the border problems. But no American forces had been in Pakistan since the previous Administration stripped most of the world of American military forces stationed overseas on FIG (Foreign Internal Guardian) missions.

"The Pakistani government asks that our involvements be kept clandestine and that our forces fly the Pakistani flag," the Secretary of State told him with some distaste in her voice.

The President's reply was immediate. "We can keep it clandestine. That's a minor problem if we can handle the news media in the process without any leaks. However, American forces always operate under the American flag. We will not provide mercenary troops for another country."

"That's what I thought you'd say," Fran Kellogg replied with relief. "And thank you for saying it. I can proceed with those caveats, Mister President. And I'll get permission to get an Army contingent into Pakistan to handle this East World weapon problem. Fortunately for our case, East World is helping the situation. The situation isn't remaining static. I got some new information in my meeting with the Pakistani ambassador a few minutes ago. East World appears to be beaming an anti-NE countermeasures signal into Pakistan on a different frequency. No details yet, but the ambassador reports that the weapon has practically shut down most Pakistani industry that uses NE robots. It hasn't affected the Pakistani military forces yet because they don't have the classified technology for NE warbots. This news isn't on the international media nets yet. I don't see how we can keep it off."

The President was savvy when it came to robotics. He'd been a warbot brainy himself during his military career. He knew that warbots required a highly secure linkage system between the warbot brainy and the warbot. This system was highly classified. It hadn't leaked for several decades. This was unusual. Only one piece of information had been kept secure for a longer period of time: the crucial neutron kernel that ensured that a fission weapon would go bang instead of melt.

Indybots weren't as critical. They could be worked by hard-wire links in remote applications and direct laser beams where line-of-sight operations were possible.

The President had first suspected that the East World weapon was interfering with the highly classified military NE warbot linkage system. However, if East World had a variation of it that could affect indybots, this made the situation far more serious. Robots of all sorts were used in advanced nations where conservation of brain-power was critical. Robots weren't as critical in some of the emerging economies where lots of hands and feet were available to do work. Those countries didn't need robot help. But when a country such as Pakistan began to make the transition from an agricultural hand-work economy to a modern industrial system, more and more robots were required to do work that was dangerous or too difficult for humans.

Thus, disabling robots struck at the very root of the economies and industrial strengths of the advanced and transitioning nations of the twenty-first century.

The President also knew and understood the news media. He couldn't stonewall them. He couldn't lie to them. He couldn't even try to provide a little amusing misdirection. They would fry him as a result, even though his popularity ran high in the polls. He would have to confront the problem.

The President made a decision that he didn't really want to make. But he was forced to do so by the circumstances. "I'll ask Doctor Hankamer to contact the Pakistani ambassador. I want to put as much of our scientific brainpower as possible on finding the solution to this new problem as quickly as I can. I know: This means we won't be able to keep the media lid on it. But you just reported that the Pakistanis won't be able to cap it if their indybots are being affected. So the story is going to get out in Islamabad anyway."

"I think our best hope is to somehow prevent the usual media feeding frenzy," Kellogg remarked.

"Yes, and I'll leave that to many media experts. But the question nags at me. Why haven't our indybots been affected in this country?"

"I'm just a highly paid foreign policy manager, Mister President," Kellogg admitted. "I'm afraid you'll have to ask someone with a lot more technical know-how than I've got!" At least she was honest about it.

The President knew now that he didn't have much time. He had to move fast and quietly. The Pakistan story was going to get out. He couldn't stop it. However, the news media probably wouldn't pay much attention to it at the moment. After all, Pakistan was a small country on the other side of the world. However, if East World expanded the scope of its anti-robot weapon to Japan, the East Indies, and Australia, things could come unbonded in the U.S.A. very quickly.

"Fran, promise the Pakistanis whatever you have to, give them as little as possible, and tell them a strike force is being sent as fast as we can get it there," the President told her. He'd made the sort of decision he'd often hated to make when he'd been a general officer. He didn't like being forced to make a decision without all the facts in line. A good decision was obvious when the facts all pointed in the same direction and the decision was obvious. However, as he also knew from experience, any manager must be ready to make the best decision possible with whatever information is on hand at the time. Time often is the one commodity that a manager doesn't have.

He also didn't dare take a shortcut around his National Security Council, although his mind was already made up. He needed their loyalty and support. One man couldn't handle the total job of the Chief Executive.

After he'd terminated his call with the Secretary of State, he called in .his personal secretary, Kim Blythe. He asked her to call the country's U.N. ambassador down to Washington for an evening briefing. He also asked her to invite the Chairman of the Federal Communications Commission to come to the Oval Office: This meant shuffling some of the afternoon's appointments. But Blythe was good at that. Finally, he called in Jeff Pickens and told the National Security Advisor that he wanted a supper meeting of the NSC. Finally, he asked the Presidential Science Advisor to come in.

When Hankamer showed up, the President told him what had happened with the Pakistani indybots.

"This looks far more serious than I'd imagined," Hankamer admitted. "I'm not sure my budget will support the necessary studies to-"

"Mark, I want you to call for a conference of no more than twelve of the country's top NE scientists," the President told him, nipping in the bud any thought that Hankamer might be able to enhance his status by doling out some big research grants on the matter. "They are to meet here at the White House tomorrow morning."

Hankamer shook his head. "That's very short notice, Mister President. I'm not sure I'll be able to get some of the top people."

"Get the ones you can. Those who drag their feet will be left out. I haven't got time to cater to prima donnas."

"Some of them will want consulting fees."

"So pay them and forget it. You have the funds. Fax them a letter of intent and turn the nitpicking over to OMB."

"What do I tell them in advance?"

"As little as possible. If they're patriotic, appeal to their better nature. If they don't have a better nature, appeal to their self-interest. They'll be completely briefed on everything that's known about this situation here tomorrow. Look, Mark, I don't want solutions. I don't want endless discussion. I don't want grant proposals. I don't want a study paper with wall-to-wall data. By tomorrow afternoon, I want a consensus from, this ad hoc commission. I want its best assessment of what's happening, what to do about it, and how to proceed immediately to do it. I want a recommendation concerning immediate steps to be taken to meet this challenge. If the industrial robots of the United States are put out of action, our economy will grind to a halt."

"I'm not so sure that most of the scientists I'll call in for this will be willing to make those recommendations that rapidly."

"If they won't, find ones who will. Tomorrow at eighteen hundred hours - sorry, six o'clock – I'm holding a press conference to announce what we're doing. I want you to be there with the most prestigious member of the ad hoc commission. Be prepared to answer questions, but do not implicate our military warbots. Understood?"

When the Chief Executive fired off orders in that manner, even Hankamer knew that they were marching orders and not a subject of argument. It bothered him to be working for a man whom he considered at times to be a military martinet. But the Big Carrot of the big academic position after his stint as Presidential Science Advisor was far more motivating than his immediate pique at being ordered around like a recruit in basic training.

"And, by the way," the President remarked as Hankamer was

leaving the Oval Office, "not one word about the request for asylum from Doctor Dongzhu, Mark, unless you want to see him killed before we get to him."

That sobered Hankamer. But he added, "Yes, sir! It's certainly going to help to have their expert in our camp. Once we know what this weapon consists of and how it works, Yankee ingenuity will be able to figure out a way to overcome it."

The President was a tactful man. He resisted the temptation to snort derisively at Hankamer's remark. The Presidential Science Advisor probably didn't know which end of a screwdriver went in the slot. Technical ingenuity was something Hankamer didn't possess.

"I agree. And don't forget the supper meeting of the NSC," the President reminded him.

"Are you going to start the rescue. and destroy mission on its way?"

The President merely nodded.

"Suppose the commission recommends a non-military solution, sir?"

"Mark, have you ever had to abort a scientific experiment?"

"Sir, I'm not an experimentalist. But, yes, while I was an undergraduate, I did have to stop an experiment that wasn't going as planned."

"Military operations are quite similar," the Commander in Chief told him. "Like many chemical reactions, they are damnedly difficult to get started because of all the ducks that have to be lined up...and very easy to stop if the reaction hasn't started yet."

"The nuclear weapons people don't think so, Mister President."

The President smiled. "Ah, but I can deliver the weapon to the intended target and decide not to toggle the final button! In which case, I bring it home again so I can use it another day, if required. Doctor, in case you're wondering, I intend to have all my options lined up in a column of ducks and ready to move to create whatever action seems to be best. That's what is known in both business and combat as 'having Plan B.' Or Plan C. Or whatever. I suspect you scientists have something similar, but you probably call it something else. You can educate me about that someday. Right now, get your commission together, Mark! And don't drag your ass! I'll see you at dinner!"

The President had a lot of reservations about Hankamer. But he couldn't cut him out of the loop this time. Nor could he bypass others in the NSC or allied agencies.

He had a different sort of worry when he called Jeff Pickens in. The National Security Advisor was an old comrade who could be trusted but who also had shortcomings. One of these was Pickens's tendency to forget to wear his woolen socks.

Pickens was afraid to take unnecessary risks. This was commendable on the part of a commander when resources of people and materiel were short. But Pickens was now working with the entire U.S. military establishment available to him. Granted, this military capability was considerably truncated as a result of the former Commander in Chiefs pacifistic, isolationist, anti-military policies. But it was still the most powerful military force in the world. It would take a few years to get the armed services back up to the level of training, motivation, and equipment necessary in this dangerous world.

In the meantime, the President knew he'd have to work with what he had and would have to keep Pickens from recommending that it be husbanded too severely.

Fortunately, Pickens was an advisor. The President knew he had people in the Joint Chiefs who believed they had to "use it or lose it."

So, the question the President fired at Pickens wasn't primarily military in nature.

"You're my security advisor," the President reminded Pickens. "I need a security assessment from you. A threat analysis. A quickie. Off the top of your head. Suppose I send a Sierra Charlie regiment into Kashmir as we've been talking about. Suppose they encounter East World forces. Give me your quick assessment of the security implications elsewhere in the world."

"If we were in the War Room, I could show you on the map," Pickens began.

"We're not in the War Room. We're in the Oval Office. You've done a briefing before without maps. I've seen you do it. And both of us carry maps around in our heads. Commence firing!"

"Nothing will happen in Europe. We've got three warbot regiments there keeping our eyes on the Bundeswehr to make the other Europeans happy," Pickens pointed out. Historically, an armed and unified Germany had the tendency to try to bring Europe under a German hegemony, and nine centuries of history showed no signs of a trend change.

"Nothing will happen in the Carib. Grenada, Panama, Cuba, and then Trinidad got the area quieted down, and they like it quiet and stable now. Keeps the tourist dollars flowing in and the trade flowing out. We're fat in the Vee Eye. The Canal is secure. And the Mexicans got their southern border quieted down and their druggers controlled."

Pickens thought for a moment, then went on. "Pacific Rim? Hawaii is the key, and Alaska is the hinge. The other hinge is Australia. The Russians, Chinese, and Japanese don't like our two regiments on Sakhalin, but it keeps them from having to fight each other while they work its resources." The National Security Advisor raised one hand and shook it lightly back and forth. "It's touchy on the Pacific Rim, but nothing we can't handle and nothing that's likely to come unbonded as a result of an operation in Kashmir. The Indonesians and Bruneis are Muslims, and we're doing very well with the Islamic nations. I guess part of it is due to the fact that we've all got more or less the same God."

The National Security Advisor looked at the ceiling, collected his thoughts, then looked back at the commander in chief. "The ABC Allianza?" He shrugged. "Argentina and Brazil keep making noises because they have big and growing economies. And military forces. But Chile is more friendly since their participation in the Sakhalin Police Detachment made them feel a part of world affairs. We snubbed the ABC Allianza's thrust northward in Operation Steel Band. So, the ABC Allianza has concentrated their attention on what we might call South World - southern and western Africa, New Zealand, and to some extent Madagascar. In the Indian Ocean, they're going to come eyeball-to-eyeball with East World one of these years pretty quick. I think they know it. So, they wouldn't be unhappy with us if we got into something with East World. They certainly aren't going to spit and fume about us going into Kashmir on a quickie."

"How about the Basket Case?"

"The Russians? Those bastards will react as they always have - part European and ⹁part Oriental. But always in a paranoid and frightened manner. It's their nature," Pickens observed. "But I'm telling you what I heard from you."

"Sometimes a commander likes to have his stuff fed back to him. Depending on the person doing it, it confirms the commander's proper assessment of the situation. Otherwise, I'd expect to hear a dissenting view."

"Well, Mister President, I'm not toadying."

"If you ever did, you wouldn't wear the hat you've now got on," the President admitted. "So, what is Ivan going to do?"

"Essentially, nothing." Pickens experience in the Persian Gulf had blinded him to the security issues of this particular situation. "And I don't think we'll have any trouble with the Persian Gulf regimes. When they're not hating each other's guts, they're kissing each other as they deposit their petroleum revenues in the bank. Our job in the Gulf is to keep them from each other's throats."

"Okay, what about East World consequences?"

"Not much of a problem if we don't actually invade India or China in the process. If it's known that we sent in only a small force, they may or may not react against that force. But they won't tickle the tiger's tail." Some of Pickens's analysis was wishful thinking brought about by the fact that he'd never served against East World forces. He didn't know their languages. He didn't know how they fought.

"Like Kerguelen," the President muttered.

"Kerguelen?"

The President realized that Pickens hadn't been informed of that super-hush operation in which no one had won and no one had lost. However, the world had been freed of the possibility of someone covertly infecting recce and surveillance satellites with virus computer programs. So, the President, who'd been there in charge of Operations Tempest Frigid and High Dragon, didn't say anything more.

Based on his security advisor's inputs, which nearly matched his own assessments, the President sat back and said, "Okay, Jeff, at supper tonight the NSC is going to make it official. Then DoD and JCS are going to issue orders for the Washington Greys to start moving into position for Operation Hell Fire."

"Uh, I'm sure you didn't choose that name, did you, Mister President?"

The Commander in Chief shook his head. "No. Do I look the type who'd hang such glorified names on very deadly missions? Let's just hope it turns out to be just a randomly generated computer tag."

Chapter Twelve

"General, I don't like this one damned bit!"

Colonel Curt Carson was tired. He was dirty. He was thirsty. He was hungry. And he was pissed off at some parts of the hardcopy orders he held in his hand.

Major General Belinda Hettrick looked tired too. But she hadn't been out in the field for several days as Curt had been. She'd been forced to stay in her office, running the 17th Iron Fist Division. Hettrick knew Curt. She recognized from his attitude and behavior that he was bone tired. But she was tired too. However, she'd gracefully accepted the inevitable. She was getting old. Her strength had never really returned after she'd been hit by the poisoned bushman's arrow in Namibia those long years ago. She'd thought she'd snapped back. She'd been able to maintain top form for many years. But those years were beginning to catch up with her now. "I didn't think you'd like parts of them, Curt. So, what do you want me to do about them?"

"I don't know whether or not anything can be done about them," the regimental commander of the Third Herd bitched. "That's why I asked to see you."

"You're right. So, stop sniveling. Nothing can be done about them," Hettrick confirmed. She resorted to an old trick she'd learned from her predecessor: Ask the recipient of the orders to read them slowly aloud. "What do the orders say? Read them aloud and listen to what you're saying."

Curt verbally repeated what he read. In printed form, it went as follows:

"This is an Execute Order. By authority and direction of the Secretary of Defense. This is Execute Order JCS-OP-41-2. This message is classified TOP SECRET.

"Objective: As an element of a joint exploration and investigation

operation with the government of the Islamic Republic of Pakistan, (a) investigate an unknown radio transmitting facility located in the Pakistani province of Kashmir on the Plains of Deosai, coordinates 34.4N, 75.4E; (b) take whatever measures are necessary to terminate its unlawful transmissions; (c) locate and extract scientists of the People's Republic of China, including Dr. Wen Ling Dongzhu and members of his staff who request asylum; and (d) withdraw with minimum hostile contact with defending troops. This activity is code-named Operation Hell Fire. This Operation is classified TOP SECRET.

"Course of Action: The 3rd Robot Infantry (Special Combat) Regiment is detached from the 17th Division and proceeds by covert military airlift means to Ghazi Air Base, Pakistan. Upon arrival Ghazi, 3rd Robot Infantry (Special Combat) Regiment operates under joint American-Pakistani military command. Amendment to this Execute Order will define unit and joint command order of battle, responsibilities, and activities. 3rd Robot Infantry (Special Combat) Regiment operates as independent special forces unit. 3rd Robot Infantry (Special Combat) Regiment operates covertly with Pakistani unit, reporting directly to JCS only on completion of the operation.

"Rules of Engagement: Cooperation with Pakistani government and military agencies, units, and personnel mandatory. Operation Hell Fire is covert in nature. Voice command warbots to be used if workable. Neuroelectronic equipment not to be used. Minimum confrontation with any hostile forces.

"International assistance and cooperation: The government of the Islamic Republic of Pakistan is experiencing problems with the nature of the radio transmissions from the target facility. Government of the Islamic Republic of Pakistan has requested joint operation to eliminate the facility. Government of Islamic Republic of Pakistan agrees to permit 3rd Robot Infantry (Special Combat) Regiment on Pakistani soil. Government of Islamic Republic of Pakistan agrees to provide logistical support at cost during Operation Hell Fire. Government of Islamic Republic of Pakistan also agrees to American transportation without hindrance of non-combatant PRC scientists from facility to United States Zone Interior upon their extraction from target facility.

"Schedule and status: This Execute Order will be implemented by 3rd Robot Infantry (Special Combat) Regiment as soon as possible. Status of

3rd Robot Infantry (Special Combat) Regiment is elevated to Red Alert. No revelation of alert status permitted.

"This is Execute Order *JCS-OP-41-2*. End of message. End of message. End of message. This message is classified TOP SECRET."

"So why are you pissed off?" Hettrick asked Curt when he finished reading it slowly.

"This is the first time the Greys have ever been under a foreign command!"

Hettrick shook her head. "Not so! Curt, I know you're growing older, and I'm told the memory goes first. Which I doubt. Other things have a tendency to go first. You and the Greys were under foreign command in Namibia, Brunei, Sakhalin, and Senegambia. Right?"

"Right!"

"I didn't notice that those campaigns slowed your style in the slightest. In fact, as I recall, you ended up in de facto command of the last three because you took command when the foreign commander dropped the dong." She sat back in her desk chair and looked at him. Then she managed a grin in spite of having a bad day at division level. "I'm also surprised that you didn't notice."

"Notice what, General?"

"Why, the fine hand of Wild Bill Bellamack, of course! Who the hell do you think wrote that Execute Order? That wording smacks of Wild Bill and what he learned running the Greys with you. He knew you were going to get that message. He knew that you'd read it very carefully. And he knew exactly what you'd do because you've *always* done it!"

Curt shook his head. "No, General, it isn't the memory that's going because of the aging process. It's the fact that the colonel has been out in the boonies for three days with the Greys. Sorry. I guess I'm bushed and didn't realize it."

"So, sit the hell down! Since when has formality existed between us?" Hettrick asked rhetorically. Then she added, "Actually, I'm the one who ought to be pissed. Operation Hell Fire looks like a job for

116

the whole damned division."

"Yeah, I get the same impression! Wild Bill knows better than to go into an operation with less than overwhelming force. So does the Commander in Chief." Curt wondered about the selection of a little more than a hundred people to go out and do a job that appeared to require more power.

"Because it's covert. Because we can move a regiment around without much notice. When a division moves, it's a major activity. At least, that's what Wild Bill told me when I talked to him this morning." She sighed. "So I'm going to sit here on my ass in Fort Hootchy-Coocha while you go out and explore the Himalaya Mountains!"

As an afterthought, she muttered, "And I was looking forward to one more grand campaign before DCSPERS makes a civilian out of me for the first time in my life."

"Sure, you don't want to come along and run Operation Hell Fire?" Curt asked her lightly. "I'll gladly go back to running TACBATT under your command. We did pretty well once. Like in Sakhalin after the earthquake."

"I gotta leave something for the kids to do," Hettrick tried to explain. "So, go on out there, schmooze the Pakistani generals, and end up running the operation. The only reason the Paks wanted in on it is because it's being conducted on their turf. You and I know you can out-command and out-lead them."

Curt sighed and shook his head. "Maybe we can and maybe we can't."

"Why the pessimism?"

"They've always worked without warbots," Curt pointed out. "We may be able to use voice-command on the Jeeps, Mary Anns, and Saucy Cans. Then again, maybe not. We could be going back to being grunt infantry, just like the Paks. That puts us on a level playing field."

Hettrick shook her head. "No, it will never be a level playing field. They don't have the equivalent of a West Point education," she pointed out. "You and I went through four years of that. What happened there helped make real professionals out of us. Maybe some of the Paks went to Sandhurst, maybe they didn't. They still cooperate closely with the Brits. The Pakistani Army is patterned after the British Army even today."

"I guess I'm going to find out how good they are and whether or not I can assume leadership," Curt admitted. Then he slapped the back of his hand against the hard copy of the Execute Order. "But what the hell is this scientist thing? The extraction of Doctor Longdong or whatever?"

"I know as much about it as you do."

"I guess I'd better call Wild Bill."

"I guess you'd better. Never get into a game unless you understand the rules and know what the wild cards are," Hettrick advised him.

Curt didn't want to monopolize Hettrick's comm terminal. Friends or not, a colonel doesn't tie up a general's line. "I'll give him a hoot on the hooter when I get back to my office. In the meantime, since the orders say 'ASAP,' I may need some help from the Iron Fist Division."

Hettrick looked at him blankly. "What for, Curt? Oh, that Top Secret mission? I'm supposed to know something about it, but not anyone on staff or in the other regiments."

"Dammit, Battleaxe!" Curt exploded, using her combat code name as a signal of his frustration. "How can I move a whole damned regiment halfway around the world in eight Chippies? Yeah, they've got midair refueling capabilities. But they'll have to be flown constantly hands-on because of the no-NE restrictions! Either I'm going to need some Chippies from the Wolfhounds and Cottonbalers, or the Aerospace Force is going to have to come through with some heavy strategic logair capability."

"And call attention to a Top Secret troop movement?" Hettrick asked rhetorically.

"Hell, Military Airlift Command moves regiments around the world every day," Curt pointed out.

"And every spook around a MAC base knows what outfit is being hauled where," the Iron Fist commander reminded him.

"JCS sure as hell must have considered the logistics of this," Curt growled. "I sure as hell don't have the authorization to whip up a chartered airlift. And I sure as hell don't want to break security by calling Brunei and asking my 'family' for help." Years ago, as a result of a joint military training operation in Brunei, Curt had been awarded the prestigious Sultan's Star of Brunei, a decoration that automatically made him a member of the family of the incredibly wealthy Sultan of Brunei. He'd been super-careful not to overstress that relationship or to use the perks in such a way that the matter would backfire. Army regulations were strict in such matters, even when such perks were part of being a "family member."

"I'm not supposed to know what's going on," Hettrick told him, "except that I was told in confidence as the division commander. Wild Bill Bellamack knows better than to yank one of my regiments out of my command without giving me some idea of what's going on. Common courtesy, and General Bellamack is a gentleman. And he didn't have to tell me why it was being done, but he did. However, that Execute Order was forwarded through me to you, and I have no authority or responsibility under it. Bellamack can probably give you all the details. On the other hand, Curt, if you want to look good, you won't joggle his elbow about airlift. Go make the arrangements. Let me give you a hint what to do. Ever hear of an outfit called Millennium Express?"

Curt had, but he searched his memory to remember when and where and under what circumstances. "Oh, yeah! Headquartered up at Williams Field, the old air base outside of Phoenix. Sort of a fly-by-night charter outfit, aren't they? I've seen their stack of old aircraft parked on the southeast side of the field. But I never got very close. Matter of fact, they're not real friendly types, I understand. Sort of quiet. I haven't got the foggiest notion how they conduct their business, or what they do."

Hettrick was quiet for a moment, then said, "Let me put it this way. And you didn't hear it from me. And I have absolutely no proof of what I'm going to tell you." She paused, then went on. "Sometimes covert operations require covert support means. Do you read me?"

Curt nodded slowly. "Yeah. I read you. Loud and clear. I recall hearing stories about outfits called Air America and Evergreen Aviation."

"There were others you never heard about."

"I'm sure."

"Call MilEx. They're in the directory."

"So, what do I ask them? Hell, I've never done this before! When we needed to go somewhere, Aerospace Force provided the airlift if we went outside the ZI."

"If I know you - and I do – you've never been shy when it came to doing things you'd never done before," Hettrick said, remembering her days as commander of the Washington Greys. Among those memories were several involving an eager, bright, and very masculine young Curt Carson straight out of West Point and Fort Benning's training center.

Hettrick also knew the nation's capital and how the people there operated. Not everyone "inside the beltway" was incompetent, bumbling, turf-happy, a lobbyist, or worse. The United States government would have collapsed in a morass of bureaucracy and boot-licking more than a century ago if that had been the case. She knew a lot of people there were honest, sincere, dedicated, and absolutely incorruptible. She'd spent a tour of duty in the office of the Army Chief of Staff. She'd also gotten to know, quite unofficially and even non-socially, a broad circle of people. She knew where a lot of bodies were buried. She knew which closets held what skeletons and how many of them. But she was extremely discreet about it. People knew she knew and respected her for not abusing that knowledge. They trusted her. And they admired her forthright approaches. Even in twenty-first-century America, she was an oddity: a female commander who had suffered physical wounds in actual overseas combat. Because of her uncompromising stands, especially in the Brunei exercise, she'd dined with the then-President many times. And she personally knew the current Commander in Chief because she'd been one of his military subordinates.

Belinda Jane Hettrick had clout and used it wisely. No one really believed she'd end up stitching quilts in Sun City when she retired a few months hence. Some people had plans. However, she was still a commissioned officer and refused to engage in any activity that posed any conflict with the responsibilities attached to that commission.

She advised her subordinate, "Curt, if a certain retired Aerospace Force general officer in Langley, Virginia, has covered the bases right and done his job the way I know he does it, MilEx will be expecting your call. They'll probably confirm who you are, and you and your staffers may have to make a quick trip up there."

In a surprising move, she swung the comm terminal around on its gimbals. "Be my guest. Key in 'MilEx' and it will autodial for you. Use full video so they see who you are."

Curt looked at her through narrowed eyes. "Dammit, Battleaxe, you had this all set up, didn't you?"

"A commander is supposed to stay ahead of subordinates," was all she said.

The image that flashed on the screen was a middle-aged woman receptionist. "Millennium Express!" was all she said by way of identification.

"Good morning," Curt told her brightly. "I'm interested in getting a quote from you on an overseas airlift."

"People or cargo, sir?"

"Both."

"And your company, sir?"

Curt shot from the hip. "I'm the CEO of the Hell Fire Chili Pepper Company near Sierra Vista."

"Yes, sir! One moment, please!"

It took less than five seconds for a large, burly, clean-shaven man to appear on the screen. There was no question that he saw and took note of the dull field insignia on Curt's collar tabs and the rumpled field cammies. It seemed he knew who he was talking to. "Good morning! I'm Woody LaRue! I'm MilEx charter flight operations coordinator! I understand you have something you want to send somewhere."

"I'm Curt Carson. I run the Hell Fire Chili Pepper outfit down in Sierra Vista," Curt said, continuing the sham. "I've got a rush job on my hands. I have to get about a hundred technicians and a lot of equipment to Pakistan in a hurry. I've got a deal to swap our Hell Fire products for some Chinese and Pakistani materials. I've already cleared this through the proper government agencies, and we're clear to ship when we can get airlift."

"Well, sir, rush jobs are our specialty! We can do it for you!" Woody LaRue was quietly confident and ebullient, certainly not guarded and reticent. "Say, I think I've heard of your outfit! Good product you make! Sure, does the job! And we're certainly all in favor of outfits working in the international market."

"Thank you for your compliments." Curt was aware now that LaRue did indeed know what was going on and had been expecting the call. The double meanings in the man's conversation twigged him about that. "I've always dealt with established airlift companies before, but we're in a hurry on this one. And we sort of need to keep a low profile because of our competition, if you know what I mean. If they knew I had this deal over there, they might blow it up in my face. I trust you can keep a confidence."

"Sure! We do it all the time! Part of our service!"

"As I said, I'm new at this because we've usually worked through established airlifters," Curt went on. "I can have my logistics staffer...uh, my transportation and shipping department, that is...get in touch with you if you tell me you can handle my business."

"Oh, we can handle it, Mister Carson! And don't worry about our capabilities. We're certificated for any cargo and we can handle pax as well. We also have the necessary international documents and clearances. And we can help you get your shipments through customs. too."

"We've already taken care of customs and such protocols, Mister LaRue. What's the next step here?" Curt wanted to know.

"Simple, sir. MilEx tries to make international shipping as easy as sending a package to Washington. We'll need to know what you're shipping in the way of cargo. Number of units. Unit weights. Unit cubages. Special requirements for things such as explosives. When you want to ship and when you want it to arrive. If you want people to go with some part of the cargo shipment. How many people you want to send. We can combine pax and cargo on some planes. We know all the shipping details required to move a unit out of the ZI. So, I suggest that our first move is for you to send your travel and shipping personnel up here so we can iron out the initial details. When can they be here?"

LaRue's relaxed use of military terminology told Curt the man had once worn Aerospace Force blue. And that MilEx obviously did a lot of exactly the sort of thing the Greys were called upon to do.

"They'll be there this afternoon," Curt volunteered. "What's a good time for you?"

"Fourteen hundred hours would be perfect. Land your Chippie over on the southeast aerodyne pad. That's out of view of most of the main ramp and no one is likely to notice it." LaRue was obviously clued into the operation.

When Curt cut the connection, he looked at Hettrick and remarked, "Well, we certainly do meet some interesting people doing interesting things, don't we?"

"Al Murray has a habit of collecting such people," she agreed. "See? I told you it would be easy."

"I can only hope the rest of Operation Hell Fire goes as smoothly," was Curt's comment.

Chapter Thirteen

"For an airline I've never heard of before, this surprises the hell out of me!" Major Russ Frazier remarked as he stretched his legs out under the seat in front of him. He and the other Washington Greys had plenty of room in the vast cabin.

"From the sound of it, Millennium Express might be another one of those fly-by-night package delivery outfits," was the comment from Major Kitsy Clinton.

"But this sure as hell isn't a cargo airplane," Edie Sampson observed. "It's old as hell, but it seems to be in great shape."

"Seven-Four-Sevens are one of those machines that last forever," Regimental Sergeant Major Henry Kester decided.

"Sort of like some sergeant majors I know," Russ said.

"No, I think Henry is a human version of the Deacon's Masterpiece," Kitsy decided.

"Huh? What have you been reading?" Russ wondered.

"The Deacon's Masterpiece was the wonderful one hoss shay," Kitsy informed him.

"Oh. Okay. Yeah. Fits him perfectly."

Henry Kester shrugged. He'd taken far more piercing humor than this during his thirty years in the Army. But he knew he was expected to retaliate, so he fired back casually, "If the quote fits, flaunt it." He too stretched out in his seat. "You young people have it easy. Contract airlift used to be sardine city."

"Yeah, Henry, tell us what it was like traveling with the Wright brothers," Edie said, maintaining the pressure.

Kester shrugged again. "Breezy. Had to lie flat on the wing. Made it damned difficult for the attendants to serve meals. It was even tougher to get to the latrine." He paused to let that sink in. Then, before one of the Greys could respond, he went on. "Flying in the old Gooney Birds was really rough duty. Almost as bad as strapping your ass into a Chippie. Same damned webbed seats that made a waffle outa your butt. By the way, since I'm the expert on ancient machinery, you should be made aware that this is a cargo airplane. One of the quick-change cargo versions. They've fitted it out with a pax kit for us."

"And well done too. It's been a long time since I traveled first class. Matter of fact, it was the Sakhalin fracas when we were hauled by Royal Brunei Airlines," Kitsy reminisced.

"Yes, Major, but that wasn't a thirty-hour flight like this one," Edie reminded her.

The MilEx 747-400 was old, but it had either been rebuilt or been well-maintained, probably both. In more than a half century of life, it had been owned by several airlines, ending up in the hands of Millennium Express.

Everyone in the Washington Greys knew that MilEx wasn't an ordinary domestic charter airline. The outfit had a ramp full of old transport aircraft at Williams Field in Phoenix. Some were cargo planes. Some were passenger planes. Some were "quick-change" passenger/cargo planes such as the one in which they were riding. And some were "surplus" military airlifters. Six of the old 747-400s had shown up on the ramp at Libby Army Airfield at Fort Huachuca to airlift the Greys to Pakistan. They had arrived within hours of the Executive Order hitting the Greys. Therefore, everyone knew that MilEx had to be owned and operated by the NIA.

Actually, MilEx wasn't owned by the NIA. The "company" was owned and operated by another of the black spook agencies with whom Al Murray's outfit maintained operational connect ions. No one would ever be able to trace the line of ownership.

The old subsonic aircraft's interior was clean, but it was also right out of a museum. And it had been configured for first-class seating throughout. Someone had been thinking. The long flight to Pakistan would have been rough on the Greys otherwise. It was tough enough on their circadian rhythms, although the Schuman

Resonators seemed to be helping.

In between cat napping, walking around the cavernous cabin to get some exercise, and engaging in relaxed chatter and shop talk, the Greys found little to relieve the boredom of the flight except the banter between them.

However, the regimental commander wasn't participating in it.

Neither was his staff.

"Colonel, you've been very quiet on this flight," Kitsy told him as she leaned across the wide aisle to speak to him.

Curt looked at her. "I've been trying to sort out this can of worms we're getting into," he told her frankly.

"The joint command matter?"

He nodded. "This shouldn't be a joint command operation. We're being sent into Kashmir to do a job for the Commander in Chief," he reminded her. "It's covert and clandestine."

"We've done that before. It's nothing new," Kitsy recalled, thinking of the many times the Greys had been sent out into a dangerous world in a hurry to put the lid on a brushfire war that threatened to get out of hand.

"That we have," Curt acknowledged. "However, I don't like the idea of sharing command with a Pakistani."

"We've operated that way before."

"True. And I realize that their military forces have to be involved for protocol purposes. And in case something goes to slime. Which it damned well could this time."

"Things can always go wrong, Colonel." Kitsy was now a seasoned combat veteran and had learned the principles and practices of command the hard way, just like everyone else. Curt knew she was going to become a fine regimental commander in his footsteps, following the tradition of Belinda Hettrick.

"That's what worries me," Curt admitted.

In the rushed hours before boarding the airlift, Curt's attention had been devoted to external matters, mostly telebriefings from the Pentagon. He knew what they knew. But still he didn't feel he had enough information.

His staff didn't think so either. Chief of staff Joan Ward wasn't pessimistic about the operation, but she was worried. Dyani, the regimental S-2, was deeply concerned because of the lack of hard data. This had affected the attitude of Russ as S-3, operations officer. Lieutenant Colonel Cal Worsham didn't seem to give much of a damn because he and his squadron would be going somewhere to lay ordnance on someone. Worsham didn't even bitch – much - about the long deployment flight, again because his Chippie and Harpy drivers had learned how to do it in the past.

The operations plan - Curt didn't like legitimizing it with that title - was more of a rough schedule of "go here, do this, then go there and do that." It had far too many holes in it. The Greys didn't have enough information to fill in those holes.

However, Curt and his troops were soldiers. They went where they were told to go and did what they were told to do. If they didn't have enough information, they knew they were expected to use their brains and exercise initiative. Thus, if they got into trouble, they had to get their own asses out of it.

They'd been told they'd be continually briefed after they'd landed and begun to trek to the Plains of Deosai.

In a hazy situation like Operation Hell Fire with its many unknowns and educated guesses, Curt didn't like the idea of doing back-of-the-envelope planning. Nor did he like the idea that he might be under the command of a Pakistani officer. The whole command structure wasn't clear to him. He was told it would be worked out by the time they got to the Pakistani Air Force Base at Ghazi.

Obviously, Playland on the Potomac was in high gear for this one. Curt knew that NIA was involved. For the first time in his career, he'd been contacted directly by Al Murray and given a highly classified briefing. At its end, he didn't know much more than when it had started except that it had come from the best information source around. General Bill Bellamack had talked to him several times, and Curt had been briefed by DIA as well. No one knew very much more than what Al Murray had told him. Curt also knew that the Department of State would have had to run a lot of interference on the diplomatic side.

But why hadn't the U.N. been brought in? This NE weapon could become a major factor in destabilizing a dangerous world.

Actually, the initial conference with Owen Pendleton and Willa Lovell at McCarthy Proving Ground had revealed more information than he'd gotten from any of the intelligence outfits.

He also knew that the main reason the Oval Office had called out the Washington Greys was to extract those East World NE experts who had apparently designed and built the weapon. Otherwise, the Aerospace Force would have done a surgical job of flattening the Deosai facility, if indeed the Deosai facility housed the weapon. Murray hadn't considered that the facility might not house the transmitter; Curt had brought it up during his briefing. In fact, Murray had listened carefully to Curt's personal strategic analysis of the situation. But the intelligence chief had been noncommittal about the validity of what Curt suspected.

Curt knew the rush deployment of Operation Hell Fire couldn't be totally covert. The only way it could have been done was to use the Navy's McCain Class carrier submarines as they had in the past. But there wasn't time. The NE weapon threatened to disrupt all the warbots and indybots on the North American continent. Russian, Chinese, Japanese, European, and ABC Allianza surveillance and air traffic satellites would certainly notice the non-scheduled flight of six airlifters from Fort Huachuca to Pakistan. There was no way this deployment could be kept covert.

How would East World react?

Murray had presented some scenarios. So had Bellamack. However, Curt was the one who would have to handle any direct reaction from East World because he'd be on the spot. So Curt was ready for anything.

Because he'd had to concentrate on these external matters, the details of getting the Greys ready to depart had been left to his staff and batt commanders. Although Curt trusted them, he really didn't know how well-prepared the Greys were. Did they have everything they might need? He hadn't had time, even on the flight, to be thoroughly briefed by his staff. So, he took the reports of "good to go, sir!" and trusted those who said it. A commander had to do that. No commander has the time to check and know every detail.

Sometimes he wished he was still running his old company, "Carson's Companions." Life had been easier then. And he could be on top of all the details that might mean life or death to those under his command.

Now he was nearly exhausted with no chance of getting a few snatches of sleep.

"We can cope with it, Colonel!" Kitsy assured him.

He was glad she was sanguine about it. It helped to know that the Greys were up and ready.

The MilEx plane was now about two hundred kilometers from the obscure Pakistani air base. Curt sat back, closed his eyes, and waited for the change in engine sounds and aircraft attitude that would tell him that the pilots had started the descent into Ghazi.

***

He was suddenly jolted in his seat and came instantly to the alert. "What was that? A baby SAM hit?" he asked Kester, who was seated next to him.

"Colonel, you dozed off. We just landed at Ghazi," Kester told him.

"What the hell, Henry! *You let me sleep?*"

Kester nodded. "Wasn't anything you had to do except sit there and fret. You been doing that for the last day or so. You're either fretted-out by now or there ain't anything left for you to fret about," the veteran sergeant told him bluntly. "Besides, just like I've always tried to tell you, sir, a soldier ought to get any sleep possible at any time. There are times when it ain't possible to sleep and stay alive.

This ain't one of those times."

Curt was the first one out of the plane. The ancient loading stairs were shaky and tall. Shouldering his duffle and making sure his Novia was slung securely over his other shoulder, he hunched his backpack more comfortably on his hips. Then he went down the long metal stairway.

The air was surprisingly cool, but it was humid. Clouds topped the hills and mountains that were all around. The air base looked like any other air base except that it was old. Two squadrons of French-made De-Launay *Vultur* assault aerodynes were parked on the ramp. They were armed with external ordnance.

Curt felt he should have deployed full regimental protocol for the arrival, displaying the national and regimental colors and lining up the Greys. But he'd been told not to. This was a covert mission. Let the enemy and the enemy spies on and around the base guess if they didn't already know. Curt guessed that the landing of six 747-400s might be enough aerial action to alert everyone for a hundred kilometers around the base.

He was wrong about that. Like people in emerging nations of the "Small World," most Pakistanis paid no attention to aircraft except tacair birds laying ordnance. In the northwest provinces, local Pakistanis would shoot back.

Waiting for him at the bottom of the loading stairs was a contingent of Pakistani officers.

Their leader stepped forward as Curt reached the tarmac. The pips on his shoulder boards resembled those of British officers. Curt saw that the man was a full colonel.

The Pakistani colonel saluted. "I am Colonel Iskander Ghulam Khan, commander of the fourth Khyber Rifles, Army of the Islamic Republic of Pakistan," the man announced in the accented English of the Indian subcontinent.

Curt returned the salute. "Colonel Curt Carson, commander, Third Robot Infantry Regiment, Army of the United States."

"Yes!"

"Excuse me, Colonel, but can we move to one side here and allow the rest of my command to debark in a rapid manner?" Curt asked as he was joined by Joan, Russ, Pappy Gratton, and Kitsy. "We've airlifted into many places, and we've learned a few things in the process. Even if this air base is secure, I don't want my troops exposed to possible sniper fire on that tall stairway."

Colonel Khan's eyes narrowed, and Curt thought that maybe it had been the wrong thing to say. Or maybe he'd said it wrong. It was both. Khan was a small, chunky man who looked a lot like Captain Mahmud Ben Hassan. Khan had obviously been better fed in his youth, however. His dark eyes flashed with momentary anger and his mustache quivered menacingly. He looked mean. "This way!" he snapped and moved to the right. His staff - majors and captains - moved quickly with him.

A round of introductions of the two regimental staffs was quickly and formally performed as the rest of the Greys stepped onto the tarmac from the plane and quickly assembled into an open formation.

"Colonel, we realize that the United States has a mixed-gender army," Colonel Khan began aggressively. "This has caused my government some concern, and this concern has been conveyed to your government. I have been ordered to request that your women obey Islamic law insofar as possible under the circumstances."

This statement bothered Curt. It enraged Kitsy, but she remained quiet. "Colonel, we'll do the best we can. What would you have me tell them to do? We're all kitted out for combat. My ladies will not-repeat, not-enter purdah."

"Keep them separated from my men," Khan insisted. "Otherwise, there could be trouble. Pakistani men are aggressive and sexually frustrated." Colonel Khan was blunt and surprisingly candid. Curt's cultural briefing had mentioned that Pakistani men tended to behave this way. However, Khan had none of the smoothness and tact that Curt had grown to expect from other officers of his equivalent rank. In every army, field officers are generally expected to behave in a polite manner and follow the general rules of protocol during their interfaces with other officers, regardless of nationality. Khan was different.

"That's your problem, Colonel Khan," Curt told him with equal aggressive bluntness. Where the hell did this guy think he was getting off? Curt wondered. What a hell of a way to begin what might have to become a team relationship between the Washington Greys and the 4th Khyber Rifles! "My ladies will behave themselves. They're ladies. As for your problems with your troops, you might tell them that my ladies aren't simpering schoolgirls. They've killed many men. They're seasoned, hardened killers with extensive combat experience. Any man who assaults them is likely to spend the rest of his life without means to satisfy his sexual frustration, if you understand me."

Khan looked at Joan and Kitsy. In their combat gear, they did indeed look hard and mean. At this point, Joan was a Valkyrie with cold blue eyes, an ice queen who wasn't about to be trifled with. Kitsy still looked like an enthusiastic but angry teenager who'd been insulted. The only prominent factors that differentiated them from Russ, Pappy, and Henry were the smoothness of their feminine facial features. Combat cammies weren't body-hugging or revealing. And the large Sierra Charlie combat helmets hid any clue of their feminine hairstyles. In a sense, the helmets were almost like hard-surfaced purdah veils, especially when the visors were lowered in front of their faces.

Colonel Iskander Khan realized he'd lost the initial engagement. That didn't make him very happy. However, the American colonel hadn't yet tried to exert direct control over him, so he persisted in his aggressive behavior. "Very well, then! Just see to it that your women maintain their discipline!"

"My ladies are ladies, Colonel. And don't ever make the mistake of thinking them otherwise," Curt remonstrated.

Kitsy finally spoke up. She might have been out of line, but she couldn't restrain herself any longer. "Colonel Khan, I'm always a lady, sir, in spite of hell!"

Khan ignored her. This made her even angrier. But having said what she'd said, Kitsy now held her tongue.

"Corne along, then! You and your staff will be briefed on the operation that lies ahead of us. It will not be an easy one!" Khan continued in his irritating, imperious manner. "But we have worked out a suitable plan that will allow your troops to provide adequate support although they aren't acclimated yet."

Curt looked at his watch and pushed a stud to give him time zone information. "Colonel, it's twenty hundred hours according to what our bodies are telling us. Twelve hours' time difference. I need to make sure that my command is suitably fed and quartered so they can rest and adjust their biological clocks. Five more airlifters are corning in with more of my personnel and equipment. It may be hours before we're ready to move out of here. My staff and I are used to working at any hour, day or night. Therefore, may I suggest that we meet after lunch? Say, at thirteen hundred hours your time?"

Curt gave Khan a perfect opportunity to mend fences by inviting Curt and his staff to lunch. But the Pakistani colonel didn't take it. "Very well! My adjutant will make arrangements for quartering your regiment. We had planned to be on our way to Kashmir this afternoon. We had expected that your aircraft would arrive in a more timely manner. And I was not aware that Americans fought only during normal business hours."

That did it insofar as Curt was concerned. The man was an aggressive boor. The commander of the Washington Greys knew that he'd have to bring up his secret weapon to handle the matter.

Chapter Fourteen

Exactly at 1300 hours, Curt showed up at the base operations building conference room. He wanted to be certain that he showed up at the appointed place on time. He felt groggy because of circadian asynchronization. It would take at least twenty-four hours to overcome that problem. And he knew that all the Washington Greys would be suffering from the same syndrome.

All six 747-400s had landed. All the Greys were at Ghazi now. All their equipment was also on the ground. The MilEx aircraft had left as quickly as they'd been unloaded and refueled.

For the first conference with Colonel Khan and the staff of the 4th Khyber Rifles, Curt had brought along his own staff. He'd also asked several other Greys to join the group. Among them was his "secret weapon." Three of them, in fact.

As a combat commander, Curt knew quite well that redundancy was helpful in a fracas. Redundancy was often spelled "reserves." And no commander ever has enough reserves.

And this was a non-lethal fracas to Curt. At least, thus far. With the short-tempered fatigue of the Greys versus the aggressive chauvinistic bombast of the Pakistani officers, Curt hoped he could keep it non-lethal. He was willing to let it become physical on a temporary basis if relations deteriorated even more than they had already. But he didn't think that a physical encounter would last more than a few seconds.

His secret weapons were certainly capable of restricting such a fight to a very short period of time.

As Curt entered the conference room, a Pakistani aide attempted to direct him to a seat at the far end of the long table. This would position Curt at the opposite end of the room from the lectern and chalkboard. It was also obvious to him that the Paks intended that the Greys sit on one side of the table while the staff of the 4th

Khyber Rifles sat on the other.

Curt would have none of it. With a brief muttered "thank you, Captain," he brushed past the aide and went to the head of the table next to the lectern and board.

He'd briefed his staff on this possibility. So, they reacted to being directed to seats on one side of the table by calmly ignoring the Pakistanis and sitting down in random order around the long table.

Colonel Khan and his staff were not in the room. Curt had expected this too. And he'd instructed his own people what to do as a result.

Khan swept into the conference room at 1305. He was followed by his staff. His initial reaction on seeing where the Greys had seated themselves was one of surprise, then anger. He said a series of sharp words in Punjabi to the aides who'd failed to follow his orders. He walked purposefully to the head of the table and remained standing as his staff came in.

The Pakistani staff was confused. They'd been instructed to seat themselves at the table in a way that would dominate the room and the meeting. As a result of the way the Greys had taken chairs at random, they milled around for a moment.

"Everyone take their seats!" Khan snapped. He had expected everyone in the room to come to their feet in respect for his rank. However, Curt had briefed the Greys about this. They'd remained seated. This was perfectly in accord with recognized military protocol, of course. Only the commanding officer of a unit offers protocol at an international military conference, and it is the guest commander who does so on behalf of all his subordinates.

When Khan's staff had taken seats, and before Khan could either take a position at the lectern or sit-down opposite Curt, the American colonel stood up. Curt gave no salute; they were inside and thus under cover. Instead, Curt properly extended the hand of friendship across the head of the table.

Khan was momentarily confused until he realized that he was expected to respond. He did so and tried to smile as Curt was doing. But again, the Pakistani colonel realized that he'd been outmaneuvered. And he also had it driven home to him that these Americans were not going to defer automatically to him.

And it was also apparent that these Americans were behaving in a cool, professional manner. This bothered the hell out of some of the Pakistani officers, who discovered they were sitting next to American women officers. It had never happened to them before. Some were stunned. Others acted somewhat resentful. A small percentage of them appeared to be offended at this disregard for Islamic law and customs in their own country. Two of them sat tight-lipped on either side of the petite Lieutenant Matsu Mikawa.

Curt was forcing the issue right at the start, and the Greys knew it.

"Welcome to Pakistan, Colonel," Khan said unnecessarily since he didn't know what else to say.

"Thank you, Colonel. I'm glad we arrived safely. But I'm not pleased by the circumstances that caused us to be ordered here on behalf of our government," Curt responded tactfully.

Both men remained standing. Curt was again forcing the issue because he believed Khan otherwise would walk immediately to the lectern, take control of the conference, and begin to dictate his operational plan to everyone. Curt wanted to stop that from happening at the beginning of the meeting. If this was indeed a joint operation, and if his orders really meant that he was to work out the details with his Pakistani colleague, Curt meant to do just that: Confer as equals. At least at the beginning. The Greys would need the logistical support and terrain familiarity of the Pakistanis.

"Colonel, I suggest we sit down and begin discussing the situation," Curt said, breaking the awkward silence. "Let's begin with an assessment of the situation, then compare our orders. Our staff members can then brief everyone concerning their areas of responsibility. From that, we can begin to plan the operation."

"I have a plan," Khan snapped.

"I'm surprised you know enough about American Sierra Charlie doctrine and capabilities to formulate a joint plan at this point. If so, I commend you on your scholarship. However, we need to make you aware of some basic changes in doctrine and operational capabilities. The East World neuroelectronic countermeasures have caused us to re-evaluate these."

Curt knew that the Pakistanis had robots, but these were utilized in both industrial and military applications quite differently than in North America, Europe, and Japan.

The Pakistani Army had a regiment of direct laser-link command French warbots mainly for internal police purposes. Like armored vehicles of old, warbots were useful in controlling the civilian population during riots and local rebellions.

However, Pakistan's primary enemy for nearly a century had been India. And Pakistan wasn't on good terms with China either. One of the major but seldom discussed issues was religion. Pakistan was an Islamic state. Islam wasn't compatible with the religions of India or the contemplative religions of China. All three countries were arguing still about who owned and administered the Jammu and Kashmir regions. Nothing had been settled. The arbitrary borders established by the withdrawing British in 1947 had cut indiscriminately across highways, railways, and the extremely important irrigation systems and rivers. Therefore, tensions always ran high in the region.

Several brushfire wars had broken out over the years. The United States had helped Pakistan with military aid funds and a few military advisors from time to time. Because of old religious and ethical hatreds in the region, nearly half of Pakistan's annual budget went to the military services.

As a result, the Pakistani Army consisted of many border guard units. Their defense doctrine was simple, based upon their national capabilities. They couldn't buy enough warbots to serve as force multipliers because of their chronically poor economy. Yet they couldn't match man for man with India or China either. Their strategy was to require that the border guards units hold back any enemy assault. Then elite non-warbot counterstrike forces would move quickly in surgical actions to cut off the enemy attack.

The 4th Khyber Rifles was one of those airborne-motorized elite counterstrike regiments.

And it was obvious that Colonel Khan took the word "elite" quite literally. In such a situation, an elite unit and its commanders have considerable political power. Several military coups had proved this over the years, and domestic politics in Pakistan rested on the foundation of military power.

Curt could thus understand why Khan behaved as he did, even taking the normal behavior of a Pakistan man into account.

And if Curt didn't knock a few pieces off the man's elite facade right at the start, it would cause trouble later. He'd had similar problems with another elite commander, the son of the Sultan of Brunei, on two separate operations. No one in the Greys would think of fragging Khan, but at the moment they wouldn't go out of their way to pull him out of the slime in a combat situation if their own butts were in a sling.

"We do not plan to use your warbots in this operation," Khan announced.

"What do you intend to use for heavy fire support?" Curt wanted to know.

"Heavy fire support? We do not need heavy fire support!"

"So, you intend to expend your valuable trained man-power in one-on-one combat with the Chinese? Or the Indian Army? Or whatever nation's troops are guarding that facility on the Deosai Plains?" Then Curt dropped his bombshell. "How do you intend to handle more than fifty Chinese Red Hammer warbots there?"

"Our reconnaissance indicates that no warbots are deployed in the Deosai facility!"

Curt shrugged. "I don't know where you get your information, Colonel, but I think you'd better look at what we've got. Sergeant Sampson, would you please set up the visual display screen?"

Before Khan could object, Edie was on her feet and deploying the portable meter-square display screen and projector. Khan had seen similar domestic Japanese units, but never one that was battery powered and ruggedized. So, he slipped slowly into a chair and watched the procedure. These Americans always had some new high-tech equipment. Khan decided it might help him control this operation better if he knew what it was and how it worked. It might provide him with better recce than he could pull down from one of the older American surveillance satellites with the old equipment his regiment had.

Curt remained standing alongside the table until Edie had switched the unit on, tuned its satellite receiver, and had a picture on the screen.

"This isn't a very good picture," Curt apologized. "Only half-meter resolution. But it's real time direct from one of our satellites. Sergeant, can you improve the resolution?"

"No, sir, not if you want real time," she explained. "I can pull down better stuff taken directly over the Deosai objective and stored, but it will be maybe two hours old. This is. an oblique. It's smeared a little because of the high angular rate. Give me thirty seconds, and I can hack a quick computer program that will clarify the image a little. On the other hand, the downlink signal informs me the target will be out of range in four minutes. Then we'll have to go to stored data anyway."

This intimidated Khan, but he tried not to show it. A woman NCO shouldn't show such technical competence, he believed. Why wouldn't these Americans keep their women under control for pleasure and babies, he wondered. But professionally, he had to admit to himself that Sampson was a technical whiz. And the little tactical satellite receiver was certainly something new to him. (It was also new to the Greys. It had come about as a spinoff of the call-anywhere satellite mobile videophone system. Its sensitive antenna and noise-canceling hyper-sensitive rf front end could pull in the weak satellite signal even indoors, just like a satellite mobile phone.)

Curt stepped up alongside the screen and pointed at an object. "Sergeant, zoom in on that, please." When Edie performed her magic with the black box, the image clearly showed the shape of a Chinese Red Hammer warbot on perimeter patrol. "There you are, Colonel, in real time as it's happening. We're going to need our warbots' heavy firepower to deal with the Red Hammers. The seventy-five-millimeter tubes with their rocket-boosted rounds on our warbots will outgun the fifty-three-milli-meter smoothbores on the Red Hammers. We can out-shoot and outrange them. We know this because we've fought the Red Hammers in Yemen and Senegambia. And we captured a lot of Red Hammers in both places. We've fought war games against them in the United States. So, we know we can take them out from a distance before making a ground assault on the facility."

"My plan uses tactical air strikes with our *Vultur* aerodynes to do that."

"Excuse me, Colonel," Cal Worsham broke in, "but the altitude of that target is above the service ceiling of your *Vulturs* unless they're carrying a highly reduced ordnance load. Our Harpies will barely hack it with a fifty percent load of Smart Farts if we can get an air refueling right after the strike. We'll be light because we've left fuel behind." Worsham was being very polite and very tactful. When he wanted to, he could be couth and speak in a normal, if loud, manner. "I've got only eight Harpies. Unless you've got a lot of *Vulturs*, we won't make a dent in fifty Red Hammers. And what I saw on the ramp this morning tells me you've got maybe twelve *Vulturs* you're counting on for support."

"We have more available!"

"Where are they? Never mind. With the weather and altitude conditions, I question our joint ability to take out the Red Hammers with tacair. My regimental colleagues will be surprised to hear me say that because I'm the commander of the air support squadron of the Washington Greys. And there isn't *any* mission in the air that we can't hack! Except when technology itself won't let us."

"Colonel Carson, do you condone such insubordination as this, interrupting you and arguing with me?" Khan asked in a nasty tone of voice, his dark eyes blazing.

"Colonel Khan, I listen to my subordinates, especially when they have the guts to speak up and tell me that I'm spouting bullshit," Curt replied.

This exchange prompted one of Khan's staffers, a large, stout major, to speak up and ask, "Even your women?"

"Even our ladies," Curt told him, correcting him.

"But they're *women!*" the Pakistani major objected.

"Yes, indeed we are! But we're also ladies," Kitsy corrected him. "Perhaps you recall that the women soldiers of the Marantha gave the British quite a fight about two hundred years ago."

The Pakistani major bristled. "A woman such as you needs to be disciplined." He drew back his hand. Clearly, his intent was to strike Kitsy.

He never got the chance. He forgot to watch his minus-x. Mickie Mikawa was sitting on the other side of him. No one saw what she did. Or she did it so fast that no one remembered. But they heard the sound of bones snapping. And the howl that came from the Pakistani major.

"Obviously," Mickie said in her delicate voice that was almost as delicate as she appeared to be, "you never learned that it isn't nice to attempt to strike a woman in anger. Or anyone else, Major."

She had broken both the radius and the ulna of the major's right arm. He stood up, holding his arm with his left hand. The arm was bent at an unusual angle.

Another of Curt's secret weapons had been triggered. However, it hadn't been his intention to do it this way.

Every Pakistani in the conference room came to his feet.

The Greys remained seated.

The other secret weapon activated. Captain Hassan Ben Mahmud said something loudly in Baluchi.

Punjabi and Baluchi are different languages. But in Pakistan, both existed alongside one another. Although most Pakistani officers spoke Punjabi and English, they also understood most of the other languages of their country because their soldiers came from everywhere.

Hassan's statement caused Colonel Khan to jerk his head around and stare at the handsome American officer. Khan was momentarily angry that one of the American women had injured one of his staff. But surprise overwhelmed anger when he heard an American officer speak a language of the region. And one that most foreigners from West World don't speak. So, Khan put out his hand and motioned for his staff to sit down, which they did reluctantly. Turning to Curt, Khan snapped, "So you not only have women in your regiment, but ignorant Baluchi peasants too?" To him the people of Baluchistan were ignorant peasants compared to the elite Punjabis who ran the Pakistani Army.

Curt simply looked him right in the eye and said, "Captain Mahmud's background is not important. He's a naturalized citizen of the United States, an honor graduate of our Officer's Candidate School, and a highly decorated combat veteran. Colonel Khan, America has a lot of people from everywhere in the world. Did you believe our military service would be different from the rest of our country?" Without waiting for an answer, Curt told his medical officer, "Major Gydesen, would you please take a look at the major's arm? It's apparently been injured by accident."

Ruth had come slowly to her feet, lifting her medical kit and keeping its Red Cross insignia in plain sight. She did this because she didn't want to provoke any additional reactions from the Pakistanis. As she moved around the conference table, she observed, "It appears from here to be broken, Colonel. Request your permission to take the major to get medical assistance."

"Please do," Curt said with a nod. Then his voice got low and mean, although he maintained his polite demeanor. "Colonel Khan, my orders don't permit me to relinquish command of my regiment to anyone. I'm responsible. We're here at the invitation of the government of Pakistan to conduct an exploratory mission into Kashmir with you. We don't intend to fight the Pakistani army. We can suffer insults. But when we're threatened, we *will* react. We prefer to counterattack before being attacked; it lowers the casualty rate. Therefore, be advised, sir, that personal and regimental honor is just as important to us as it is to the Fourth Khyber Rifles. And like your officers and regiment, we don't demand respect; we've earned it as you have. Furthermore, we're professionals just like you. I suggest that we all begin to act like professionals. And that we get busy planning our joint exploration?"

Khan was quiet for a moment, then finally agreed. "Very well. Let us proceed as equals, then. But you will be well advised to remember that you are in Pakistan, not the United States of America."

Chapter Fifteen

"It's a damned good thing you and Taisha were late getting here," Curt told Colonel Owen Pendleton.

"Sorry, Curt. Orient Express Flight Nine was late getting out of Las Vegas. Then the Chairman of the Pakistani Institute of Science wasn't at the Islamabad Airport to pick us up," Pendleton said wearily. "I was bushed when we landed, but the drive from Islamabad here woke me up!"

Pendleton and Taisha had deliberately not traveled with the Greys. The deployment phase of this mission was far too open as it was. Murray had decided that both Pendleton and Taisha would travel with civilian passports on commercial hypersonic aircraft. Bookings were made at the last possible moment after an official invitation had been received from the Pakistani Institute of Science.

Dr. Rosha Taisha looked both tired and tense. "Colonel, that road was excellent and traversed country that was relatively benign in comparison to the norm in this part of the world."

"It wasn't the road or the terrain, Rosha. It was the driver," Owen admitted.

"I thought he was a good driver. We didn't have an accident, did we?"

"I thought we would a couple of times."

"You must remember, Colonel, that the roads in Asia are used by everyone and everything to go everywhere."

"Why the hell do they have to conduct a cattle drive along a main highway? By the way, Doctor, we're here as civilians. Please don't refer to me by my military rank," Owen reminded her.

"Sorry, Doctor. It's my programming."

"So why do you say it was a good thing we were late, Curt?"

Pendleton asked the commander of the Washington Greys.

"Because you missed the fight. But the delay gave me the opportunity to postpone final mission planning with Colonel Khan," Curt told them. "Come inside. The staff is waiting, and we'd better get a few of our ducks lined up before we have to tangle with Khan tomorrow morning at oh-nine-hundred."

"I'm not sure I'm thinking straight, Curt," Pendleton admitted. "It's seven o'clock in the morning to me, and I didn't get much sleep. Can Rosha and I get some rest before we have to make life-or-death decisions?"

Curt shook his head and held the door to the barracks open for the two of them. "You haven't met Colonel Iskander Khan yet. He's hell on wheels with turbo-boost. All he wants to do is smash his way into Deosai, blow the place up, and kill a lot of Chinese or Indian troops. And he's not very happy that he's got to support our mission to get the Chinese scientists out of there. He dislikes the Chinese only a *little* bit less than he hates the Indians. And he's not at all scientifically literate."

"What's this about a fight? And doesn't this place have any air-conditioning?" Owen asked as they walked down the long hallway lit only by dim sixty-watt light bulbs hanging from the ceiling.

"Welcome to the Small World," Curt remarked. " 'Air-conditioning' means opening the windows and letting the flies and mosquitoes in. This is an old British Royal Air Force barracks. It's been here since World War Two. I thought you already knew that nothing is too good for us, and that's exactly what we get. As for the fight, there was actually two of them. The first one was between Khan and me; he thinks he's running the whole show."

"Well, that certainly isn't the case! The Paks are in a support role!" Owen insisted.

"I'll let you tell Khan that."

"What was the other fight?" Dr. Rosha Taisha wanted to know.

Curt paused before they entered a door into a dayroom. He grinned. "Some of the Pakinstani officers didn't like the idea of fighting alongside the ladies of my regiment. They're sticklers for Islamic law in this country. One of the Pak officers insulted Kitsy Clinton. That was a big mistake because Kitsy is a lady and is never rude to anyone unintentionally. He didn't like what she said. When he raised his hand to strike her, Lieutenant MIkawa's hand somehow got in the way. He broke his arm. The meeting quieted down after that. Colonel Khan started to listen. Seems like he'd gained some measure of resect no only for us but for the ladies of the Greys. Amazing what a little violence will do when confronting violent men."

Taisha shuddered. "Violence! Why is there so much violence?"

Curt knew she'd seen far too much of it in her lifetime. It had once warped her mind and driver her to attempt to control human beings with neuroelectronics. She'd become violent in her own way. Although she'd gone through extensive NE rehab at Fort Benning's Martin Army Hospital, Curt suspected that her mostly deeply seated and personally held paradigms hadn't been completely reprogrammed.

"Because that's the way the universe operates, Doctor. As a scientist, you're probably aware that the use of physical force and violence exists even down to the bacterial level," Curt advised her.

"But it doesn't *have* to!"

"Then life would end because organisms wouldn't be able to eat," Pendleton told her philosophically.

"But we don't have to kill to eat! Many of the world's most advanced cultures are vegetarian!"

"Doctor, we can argue philosophy when this operation is over," Curt told her. "We need a high-energy omnivore diet so we can protect non-violent vegetarians."

"My ancestors didn't fight to get to the top of the food chain just so I could be a vegetarian," Owen Pendleton muttered.

The regimental staff of the Washington Greys looked tired, but most of them had gotten their second wind. They greeted Pendleton and Taisha with as much warmth as their fatigue would allow.

In spite of their weariness, they still maintained a spark of humor and perspective because Joan Ward greeted Pendleton with the remark, "Colonel, we're less than a thousand kilometers from one another in the United States. We've got to figure out an easier way to see one another than coming halfway around the world!"

And in spite of his circadian asynchronization, Pendleton fired back with equal humor, "Yes, I agree we've got to stop meeting this way!"

After they'd all seated themselves in somewhat rickety wooden chairs around the worn and battered table, Curt said, "I want to keep this short. We all need to log some sack time so we can be high, tight, and good to go twelve hours from now when we tangle with the Paks again. First, I want to remind everyone where we stand and bring our two scientists up to speed."

"I think that's perfectly clear," Major Russ Frazier growled. He was unhappy with the situation and with their forced "allies," the Pakistanis. "Colonel Khan believes he's going to run Operation Hell Fire his way. And to hell with anyone else because it's on his turf!"

Curt knew his S-3 operations staff officer was an aggressive type. Russ Was naturally aggressive and had been trained by an aggressive superior officer. He'd been one of the first effective Sierra Charlies. Russ had never bitched or sniveled about leaving the safety of a warbot brainy's linkage couch in the rear area. When he got into combat, the blood lust rose in him. He didn't love killing, but it didn't bother him either. It was just something that went with his job. And he liked his job. "Look at it this way, Russ," Curt told him. "We made some progress this afternoon. We got Khan to back down to a position where Hell Fire is an equal opportunity operation."

"Yeah, but they will be more equal than we are."

"Russ, handling this interface with Khan is my job," Curt reminded his operations man. "I'll do the best I can to intimidate and otherwise humiliate him, so he isn't so damned macho. Hassan has already briefed me on some secret buttons to push to get an Islamic man to behave. Basically, Khan doesn't understand that the operation has three elements."

"He only wants to go in there, bust up the Deosai facility, and kill East Worlders," Hazier observed.

"Knowing the history of religious intolerance in this region and the indiscriminate slaughter that's gone on for centuries, I can understand the man although I can't empathize with him," Curt admitted. "But I have to work with him. So, when handed a lemon, I'm going to make lemonade."

Major Russ Frazier was still worried. "Colonel, what if the Paks get in the way? They're not really anxious to cooperate. Hell, they want to do it their way. Suppose we get into Deosai with them and they slip it to us greasy?"

"Major, did you ever hear of 'friendly fire'?" Henry Kester wanted to know. "Usually, it ain't."

"There's no such thing as friendly fire," Joan added.

"Well, I've taken friendly fire from Kelly and the Wolfhounds," Russ replied, and paused for a moment while he thought about what Henry and Joan had said. "I sure as hell won't blow away a Wolfhound unit because they made a mistake and shot into us. They're on our side, except when they try to grease our skids in a field exercise. On the other hand, I remember the Sonoran militia shooting at us until they got the ungarbled word. We parted their hair a little and they got the message loud and clear. We took a lot of friendly fire on Sakhalin Island too. Colonel, I presume the same ROEs are in effect for this fracas?"

"I won't make it official," Curt told him. "I don't have to. The standing orders are and always have been simple: If the Greys take incoming, they shoot back."

This bothered Pendleton. "Suppose the incoming is a mistake?"

"Those standing orders tend to minimize such mistakes," Frazier told the scientific officer. "Those who make such mistakes sometimes don't get the chance to make more of them. Consider it evolution in action."

Owen Pendleton wasn't an antimilitary weenie. Once he got the music straight in his mind, he'd march to the drumbeat. He had proved this more than a decade before in Zahedan, Iran. So, he just nodded. "Okay, as long as everyone knows..."

"I'll make sure my counterpart on Khan's staff knows," Russ promised. "It'll make the operation easier. And we'll feel less guilty if we have to blow the shorts off a few Paks who shoot at us 'by accident.' "

"The other two elements are scientific and defensive," Curt went on, not wanting to let this Papa briefing degenerate into a bull session, as it often did when the Greys were tired or stressed-out. "We have to allow Owen and Doctor Taisha to see what's in that Deosai facility. Edie, as our chief techie, I'd like you to work with them once we penetrate the facility."

"Yes, sir! Can I have some backup from one of the assault platoons in case the Paks decide to go hyperbolic when they get in there?"

Curt nodded. "Everyone will be briefed. Nothing technical is to be damaged or destroyed until the scientific team says it's okay to do so."

"That's where we're probably going to have trouble with the Paks," Edie remarked. "They'll probably want to blow up the whole facility right away."

Russ shook his head slowly. He had an evil grin on his face. "Nooooo, not exactly! Colonel, you'll advise them of our standing orders you just discussed with he us?"

"It will be done," Curt promised her. Then he went on. "And I usually don't argue with my chief techie NCO. But Edie, we'll have the biggest hassle with the Paks when we round up the Chinese scientists and try to get them out alive," Curt looked around at the others on his staff. "That's going to require the efforts of a joint military-scientific team."

Curt switched to speaking Mandarin Chinese. He'd been one of the few West Point cadets in his class who'd chosen that as a second language. He knew his Chinese was rusty and that he probably had a terrible American accent, but he spoke directly to Taisha in Mandarin. *"Doctor Taisha, from your background I know you must speak this language. Therefore, I will be the military part of the extraction team and you will handle the scientific side. Is this agreeable to you?"* Actually, that isn't precisely what he said, but only the closest translation possible in English.

Doctor Rosha Taisha jerked upright in her chair, her eyes suddenly blazing. She did indeed speak Mandarin. Her father had been a Chinese scientist. She'd been raised in Beijing. Her youthful memories and the terror had created personal demons that had dogged Taisha for decades. She'd finally been forced to confront them and they'd driven her into catatonia. Only the neuroelectronic rehab specialists of the United States Army had been able to draw her back to the real world so she could make peace with those demons and continue living with herself. It hadn't been easy for her. The memories were there, but she'd learned to ignore them.

But Taisha answered Curt in English. "Colonel Carson, it has been a very long time since I spoke that language. I am not sure I can remember how to say some things. However, I do understand most of what you said. It is not necessary for me to agree to handle the scientific side of the rescue of Doctor Dongzhu and his colleagues. It is already my assignment from Colonel Pendleton. And I shall carry it out."

Curt noticed that Taisha suddenly spoke in phrases that were somewhat stilted, forced, formal, and precisely correct English.

She was apparently facing something she'd rather forget.

However, if forgetting it made her an ally rather than an enemy, Curt was willing to allow her to do so. Therefore, he didn't push the issue any farther.

"Okay, Doctor, we'll take it from there once we get inside the Deosai," Curt told her easily. As a result of her behavior, however, he wanted to keep surveillance on her J.I.C.

"I have some additional information," se went on, lapsing back into the comfortable English she'd used at McCarthy. "A different message has appeared on the ten-hertz signal."

"And?" Curt prompted her when she hesitated.

"Doctor Dongzhu says that he'll have the signal turned off if he knows when we'll begin the final assault," Taisha reported. "He says it will allow us to use neuroelectronic equipment during the rescue."

"How are we supposed to get that information to him, for God's sake? What did he do? Leave a telephone number where he could be reached?" Lieutenant Colonel Pappy Gratton snapped. He hadn't spoken up during the briefings thus far. However, if anyone was an expert in communications, Pappy was. No matter where a Grey might be on leave or pass or TDY, Pappy could manage to establish communications with that person. Curt knew that Pappy had located him many times in the past when Curt thought he'd managed to disappear from the world.

"Colonel, he did just that," Doctor Taisha said bluntly. "The message says if we call eight-six, one, eight-six, one-one, two-nine-five, it's a direct link from Beijing to Deosai."

"Ask a simple question, get an obvious answer," Pappy muttered, then added, "Of course! We forget the whole damned world is wired now! If it isn't landline, it's comsat. Obviously, the Deosai facility has its comm link to Beijing!"

"That's the PRC country code and the Beijing city code," Edie confirmed.

"And sure death if we call," Captain Dyani Motega, the regimental S-2, pointed out firmly, "Colonel, do they think we're stupid? That we'd give away important intelligence data? That we'd tell the Chinese we're coming? And when?"

"The thought had occurred to me too, Dyani," Curt agreed. "Doctor Taisha, have you reported this to Washington?"

"No, but Colonel Pendleton did."

"I talked with General Bellamack," Own admitted.

"And did he have any recommendation?"

"Nope. He thanked me, and that was the end of the conversation."

"What do you think about it, Owen? DO you know Doctor Dongzhou, but I know his papers and his work. Rosha hasn't met him either. But she says she can identify him from the pictures that have appeared in the journals," Owen remarked.

"I want to talk to General Bellamack about this. Edie, can you patch a link through Grady to Georgie to Fort Fumble?" Curt asked rhetorically, knowing that Edie Sampson could do wonders with the primitive comm gear they'd brough on this mission.

"Yes, sir. The general should be in his office now." Edie had made a quick calculation of time zones in her head. It was 0830 in the Pentagon.

"Make is so," he told her.

She took the tacomm brick from her waist and began to work it.

"Colonel, maybe we *should* give the Chinese a call," Dyani suddenly said.

Dyani Motega continually surprised Curt, and it was therefore not so much of a surprise on this occasion. He knew she could think in very devious ways. She was an expert in scouting, and therefore an expert in deception. Except that she'd never deceived him. "Why?" was his simple question to her.

"The Chinese have an outstanding intelligence network second to none, not even the KGB," Dyani pointed out. "Our deployment was certainly noticed. The flight of Colonel Pendleton and Doctor Taisha might have been detected too. Doctor, when did that message appear on the ten-hertz signal?"

"Two hours before we departed McCarthy," Owen told her.

"Then the chances are good they knew the two of you were coming," Dyani went on.

"So why do you say we should respond by calling them?" Curt asked again.

"Deception, sir. Somehow, they must know that the decision has been made to assault Deosai. But they don't know *when*. So, we'll tell them. But the time we give them will be two to three days *after* we're actually scheduled to initiate it!"

The room was silent for a moment. Then Curt spoke up. "I can't authorize us to do that. It might jeopardize the success of the mission."

"Colonel, they're going to see us coming in the aerodynes if they're using their surveillance satellites," Russ pointed out.

"It's only two hundred fifty klicks from here. That's less than an hour's flight. Mighty short reaction time on their part," Joan remarked.

Curt sighed. "So, we set them up for a later time. That will confirm their intelligence data. That also puts them on yellow alert in case they think we're lying to them, which we are. Dammit, this is the sort of hide-and-seek game I don't like to play because I don't have enough of the tactical factors under my control." He turned to his tech NCO. "Edie, belay that last order. Cancel the call."

"Yes, sir."

He turned back to his staff. "Our best answer is no answer at all," he told them. "Why let them know we got the message? If I get a call from Fort Fumble about it, I'll do whatever General Bellamack wants, providing I don't think it's too damned dangerous." He stood up. "Besides, I'm too damned tired tonight to make a critical decision of this sort. Let's sleep on it. We've tot a busy day tomorrow. Except it's probably tomorrow already. Hell, I don't know. My circadian is all screwed up anyway right now. Under those circumstances, we could be missing the one obvious and important data point in this whole damned sheep screw."

HE was right about that.

Chapter Sixteen

"Mister President, we must respond to the latest message from Doctor Dongzhu!" Dr. Mark Hankamer was very insistent. "We must let him know that we're on our way to rescue him!"

The President had expected this from his science advisor. The man was an academician, and he had practically no feeling for the realities of the world. The President would make the decision about responding, of course, but he had to keep some peace on the scientific side of the house at the same time. He wasn't going to authorize a response. However, he wanted to assure Hankamer that all the factors had been carefully considered. The President was a prudent person. More than thirty years' service in the United States Army and the command of several international military operations and humanitarian missions had made him a tactful as well as a tactical man.

"Doctor, I hope you realize that we don't have to do anything, including sending American troops into a foreign country to destroy a new weapon system!" was the response from National Security Advisor Jeffrey Pickens. "We're not exactly on solid ground here anyway. If that Deosai Plains facility is indeed a weapon against our neuroelectronic systems, we should let the Aerospace Force drop a kinetic kill weapon on it. Or we ought to get to work and use our brainpower to counter it."

"I'd expect that approach from a former military officer!" Hankamer countered with venom. "I do *not* favor attacking it anyway. The least we can do is what we're doing: Send in an exploratory expedition to find out what is really is and bring out the people who built it."

This argument had gone back and forth for two days now, and the President was growing weary of it. He had other matters to attend to. This East World Deosai operation was causing dissension in his staff. Thus far, thank God, he'd managed to keep it from the attention of the world press. The other side, probably East World, wasn't trumpeting it to the news media. And it was to the advantage of the United States to keep it quiet until he could report on it. His military background told him to act, then explain.

I also told him not to dither. It was always possible to change an operational order. Modern communications no longer made a mobilization equivalent to a declaration of war as it had at the start of World War I. The previous President had actually called off an operation in Yemen right in the midst of a major battle at Sana'a International Airport.

This President wouldn't do that sort of thing, however. Ordering a retreat during an engagement caused unacceptable human as well as political and diplomatic losses.

The President had set in motion the necessary actions to initiate Operation Hell Fire. It was proceeding on schedule. The new message from Dongzhou was unanticipated but gave him no reason to change the operation at this point. The question of what to do about the message was now the issue, and it was dragging in other issues he thought had been settled the day before.

"American ingenuity is the best weapon we've got," Pickens argued. He didn't realize he was, in effect, taking on the man who was the White House bastion of that group that believed it had the monopoly on ingenuity.

The President sat back and watched this assault. He wanted to see what would happen when his security advisor made a frontal attack upon the well-fortified position of his science advisor. The result would tell him much. One of the two men would lose. The President had reservations about both men. However, he'd acquiesced to political pressures from both academia and the military to have both men on his staff. Maybe the loser would create a suitable excuse for the President to activate the letter of resignation all Presidential staffers had deposited in the center drawer of the Presidential desk.

The President didn't want losers on his staff. He was a graduate of West Point. But he knew about Jonas Ingram standing on the steps of Bancroft Hall at the Naval Academy and shouting, "The Navy has no place for good losers! The Navy needs tough sons of bitches who can go out there and win!" The President felt the same way about the United States of America.

"We invented neuroelectronics," Pickens went on. "We developed the direct interface between the electronic computer and the human nervous system. We know more about it than anyone else!"

"The American NE industry might argue with you about that, General!" Hankamer broke in.

Pickens was a retired general, one of those who can-not abide being interrupted, especially by a civilian. He fired back acidly, "Even the Japanese haven't been able to keep up with us in neuroelectronics. The bastards are great copiers! Always have been! So, we ought to be able to handle this problem as an opportunity to forge ahead and stay ahead."

"What do you have in mind?" Hankamer tried to draw Pickens out in an attempt to discover a weak point where he could counterattack. Hankamer didn't think of it in military terms as Pickens might, but in the paradigms of the academic world where conflicts were as intense and decisive.

"Well, hell, it shouldn't take long to analyze what East World is doing. We have their signals. We only need to apply our reservoir of brainpower to come up with both a countermeasure and a new direction for neuroelectronics. I used to read Rudyard Kipling. That man had a lot to say about the military as well as about the world in general. Do you remember what he said about technological warfare? Remember *The Ballad of the Mary Gloster?*"

Hankamer had read Kipling as part of a mandatory assignment in a sophomore English class many, many years ago. He considered Kipling to be an atavistic, jingoistic British bigot. He didn't know that the power-novelist had been born in Bombat and had thought of himself as a man of India. "No," Hankamer replied, knowing that his answer would subject him to a Kipling quotation. However, Hankamer did it in the hope that he might be able to twist the Kipling quote for his own purposes.

"It was about a sailing ship designer," Pickens told him. "Others were worried about rivals duplicating the ships of this genius and beating out the Brits in the maritime trade. Kipling's hero says, *'They copied all they could copy, but they couldn't copy my mind; so I left 'em sweatin' and schemin', a year and a half behind!'* And that' what we've got to do, Doctor! Keep moving ahead! Quit reacting to competition!"

The President found himself agreeing with his security advisor.

"We're not talking a year and a half, General!" Hankamer came back at once, seeing the opening and moving right into it. "We're talking years! What do I have to do to convince you that scientific research such as you're talking about can't be done under pressure or on a schedule? And my colleagues may not be able to find a countermeasure or even a new approach to neuroelectronics! We don't understand much about the human mind in spite of what NE has taught us. We don't understand much about neurophysiology! When neuroelectronics broke over us, it demolished all the existing theories of neurophysiology! Forty years later, we're still trying to normalize the theories with the new reality!"

"So, you believe that will be helped by getting Dongzhu and his colleagues out of Deosai?"

Hankamer nodded. "We need their expertise. They'll prevent us from duplicating their work."

"But if we didn't have to get them out of there, we wouldn't risk American lives by sending in Sierra Charlies! The Aerospace Force could make quick work of the situation! That's why we've built a hypersonic bombing capability with kinetic weapons." Pickens wasn't a dove, but he didn't like the idea of ordering soldiers into a situation where they could be killed. He was a "peaceful" general. He'd been perfect for the command of such areas as the Persian Gulf, where the main American military objective was to cow into inaction the various warring tribes that ran the nations there. He'd therefore done a reasonable job as Army Chief of Staff in a period when he'd only had to order troops into combat once. And he'd done that through a subordinate, General Wild Bill Bellamack, during the Senegambian bloodbath.

157

The President sat up in his chair and placed both hands on his desk. "I see a basic disagreement between my science advisor and my security advisor. So, let me ask my intelligence advisor: Al, should we respond to Doctor Dongzhu's message?"

Al Murray had sat quietly listening to the exchange. It wasn't necessary for him to contribute to it. He had his own analysis of the situation based on a great deal of information. He knew he didn't know everything. He knew his information was probably incomplete. Intelligence data is always incomplete. But he had a lot of it. "No, sir," was his brief response.

"Why?"

"I speak as a former general officer and as your chief spy," Murray told his boss. "The lives of more than a hundred crack military troops are already involved. Therefore, one does not tell the enemy anything in a situation such as this. Besides, the message may not be real."

"*What?*" Picken's couldn't believe what he was hearing.

"Nonsense!" Hank snapped. He'd staked a great deal of clout on the validity of the messages being passed along to him through his colleagues in the academic community.

Murray pursed his lips. It wasn't often he revealed his thoughts by his facial expressions. "One of the responsibilities of my job it to evaluate all the potential situations presented by a given set of circumstances. Then I have to look at possible consequences. It's a game of 'let's suppose.' It's based on a long history of affairs not being what they initially appear. Mister President, I have no intention of getting myself and my agency in a position where I must give you the lame excuse that we didn't think of something. As a result, I have to ask myself and my people some very basic and often uncomfortable questions. For example: Why is East World doing this now? What do they believe they'll gain? Does anyone in this office believe that this apparent weapon is *not* destabilizing? Why would East World want to destabilize the international situation at this time? They were caught with their hands in the cookie jar in Yemen. French and American military stopped them cold in Senegambia. Given those questions, one must then ask: Is East World really doing this? Or is someone else doing it? And why? What's to be gained? And at what cost? And what are the chances of winning?"

"Oh, hell, Al! It's obvious!" Pickens exploded. "The goddamned East World nuts want to run the world! They've been on the bottom of the heap for more than five hundred years and they want to be king of the hill again. So they've come up with a weapon that wipes out our warbot capability because they haven't got any of their own to speak of! They really don't need warbots. They've got all the human cannon fodder they can use, even on a nuclear battlefield."

"Suppose East World isn't behind this. Then who is?" the President asked his security advisor, whose job it was to be on top of all the potential security problems and the threat analyses.

"It may be the damned Muslims! Hell, I spent years among them in the Middle East!" Pickens replied with authority in his voice. He'd been with the 21st Robot Infantry, the Gimlet regiment, and had survived the Middle East arms scam. He'd been the obvious choice for command of that regiment. Because of outstanding subordinates, the Gimlets had been reorganized and revived. Then the Powers That Be had felt that Pickens had unique knowledge of the Middle East, just as Douglas MacArthur had had about the western Pacific region. So, he'd been bucked up to theater command there. By keeping his nose clean and not giving any opportunity for any of his enemies to catch him committing sins of commission or omission, he'd climbed the greasy pole of power in the Pentagon. Finally, it was thirty-five-and-out because he'd been tapped as National Security Advisor. As a result, Pickens was highly biased and suffering from manageriosclerosis.

"Those people will lie, cheat, steal, or schmooze to get whatever they want!" he went on pontifically, venting his general dislike of the Islamic people who worshipped God in a way different from his Southern Baptist beliefs. "They're devious and not to be trusted. Look at the grief the Pakistanis are giving us about letting the Greys take the Chinese scientists out! If those are really Chinese scientists at Deosai! Why are the Paks behaving this way? Mister President, the Chinese may have nothing to do with this situation. Those scientists could be from India! The Paks hate the Indians."

Pickens didn't have all his ducks lined up as neatly as Murray or even Hankamer. So, he shot from the hip. He was making up a lot of it as he went along. And it was tempered by too many years of being in a command position among peoples who felt subjugated. "Or there may be no scientists at all. This could be a prologue to another Indo-Pakistani war. This time, the Paks are trying to get the United States involved. I'm willing to bet that the Paks won't let the Greys get as far as Deosai. That's damned rugged country. It's also close to the vague 'cease-fire line' with India. The Greys will probably be ambushed by the Indian Army or the Sikhs first. Then what do we do? If you want an alternate-view scenario, Mister President, I've just given you one."

"I've got to concur with Jeff," Murray put in. One of his own scenarios closely matched it. He'd gotten some fresh insight into the situation as a result of recent contacts. But he hadn't brought up the matter in front of Pickens and Hankamer because he didn't trust them if he revealed his source. Pickens himself could have raised hell in the military sphere. Murray always protected his sources.

The President looked at the NIA chief. He decided to get together with the man privately and covertly after the others had left. The President had only a few brief questions for Murray, but they had to be answered in private. "Jeff," the President said to his security advisor, "will you prepare a written threat evaluation covering what you've just proposed as an alternate scenario, please?" He knew that Pickens was a bigot. But the security advisor might have touched on a valid scenario. The President didn't want to let it slip past just because the man was acting somewhat irrationally. In addition, Murray had indicated that some validity attached to what otherwise might have been evaluated as a wild guess.

"Certainly, Mister President!" Pickens suddenly considered that perhaps he'd gone too far. Maybe he should have kept his mouth shut. On the other hand, if he hadn't and if his worst fears had materialized, he'd be in trouble if he hadn't raised these points.

Pickens really wasn't comfortable in the position of National

Security Advisor. He'd taken the job with the assurances that he'd be amply supported with data and assistance from certain cliques within the armed services. He didn't like to get into positions like this one. He knew he was shooting from the hip. But he was too insecure and too short-tempered to restrain himself under these conditions. After all, he was privy to decisions that shaped the world and affected the lives of millions of people. It was almost too awesome for him to think very much about it.

The President had other items on his daily agenda. He could see from looking at his communications terminal that his secretary was frantically signaling him about being late for the next appointment. Well, the new judge of the Third Circuit Court of Appeals could damned well wait a few minutes, the Chief Executive decided. If the nation got into a shooting war with either India or China - both of whom had nukes, warbots, and military space capabilities - the matter of the Third Circuit of Appeals might be moot.

Abruptly, the President told the three, "I've got to break this off. Thank you for coming early on a very busy morning. I'll be in touch with all of you. And Jeff, I'd like to have your analysis by fourteen hundred hours today."

"So what do we do, Mister President?" Hankamer wanted to know as he slowly stood up.

"Why, precisely what we're presently doing," the President told him. "No change in plan. No addendum to the plan."

"You aren't going to answer Doctor Dongzhu?"

"No. Not at this time. And I expect everyone present to maintain confidentiality. I do *not* want any leaks. If leaks occur, I will know where they cam from." No one could mistake the resolve in the President's voice.

Murray left with the other two but used the revolving-door technique. He came back through another door within a minute. "Yes, Mister President?" Murray had gotten the signal.

"Just a quick one, Al, then I *must* get on to other matters. I take it your contact is within the military forces of Operation Hell Fire."

"Yes, sir."

"Who?"

Murray told him.

The President nodded. "Good! I trust him. And he has an excellent talent for both tactical and strategic thinking. Furthermore, he's on the spot with his arse bared to the breeze."

***

Half a world away, the NIA's intelligence source didn't have that part of his anatomy uncovered. He was under a sheet because the temperature dropped quickly at night at the Ghazi air base. But he was keeping warm enough by exchanging body heat and the wonderful feeling of gentle skin to-skin contact.

"Was it right for you to call General Murray directly?" Dyani asked him.

Curt nodded. Command was indeed lonely. Dyani made it less lonely. Sometimes just her closeness, her presence, her touch were enough. Both were too exhausted that night for anything else. They needed no excuses. Neither expected more from the other. Danger was in the air all around them, but they weren't expected to be on guard against it right at that moment. So, they enjoyed one another's touch and presence. Curt had learned that real, caring love was more than sex. And he knew exactly how he felt about Dyani and how she felt about him. "I also told Wild Bill Bellamack. I can trust him too."

"Yes, you had a contract with him when he was regimental commander," Dyani recalled.

"I still have a contract with him," Curt pointed out.

"As we have a contract with each other."

"Several," Curt reminded her. "I'm going to be counting heavily on you for recce and scouting."

"I won't let you down. I never have."

"You never have," Curt agreed. His reply was something he'd learned from her: a phrase with many meanings. "Thank you for telling me your fears about the Indian Army. And the Sikhs. And the chance we might be the sucker bait in a new Indo-Pakistan war. And for not insisting on getting the credit."

"Who cares about the credit? It's my job. It's my duty." Duty ranked very high on Dyani Motega's list of priorities.

"Get some sleep," he told her.

"I will if you stop shaking."

"Am I shaking?"

"A little."

"I always shake a little bit the night before an operation," he admitted.

"I know. Stop caring so much. Stop worrying about me. About the Greys. We can handle anything that comes our way tomorrow. Here, let me help you relax a little. Does that feel good?"

"Yes. Very good. You're good at anything you do."

"I've had some outstanding teachers. Including you."

Chapter Seventeen

"I hope now you're rested after your long flight." Colonel Iskander Khan was downright courteous and solicitous as the Papa briefing began.

Curt knew then that Khan had received a call from the Pakistani Army Chief of Staff, General Muzaffar Rahim. The COS in turn had received a call from the Pakistani JCS Chairman who in turn had been contacted by the Minister of State for Defense. The commander of the Washington Greys had rattled the long chain of command and control last night during several secure communications through military channels to the United States. Curt had reported quite properly and had made careful requests. The chain had thus been jerked. The links transmitted the message by long concatenation to Colonel Khan.

"Thank you, Colonel. Yes, we're in much better condition today," Curt replied politely. He looked at Owen Pendleton and Rosha Taisha, who were present. "Now that the scientific leaders of the expedition are here, everyone involved is present. And we can proceed to conduct cross-briefings. Everyone must have a complete understanding of the expedition's objectives and the security capabilities of our two regiments."

Khan knew more about the whole affair this morning because of the communications that had come down from Islamabad. Khan had been informed that Colonel Owen Pendleton had shucked his military rank for this operation. And he'd been given a full dossier on Rosha Taisha. They were American military scientists leading a scientific expedition that was a military operation. It was being disguised for many reasons, some of which had been revealed to Khan. The military units of both nations were under orders to provide "security" against Kashmir guerrillas as well as possible harassment by Chinese and Indian troops in the rugged mountains.

Khan didn't really like the duty, and he didn't like being

responsible to an American military officer operating under cover as a civilian. But since his government was happy playing games with the Americans, he had no inclination to play other games instead. Islamabad had informed him that a successful "expedition" would do wonders for his career and promotion possibilities. The military services were Number One in Pakistan. And Khan was clawing his way up the greasy pole of success in the Pakistani system. So, he'd decided to become much more cooperative. But he gave no excuses for his previous behavior. That just wasn't done in Pakistan. A merchant in the bazaar might be allowed to apologize to a good customer under certain circumstances, but not an Islamic warrior.

Khan also knew now that Colonel Curt Carson was advised by a Baluchi officer in the Washington Greys. Captain Mahmud understood how things were done in this part of the world. In short, Khan couldn't count on Carson's ignorance of regional mores.

"This has become a scientific expedition," Khan put in, revealing to Curt again that he'd received orders and briefings from higher up on the Pakistani chain of command. "Therefore, Doctor Pendleton should now tell us why the United States wants to investigate a site on. the Plains of Deosai. Doctor?"

Pendleton didn't have a Ph.D. He didn't need one. He could have taught Ph.D's and often did. Usually, Owen corrected anyone who addressed him as if he had his doctorate. However, this time he didn't. If Khan believed it, it might help in an otherwise difficult cross-cultural situation. Muslims still regarded learning and the possession of knowledge with respect.

Pendleton stood up and gave a thirty-minute briefing on what had been discovered at McCarthy Proving Ground. He showed high-resolution satellite images of the Deosai facility. He went on to say, "We believe the radiation from Deosai poses a serious security threat to the nations of the world. It destabilizes the international security balance. It can have significant economic impact on industrial operations that use neuroelectronic robots. This includes the Islamic Republic of Pakistan because of the increasing number of robots being used in modern industrial operations that are hazardous to any human beings present. The radiations also could destroy the humanitarian progress in neuroelectronic mental therapy. We already know and understand a lot about the effects of the Deosai transmissions. But we need to find out how such a powerful signal is being generated without an obvious input of large quantities of power. We also seek to learn why the facility was established on the Plains of Deosai."

The satellite images faded from the display screen, and Pendleton concluded by saying, "And finally, Doctor Wen Ling Dongzhu and his colleagues have asked for rescue and asylum. Doctor Dongzhu is the Director of the People's Institute of Intelligent Machinery Development in Beijing. He has informed us in the United States that he and his staff have been forced against their wills to construct the Deosai facility. They wish to defect to the United States. Therefore, we intend to bring them out of Deosai. We believe this move will be resisted by the People's Liberation Army of the People's Republic of China. And possibly by the Indian government and its Army, if India is involved as our intelligence agencies believe. This is why the Third Robot Infantry Regiment of the United States Army was ordered to provide protection and security for us. Colonel Carson, will you and your staff please brief us on the status and capabilities of the Washington Greys?"

Curt and his regimental staff were ready for this. Actually, he and Owen had established the agenda last night. So far, it was working.

A full regimental status briefing is almost the ultimate "dog and pony show." Curt kicked it off, then turned it over to his chief of staff, Joan Ward, who gave an overview of the regimental organization. She then allowed Gratton, Dyani, Frazier, and Harriet Dearborn to give the status of personnel, intelligence, operations, and logistics in order.

For the first time in many years, the Greys had a full Table of Organization and Equipment, the TO&E. The deployment had been Class One: full capabilities. The Greys had all of their 137 people in Pakistan.

As Dyani reported, the neuroelectronic birdbot recce platoon wouldn't operate their birdbots on this mission. The threat of the

Deosai NE countermeasures was too great. Therefore, the possibility of the loss of birdbots and the birdbot brainies who ran them was too great a risk. As a result, the birdbots had been left at Fort Huachuca. The members of Captain Dale Brown's Black Hawks had been tasked to ride as observers in the eight Harpies of Major Paul Hands's tactical air support company. To familiarize themselves with the Harpy aerodyne and the view from the aux seat, the Black Hawks had deployed aboard the Harpies to Pakistan. It had been a grueling flight for the former birdbotters. However, they were performing well in spite of their new assignment.

Major Russ Frazier's briefing wasn't as sanguine. "The guiding principle of the Deosai operation will be surprise. If those troops with their Red Hammer warbots in Deosai know we're coming, they'll be ready for us. We don't know how many soldiers are there, but our intelligence sources estimate that at least fifty Red Hammer warbots are deployed at Deosai. This makes it a formidable defensive position. An assault on such a strong defensive position can be very costly. Although it's true that any defense can be overcome if the attacker is willing to pay the price, that price may be too high for our limited capabilities. A prolonged siege of Deosai may allow the Chinese or Indians to bring up reinforcements. This could escalate this expedition into a major armed conflict. It might also permit the Chinese to kill or otherwise make Doctor Dongzhu and his colleagues unavailable for rescue. When we discuss the operational plan, I recommend that a surprise attack be planned."

Curt was pleased with the analysis Russ had made of the situation. Frazier might be an aggressive fighter, but this didn't keep him from thinking. The man had mellowed considerably over the years. He'd objected to being pulled out of the command of TACBATT and slipped into the S-3 slot, but it had helped him mature. And Curt knew of no one else in the Greys who could fill that important staff position.

"We believe that the only way to achieve surprise will be to use a vertical envelopment with a tactical airlift. Furthermore, we should not spend any more time than we have to in that high mountain environment. We must get in there fast and get the Chinese scientists out quickly. Then we must withdraw rapidly once the scientific team has completed its studies. However, we face a serious. problem in deploying the entire regiment by air. We don't have enough Chippewa aerodynes to do it. This is because the Chippies must operate with reduced loads of both fuel and cargo to clear the six-thousand-meter Pangi Range on this side of Deosai. And they may not be able to lift off at the high altitudes of Deosai. This operational problem needs to be addressed in our joint planning today." Russ had dropped the bombshell that had worried Curt. It also meant they might have to depend upon some sort of assistance and support from the Pakistanis. Maybe the 4th Khyber Rifles wouldn't be enough support.

Major Harriet Dearborn completed the staff presentation by reporting that the Greys had enough consumables to operate for one hundred hours once they left Ghazi. Therefore, unless logistical support could be obtained, the Greys would have to get into Deosai and get out again in about four days. This emphasized Frazier's observation that the mission had to be fast, stealthy, and surgical.

No one present could possibly have missed the fact that the Americans knew very well that this was not a scientific expedition as its cover proclaimed. It was a military operation. Its objectives were to find out what was going on, destroy the facility, get the Chinese scientists out, and then withdraw quickly. Preferably without starting a war in the process. No one in the room wanted a war either. They'd probably be the first ones to die.

In the environment of the conference room, no one kidded themselves about any of this.

Even the staff officers of the 4th Khyber Rifles sobered considerably as information was laid out before them. They were, however, a bit more willing to take risks than the Americans. After all, they were Muslims. If they didn't believe openly that their death in battle would permit them to enter paradise, they secretly harbored that hope.

The briefing of the 4th Khyber Rifles was done a little differently. The staffers didn't make presentations; they were present to answer any questions that Khan deflected to them. Colonel Khan was in charge. Definitely in charge. In the 4th Khyber Rifles, one listened to the Top Man: Colonel Khan.

Curt recognized Khan's organizational and management technique as classical linear command doctrine. Reports came up from below to the top, and orders went down only from the top. This worried Curt. He was used to subordinates being ready, willing, and able to take the initiative if the situation required it or the command chain was broken or too long.

But Curt knew how to counter such a linear command doctrine too. He'd fought against enemies who had used it.

"The Fourth Khyber Rifles is a tactical strike light infantry regiment of eight hundred men," Khan told them. "We have sixty Brazilian *Urutu* armored infantry vehicles and eighty air-transportable SAR Viper two-man all-terrain vehicles. Since we are always within a few hundred kilometers of any potential border action, this configuration allows us to move rapidly on the ground. If an urgent need exists for immediate response, we can go by air. Our *Urutus* and their drivers can follow in a few hours on the ground. We are thus experts on rapid vertical envelopment tactics. And those tactics are what we shall have to use to assault Deosai."

That was about as much as Khan was willing to tell about the 4th Khyber Rifles. He immediately took control of the meeting by outlining his plan. As he did so, he told himself that he should have done this yesterday. He would have if the Americans hadn't been so adamant about following their protocols.

"We shall move our *Urutus* in convoy up the Karakoram Highway," Khan told them. "The Americans will accompany us with their artillery and mobile assault warbots. The ground force will bivouac at Skardu on the western edge of the Deosai Plains. The air transport-able elements of our two regiments will proceed by means of Scorpion and Chippewa airlift aerodynes to assault Deosai from the southwest over the mountains. The assault will be coordinated so that the ground element and the air element strike simultaneously."

Curt reacted immediately. "Colonel Khan, I don't like your plan. It splits my forces and requires coordination of two prongs of an assault in extremely difficult terrain."

Khan looked at Curt imperiously because he'd maneuvered himself back into command of the situation. "Colonel Carson, your staff admitted that you don't have the capability to airlift your regiment into Deosai in one wave. We do not have the airlift capability to do it for you or to airlift the entire Fourth Khyber Rifles. Do you have a suggestion that would eliminate your objection to my plan?" Khan didn't think Curt did.

But Curt proved him wrong. "We'll take our forces into Deosai in a series of stealthy waves. We bivouac in camouflage until we've concentrated our forces for a unified assault."

"And how long do you think that will take? And how do you intend to supply them in the meantime? And how do you plan to keep them from being detected?" Khan wanted to know.

"I don't know how long it will take," Curt admitted. "Let's get our staffs together and let them work it out. That will tell us the percentage of our flights that will be required for logistical purposes. As for maintaining stealth, how to do you propose to hide a convoy of nearly two hundred military vehicles on the only road through the mountains? That's a convoy more than five kilometers long! As for hiding a ground force in those hills up there for a day or so, we can certainly call for ECW and other measures that will keep the enemy unawares until they find out. If they discover us before we have all our forces in place, we'll have Plan B to confuse them. But we must *not* reveal our actions or intentions by sending vehicles up the Karakoram Highway. We can stealth aerodynes and spook enemy air defenses; we can-not hide those vehicles on that highway!"

Dyani scribbled something on a slip of paper and passed it to Curt. When he looked at it, he saw it said, "Request private staff meeting. Have idea."

This was so unusual on Dyani's part that Curt crumpled it and remarked to Khan, "Colonel, may I request a fifteen-minute recess? My staff has some concerns they wish to discuss privately with me."

Khan had seen Dyani pass the note to Curt. This confused him because it was something that no woman in Pakistan would do, even if she happened to be the prime minister. So, he decided he'd better see what resulted from such a private meeting of the Greys' staff. Certainly, he didn't seem to be making much progress. Maybe these forthright women would put some sort of pressure on Carson the way his wives did (but only in private) on him. Maybe they'd bring Carson around to Khan's conservative plan. "Fifteen minutes, Colonel."

The eight Greys and two McCarthy warbot scientists stepped outside into the morning sun and walked about a hundred meters from the building. Curt then turned to Dyani and asked, "What the hell is going on, Dyani?"

"Sir," she answered formally and forcefully, "it occurred to me that if the Fourth Khyber Rifles want to go in by the Karakoram Highway and aren't worried about being detected, why not let them?"

"Because it will split our already small operational force," Curt explained.

"Yes, sir, but we could take the Deosai facility ourselves if we're airlifted into position while the Khyber Rifles are coming up the road," she explained. She was unusually loquacious right then. She knew she had to explain a reasonably complex idea to Curt and the rest of the staff in a very short period of time without maps or visual aids. "If the road advance of the Rifles is detected, that will distract the Deosai troops. It will draw attention away from us. It will make it easier for us to deploy. If the Deosai troops and warbots ambush the Rifles, they'll leave their rear unguarded. If they don't and hope to defend against only the Rifles, we can hit them from behind. Basically, sir, the problem of the Fourth Khyber Rifles can be turned into an opportunity for us."

Curt smiled. Dyani had an unusual perspective because of her heritage as a Crow Indian. She rarely thought in terms of frontal attack. In combat, she was the one who always managed to outmaneuver the enemy. But with Curt and the Greys, she was scrupulously honest and straightforward. "Captain Motega, you are

171

indeed a sneaky individual!"

"Yes, sir. Thank you, sir."

Curt looked at his operations staffer. "Russ, what do you think?"

"I think it will work just fine, sir."

"Harriet? Any logistics problem you can see?"

Dearborn shook her head. "No, sir, unless we can't get out of there after four days. We might get a little hungry."

Joan Ward reminded all of them, "The chances of that are slim. Cal Worsham and Tim Timm will bust their butts to put aerodynes over us for logistical air drops. If everything goes to slime, they'll airlift us out. If they can't for some reason, we can always walk out."

"Hell of a rough walk through some damned rugged mountains!" Pappy Gratton groused.

"No, sir. In case you haven't noticed, Kashmir is one of the favorite backpacking locales in the world," Edie Sampson pointed out. "Lots of trails and backpackers. If civilians can do it, we sure as hell can!"

"Most of us will ride anyway," Henry Kester remarked. "We can't burn up all our vehicle fuel sitting around waiting for the Pak attack."

The more Curt thought about Dyani's plan, the more sense it made. "I like it," he told all of them. "Unless you have strong objections, that's exactly what I'll tell Khan we're going to do. But I'm not going to tell him maybe he's getting set up here as the diversion to keep the enemy off our necks. But the plan will keep his unit together and not threaten his command. And if he can't hack it or gets detected and ambushed, that's his problem. The Greys can hack it! We can get in there stealthy. We can remain under cover until the attack. We can execute Plan B if we have to do the job alone. And we can keep our 'dynes ready to lift us out."

Henry Kester raised his hand and said in a cautionary tone, "Colonel, we've got time to put in a request for some additional airlift support for our withdrawal. I'm sure General Hettrick will detach the AIRBATTS from the Cottonbalers and the Wolfhounds.

They can get here in time for our withdrawal four days after we go in. I'm sure recommending that you call for some additional help from the Iron Fisters. J.I.C., you know."

This was a damned sharp group of people, Curt told himself.

"Owen?" Curt asked the warbot expert. Pendleton hadn't said anything since his own briefing.

Pendleton shrugged. "Curt, we really are the scientific expedition. All two of us. On the other hand, you understand the military angles. We'll ride with you however you want to plan it."

"Okay, let's go back, schmooze Khan, and sell him on those parts of the Dyani Plan he needs to know about," Curt told them all. He checked his watch. "Hell, we might as well relax. That took only five minutes, and we've got fifteen."

"Yeah, someone might think we're professionals and had maybe done something like this before," was Henry's comment.

Chapter Eighteen

"Mustang Leader, Grey Tech has your beacon!"

"Roger, Grey Tech. We've located a landing spot. We also found a bivouac area. Keep it low on the approach J.I.C."

Dyani and Harlan Saunders' Scouts had been the first wave into the Plains of Deosai. Their job: Fine a suitable staging area within ten kilometers of the target in a place where they could remain camouflaged until the assault began. They'd done it. Curt had had no doubt that they could or would.

The huge mass of Nanga Parbat certainly dominated the Pangi Range of the western Himalayas, Curt decided. He watched the high peak appear and disappear behind ridges and hills that would have been major mountains anywhere else in the world. No wonder this was the world paradise for mountaineers.

Fortunately, the plethora of mountains, peaks, ridges, and valleys of the tortured landscape around and under the incoming Chippies was helpful. They would produce confusing return signals to anyone watching radar and other air defense detection systems. The terrain would produce plenty of ground clutter.

But Cal Worsham and his pilots were taking no chances. The Chippies were being flown nap of the earth under manual control. That was almost a requirement because the loaded aerodynes were at their service ceilings. The terrain was between five thousand and six thousand meters above sea level itself. So, the inbound Chippies were flying up the valleys and just skimming the ridges of the mountain passes. It was also no easy task. Instead of being "part of the system" in neuroelectronic linkage, the human pilots were monitoring the autopilots and providing correction control inputs. Basically, this was the ancient way of flying an aircraft. All of Worsham's pilots had learned to do it as beginners. Some of them were rusty. But flying an airplane is a lot like riding a bicycle: Once you learn how to do it, the paradigm becomes a non-erasable memory that can be called up in full at will at any future time.

From his seat on the right of the pilot, Curt watched the terrain with concern. Not only was it rugged beyond belief, but it was extremely high.

"Are you sure you can get this bird out of our bivouac area, Nancy?" Curt asked his pilot.

Lieutenant Nancy Roberts nodded. She was flying the Chippie directly by hand-eye-foot with direct control inputs. The only job for the complex artificial intelligence equipment aboard was to keep the Chippie stable. It also automatically set the various power and slot parameters to keep it in the air. The aerodyne couldn't stall, but it was nearly at its lift limits. "If the charts are right, I'll get it in. And I'll be empty coming out. Also burned off an hour's fuel coming in. I'll be all right. It's getting *you* out of there after Operation Hell Fire that may be difficult, Colonel! I'm mostly worried about a malfunction. I don't think there's enough room down there to land a butterfly."

Nancy had fully recovered from the injuries she'd sustained in Yemen, where she'd had to make an emergency aerodyne landing. Her Chippie had blown up and burned just after she'd undergone a rapid NE delink and gotten out of it. She'd suffered burns from the explosion and some neurological trauma from the rapid delinkage.

"Depends on how the operation proceeds," Curt reminded her. It was much easier to converse with her out of linkage. "We'll burn that bridge when we come to it."

The entire Third Herd wasn't being airlifted into the staging area south of the Deosai Plains. With limited airlift capability caused by the 5,600-meter altitude of Deosai, Curt saw no need to haul along the SERVBATT. So only the TACBATT under Kitsy Clinton and the AIRBATT under Cal Worsham were involved.

Ruth Gydesen's BIOTECO was along, however. If any Greys were wounded or injured, Curt wanted bio-tech help on hand. Even a one-hour flight back to Ghazi might be too long. He'd read the history of the poor, bloody infantry. He'd tried to learn the lessons learned over the past century about rapid field medical aid. And he'd had his own experiences with the Washington Greys when they'd discovered the hard way that infantry required medics. The quicker the bio-techs could get to work, the greater the chances that a wounded person would survive.

Curt wasn't about to ask forty-two Greys to go out in the Himalaya Mountains on an assault against an un-known enemy unless bio-tech help was right at hand.

The warbots were something else. Field-level maintenance and repairs could usually keep them fighting. If not, they could be shut down until they could be air-lifted back to Ghazi where the technicians of SERVBATT could minister to them. A warbot spurting red hydraulic fluid on the ground isn't as urgent a matter as a Sierra Charlie leaking red blood.

Warbots would just quit; they could be restarted from scratch once they were repaired. But if Sierra Charlies stopped working, they wouldn't respond to an arctic boot.

Communications were key. In fact, Curt needed to report back to Joan Ward, whom he'd left in charge at Ghazi. Joan had seen her days in combat, and she'd grown tired of it. Yet she was an outstanding chief of staff. This bothered Curt because it would have pleased him to have Joan as one of those contenders for regimental command when he moved on.

"Grey Chief, this is Grey Head," he called via tacomm. It seemed strange and even antiquated to use voice tacomm again. But no one wanted to take any chances using NE devices of any sort this close to an anti-NE weapon. "We're about twenty klicks out of Hell Fire Forward. How do we look? Is our vertical detection cross section low enough?"

"Grey Head, if I didn't know you were stealthed, I wouldn't know where you are!" Joan's voice came back. "You don't show up on any ground-based radar, lidar, or i-r. Your vertical DCS is practically nil according to the latest satellite data. We're getting better returns from birds!"

This made Curt feel better. He'd worried about maintaining stealth in this environment. The snow-covered mountains all around them meant that the Chippie infrared differential signal was greater than normal. However, he'd been assured that "suitable national technical means" would be used to conceal the final deployment of Operation Hell Fire. This meant that NIA and Army Countermeasures were Doing Something tip there in orbit over their heads. Curt didn't have to know what Something was, only that it was working. Thus far, it was.

"Okay, as soon as we're on dirt, we'll set up the ground-wave comm and stay off the air," he told her. The Greys had been supplied with a new communications system. It had quietly arrived in a MilEx cargo air-lifter the night before this deployment. The quiet civilian techie (probably an NIA engineer) hadn't told Edie Sampson much about it. "It uses some of the principles discovered back at the start of the twentieth century by Nicola Tesla," was all the explanation she was given. It was a matter of "Do this and then that. It will work. If it quits working or if you have to abandon it, activate this guarded switch. You'll have thirty seconds to get far away from it."

Curt had let it stand at that. The less the Sierra Charlies knew about real black technology such as the new comm system, the better. If something happened and they were captured, they couldn't spill their brains about it because nothing related to it was in their jellyware RAMs.

The same with their special infrared stealth cammies that had also arrived on the MilEx flight. These were experimental combat clothes intended to reduce a human being's infrared signature. The Greys had tried to check it out, and it had seemed to work. Furthermore, it was warm, a blessing in view of the high mountain environment into which they were deploying.

"How are the Khyber Rifles doing?" Curt asked her.

"They're late getting off," Joan told him.

"Figures. Are they on the road?"

"Affirmative! Grinding along at about forty klicks."

"That's damned slow! Far slower than planned."

"I guess that road is worse than the stuff we hacked in Sonora."

"Okay, Joan," Curt told her, "keep me advised of their progress. And stand by for possible additional logair flights. If we have to stay quiet in the hills here until Khan gets positioned, we may need to be replenished in the chow department. Doesn't look like there's much to chew on outside. Pretty barren."

Because of the strong personalities and different leadership styles of Curt and Colonel Khan, it had come as a great relief to him when they'd agreed on the operational plan.

The 4th Khyber Rifles of 1he Pakistani Army would proceed northward on the Karakoram Highway to Gilgit, where they'd turn east to Skardu. This would put them on the northwest edge of the Plains of Deosai. Khan knew that this movement would undoubtedly be detected by East World. However, he wasn't concerned about it. "The East World forces at Deosai may see us coming and they'll get ready for us," Khan had said. "However, they can't reinforce Deosai by the time we get there. Carson, I like your concept of moving your Washington Greys into position in stealth and then hitting Deosai from the rear when we begin our assault. That will make it easier."

It would take thirty-one hours for the Khyber Rifles to reach Skardu and launch their assault. That gave Curt two daylight periods in which to airlift the Greys into position. He wouldn't ask his aerodyne drivers to fly the western Himalayas at night. The crazies in Worsham's squadron were hot to do it, but the altitudes were too high and the charts too unreliable. Curt didn't want any Washington Grey to end up as a smoking hole on a mountainside.

If the Khyber Rifles were delayed or halted, Curt had Plan B ready. The Greys would hit the Deosai facility on their own in a surprise attack. If the Khyber Rifles showed up later, or if the Greys got additional support from other units of the Pakistani Army, that would help the withdrawal from Deosai. Again, Curt and his staff had planned several withdrawal routes, one being along the incoming route of the Rifles through Skardu and down the

Karakoram Highway. The other ground routes were over high Himalayan passes. Curt didn't like to think about what was involved in using them.

The high altitudes had him worried. The Washington Greys hadn't lived and fought at 5,600 meters. At that altitude, nearly half the Earth's atmosphere was below them. Atmospheric pressure was about half that of sea level, which also meant that roughly half the oxygen was available.

Aerodyne pilots were required by regulation to use supplemental oxygen when flying above four thousand meters by day and three thousand meters at night.

The only supplemental oxygen Major Harriet Dearborn had been able to get on short notice was given to Major Ruth Gydesen's bio-tech unit. In the meantime, Dearborn continued to search for more supplemental oxygen kits and request additional ones from the States. Although minimal logistic support of Hell Fire was planned, the Chippies were available if needed for additional supply flights. The entire Operation Hell Fire was planned so the Greys would spend less than one hundred hours in the field. This would allow them to rely on their tactical logistical stores.

Curt brooded over all of this as he watched the Himalayas slip past. He didn't want to chatter on the tacomm. That might be picked up by the East World forces. Silence was golden. And just about as easy to get most of the time, he told himself. Except now when he needed someone to talk with. Nancy was busy with her hands full of aerodyne. And the other Greys were down on the cargo deck. So, he didn't have any way to relieve his own tension.

If this was one of the legendary situations that illustrated the loneliness of command, Curt was beginning to believe that command was for someone else. He never really liked going into combat. As a platoon and company commander, it had been easier. He'd followed orders from General Carlisle, Belinda Hettrick, or Wild Bill Bellamack. Now he was on his own.

Silver eagles on his collar. tabs, the command of a legendary regiment of the United States Army, and all the perks of such command hardly made up for the other factors that bore down on him.

Curt Carson never liked the idea of issuing orders that might result in the deaths or injury of his friends, colleagues, and comrades.

He'd come to grips, he thought, with the problem of giving such orders to a loved one. That had probably been easier than learning how to live with ordering his friends and colleagues into danger. He and Dyani had been able to talk it out. On the other hand, it was difficult for Curt - and all other commanders - to get truly intimate with subordinates who had their own lives, dreams, plans, aspirations, and desire to live.

He tried to put it out of his mind. His thought patterns might be affected by the altitude, he told himself. However, within minutes, Nancy would have the Chippie on the ground. Then his problems would change from problematic ones to real ones.

Which they did.

The landing was fast and hard.

"Sorry, Colonel!" Nancy apologized. "I've never had to land at fifty-six hundred meters with max permissible load before! It sinks *fast!*"

"Apologies not required but accepted if it makes you feel better," Curt told her. "Shag back to Ghazi for the next load as quickly as you can."

Roger that, sir! Good luck!"

"The same for you. Be careful. Fly low and slow."

Curt moved down the ladder from the flight deck, collected his pack, and trotted out the open cargo ramp behind his staff and Kitsy.

And he was immediately aware of the altitude.

Curt was in outstanding physical shape. He ran several kilometers every day. He worked out in the gym regularly. He was unquestionably in the best physical condition that a human male could be.

And he found himself panting with exertion just from trotting out of the Chippie with his full combat pack.

Captain Nellie Crile, the regimental chaplain, was on his knees in the cold grass of the mountain meadow. He was vomiting. Between his retches, he gasped for breath in the sort of hollow rattle Curt had come to expect from dying comrades who'd gone into Cheyne-Stokes breathing.

Bio-tech Sergeant Ginny Bowles was at his side. She didn't look very good either. But Curt knew Nellie was in good hands, so the regimental commander concentrated on being the regimental commander. He had other jobs to do, and he knew he had to concentrate on those to the exclusion of anything else. Everyone had their specific job to do, and he was no exception.

Dyani and Harlan were directing people to bivouac spots where they could camouflage themselves and the warbots.

Curt took a moment to look around and get a feeling for the site and the terrain.

They were in a beautiful, grassy mountain valley with high, snow-covered ridges and peaks all around. Curt knew from satellite imagery that the 5,600-meter elevation of the valley would be far above the timberline in the Rocky Mountains. However, clumps of hardy trees were scattered around the valley. Low bushes resembling scrub oak offered many locations in which to hide people and warbots. The terrain in the valley was terraced like a rice paddy. People once must have lived here. No, perhaps "survived" was a better word. Even in April, the air was cold in the bright sunlight.

Curt could see no signs of human habitation. However, that didn't mean that people didn't live in this valley, he reminded himself. Even at its very high altitude, the valley was fertile. People are adaptable. Therefore, people must have lived here and probably were still living here.

"Mustang Leader, this is Grey Head," he called to Dyani via voice tacomm.

"Right behind you, Grey Head!"

Curt turned to see Dyani about ten meters away. "Sorry," he said directly to her. "Didn't see you."

"That's the general idea," Dyani told him. Her attire - Uniform, Experimental, Infra Red Suppressive, Camouflage, American Woodland, green and tan, mottled, Mark X1 Mod 0 Test Beta - had been subtly altered by her to blend even more closely with the greenish-brown and splotched white of the snow-specked valley. She'd used mud. He thought the mud was redolent with an objectional odor. Curt told himself that this valley must have received the recycled grass of many cows over the centuries.

"Let's hope East World doesn't have chem sensors," Curt told her. "What did you fall into?"

Dyani wrinkled her nose. "Must be the mud. I can hardly stand it myself. But we've got work to do. I can change clothes later."

"Better bury those," Curt suggested, and got back to command business. "If you haven't already done so, please put out scouting patrols. I want to learn whether or not anyone lives nearby."

"Zeb Long and Clara Lewis are already out and about," Dyani reported. "As quickly as we get everyone camouflaged, I'll go out with Harlan and Sid Johnson."

"Take some help with you," Curt told her. "Get with Kitsy. I want three shifts of patrols using everyone. In the first place, I don't want people sitting around here and stewing for the next twenty-some hours."

"They aren't scouts," Dyani pointed out.

"So? Everyone's cross-trained," Curt reminded her. There are six Sierra Charlies in RECONCO who are scouts. Make them patrol leaders. That gives us two patrols out at any given time, each led by a trained scout."

Dyani didn't argue. "Yes, sir."

"You don't look well," Curt observed, noting the stress in her expression. Curt could read Dyani very well.

"I'm all right. I had a headache shortly after landing. I have it under control," she admitted.

"See Ruth about it," he ordered her.

She shook her head slowly. "I'd like to defer that until I've done my job and gotten the patrols out. Ruth will use chemotherapy. I don't want chemicals affecting me under these conditions."

That was classic Dyani, the superwoman who had complete control over her mind and body. Except when she didn't realize it because of new environmental factors. Curt was feeling the effects of the high altitude. And other effects that might be caused by the proximity of the NE weapon on the Deosai Plains just across the low ridge to the north about ten kilometers away.

"I don't want to take chances with our physical or mental health, Captain!" he told her sternly, letting her know in a firm manner that this was business and duty. He was giving her an order; he expected her to carry it out. "We're out in the hills on a combat mission with minimum support and facing an unknown weapon. You're my chief scout and Ess-Two. Please do as I tell you!"

His tone was surprisingly sharp. Dyani reacted to it in a like manner, which was unusual for her. Her face got hard and she pursed her lips tightly. Curt thought he was about to see her lose her temper for the first time. But instead she merely snapped back, "*Yes, sir!*" And she turned on her heel and walked purposefully away from him. Curt didn't notice right then, but Dyani tended to stagger a little bit instead of moving with catlike grace.

Curt felt anger well up inside of him. Dyani had reacted as a subordinate but in a manner extremely uncharacteristic of her. She'd acted as if she was under extreme stress.

He went looking for Russ. Frazier was supposed to set up the command post that would house the four other people of his truncated combat staff plus Pendleton and Taisha. Curt was bloan about by the downwash of operating Chippies as they landed, disgorged their loads, and staggered back into the air for the return flight to Ghazi for another load. At one point, he became disoriented, but he didn't recognize it. He finally saw Pendleton and Taisha sitting on the ground under a clump a trees.

Both were breathing deeply. Pendleton was blue around his lips. Taisha seemed to be a bit more hardy.

Curt didn't believe it was cold enough to cause Owen's lips to turn blue.

"Curt, I've got to lie down!" Owen told him.

"What the hell?" Curt was at a loss to explain what was going on.

"Colonel," Taisha told him, "I've been in high mountains before. I survived coming through mountains like this after Zahedan. And I'm a doctor, so I understand something about what's happening. Unless someone gets some oxygen and other therapy to Owen – and to anyone else with symptoms of mountain sickness – we won't be fit to explore Deosai and your people won't be fit to fight!"

Chapter Nineteen

"Altitude sickness. Mountain sickness. Hypoxia. It's all the same," Major Ruth Gydesen, the regimental medical officer, told Curt and his officers as they gathered in the temporary regimental CP.

It was early evening on the first night the Washington Greys had spent in bivouac at 5,600 meters up in the western Himalaya Mountains of northern Pakistan. They'd been bivouacked in the high mountain valley for as long as twelve hours in the case of Motega's Mustangs.

None of them were feeling very well. Most complained of shortness of breath. This was unusual for people who were in top physical condition. Others remarked that everything they did required far more physical exertion than before. Some had become lackadaisical.

"The effects of altitude sickness vary from person to person. Usually, one begins to feel it at about thirty-three hundred meters," Ruth went on. "Father Crile probably wasn't in the same good physical condition as many of you. In addition, he's a little bit hypothyroid. In his case, that's not a problem because he doesn't work NE linkage at all. So, his metabolism is susceptible to the causes of the syndrome. And each of you will react differently to it. That's why I wanted to give you a bio-tech briefing. I want you to be aware of what can happen to you. You need to know what the early symptoms might be. It's going to be up to you to watch yourselves and your subordinates. Altitude sickness can be lethal under certain conditions."

She paused to allow this statement to sink in, then went on by way of explanation. "Basically, altitude sickness is caused by a lack of oxygen to the brain and the central nervous system. Pilots suffer from it if they fly at altitudes higher than three thousand meters without supplemental oxygen for more than an hour."

"Then how the hell do the East Worlders in the Deosai facility manage to live with it?" Russ Frazier wanted to know. His normally aggressive personality was even more so right then.

"They're probably acclimatized to it," Ruth told him.

"How can you become accustomed to half the oxygen you normally use?" Kitsy asked. She was feeling the altitude, but not as badly as, some of the other Greys. She didn't know why.

"Mountaineers do it, but they ascend only a thousand meters per day to get used to it. We didn't have that luxury. But I've learned over the years the human body is incredibly adaptable," Ruth told her. "Unconsciously, a person readjusts body and blood chemistry and creates a larger percentage of oxygen-carrying red blood corpuscles."

"How long does that take?" Lew Pagan asked.

"Six to eight weeks."

"Oh, great!" Curt exploded. He was tired, weary, fatigued, and drowsy. "We're going to be here three more days. What the hell can we do, Major?"

"First, you and your troops should rest," Gydesen told them all. "Drink lots of water and liquids such as fruit juices. Force yourself to eat, preferably foods that are rich in potassium and sodium bicarbonate. Let your warbots do everything they can for you."

"All right, let me ask that question differently," Curt fired back. "What can you and BIOTECO do to alleviate this condition? Give us portable oxygen tanks to carry?"

Ruth nodded. "No, supplemental oxygen won't help in the short term except in cases like Father Crile's. I've got him on supplemental oxygen at the moment. He's going back to the lower altitude at Ghazi on the first flight out tomorrow morning. Yes, I've requested more oxygen from Harriet Dearborn. But more oxygen isn't the answer, and lack of oxygen isn't your biggest metabolic problem. It's acidosis."

"What the hell does an upset stomach have to do with it...except that some of us can't keep our food down and others aren't hungry?" Russ fired back.

"Russ, one of the symptoms of this malady is irritability and irrational behavior," Ruth explained, trying to counter the man's naturally aggressive tendencies. Those traits hadn't improved since he'd been kicked upstairs to S-3. Frazier liked a fight. Thus far, he'd controlled his frustrations about being a staffer. Ruth saw trouble with Russ unless he could overcome the personality trait that had made him an outstanding combat officer. "Unless we do what we can to help ourselves in this, we'll use up all our energy fighting with each other instead of the East Worlders! You're all mean, nasty, deadly people when the veneer of civilization is stripped away. Fine! That's what makes a Sierra Charlie! But let's for God's sake remember who we're really fighting!"

She stopped, took several deep breaths, and went on. "Acidosis is an imbalance of your blood acid-base condition. It's caused by an excess of carbon dioxide and the inability of your bloodstream to remove it from your body. Red blood cells like carbon dioxide more than oxygen. If enough oxygen isn't present to replace the carbon dioxide, your blood loads up with C-O-Two. It goes acidic. Your nervous system reacts by trying to take in more oxygen and get rid of the excess C-O-Two. You go into deep, racking, labored breathing that sounds a lot like the death rattle you're all familiar with. So, when you start deep panting, stop what you're doing, sit down, and rest."

"I'm supposed to do this while someone is shooting at me?" Kitsy asked.

Ruth shrugged. "You're just going to have to do the best you can, Kitsy. If you're hyperventilating like I just described, you won't be able to hit a robot with a rock at three paces, much less shoot at someone and hit. So, you've got to learn to pace yourselves."

"What? How?" Captain Larry Hall wanted to know.

It was Captain Hassan Ben Mahmud who answered. "I grew up in the high mountains west of here around Zahedan and western Afghanistan. I didn't have much to eat. I wasn't on the sort of high-energy diet that we enjoy. But I learned how to pace myself on a marginal diet to save something for when I really needed it. Wasn't easy. And you've got to learn how to do it overnight. So, eat everything you can. To hell with your diet or the Army regs on obesity! You won't get fat in four days! Rest when you can. Conserve your energy."

Lieutenant Dan Power, one of the newer Greys, tentatively asked, "Are we sure this syndrome isn't caused by whatever they're doing over the ridge? Are we sure it isn't an offshoot of their neuroelectronic weapon?"

"No, we're not," Curt replied for Ruth. He'd asked some piercing questions about this weapon when he was being privately briefed by Murray, Pickens, and Bellamack. One of his concerns was about the weapon's possible side effects such as circadian asynchronization. He'd asked what other physiological and psychological effects had been identified. No one knew. So, Curt admitted, "We don't know."

"Why didn't someone think about the possibility of altitude sickness?" Kitsy Clinton wasn't trying to nail Ruth to the wall for this oversight, and she'd tried to be careful how she said that.

"Because three days ago we were sitting fat and happy at fifteen hundred meters altitude in Fort Huachuca with no idea that we'd be up here tonight," Ruth shot back quickly. "However, I've always tried to anticipate your biotechnology needs. So, I do have some pharmaceuticals that will help. If you have trouble sleeping tonight- and some people will - or the instant you begin to feel bloated or get a wet cough, any of my staff will put you on two hundred fifty milligrams of acetazolamide. That's a mild diuretic that will keep you from coming down with pulmonary oedema, which is damned serious. I'll also clear all of you for mild painkillers if you start to feel like you've had too much to drink at the Club."

"Hell, I wish we had a Club here!" Russ groused. "Then I'd have an excuse for this hangover."

"Exactly! Come see me after this bio briefing, Russ," Ruth told him. "I'll fix it so you get a good night's sleep without the headache. By the way, don't worry if you have to urinate a lot. That's better than retaining fluids. So, drink lots and lots of water, especially if your urine isn't clear and light-colored."

"Damned hard to see at night," Kitsy said.

"Just don't get dehydrated, Kitsy," Ruth warned. "Or you'll end up being evacced. Now, make sure you and your troops eat well and often. The MREs are well-balanced. You won't suffer electrolyte imbalance if you eat anything and everything in the meal pack."

"I can't *stand* some of the crap they put in those MREs!" Larry Hall complained.

"Eat it all, Larry, or you may go down the hill in an outbound aerodyne," Ruth told him. "I can help some of you rebalance your body and rechannel some of your symptoms with neuroelectronic reprogramming."

"Not a chance, Doctor!" Curt broke in. "We're not going to use NE equipment this close to a potential NE weapon!"

"Colonel, I respect your orders, but I'm also your chief medical officer," Ruth snapped back. He could see she was also under stress and reacting strangely. "If I determine that hard-linkage NE therapy isn't contraindicated, I'll use it. In my opinion, the chances that the NE weapon might interfere with a hard-wired direct linkage are slim. However, be assured that I'll use NE therapy with great care under these circumstances."

"I can try to teach you a few exercises that may help," Dr. Rosha Taisha put in. "Doctor Gydesen, I can reprogram your equipment to completely overcome the altitude sickness syndrome."

Curt shook his head. "Not a chance, Doctor Taisha. Doctor Gydesen is my medical officer. What she intends to do is accepted therapy. She and her staff are prepared to handle any problems that might arise. So, I can't allow the use of experimental procedures in a pre-combat situation!"

"I'm willing to let Rosha try it on me," Owen Pendleton suddenly said.

"Not a chance, Owen!" Curt maintained.

Pendleton looked Curt squarely in the eye and replied, "Colonel, you may be in overall command of Operation Hell Fire, but technically I'm a civilian scientist on this mission. If I want to carry out a scientific experiment, I don't need your permission. I'll do it!"

Curt realized that he was succumbing to the symptoms of mountain sickness. himself. "Owen, you've always been a brave man with a mind of your own. Hell, I can't stop you. On the other hand, I won't tell you it's okay to do what you want to do. But if you do it and find yourself in deep and slippery slime because you've blown your mental fuses, I've got to figure out how to conduct the scientific investigation of Deosai."

"I know what I'm doing," Owen insisted.

"We know what we're doing," Taisha insisted as well.

"One last thing, and then I want to wrap this up because it's late and we all need lots of rest," Ruth said. "Don't panic if your tent mate suddenly stops breathing. If breathing doesn't start again with a huge intake of air after ten to fifteen seconds, then get busy with CPR and yell for a bio-tech. However, I don't expect anyone to stop breathing. Most of you will spend the night with your hearts pounding up around a hundred per minute and your breathing being deep and even irregular. If you can't sleep, my staff and I aren't far away. We'll be up most of the night anyway, I suspect."

At 2100, Curt made the rounds of the camouflaged bivouac with Henry Kester. "First the people, then the warbots, then the guns, and *then* we can hit the sack. Henry, don't tell me you aren't feeling this altitude?" Curt said to him. Surprisingly, the older man didn't appear to be suffering from shortness of breath.

"Oh, yeah, I'm feeling it, all right," the chief NCO replied. "I just feel older, that's all. And since I feel older than most of you most of the time anyway, it ain't nothin' new. Just more of the same."

"How's your heart?"

"It was pumpin' just fine the last time I paid attention to it. I don't think it's quit since."

The Greys had bivouacked in stealthed and camouflaged positions that were well hidden in the beautiful valley. It was a cloudless night. Curt had never seen so many stars, not even in the clear desert skies of Arizona. Now he knew why astronomers preferred to place their observatories on top of mountains. Half the Earth's atmosphere was below this altitude.

At the end of the inspection, Curt found himself breathing deeply but not panting. He'd used some of the self-control Dyani had taught him. He hadn't allowed himself to get into an acidotic condition. He couldn't measure his blood chemistry, of course. But what Ruth had told them about the symptoms of acidosis allowed him to recognize the early onset signs and take precautions by breathing properly.

"I'm worried as hell, Henry," Curt confided to his old NCO who'd been with him since he'd joined the Greys fresh out of West Point. "We've got an unknown enemy with unknown weapons over that ridge to the north. Day after tomorrow, we've got to go in there and probably fight them. I'm not so sure that we'll be in good shape. We could lose this one."

"Bullshit, sir!" Henry shot back vehemently. "When the jackets start flying and we've gotta perform, we'll all be surprised as hell at the reserves inside us. Hell, Colonel, it's always been that way. I don't recall a single fracas where we believed we were really ready to fight. That's in spite of our gung-ho good-to-go attitude. Deep down inside, everyone always wonders and doubts. Hell, nothing's gonna come unbonded tonight, Colonel. Get a good night's sleep if you can. The warbots are out on the perimeter, and Captain Motega reports the valley is dean. Why don't you do like you told everybody else? Rest and get ready."

"Because I'm the regimental commander, Master Sergeant."

"And you're a damned fool of a regimental commander if you don't, Colonel."

Although Henry could speak privately that way to Curt and get away with it, Curt's oxygen-short brain caused him to react momentarily with anger. But he spotted it and stopped it. "I think I'll ask Major Gydesen for some of that painkiller. I've got a hell of a headache," Curt observed instead. "Good night, Henry."

Curt stopped at the M-660E Bio-tech Support Vehicle and went in. Ruth, Helen Devlin, and Bill Molde were busy around Captain Nelson Crile. He was wired up with NE equipment. The regimental chaplain was no longer blue around his lips, and he seemed to be sleeping comfortably.

"Hi, Colonel! We have Father Crile stabilized," Helen reported to him when she saw him in the doorway. "Don't worry. We're just doing NE monitoring, not programming."

"I wasn't worried. Any other problems with anyone else?" Curt asked.

Ruth shook her head. "I've handed out some analgesic tablets. No one has qualified for the acetazolamide yet. But I'm worried about Pendleton."

"How so?"

"Taisha asked me for some of the psychoactive drugs we have in stock to help warbot brainies who go KIA."

"I thought you had NE programming for that now," Curt observed. "At least, I remember you used something like that on me once."

"Belt and braces, Colonel! Always have a backup!" Captain Molde said. "We don't throw away anything that works, no matter how good the new stuff is! Hell, we still have morphine in our supply locker. Okay, Doctor, the Father is looking good. All vital signs within normal parameters."

"What's this about Taisha and psychoactive chemicals?" Curt asked, picking up the thread of Ruth's conversation. This bothered him. Taisha had *always* been prone to play around with the minds of other people.

"She asked for five milligrams of chakrazol. She explained that she wanted it to clear away some cholinergic neural inhibitors between Owen's conscious mind and autonomic nervous system," Ruth told him casually.

"And you gave it to her?" Curt asked in amazement.

"Of course! She's a doctor, Curt," Ruth reminded him. "She explained to me exactly why she needed it to facilitate Owen's NE reprogramming. I won't get technical with you, but chakrazol acts something like ethanol. It removes some inhibitions, but in a more controlled fashion that doesn't interfere with NE probing and reprogramming. Five milligrams are about a tenth of what I've used on some KIA cases."

"I hope you're right."

"I'm right. I'm also a doctor. I'm supposed to heal, not experiment," Ruth said. "Owen Pendleton has his neurons all lined up. He'd make a good warbot brainy if he wasn't such a hot AI mentor. He-"

The regimental medical officer was interrupted by a yell. It came from the forward compartment of the BSV.

"And I may have been wrong in this case," Ruth finished. She bolted for the door through the bulkhead.

Curt was right behind her.

Taisha was standing alongside a treatment cot with a very surprised expression. Owen Pendleton was sitting straight up on the cot. He was wide-eyed and sweating. NE sensor and effector wires hung around him. Apparently, his sudden action had pulled them from their connections in the wall-mounted equipment.

Curt almost grabbed Taisha in a fit of anger. But he stood his ground as Owen gasped between deep breaths, "Jesus, what a vivid nightmare!"

Taisha was busily reconnecting wires. "I should have been ready for that."

"Okay, what the hell are you up to, Taisha!" Curt growled in anger.

"Owen was in REM sleep state," Taisha explained as she reconnected Pendleton to the NE equipment. "We were using a combination of NE programming and chakrazol to lower inhibitory synapse responses. That would allow him to exercise direct control over his metabolic balance. Electronic yoga, if you will."

"Damned bad dreams too!" Owen added, wiping his face with his hand. "I was in a house. It was an old house. I've been familiar with it in my dreams for years. I was helping move the walls! Then the house started to fall down on me…"

"The house is your symbolic body," Taisha explained to him. "I was helping you outside with NE to move the walls around. You had to get to the symbolic electrical circuits and plumbing."

Owen shook his head. "Wow! Vivid! Even better than the X30 VR sim! Scared the shit out of me! But what the hell were the faceless little men running around trying to move things the way they wanted?"

Taisha suddenly put a hand on his shoulder. "What little men?"

"Just what I said, Rosha."

She started unplugging NE circuitry from him. "I'm not a certified psychological dream interpreter," she said with concern in her voice. "I can speak about the images that are clearly classical ones. But I hesitate to speculate on this new factor you just reported. So, I'm aborting the chakrazol and NE therapy."

"You haven't administered the chakrazol yet?" Ruth asked.

"No, Owen didn't need it yet."

Curt decided that Dr. Rosha Taisha *had* changed. In the past, she would never have admitted such things. Nor would she have aborted an experiment. She would have charged ahead to explore, thinking little about the possibility of ruining a subject's mind.

Curt was no NE expert, but he'd been thoroughly briefed on what was known of the Deosai NE weapon. So, he asked, "Could the NE coding that's riding on the six-hertz magnetic pulse be getting in here? We're pretty close to the weapon."

Taisha shook her shaved head. "No. I did a frequency sweep before we began tonight. We're close to the transmitter - if it is indeed a transmitter. Nothing showed up here. But the radiated signal may be resonated with the Schuman cavity. This could happen if the signal was beamed upwards to take advantage of the ionosphere."

"I know something about that weapon," Curt admitted. "I know it's got all sorts of nasty little side effects we haven't had time to explore yet. That's why I don't want anyone screwing around with any NE equipment. I couldn't give you orders not to, Owen. Or you, Doctor Taisha. But now maybe you'll listen to some of the things I've got to say. And pay attention to some of my concerns for everyone."

Taisha looked squarely at him. For a moment, he thought he detected the old Rosha Taisha behind those almond eyes. Coolly, she told him, "Colonel, you take care of the external battle. We'll fight the one inside of all of us."

Chapter Twenty

"You didn't sleep very well, did you, Kida?" Dyani was perceptive. She knew her man looked weary. Furthermore, she saw that he was reluctant to cat breakfast.

Having breakfast together had become a tradition with them. It had started during the Sakhalin Police Detachment operation. Breakfast together was an event to start the day wherever they might be. Often, it wasn't possible when Dyani was OOD or they were on field exercises. Or when Curt was on TDY. However, breakfast was the one time of day when they were both likely to be unencumbered with their individual responsibilities. So, it became their quality time together.

This didn't mean they weren't together as much as possible when they could find the time.

However, they'd also struck an agreement: They were "First among Equals." In this regard, they were typical Washington Greys. Not only had the Army pioneered the mixed-gender military unit in the warbot period, but also the mixed-gender Sierra Charlie doctrine. The former allowed men and women to fight together in a non-lethal environment using warbots. This had overcome the strong objections of many early non-military "experts," and even the ultraconservative reluctance of the male generals. Then the Washington Greys had discovered that the all-warbot doctrines, strategies, and tactics broke down in limited warfare. As a result, the ladies of the Greys took off their warbot linkage harnesses, picked up Novia assault rifles, and stood shoulder to shoulder in battle with the men.

However, in spite of Rule Ten or even because of it, it was inevitable that serious relationships would develop between men and women who faced death and dealt death together. Army Regulation 601-10 prohibited physical contact between personnel of the opposite sex except on official business or when Rule Ten was suspended by the unit commander in non-duty situations.

Curt had been through his own hell with this - not as a unit commander faced with difficult decisions, but because his relationship with Dyani Motega had grown far beyond merely the release of sexual tensions. Other Greys of both sexes had had a similar experience. Each had handled it differently. A field manual couldn't be written to explain it by the numbers in typical Army field manual format.

One factor that made the situation different was that the men and women of the twenty-first-century American Army went through NE warbot training. That intensely personal experience had forced them to deal with their responsibility to and for themselves. It had converted them from adolescents to adults.

Both Curt and Dyani had faced up to the awful thought that either of them might be killed or maimed in the next combat skirmish. They believed they loved one another in a way that was unique in history - a common fallacy in such circumstances, although they wouldn't admit it. But they also knew that other relationships with other partners not only *should* be developed but *had* to be developed. Life had to go on regardless of what happened to either one.

There were nights when they weren't together but were with others. Yet they each knew the other would return. This was their insurance against the possibility that the other might not return some day.

A hundred years before, the mere concept of a mixed-gender military unit was grounds for prolonged and heated debate in Congress. And in bars and homes around military bases. In common with other social matters, people themselves worked out the problems and solved them. Only a few nations were left in the world where governments attempted to legislate basic human behavior. Those governments would fall or evolve in the turbulent New Millennium.

Both Curt and Dyani knew there would come a time when they'd agree to make it exclusive and permanent. But that time wasn't yet.

So, they enjoyed what they had while they had it. That was true even when it was on a frigid April morning more than five kilometers above sea level in an environment that taxed both mental and physical stamina.

"I sure as hell didn't sleep, Deer Arrow. I was listening to you snore," Curt told her.

"I don't snore."

"Damned good imitation, then. I was listening to your breathing."

"Did it stop?" Dyani's sense of humor had grown both sharp and subtle. And she'd become less stoic and more loquacious as she'd grown from a girl to a woman.

"Not that I heard. How's the coffee?"

Dyani looked at the steaming container perched on the catalytic heater. "Muddy. Cloudy. The river water checks out clean. But it's full of microscopic particulates of some sort."

"Funny. This coffee tastes pretty damned good even if it looks like hell," Curt observed, wondering if maybe his sensory perceptions were being affected by the altitude too.

"It brewed fast. The crystals went into solution rapidly. But I do have to worry about getting it too hot. Water boils at about eighty degrees up here," she observed.

It was wonderful to engage in small talk about nothing really important. Lately, too much of their time had been involved in life-or-death decisions. Or serious debate whose outcome could affect their lives and those of their friends. Or the even more serious business of security and planning. The breakfast break was not only welcome but important to both of them.

"Pretty place," Curt observed, looking around. "People spend perfectly good time and money to come here just to bust their asses battling the environment and climb the mountains."

"Don't belittle their tastes, Kida. Not everyone likes to wallow in conspicuous consumption when not fighting to preserve it."

"I'm glad you learned to enjoy that with me."

"We've taught each other a lot of things," Dyani reminded him unnecessarily. "But I still like being out in the wilds."

"I get enough of good old Mother Nature in the raw. When I get the chance, I like to control some of it."

"And that was as difficult for me to learn as it was for you to learn how to control your spirit."

"I wish we had a better term than spirit, but I think I know what you mean. Maybe I'd understand it better if we could define 'spirit' more tightly. I don't think I do a very damned good job of controlling it sometimes."

"You try. That counts."

He took a couple of swallows of the tepid coffee, then asked, "Do you still doubt the change in Rosha Taisha?"

Dyani looked troubled. "I have difficulty understanding how the terrible demons in her mind could have been banished. I've touched them. They frightened me, even though I knew I could defend myself against her."

"NE technology can do a lot of wonderful things, Deer Arrow. We see only the destructive applications of it."

"Kida. I don't understand how she could have driven out those demons – or allowed them to be driven out – and still remain Rosha Taisha. I worry that they're still buried deep within her. I'm concerned that they'll burst forth because of some unexpected stimulus. And I don't know what that is."

"I'll watch her," Curt promised.

"I think we both will," Dyani added. "Drink some more coffee. You need the stimulant as well as the fluid. Both will help altitude sickness."

"Did you dream last night?"

"Vividly. Very old dreams. Dreams of another time and place long ago."

"Can you be more specific?"

She shook her head. "No."

"Do you believe in dreams?"

"Are you asking me if I believe what goes on inside my own mind when I'm asleep? Of course I do! But I sometimes don't know what it means. The symbology is different," Dyani admitted. "That's another reason why I wonder about Taisha. She tries to act like an old medicine man without the training to do so."

"Maybe she has equivalent training."

"If so, I didn't encounter it," Dyani stated firmly.

"You're weird, woman," Curt kidded her.

"And you're a stud, sir!" she fired back. "And no more jibes about superwoman. Not until we get back to a lower altitude..."

Curt's tacomm beeper sounded. He reached over to where he'd stowed his equipment harness, picked it up, and toggled it. "Grey Head here!"

"Grey Head, this is Grey Day," came the verbal reply from the OOD, Lieutenant Mickie Mikawa. "Patrol East reports the valley is inhabited."

Dyani quickly grabbed her tacomm and switched to another frequency and hop pattern. "Scout Zeb, this is Mustang Leader!" She knew that Patrol East was under Sergeant Zeb Long. Dyani wanted first-hand information, which was why she bypassed Curt and Mickie. "Report your contact with inhabitants!"

"Grey Day, Grey Head confirms that Mustang Leader is now in contact with Patrol East. I'll get the data direct. Continue to monitor this freak!" Curt told his OOD.

Dyani's tacomm brick squawked, "Mustang Leader, this is Patrol East. Affirmative. We have made contact with inhabitants of the valley. A group of ten farmers with their wives and children. They're on their way out to their fields."

"Dyani, didn't your patrols make a sweep of this valley yesterday when we were deploying?" Curt asked.

"Yes, sir. We found numerous vacant farm hovels. Hassan reported that these dwellings are the usual Kashmiri houses made from wooden logs. But the patrols found no inhabitants," she replied concisely.

And before Curt could issue the order, she said into her tacomm, "Patrol East, bring in those inhabitants under armed guard! Attention all patrols, this is Mustang Leader! Bring in under guard all people encountered during your sweeps! Be careful! These people may be armed and dangerous when first encountered! Search them for weapons before bringing them in!"

Curt didn't wait for Dyani's patrols to report receipt of orders. He was on his feet at once. Grabbing his helmet, pack, and Novia, he took off at a carefully paced walk toward his camouflaged OCV.

He was breathing hard when he got there in spite of keeping his physical exertion down to a purposeful walk.

Mickie Mikawa was there with the OOD brassard on her arm. So was Sergeant Charlie Koslowski, the NCOOD. Major Russ Frazier stepped in a few seconds after Curt arrived.

"Kos, get Henry and Edie over here ASAP!" Curt snapped. "Mickie, you and Kos are relieved of day duties. I want you to put together a detail and mount an armed guard on the people the patrols will be bringing in."

"Yes, sir!" Koslowski replied, stripping off the brassard.

Mickie removed the OOD brassard. "Are they prisoners, Colonel? And if they're civilians, how should they be treated?"

Curt had no doubts that Mikawa could be as tough as anyone twice her size. But he didn't want to unlawfully detain civilians. On the other hand, they could compromise the unit's security if allowed to roam free.

"Erect an enclosure. Put them in it. Make sure they have food, water, and sanitary facilities. And stand by to bring them out one by one for interrogation," he told her.

"What the hell is wrong, Colonel?" Russ asked.

"Patrols have encountered civilians. Maybe they're civilians. Maybe not. They weren't in this valley yesterday," Curt explained.

"Spies!" Russ growled. "If so, we'll be treating them too damned good! Spies caught out of uniform used to be shot!"

"We don't know yet that they're spies, Major," Mickie told him as she hoisted her pack. On her, the pack looked huge. She picked up her Novia. "So, I'll treat them as unidentified refugees in a combat zone."

"And if they start to run, blow their shorts off!" Russ suggested.

Mickie gave a sweet smile that belied her samurai character. "Sir, one bad move, and they're vulture food!" Then she was gone with Koslowski following her.

Henry and Edie arrived. Edie was panting with exertion. Henry was trying not to.

"Edie, get me a comm patch to Fort Fumble and another one to Colonel Genghis Khan," Curt told his chief tech sergeant, using the nickname for the Pakistani officer that had sprung up among the Greys. Curt was too weary and fatigued to bother with international protocol right then. He was really concerned that Operation Hell Fire had been discovered and that the enemy might be practically within the camp.

"Yes, sir! The Harriers are probably sitting down at Ghazi on yellow alert and running out of comic books to read. Or they're about to take their morning shower, which makes this a good time to blow the horn on them. How about calling in some Harpies J.I.C.?" Like the other Greys, Edie appreciated the pilots of AIRBATT in spite of their elitism. However, she wouldn't hesitate for a moment to give them some hassle that would cause them to pee in their pants. Everyone knew that jumping into the shower during a yellow alert caused the klaxon to go off.

"Get the Harriers up on the net and move them to red alert. I don't want to scramble them yet. We don't have targets for them," Curt pointed out. "Russ, coordinate with Dyani. Locate all those hovels on the holo chart. Treat them as target coordinates for Saucy Cans.

Or even Mary Anns if they're close enough. And I want tightened security on the passes leading into this valley. Any incoming personnel are to be stopped and brought in."

"What if they shoot back?" Russ asked unnecessarily.

"Mister, you ought to know better than to ask a question like that," Curt told him bluntly. "Stealth and camouflage rules are shit-canned at that point. Henry, get with Hassan. Maybe he speaks the same language as these peasants. I'd like you to monitor the interrogations. Bring to me anyone you think I might be interested in questioning further."

Kester didn't even acknowledge verbally. He just gave Curt the high sign and ducked out of the OCV.

"Let's see...who the hell isn't doing something right now?" Curt asked himself aloud. "Okay, Edie, call Kitsy in. And give me a personnel availability sheet."

"Morning report coming up on the screen, sir!"

"Good!" Curt studied the list that came up on the OCV's projection screen. "I want to get a detail up on the ridge with me so I can have a careful look at the Deosai facility. We may have to move against it earlier than we thought."

"Yessir!"

Curt was in his element now. He was a master tactician. But even as he was putting together a fast ops plan in his head and spitting out the orders, he knew he'd call a Papa briefing once they got the civilian "farmer" matter squared away. He was turning over in his mind the strategic and national security aspects of having to go into Deosai without the Paks. The political situation in this part of the world was squirrelly and getting worse. Whatever decisions he made and whatever the Greys did might have worldwide repercussions. It might be very easy to start West World and East World up the ladder of escalation to a general war.

West World had been lucky thus far in Yemen and Senegambia. East World had won the first and lost the second. Thus far, these operations hadn't shaken the status quo. But they might have brought the world situation closer to a flash point.

"Grey Head, this is Patrol West," came the report from Sergeant Clara Lewis, who as an experienced member of Saunders' Scouts was leading one of the two patrols out in the valley at the moment. "We've apprehended six farmers with their wives and about twenty kids heading toward the fields. These people sure have a lot of kids! Must be nothing much else to do up here at night!"

"Are they armed?"

"Negatory! But we made them put down their farm implements," Lewis's voice replied. "I don't look forward to being ventilated by one of their pitchforks."

"Pitchforks?"

"Yes, sir! Made in China. Kids are apparently made here. They're kind of dirty, but they're just like kids everywhere. Sort of cute in an Oriental way."

"Bring them all in, Sergeant! Hassan and Kester are running the interrogations," Curt told her. "And keep the adults under close supervision. If they're a spy team, they probably brought the children along to help their cover and draw our attention from the adults to the kids." Curt knew the battlefield affection American soldiers always had for children who, by no fault of their own, were caught up in the maelstrom of war. Even Curt felt sorry for refugee children, especially those who happened to be born in this isolated part of the world where everyone was poor. "Russ, see if some of the assault units can break out MREs and give these people a hot meal. Especially the children."

"I'll assign that one to Lew Pagan," Russ decided. "It's about time he did something other than lie around on his dead ass consuming his rations! And he's got nine people with nothing to do until we mount the assault."

Kitsy came into the OCV breathing hard. "Wow! I didn't think the altitude was affecting me! But it just did!"

"You okay?" Curt asked solicitously. Kitsy always looked like a teenaged student reporting in for ROTC class. He figured her immunity to altitude sickness was partly caused by the fact that she had less mass and therefore required less oxygen.

"Yes, sir! What's up?"

Curt held a quick briefing for those still in the OCV. He concluded with, "Kitsy, get a platoon together. We're going to go up the ridge to the pass and have a look at Deosai. We'll need to plan for a quick assault contingency."

"Yes, sir. How do you think it would be different from the planned assault?"

"We won't have the Paks to provide diversion."

"Right! Must have unplugged my brain and left it in the sleep sack when I got up!" She shook her head slowly. "All neurons are firing. Even the solid-state ones that jump-start my neck. Uh, Colonel, in case we need fire support from the Mary Anns or Saucy Cans, can we go up that ridge blooming beacons?"

"So Russ can see us and Larry won't fire into us? Sure."

"What if the Chinks can see our beacons?"

"They didn't capture any of our classified transponder chips in Yemen or Senegambia," Curt pointed out. "And if they do put fire into us, all bets will be off anyhow. We'll have to commence the assault right then."

"Then we should go up that ridge with as many Sierra Charlies, Jeeps, and Mary Anns as we've got," Kitsy suggested. "I don't think we'd want to be pinned down by a superior enemy force while we're waiting for our own troops to come up and support us."

Kitsy was thinking more and more like a field commander. Curt decided.

"Okay, pick your people and let's move out. On to Bear Mountain Bridge and the capture of Poughkeepsie!" Curt told her with a grin, using the old and familiar battle cry of West Pointers on a tactical exercise.

This one threatened to be far more lethal than walking through Bear Mountain State Park.

Chapter Twenty-One

"Damned good thing we could ride Trikes up here!" Major Russ Frazier pointed out as they halted their PTVs just south of the ridge line. "What with this altitude, I'm not sure we could have made it! Even if we'd taken a couple of days!"

"Debouch the Jeeps," Curt ordered, ignoring Russ's sniveling. "Kitsy, deploy the Mary Anns this side of the ridge line in defilade and camouflage."

"Yes, sir!" Kitsy snapped back, gung-ho as usual in spite of the altitude. "I'm going to roll a couple of them along the military crest on higher ground. They can depress their twenty-fives to fire downward if they have to."

Curt whipped the tacomm brick off his belt, removed his helmet, and donned his field cap. "Is it me?" he asked his two officers. "Or did someone fall into some yak shit on the way up here?"

Both Russ and Kitsy were wrinkling their noses. The stench was awful.

"I think it's these damned anti-i-r cammies, Colonel," Kitsy guessed. "I began to notice it last night. I thought I needed a shower. But I wasn't about to skinny-dip in the river that runs through the bivouac. Damned water would probably freeze if it wasn't running!"

"Why are our uniforms stinking?" Russ wondered. "And what the hell can we do about it if they are?"

"Maybe wash them when we get back," Kitsy suggested.

"Or bury them and crawl into regular cammies," Russ added. "Burying them may be the only alternative if they keep getting worse."

Smelly uniforms were the least of Curt's worries right then.

"Owen, how did you survive the ride?" Curt asked the warbot expert.

Pendleton was limping a bit and very short of breath. "I survived. I had to remind myself not to hyperventilate. There were times when the path was a little scary. And I confirm that it's your uniforms that are smelling."

"Got any idea what causes it?"

Pendleton shook his head. "I'm a warbot AI mentor, not a chemical engineer who specializes in textile treatments. I'm just glad I'm not wearing those threads. It's bad enough being in your vicinity."

"Well, I'm sure as hell not going to ask everyone to strip to their skivvies up here," Curt muttered. The air was cold, and a frigid wind blew over the ridge line. "Doctor Taisha, how about you?"

Taisha had donned a parka and hood. "I am all right, Colonel. I have to keep my head covered to conserve my body heat." Because of her work in neuroelectronics at McCarthy Proving Ground, she'd shaved her head, and continued to do so even in the field.

"You should get a wig to wear when you're not working," Curt suggested. Although a bald woman had a certain exotic appearance, a woman's hair was still one of the primary sensual attractions of the gender. It also served to maintain skull and brain temperatures. Studies had shown that female metabolism was subtly different from that of a male, as any husband could attest. Female thermostasis was controlled slightly differently in the brain. Thus, a head of hair was probably as much a metabolic survival factor as it was an attraction to the opposite sex.

"I would rather continue to shave," Taisha admitted. "It helps me separate my present life from my former one."

Curt raised the tacomm brick to his face and spoke into it. "Grey Tech, this is Grey Head."

Edie Sampson's voice came back. "Grey Tech here, Grey Head. Read you five-by!"

"We're on the ridge," Curt reported.

"Roger that! We see your beacons!"

"No problems coming up except we had to make our own road," Curt reported. "The dozer blades on the Mary Anns helped. Had to winch only twice to get through. Sort of like operating in the Kofa Mountains except this is a lot higher and colder! What's the status on the civilian roundup?"

"We have ten men, ten women, and thirty-seven children, all boys about ten to twelve years old," Edie reported back. "We've sequestered them in an area guarded by Jeeps. We've fed them. Wish we could give them a bath."

"The stink may be your own anti-i-r cammies," Curt told her. "We're really pretty ripe up here after that climb. Don't know why yet. How is Hassan coming with the interrogations?"

"Not very well," was Edie's somber reply. "Captain Hassan can't speak the local language. He reports it isn't Arabic, Punjabi, or Baluchi. To me, it sounds sort of like Chinese with its singsong delivery. But I'm no language whiz, Colonel. I've got my hands full just keeping the Greys talking to one another in Army jargon!"

"Okay, Edie, please let me know at once if Hassan makes any breakthroughs or somehow gets some information out of those people," Curt responded. He was concerned because these strange people had suddenly appeared in the valley when they hadn't been there yesterday. On the other hand, he knew nothing of the local customs. Neither did anyone else from whom he'd tried to get a cultural briefing. Kashmir is one of the places in the world that is strategically important but culturally insignificant. Too bad, Curt decided, because some of the oldest of the early civilizations had gotten their start in these rugged valleys.

He picked up his infrared and passive laser imagers. "Russ, grab the passive radar unit," he told his ops staffer. "Kitsy, you bring the data recorder and keep your eagle-type eyeballs peeled for any security patrols along this ridge. Dyani, you just bring your calibrated eyeballs and your scout's memory. Owen and Taisha, follow me. We'll check out this Deosai facility with real-time close-up imagery."

The group was careful as they reached and topped the ridge line. Curt warned Pendleton and Taisha about becoming good targets against the skyline. So, they quickly went over a diagonal saddle and positioned themselves down the northern slope where they could see the rest of the Deosai Plains to the north.

"What a beautiful place!" Kitsy breathed, somewhat overwhelmed by the magnificent panorama. Kitsy was a Southern girl who had been raised on the flat coastal plains of South Carolina. Even the American West had been something new to her, but she liked it.

Although she'd been in more than a half-dozen spectacular places in the world with the Washington Greys, she'd never seen a high mountain basin such as the one that lay before them.

It reminded Curt of the high mountain parks of Colorado.

Dyani saw it through somewhat different eyes. It was a place where things could be hidden. It was a place where combat would be one-on-one at close range. It was a place where a person could die without being in battle.

The sunlight was very bright because of the altitude. The air was extremely clear. Visibility must have been at least a hundred kilometers. But the deep blue canopy of the sky was broken by clouds that hugged the high white mountaintops of the western Himalayas. The Deosai Plains weren't a level basin. They were cut by low ridges. Several streams ran through them to join the Indus · and the Ganges. The Plains of Deosai were the watershed roof of the Indian subcontinent.

That very bright sunlight glinted off several objects down in the valley.

"Have a look in the visual," Curt instructed Dyani. "Russ, see what the passive radar shows. I'll check passive laser illumination." He'd passed the word that morning to Washington. Orbiting satellites would provide constant ultraviolet laser illumination of the Deosai Plains from high above. He had the visual sensor that was tuned to the ultraviolet laser frequency. The u-v wavelength had been selected to penetrate the ionosphere and ozone layer. It was of such low power that detection was nearly impossible unless one had the sensor precisely tuned to that frequency.

What he saw was familiar. But he was seeing it from a new angle now. The satellite images taken vertically and on the oblique had been computer-processed, and Curt had seen these images with the point of view shifted to ground level. Now he was seeing the same scene for real, not as a creation of various megacomputers buried beneath the ground on the other side of the world.

The long two-story barracks were where they should be.

The large cube-shaped building had cables festooned on it. These had been below the resolution of the satellite images.

Curt saw that these cables ran on poles to what appeared to be a huge antenna.

As he studied it, he saw it was a rhomboid antenna with legs that were several kilometers in length. These legs filled most of the Deosai Plains. Again, because the antenna cables and elements were only centimeters in diameter, they'd escaped the view of even the high-resolution satellites and the hypersonic recce craft.

"Check out the antenna," Curt muttered to Russ and Dyani. "I'm no EM comm expert, but it looks like a rhomboid to me."

"It is," Russ confirmed. "Let me check the orientation of the open end."

"I'll bet the alignment checks with the bearing for the great circle route to McCarthy," Owen Pendleton added. He was busy working his personal computer. "That should be three-five-zero degrees true."

"What's the magnetic variation?" Taisha asked.

"About twenty-eight west," Owen read from his computer screen in his palm. "Alignment should be three-two-two magnetic."

"I see the open end on the other side of the valley. If it isn't three-two-two, it's pretty close!" Russ confirmed. His radar sensor, receiving the return scattered from a radar pulse transmitted from orbit, was capable of resolving the antenna wires and poles once Russ knew they were there to look at.

"Okay, that confirms the NE weapon uses a six-hertz EM transmitter," Owen observed, looking at the radar display. "Man, I'd like to see the loading coils on that sucker! Quarter wavelength antenna would be halfway around the world. Yeah, that figures! They won't need loading coils! They're exciting a resonant cavity. Sort of a super magnetron using the whole damned Earth as part of it."

"We'll still need to confirm that," Taisha reminded him.

"Where the hell are they getting the power to ram such a strong signal all the way around the world?" Russ wondered aloud as he began recording the sensor data.

"Wouldn't take much, Russ," Own explained. "Maybe a couple of kilowatts at the most. Remember, they're working inside a resonant cavity! And at that frequency, they can count on a sizeable ground wave too."

"What about that ground wave, Owen? Could we be in it right now? IF so, how might it affect us?" Curt was anxious about such unknown factors. Because they were unknown, they didn't fit in with his military approach to this operation. If unknowns existed, Curt tried to make them knowns before committing lives to action.

Pendleton shook his head. "No. Rhomboidals are highly directional. Most of the energy is going out the open end of the rhomboid on the other side of the valley. We're probably out of the black lobe. That's very weak and directional anyway. One of the reasons you want to use a big rhomboidal at lower frequencies is because the design is so efficient when it comes to directing radiation."

"So where are they getting the power input, Doctor?" Dyani asked, an obvious but embarrassing question.

Pendleton shrugged. But it was Taisha who remarked, "Look for some buildings that appear to be mine shafts."

"We didn't see any on the sat images," Curt said. But he started looking.

"We're not the only ones who know how to use stealth and camouflage," Taisha pointed out. "If you recall, at Battle Mountain most of the electrical power came from hot springs. The land-line power was merely to handle peaking. The holes to tap the thermal sources were very well hidden."

"Now, you're making real good inputs, Doctor!" Curt told her. But he looked up from his laser binocs and shook his head. "I can't see anything. Would you like to take a look? Maybe you can spot something that I can't because of your stay at Battle Mountain."

"I don't like to be reminded of that, Colonel," Taisha told him in a low voice that was still sharp. "I have grown beyond it."

"I hope so. And I didn't mean to demean you or taunt you, Doctor. In any event, you're the real expert now. Have a look."

As Taisha took the laser binoculars and began to scan the Deosai Plains, Curt turned his attention to the details of the assault plan. Now he'd seen the terrain. That always made him feel better. He knew the ground on which he would have to fight the regiment.

"Russ, when you've had a good look, let's check the validity of our planning for Operation Hell Mover," he told his S-3, using the ops code they'd come up with in Ghazi for the final assault.

"I've seen what I need to see for right now," Russ replied, putting down the radar scanner. "Pretty much confirms when we've seen on the high-res sat images and what we've worked with on the computer-generated holos." He pointed over toward the northwest side of the park. "That's where Colonel Ghengis Khan and his Khyber Rifles are scheduled to come in tomorrow at dawn...if they get to the jump-off point in time. Right up the Sind River valley."

"How does this saddle look to you as a jump-off place for our rear assault?"

Russ thought about it for a moment, then announced, "I'd like to get in closer if I could do it without being detected. The farther we have to move to make the as-sault, the greater the chance of being nailed by artillery."

"We've got counterbattery fire capability with the Saucy Cans in the bivouac behind this ridge. They'll fire over it," Curt pointed out, indicating the long spine of raised ground.

Russ shrugged. "Okay, I guess we can hack it. What is it? About three klicks to the facility from here? About ten minutes if we can go high-mobile mode."

"Would you recommend it?" Curt asked, a pointed question of a commander seeking to get his subordinate to commit.

Russ shook his head. "No, sir. I like to close with my enemy before I try to blow his lips off."

"I agree with you on that. But would you take the chance of being spotted while maneuvering into a close-up final assault position? If you're caught in the open, what then?" Curt had already decided what he wanted to do. However, he was probing Russ to see if the man had any better ideas or seen something Curt had missed.

"If I had to take that chance, I'd do it. I might sustain some casualties if it went to slime while the battalion was in the sneak phase. But I think that's counterbalanced by the lowered risk of casualties by attacking from a close position."

Curt knew that Russ Frazier was an aggressive man. He'd proved that many times while leading a platoon, a company, and TACBATT itself. But Curt could never forget the look in the man's eyes when he was in a fight. Russ loved to fight.

But what mattered to Curt was that Russ Frazier had always been and was still willing to do something Curt could never do. Russ would waste people when an alternate plan might assure success and less killing.

That was one of the reasons Curt had booted Russ up to S-3 on staff. There Curt could exercise close control on Russ's operation plans, and Russ wouldn't waste any more Sierra Charlies in Frazier's

Ferrets.

"We'll stay here tonight," Curt decided. "We'll maintain our bivouac back in the valley. The Chippies need a place to squat, and they can't do it on this hogback spline. I also don't want to pull out of there and leave those 'peasants' in my rear before I know who they are. We'll move that bivouac when we take the Deosai facility. See any problems other than what you've already commented about, Russ?"

"Yes, sir. You're splitting your forces."

"Not any more than they would be anyway. I'll leave Larry Hall in charge of the bivouac. He's got the Saucy Cans placed and zeroed from there anyway."

Since he'd made the decision to stay on the ridge, he wanted to check it for security. He'd let Kitsy recce security while he concentrated on scouting the Deosai facility. But whether on recce or overnight, Curt didn't want any possible enemy assault on their flanks along the ridge line. "Any reaction to our presence here, Kitsy?"

"No, sir, or you would have heard from me," she replied professionally. "All sensor scans are negative. If anyone's out there waiting to bushwhack us, they're not putting out in any spectrum. Including olfactory."

Curt's uniform was really beginning to stink now. So was Kitsy's. "Yeah, we're prime targets for chem sensors, aren't we?"

"Sir, you would have to mention that! No, sir, we're not. The chem sensors on our Jeeps have reached overload."

"Shit!" Curt muttered.

Kitsy overheard him. "No, sir, we smell worse than that. And I'm damned near ready to puke because of it. If we can't shuck these damned stinking clothes, I'm likely to have a mutiny on my hands with TACBATT."

"You didn't figure on fighting naked up here, did you?"

"That might be fun under other circumstances. And in a very

different environment," Kitsy replied with a coy smile. "But no, you taught me always to have Plan B. So, like the efficient little Girl Scout I may appear to be, I did just that. I had TACBATT stuff regular cammies in the carry bins of their Jeeps and Mary Anns. 'Just in Case.'"

"So you and TACBATT want to change out of the i-r cammies?"

"Yes, sir! Please?" Kitsy could really be effective when she wheedled. She was being that way now.

"And you didn't think about your commanding officer?"

"You bet I did! Dyani's got your change-out!"

"In addition to my own," Dyani put in.

"Okay, everyone except outguards and warbot pickets down off the ridge," Curt ordered. "Change clothes by the numbers. And don't get caught with your pants down!"

"Body armor?" Kitsy asked.

Curt paused for a moment. Body armor wasn't uncomfortable to wear. This was a good time to put it on. On the other hand, they weren't facing the possibility of combat today.

But it was a cautionary matter. Belt and braces. Plan B. J.I.C.

"Yes. Body armor for everyone. Including Pendleton and Taisha."

That decision saved Curt's life.

Chapter Twenty-Two

Curt heard the round hit the side of the Mary Ann next to him as he was pulling on his pants.

He didn't hit the ground. He'd just put on his body armor. That would stop anything up to a 10mm Magnum round.

Sporadic firing broke out all around him on the ridge.

The Mary Ann next to him quickly swiveled its 25mm autocannon over his head and fired a round.

The muzzle blast nearly deafened him because the barrel was right over his head.

This was accompanied by the tearing roar of the 7.62mm autoguns on the Jeeps.

Then he heard the staccato ripping sound of Novias being fired in burst mode.

It didn't take him more than a few seconds to pull on his cammie jacket, strap on his equipment harness, put on his helmet, and grab his Novia. It was as though he did it all in one continuous, sequential movement.

Curt dashed around the Mary Ann to where Russ and Kitsy were. Both had donned armor and fresh cammies that didn't stink.

The blood lust was in Russ Frazier's eyes. He was firing his Novia with precision into the trees that sur-rounded them on the ridge.

"Kids!" Russ Frazier bellowed, not even bothering to use tacomm. "Bunch of damned kids snuck up and ambushed us!"

Kitsy was trying to talk on her tacomm.

Her Novia was in her right hand. At her feet was a small, crumpled human form. It was wearing a baggy, ill-fitting grey-green pair of pants and a shirt of the same color. A nondescript cloth cap was on the ground where it had been blown off the small person's head. There wasn't much left of the head. When a 7.62mm Novia round hits a human head at less than three meters, it does irreparable damage of considerable magnitude.

"Dammit, I don't care if they are boys! Those kids are shooting at us and killing some of us! If your targets aren't Greys or our warbots, open fire on them!" Kitsy was trying to act like a battalion commander. But there was a catch in her voice. She was upset. "The little bastards damned near got Frazier and me before we saw they were armed!" she added, but not into the tacomm.

A small form not much bigger than Kitsy but considerably younger dashed out from behind a tree. He raced toward them firing an A-99 submachine carbine from the hip. As he did all this, he managed to roll a grenade toward them before Russ cut him in half with a Novia burst.

Curt took Kitsy down as he went for dirt. Russ spun on the heel, firing as he turned, and dropped.

The grenade went off a few meters away.

But it had rolled behind a rock that deflected or stopped the frags. The only effect that hit the three of them was the concussion wave.

Kitsy rolled over on the ground and looked at Curt. For the first time in a combat situation, Curt saw tears in Kitsy's eyes. "Kids!" she gasped, out of breath because of the exertion and altitude. "Curt, they're sending kids against us! The boy I shot wasn't more than ten years old! Goddammit, how the hell are we supposed to fight and kill kids? That's who we're saving the world for! Jesus, I didn't sign up to be a baby killer!"

"Let's get this skirmish under control, Major," he told her in a level, professional tone of voice, trying to yank her back to her duty as an officer. "Then we can get some answers. What orders have you given?"

She didn't move, "Only what you just heard me issue on the tacomm, Colonel. And damn your cold, hard hide! But thank you for being cold and hard right now. I was having a little trouble with that."

"I know you were. That's why I did it," Curt told her briefly, got to his feet, and helped her up.

A-99 rounds were still flying, but the mad minute was just about over.

"Casualties?" Curt asked.

"I don't know yet," Kitsy admitted.

"Let me know when you get the information. Russ, are you okay?"

Frazier was on his feet, and he was still firing his Novia out into the cover around them. He kept on firing until he'd used up the clip of fifty rounds. Then he lowered his Novia, dropped to his knee, and inserted a new clip. As he did this, he quickly turned his head to Curt and Kitsy. "As Henry tells us: When in doubt, empty this clip."

Russ Frazier had gotten his jollies, Curt realized.

I was over in about three minutes and two Novia clips. Curt hadn't fired that many rounds since he'd spent the day at the rifle butts in Fort Huachuca several weeks ago.

When the firing tapered off, Curt looked around. "Dyani? Where's Dyani?" he suddenly asked.

"She took off when the firing started," Kitsy recalled. "We just had enough time to get the Novias unlimbered and order the warbots to fire. But she took off right away."

"Get me a report of casualties! Now!" Curt snapped. "Russ, who and what hit us?"

Frazier knew the fight was over, but he didn't sling his Novia. He carried it at the ready in the crook of his right arm. "I don't know yet. Maybe an infantry patrol. Non-warbot for sure. We didn't think a patrol at first. Three kids walked up to us like they were lost or lived here. They looked a lot like the ones we rounded up in the valley this morning!"

"Dammit!" Curt swore and toggled his tacomm. "Grey Base, this is Grey Head!"

No answer.

Curt repeated the call-up.

Finally, the harried voice of Hassan snapped back, "Grey Head, Grey Base is under fire right now. Can I call you back when we grease their skids?"

"Who hit you? Was it the kids we brought in this morning?" Curt wanted to know.

"Affirmative." Pause. "Okay, one less little bastard to harass us! Affirmative! Turns out they'd carried Mini A-99s in their shorts or something. Real short barrels. And some grenades. I don't understand the grenades. The handles are held down by rubber bands. Even if the pin is pulled, they won't go off." Another pause and dead air. "Sorry, Grey Head, got some work to do here. Back in a sec!"

Curt had intended to warn Hassan about the boys. The earlier report that the children were all boys who looked about ten to twelve years old hadn't made any impression on him then. Now it did. He wondered what was happening to the adults they'd picked up. Were they decoys intended to be slaughtered when the ambush started? Or were they the commanders?

He didn't have time to reflect on the possibilities. Dyani came out of the woods with First Sergeant Tracy Dillon. They'd captured two of the youthful soldiers.

Dyani's first words when she got within talking range were, "They got Harlan." It was a flat, almost unemotional statement on her part. But the way Dyani said it told Curt that she was pretty badly shaken.

"Does he need a bio-tech?" Kitsy asked.

"No. He didn't even know what hit him," Dillon added. He prodded one of the boys. "We would have brought in three. But one wouldn't cooperate."

"I...I had to kill the boy," Dyani reported. Normally, Dyani wasn't reticent about killing someone who was about to kill her. She'd done it coldly and methodically in the past. She wasn't someone to trifle with in a combat situation. But obviously this was something different.

Curt looked at the two boys. They were definitely boys, not young men. They hadn't reached puberty yet. They were the sort of youngsters Curt had seen in Sierra Vista playing softball on the school field, riding bikes down the sidewalks, and engaging in horseplay outside the grade school.

But these boys were different. They look hard and defiant. Obviously, they didn't like the fact they'd been taken prisoner. They looked ready for the worst.

Curt faced them, his Novia at the ready and pointing at them. He knew that youngsters could react in irrational and unpredictable ways. "Do you speak English?" he asked.

The boys spat at him and remained silent.

"Urdu?"

Again, they spat.

So, Curt lapsed into Mandarin Chinese and asked the question again.

This caused one boy to react. Surprise showed on his round face. No one other than his parents and superior had · ever spoken to him in anything like his native language. The boy apparently didn't understand some of what Curt said, but he caught enough of it.

The boy replied in a Chinese dialect that Curt had trouble understanding, although he could get the gist of it. "How can you speak as they do on Radio Beijing? I have never heard a West devil speak that way before!"

"Are you a soldier in the Chinese People's Liberation Army?" was the first full question that Curt fired at him. This was critical. If the boys were soldiers, he had to treat them according to the terms of the Geneva Convention. Maybe the Chinese didn't always follow the Convention, but Curt didn't want to be the American who broke it.

"We are members of the People's Red Scouts!" the boy announced proudly.

"What the hell are the People's Red Scouts?" Curt had lapsed into English because he didn't recognize that organization.

"That's the Chinese version of our Boy Scouts, Colonel," Russ explained in English.

"Except we don't send our kids out to fight wars," Kitsy pointed out.

Switching back into Mandarin, Curt told the boys, "I am required by international law to ask your name, rank, nationality, and date of birth."

"We tell you nothing! Kill us if you want!"

"Are you soldiers?"

"Everyone in the People's Republic is now a soldier!"

"If that is so, things have changed. Why?"

Curt had come up against the People's Liberation Army on Sakhalin several years before. The PLA had been professionally led albeit conscript-manned. The Chinese had been both surprised and revolted by the presence of women in the United States Army. In spite of the severe overpopulation problem, the government of China followed the old ways and wouldn't even consider using women. They had in the past, of course, during the days of Mao and the Long March. But those had been guerrilla campaigns. Under those conditions, anything goes. But this wasn't a guerrilla operation on the Plains of Deosai.

Curt also knew of the gentle and protective care Chinese families provided for their children. Finding Chinese-speaking boys out on the frontiers of China acting like cannon fodder was something new to Curt. This possibility hadn't been mentioned in the NIA and DIA briefings preceding this operation.

Curt realized that East World was making a strong strategic move here at Deosai. He didn't understand the full consequences of it or even its basic purpose. The pieces to the puzzle were lying on the proverbial table in front of him. He couldn't make a pattern out of the pieces yet.

He also realized that he was used to thinking of strategic operations in terms of a chess game. That had been the policy of, a military leadership that had spent decades preparing against the Big Red Tide headquartered in Moscow. The Pentagon had realized that the Soviets had planned a three-pronged "peace offensive" consisting of *perestroika*, then *glasnost*, and finally *usterenny* or "acceleration." The Soviets were also chess players. So, Americans had become chess masters.

The Chinese, on the other hand, were masters of an-other strategic game known as *I-Go* or simply "Go." It had been developed at the behest of an ancient Chinese emperor to teach his imbecilic son the principles of power strategy. Curt had played Go. He wasn't an expert. But he wasn't a chess master either.

And he didn't yet understand the various tactical and strategic moves of the PRC and East World in this new worldwide game of Go they appeared to be playing.

The two boys didn't answer Curt's last question. Instead, they spat on him.

And one of them made a big mistake. He quickly tried to reach into his shirt.

Both Dyani and Dillon fired.

"I hated to do that," Dillon remarked.

"So did I. But look what he reached for under his shirt."

Each boy had two small grenades, each in its little cloth pouch in his armpits.

"They were going to commit suicide anyway. And take as many of us with them as they could." Kitsy was having trouble believing all this. "What kind of enemy are we up against? What kind of people would send children out to fight their battles and die without remorse? What the hell kind of war are we in here?"

"Major," Curt reminded her, "I don't know either. I only know that we're not in the middle of it. If they send boys to kill us, we've got to fight back as if they were seasoned adult professionals."

"Doesn't this bother you?"

"Yes. It does. Deeply," Curt admitted. "But dammit, we're now in a fracas out on the edge of the world. We either do what we were sent to do or we'll be killed here by boys and God knows who else. So let's bury our disgust. And these kids. And get on with it. We can work out our personal problems with this later."

Kitsy was breathing hard. It might have been partly due to the altitude. But she was teary around the eyes. Her reaction to this was unanticipated by Curt. Then he realized what was happening.

"We may be up against several new East World weapons here, ladies and gentlemen," he told the Greys clustered around him. "We encountered the East World troops in Yemen. And they encountered us. We met them again in Senegambia. We probably haven't studied them as much as they've studied us. They tried to duplicate our warbots, and they did."

"Hell, their Red Hammers are no competition for our Mary Anns and Jeeps," Russ sneered. "We've greased their skids every time they've used Red Hammers against us."

"That we did," Curt admitted. "But these people are smarter than hell. If they can't beat us on the technology part, they'll try to beat us on the psychological front. I think we've just encountered their countermeasure weapon against the ladies of the Sierra Charlies regiments."

"What?" Russ didn't fully understand what Curt had just said.

"Look at the reaction of Kitsy. And Dyani. And I'll bet the same reaction from every one of our ladies," Curt pointed out. "Extreme revulsion and hesitation to fight and kill children. Ladies, have they found a weak point? Or not?" Curt directed his question directly at Kitsy and Dyani.

"Yes, but we may be tougher than they think," Kitsy replied, apparently steeling herself to accept the inevitable during this operation.

"It's a weak point only if we permit it to be," Dyani said quietly. "Some Amerindians would slaughter enemy women and children as easily as they'd killed warriors. Crows and other tribes were primarily interested in counting coup. But we also fought against tribes that weren't interested in that kind of symbolic victory. They Crows would take women and children as hostages to get our own back in a trade. And I think my ancestors probably killed enemy women and children when they were used as warriors against us. So, Colonel, if we have to fight boys, we'll do it."

"I agree," Dillon said. He was from Montana. He knew the Indian ways. "But I don't think our ladies will like it."

"Damned right we don't!" Kitsy snapped. She seemed to become Major Kitsy Clinton again, leader of the tactical battalion of the Washington Greys. She picked the tacomm off her belt. "Puma Leader, this is Cougar Leader! Report casualties! And give me your estimate of the situation ASAP! We need to regroup and prepare for another assault!"

"Captain, see to it that these boys are buried. And the rest of them around here too," Curt told Dyani.

"Yes, sir, once I get the new security procedures set up," she told him. "Sorry this happened, Colonel. I admit I wasn't expecting to be attacked by boys."

"None of us were." Curt turned his attention to his tacomm. "Grey Base, this is Grey Head! Give me a sit-rep, please!"

It took two calls to get a reply from Edie Sampson. "Grey Head, this is Grey Tech. It was one hell of a furball, sir! And the first person who says that life in the rear area is safe and secure is going to catch hell from me!"

"Save the personal comment for after the debrief, Sergeant!" Curt admonished her. However, he was happy to hear her respond in that sanguine manner. It meant that the Greys had prevailed down in the valley. "Is the furball still balling?"

"No, sir! We greased their skids in about five minutes! I didn't like it. I didn't like shooting the boys, but they were mean little bastards anyway. Tougher than hell and deadly because we originally pampered them and didn't think they were. But when they shot the adults we brought in because the old people got in the way, we didn't have any qualms about wasting the little bastards."

"They killed the adults they were with?"

"Yes, sir. Slaughtered them. Threw the bodies over the wire we'd strung around their compound. Climbed over the dead bodies. Nasty tactics. But that slowed them down. Gave us time to lock and load. At that point, we weren't real gentle with them. Captain Mahmud said to tell you everyone's okay except Henry took a Chinese round in the left arm. None of us was wearing body armor. We are now!"

"No other casualties?" That sounded amazing to Curt.

"No, sir! Captain Hall's people were in the LAMVAs siting the Saucy Cans. So, they used the fifteens on the turrets. The Jeeps were on the ground and fired up, and they got a lot of the rest. Lieutenant Mikawa was a holy terror, sir. She may be small like me, but she's just as mean and nasty."

Curt knew he'd get the full report later. Right then, there wasn't time. "Okay, stay put for right now. I've got to find out where the Paks are. And report some of this to Fort Fumble. Stand by to move everything but GUNCO to the top of the ridge. We may have to kick off an assault today, and to hell with the Paks!"

"Yes, sir! We'll move out as soon as…Goddamn! Sonofabitch!"

Her transmission was interrupted.

A few seconds later, the sound of an explosion reached the top of the ridge from the valley below.

Chapter Twenty-Three

"Edie! What's going on down there?" Curt forgot all about tacomm protocol. The explosion had come from the valley in which the vehicles, the Saucy Cans, und the Bio-tech unit were bivouacked. His top technical NCO had cut off her transmission. Edie Sampson was an old, old friend and comrade. Curt blew his cool for a moment.

Another explosion was heard.

"Dyani, can any of your scouts see anything down at the bivouac?" Curt snapped.

"Negatory! Trees are in the way! Obviously, two explosions!" Dyani replied at once. "I'll send two scouts down!"

"No, no! Let's see if we can make contact before sending anyone down there!" Curt decided. Then into his tacomm, he called, "Grey Tech, this is Grey Head! Assassin Leader, this is Grey Head! Anyone in bivouac, answer Grey Head!"

"Grey Head, Panther Leader here!" said the voice of Lieutenant Dan Power. "Read you five-by! Not to worry! We had a little disaster here courtesy of the boy wonders of Deosai!"

"Panther Leader, Grey Head!" Curt broke in, somewhat relieved. "Can you give me a sit-rep?"

"Negatory, sir! We've got a little mop-up in progress! We might lose someone or something yet unless we kill some of these little bastards first!"

"We heard two explosions up here on the ridge! What were they?" Curt persisted.

"An ACV and an Em-six-six-four log van! They blew up!"

"Mister, vehicles don't just blow up! What caused it?"

"We don't know, sir! Now, with all due respects, get off my bot, sir!

I've got some nasty work to do here. Panther Leader out!" And the tacomm went dead.

"Goddammit, I ought to have his bars for that!" Curt exploded.

"Colonel, if you bust him, you should bust me!" Russ Frazier remarked with a growl. "I've lipped off to you worse than that in combat! And I've heard you take a few disrespectful swipes at commanders a few times myself!"

"That was Dan Power. He's a good man," Kitsy added. "The way he talks, he's got his hands full of combat at the moment."

Curt tried to catch his breath. The worry of command, the adrenaline rush of combat, and the high altitude were all getting to his capabilities for rational thought and cool command decisions. He knew the Greys now fighting down at the bivouac would get back to him as quickly as they could. So, he called, "Pendleton? Where are you?"

Owen Pendleton and Dr. Rosha Taisha came out from behind some rocks where they'd taken cover during the firefight. Pendleton was unarmed, being the "scientific leader" of the expedition. But, as he came up to Curt, he remarked, "Right here! And I think we'd better knock off this crap about a scientific expedition, Curt. You'll need every gun you can get. Give me a Novia. I've never fired one, but that won't stop me. I never fired a gun before Zahedan, remember?"

"Yeah, I sure do!" Curt recalled the AI mentor's exemplary performance those many years ago. "But we don't have any extra Novias here on the ridge. Our reserves are down at the bivouac."

"Colonel," Sergeant Tracy Dillon said quietly, "I'll go get Lieutenant Saunders' Novia. We'll need to tag the coordinates of his body for pickup anyway. And I'll cover him up."

"You don't need to do that, Dillon," Dyani told him. "Yes, Dyani, I do. He's a real mustang. He came up through the ranks like you. I owe it to him. Besides, he'd want Colonel Pendleton to use his Novia instead of letting it lie there with him when he can't use it any longer." Without asking further permission, Dillon. headed out into the trees again, his own Novia at the ready.

"Damned if I'm going to let him go alone," Battalion Sergeant Major Nick Gerard growled. "Harlan was a good buddy of mine too." And without asking permission from Kitsy, Nick followed Dillon.

Curt swallowed hard and tried to remember what Dyani had taught him about self-control. Another Grey had joined the list of honored dead. Harlan Saunders wouldn't lie there long. Dillon would beacon the body for later pickup. If possible, the body would be returned to the States. It wouldn't be left there. Like the French Foreign Legion, the Washington Greys never abandoned their dead on the battlefield.

It was time for action, not contemplation. There wasn't a whole hell of a lot he could do about what had happened thus far. But Curt knew he could gain control of the situation again if he took control. So, he proceeded to do that.

"Kitsy, get me a sit-rep on our personnel and units up here on the ridge," Curt told her, and continued to snap out orders. "Russ, if you can't get through to Ghazi to spool-up the Harpies, keep at it until Grey Tech gets online again or you manage to get through by skip. We're not going to fuck around up here on this ridge waiting for the Paks. I want to move against Deosai now while we still might have some element of surprise left. And while we still have personnel and equipment to do it! Damned if I'm going to sit here and-fend off these god-damned attacks from the Red Scouts for the rest of the day and all night!"

As they quickly moved away to carry out his orders, Curt toggled his tacomm again. "Grey Tech, this is Grey Head."

Silence.

"Okay, if I can't get to Fort Fumble through a patch in the OCV, I'll try direct," Curt decided. From another pouch on his equipment harness, he pulled forth a much smaller communicator. Its antenna was different. Curt pushed a control and began to sweep the antenna across the sky.

Owen noticed the unusual appearance of the unit. "Planar-array antenna?"

"Yeah. The next great advance in tactical communications," he explained to Owen. "Direct satellite communications. It's sending out a pulse signal now. If it gets a response from a comsat up there, it lets me know and locks on. The planar array is automatically programmed to stay locked on the comsat. So, I can move this sucker any which way and not lose narrow-beam lock. Aha! There we go!"

A green light glowed.

"Tiffany Main, this is Hell Fire One. I say code: Three. Seven. Four. Alpha. Six. One. Zero. Password: Kit. Call Wild Man One." Curt said this all slowly and carefully into the little unit's face.

No human ear heard the signal. It went to Tiffany, a computer complex deep beneath the bowels of the nation's capital. Curt had spoken slowly and distinctly so the computer voice-recognition circuitry would match his voiceprint and understand the codes.

It was new to the Army. But it had been used for several years by the NIA. It was one of Al Murray's "national technical means." Curt had decided to call it the "NTM-1."

A lag of about two seconds followed.

"Wild Man One here!"

"Wild Bill, this is Grey Head!"

"Where the hell are you? We've been trying to reach you for hours!" the voice of General Bill Bellamack replied.

"Sorry to wake you, General. I'm on a ridge overlooking Deosai as planned," Curt reported. "We've been hit twice, almost simultaneously. East World is using boy soldiers. About ten years old, most of them. I know you'll tell your spooks but be sure to tell the Chief Spook too."

"Boys? That's unusual for them," Bellamack replied.

"They must have learned it from India. The Brits ran up against women and young boys as troops a couple of centuries ago out in this part of the world," Curt reminded his former regimental commander. "I believe the stealth portion of this operation has been compromised. Therefore, I'm initiating the assault on Deosai immediately I can get the rest of my assault forces in position."

"You're not waiting for the Paks?"

"That's an affirm. I am not waiting for the Paks. As soon as I get regional tacomm back, I'll call Khyber Head. Right now, Edie is involved in the mop-up of a fight in the bivouac. Never mind the details. I'll give you my full report when I can. Just wanted to let you know what had happened here. NSC should know about it too."

General Wild Bill Bellamack, now the Army's top general, didn't even try to argue with Curt. Once, Bellamack had commanded the Washington Greys. During his command, he'd run the regiment but Curt had led it. Bellamack handled the command role while Curt provided the tactical brains. The two men still believed their original contract held. They would support one another. Neither would shoot into. the other's goal without checking first.

Some people don't understand the Old Boy Network of the military services. It's not a mechanism for maintaining power. It's built upon years of gaining trust in another person. As such, it's a natural consequence of the saying that one should try to do business with one's friends rather than one's enemies. Or unknown entities. Such networking exists in the business world, but it's far more powerful in the military services, where lives are at stake.

Curt didn't know it yet, but he was part of that network now. And what he did on that ridge in the western Himalayas merely confirmed what others knew of him as an honorable leader.

"Roger that, Grey Head! You're on the spot. Do it! I'll support you from here! The word will get to the Man when he wakes up later this morning."

"Uh, yeah, I sort of forgot that we're twelve hours out of synch, Wild Man," Curt apologized. "Sorry about that, sir."

"Grey Head, if I wanted a nine-to-five job, I wouldn't be where I am," Bellamack told him bluntly. "Let me know how it goes and what you need from me."

"I'll do that, Wild Man! We're off the line here now!" Curt flipped a switch, folded the little antenna, and slipped the unit back into his pouch.

"That," said Owen Pendleton, "was great!"

"Yeah, the guys in the spook shops turn out some good stuff. I'm glad we get it when they move on to something better," Curt observed.

"What else have you got in your magic pouch?" Pendleton wanted to know.

"Blue smoke and mirrors mostly," Curt told him. "Why don't you guys get busy and invent a peace ray? Then I could beam it at Deosai and we could all go home with no more fuss."

"Ah, we're working on something," was all that Pendleton would say right then.

"Yeah, looks like we'll need it if this NE weapon thing down there is for real," Curt mused. "If East World can do it, it won't be long before everyone can. And we'll have to scrap all the warbots."

Colonel Owen Pendleton looked out over the Deosai facility. "Well, that depends on what we find when we get in there. But if you want my unvarnished opinion, it looks like this may be the end of the warbots. At least, the NE ones. Hell, I may have to go find a new job!"

"We will always have a job, Owen," said Rosha Taisha. "We have only scratched the surface of the human-machine interface. There is much to be done. And this will help us do it."

Pendleton looked at her. "Maybe. But technology continues to accelerate and progress. I wish I were as confident as you are, Rosha."

"You'll see," was her cryptic reply.

Curt wanted to ask her about her remark. She always made cryptic remarks. Dyani did the same. He'd learned not to let such remarks pass. But before he got the chance to say anything, his tacomm brick squawked.

"Grey Head, this is Grey Tech!"

"Thank God!" Curt breathed and whipped it up to his ace. "Go ahead, Grey Tech. Are you all right?"

"Hell, yes, sir. Why shouldn't I be? I was left in the rear area out of harm's way to run the regimental communications," Edie's voice replied. "Sorry for the interruption. We had a couple of things blow up on us and a bunch of unruly boys to take care of. Henry's in Bio-tech right now. Nothing serious. But he gets another Purple Heart, damn his tough old hide! Izzy Greenwald got it too, but he'll be okay when they put a plug in him to fill the hole. To bring you up to date, we're now all in body armor. We have a pile of dead boy soldiers here. They paid the full retail, price for playing with guns when they were too young. I'm not trying to be funny about it, Colonel. It's damned tough to shoot kids who ought to be playing hide-and-seek instead of war games with live ammo. Sir, I think we've been compromised. Hassan the Assassin wants me to tell you he thinks we ought to go in and hit Deosai before sundown. Otherwise, even in spite of the Chinese fire drill, they'll be ready for us tomorrow."

She stopped talking. Curt had let her talk. He knew his redheaded chief tech sergeant whose red hair was slowly becoming streaked with a little grey. She needed to let off some steam.

"Okay, glad to get your report. Pass the word to Hassan," Curt told her, feeling greatly relieved. "Move out the Assassins to join us here on the ridge ASAP. You are to join us too. Bio-tech and GUNCO are to remain there. We'll need a firm patch through to Hellcat Leader for fire control. And I'll want a firm patch through to Ghazi as well. We're going to need tacair within hours. And I want it overhead and ready."

"Yes, sir! Got that! Will do! We've also got a call-in from Khyber Head, and he wants a call back," Edie went on, more smoothly now as the excitement of combat drained from her.

"Set it up," Curt told her. "By the way, how did those kids blow those two vehicles? I didn't think they were carrying high explosives."

"They were," Edie told him. "Remember the report was they were carrying grenades with the arming handles held down by rubber bands?"

"Roger. They wouldn't go off even if the pins were pulled."

"Yeah, but they did. They're the nastiest little anti-vehicle mines I've ever seen," Edie reported. "Even more so than the wadi mines we ran into in Yemen. The kids take the cap off a vehicle's fuel tank, pull the pin on the grenade, and drop it in. Put on the cap and get out of there. At some unknown time in the future, the turbine fuel eats away the rubber band. The grenade goes off in the fuel tank."

There was silence on the tacomm for a moment. Then Curt agreed, "Yeah. Nasty. Real nasty. But I'll bet the kids didn't think up that one. Must have been trained to do it. They only seemed to know how to kill."

"Yes, sir, but they didn't do a real good job of that either. Not against professionals. But that was one time I wasn't real proud to be a pro. Okay, Grey Head, your patch through to Khyber Leader is coming up!"

Curt caught his breath. Dyani came up to him and told him, "We got them all, Colonel. About twenty-six dead Red Scouts. But no adult leader. They must have been sent up here on their own."

"Maybe their leader was with them but didn't get in the fight and went back," Curt mused. "If so, that means we've got to act fast."

"I'd like to go down now and begin to probe their defenses," Dyani remarked.

Curt didn't want to send her down there without support. "Wait until we move out. And that's a direct order, Deer Arrow!"

Dyani looked directly at him and her mouth twitched. She didn't like the order. But she would obey it. She didn't know what Curt had in mind. "Yes, sir! The Mustangs will be ready, sir!"

"I know you will. And I know I can count on you too." Curt told her. "While you're waiting, get the recce Harpies off Ghazi. The ones with the Black Hawks riding shotgun as observers and spotters. We'll need them overhead in about ninety minutes or so. Edie has set up the patch through the OCV. So, make it so and take a little of the burden off yourself and your troops. Don't forget, you're short an officer now."

"Yes, sir. I'm taking over Harlan's platoon for this." She paused, then added, "And I won't forget my other responsibilities too."

"Including the ones to each other?"

"Especially including those, Colonel!" And she was gone.

His tacomm beeped. "Grey Head here!"

"Grey Head, this is Khyber Head!" the voice of Colonel Iskander Khan came back. "Are you in position?"

"Affirmative!"

"Remain in that position. We have not progressed as planned. We will be eight hours late arriving in Skardu. I do not want to assault at night. Therefore, the operation has been delayed for twenty-four hours," Khan told him.

"Khyber Leader, I can't delay. I have been under attack," Curt reported. "I believe the security of this operation has been compromised. Therefore, I am initiating Operation Hell Mover at once. I will keep you advised so you may continue to move at night and support us if we haven't breached the objective by this evening."

He was greeted by silence for fifteen seconds. At first, he thought that the link had been severed. Then Khan came back, and his voice revealed his anger. "Grey Head, this is a joint operation!"

"Then shag your ass and get the hell up here, Khan!" Curt snapped. It had been a rough day. It was going to get rougher. He wasn't about to spend any more time arguing with the Pakistani colonel. "I'm not waiting for you! I can't!"

"You can't take Deosai alone!"

"Want to bet?"

"This is a breach of the agreement between our governments!"

"Maybe, but my government didn't send us up here to be slaughtered while waiting for you!"

"I won't let you do this!"

"And how the hell are you going to stop me?" Curt was angry, but even in the heat of his anger he realized that the Paks could make it difficult if they wanted to. But only later, when the Greys were withdrawing and leaving Pakistan. However, Curt would cross that bridge when he got to it. Right then, the Greys were vulnerable as hell where they were. He knew they couldn't stay there.

"This is an insult to the Islamic Republic of Pakistan!"

"Bullshit! It's saving your ass! Or do you want to answer for the massacre of the Washington Greys?" Curt had lost patience with the Pakistani commander, who had believed from the start that he was running the operation. However, Khan and his regiment hadn't showed up when and where they were supposed to. Curt wasn't going to stand still for that and continue to take losses from ambushes.

"Assume a defensive posture! They can't prevail against your warbots!"

"Yeah, but they can and have killed my people!" Curt told him. "And I'm not going to stand still for any more of that. We're an offensive outfit. We're going to attack. Besides, what the hell are you sniveling about? We're going to go in there and do your job for you! And I'll bedamned happy to let you have all the glory you want afterward. I've had all the goddamned glory I need in my career! This regiment is going to do the damned job and get the hell out of here with everyone if possible. You see, we don't go to paradise if we die in battle! So, shag your ass, Khan. If you get here by sundown, you can join the victory celebration in the Deosai facility! We're not going to fuck around any longer! Grey Head out!" Curt snapped off his tacomm and replaced it in his harness with a decisive movement.

"Damn, I hope I did the right thing!" he muttered.

But Dyani had overheard him. "Right or wrong, we're with you!

And we'll do it! We're ready as soon as the Assassins join us! What's this about not going to paradise?"

"No, we go to a place called Fiddler's Green. That's halfway down on the road to Hell. I think we're already there."

Chapter Twenty-Four

"Colonel, I'm sorry it took so long for us to get here," Hassan apologized. "It was damned difficult to come up the hill."

Hassan's Assassins were more than an hour late arriving on the ridge line. The sun was now getting close to the western horizon.

"Why?" Curt asked. Earlier, a lot of time had been spent making a road up from the bivouac.

"We had to make our own road in the process!" Hassan explained.

"Make your own road? Why didn't you use the one we made getting up here this morning?" Curt demanded.

"Sir, you made a road?"

"Damned right we did!"

"We didn't know that! And we didn't see it!" Hassan said.

"Why not? We took the fastest route up here!"

"Well, that's probably the reason, sir," Hassan explained. "I'm used to maneuvering in hills like this. So, I took what appeared to be the easy route…"

"So, we chose different routes. Great!" Curt snapped in exasperation. He knew it was his fault for not informing Hassan of the existing road. "Well, hell, there isn't too much we can do about that now. You're here. But the assault probably can't be made in daylight."

Curt turned to his S-3. "Russ, when does the sun go down? How much daylight is left?"

Major Russ Frazier checked his hand computer. "Got about eighty-three minutes up here on the ridge. Less down on the Deosai Plains. Twilight will last another seventy-two minutes."

"What sort of moonlight conditions will we have? It was pretty damned dark out last night."

"We've got a last-quarter moon. It won't rise until about midnight local."

"That's what I thought, but now I'm sure of it." Curt had gathered his officers and lead NCOs around him behind the ridge. He looked at each of them. "We've got to come up with a revised ops plan here. And fast. Let's consider the parameters we have to work with. It will take us about thirty minutes to close the gap between the ridge line and the Deosai perimeter. We can do it all at once. Or we can deploy to combat positions with small units moving slowly over a period of time."

"Small units moving slowly will attract less attention," Kitsy observed.

"I think so too. But it will take longer," Curt told her. "Can we take longer to deploy? What are the pros and cons as you see them? Everything works backward in time from the final assault. When do you think we should trigger it? I'm asking for the best ideas from each of you."

"Colonel, we can fight as well at night as in the daylight," Dyani said. "We're not dependent upon sunset or moonrise. In fact, they may work against us."

Edie Sampson spoke up. "The Chinese may not have good night sensors. They didn't in Sakhalin. We didn't encounter any East World night sensors in Yemen or Senegambia. And if they've gotten them since then, they can't be very advanced, I know how to spoof them."

"The best time to make a non-daylight assault is two hours before dawn when the enemy is sleeping, or the night guards are weary. The next best times are in the deep twilight," Hassan pointed out, calling on his extensive memory. "The unaided human eye is at its worst about an hour before sunrise and an hour after sunset. Everything becomes a different shade of gray. Color vision goes to hell. That's why most automobile accidents in rural areas occur during those twilight periods."

"It's going to be tough to keep the warbots stealthed," Captain Lew Pagan interjected. "Maybe we ought to pull the old Alpha-Bravo assault. Move the warbots up to form the Alpha fire base and attract attention while the Bravo maneuvering unit sneaks into position on the flank. The warbots will draw fire and take the incoming. The East Worlders will probably deploy the Red Hammers against the Mary Anns of the Alpha Unit. That's no contest if we have good targeting information for Larry Hall's guns. And if the Harriers are overhead to lay a little ordnance, the Red Hammers are so much scrap metal. If the Saucy Cans don't do the recycling job first, like they did in Yemen."

"We can initiate the assault with a Saucy Cans barrage followed by a Harpy operation," Russ suggested. "Then open up with the Mary Anns of the Alpha fire base. Classic fire-and-maneuver tactic."

"That's almost standard Sierra Charlie doctrine. We've read Patton. They've read Patton too. Will they be expecting that?" Kitsy wanted to know.

"No. They won't be expecting us to launch a night attack at all. Which is precisely why we'll do it!" Curt decided. He recalled military history. "The Chinese don't like to fight at night. So, we will."

"Sir, they ambushed you at night on Sakhalin," Hassan recalled.

"And they conducted small squad operations at night in Korea too," Curt replied. "But their big human-wave attacks with bugles and yelling occurred during the day. They probably would have done the same at Sinegorsk on Sakhalin if we hadn't intercepted the Soviets first. The best Gee-Two I've got says they don't have night-fighting equipment. They can't afford to equip their mass armies with it. Furthermore, night-vision stuff may be ancient tech to us. But it's the highest of high tech to the PLA. Their conscript soldiers don't have enough technical savvy to keep it working."

"The Chinese aren't stupid," Taisha said. "They built the Deosai facility. And they developed the NE weapon we're going after. I'm not standing up for the Chinese because I'm part Chinese. However, the Chinese have developed a lot of the technology we now use.

Like gunpowder. And wind power in the form of the windmill."

"True," Curt told her. "But they didn't do what they should have done, which is reduce it to practice and encourage widespread use. They're scientifically brilliant in many ways, but Chinese kids don't grow up surrounded by technology the way we do. We don't think anything about trying to fix something that's busted. We may not fully understand the technology behind the gadget, but we'll give a try at fixing it. The Chinese don't. Neither do the Sovs. And especially the Islamic men. I don't know about the Indian Army. My guess is that the Indian Army people still maintain the basic British outlook we share with them: Anything can be fixed, especially if it's in short supply."

He paused and got the discussion back on track. The Greys were smart, educated people. However, they tended to convert their Papa and Oscar briefings into philosophical bull sessions. Curt turned the present discussion into an Oscar briefing.

"Okay, let me put up a straw man here. We spend the rest of daylight here on the ridge getting ready. Thirty minutes after sunset, we move out in two detachments. Alpha Detachment will be under the command of Major Clinton. It will consist of the massed Mary Anns of TACBATT and Pagan's Pumas to operate them. Bravo Detachment will be under the com-mand of Major Frazier. It will be the maneuver unit with all the remaining Sierra Charlies and the Jeeps. The Harriers will be overhead with the Black Hawks running recce in the right seats. I'll accompany Bravo. The Mustangs will serve as our point element. Owen, you and Taisha will be with me."

He looked at Kitsy and told her, "Major Clinton, your job is to get the Mary Anns within five hundred meters of the south side of Deosai. Your targets will be the Red Hammers and the barracks. You'll have artillery support from the Hellcats and tacair from the Harriers. I want Alpha to appear as the main attack."

"I think we can make enough noise and nuisance to qualify," Kitsy answered, gung-ho as usual.

"Bravo will maneuver into the best position on the east side of

Deosai for a stealthed assault on the main facility building," Curt went on. "We'll have to coordinate this closely so Alpha and Bravo don't shoot into one another."

"And so, the Hellcats don't burst on you or the Harriers lay ordnance on you," Kitsy put in. "Where will Edie be?"

"With me," Curt told her. "Sergeant Sampson, leave the OCV here in stealth and camouflage. Set up the necessary comm and tac display patches. I want you with me working remote. I don't want to haul the OCV cross-country with Grady inside. Better it stays here."

"That can be done, Colonel," Edie responded, making notes on her hand pad. "Messy patch, but no one ever told me this job would be easy. Could Henry come up from bivouac to run the OCV?"

"I suspect not. That's up to Major Gydesen."

"Henry is pissed at getting shot by a boy," Edie explained. "And when he wasn't looking too. If we can get him up on the ridge, it would make me feel better. I don't expect my comm and display gear to go tits-up, but…"

"Okay, we'll get him up here," Curt decided. "With two roads to choose from, he should make it within the hour if Major Gydesen will release him." Then he made another decision, keeping his TO&E in his head as he did so. "Larry Half will run the show at the bivouac when he isn't putting seventy-fives into Deosai."

He checked his watch. "Okay, timeline. Sunset at eighteen-thirty-three. Push off from here at nineteen hundred hours. On final assault positions no later than nineteen-forty-five. Saucy Cans barrage commences at twenty-hundred hours. Alpha opens fire no later than twenty-fifteen. Bravo begins to move in at twenty-thirty."

Curt paused I and looked around. His lead officers and NCOs were waiting. The regimental commander had laid down an operational plan. Curt's leadership methodology was known to them. When he set up a straw man such as this, they knew they'd be asked for their inputs. But they waited until they were sure Curt had finished.

He had. So, he said, "I'm now entertaining comment, complaints, criticism, critique, and questions. Does that straw man plan sound reasonable? Can you hack it? Any problems? Any questions?"

"Yes, sir. Question. What's Plan B?" Kitsy wanted to know.

"Let's figure on several. Let me trot out a possible Plan Bravo One. It says if you're fired upon early, fire back. Then we move all times up accordingly and shove the assault down their throats from that moment on. Plan Bravo Two: If anyone gets stuck between here and there, we abort the operation."

Curt sensed dissatisfaction with the latter. "Sorry if you don't like it. It's better than Plan Charlie. That will be a withdrawal under fire because Colonel Khan was right, and we can't hack it alone."

Curt had revealed Plan C for a good reason. It would get a reaction from the Greys.

"Sir, our colors do not run!" Kitsy maintained indignantly.

That was what he wanted to hear.

"How about the withdrawal plan for later? After we've looked around and destroyed the place?" Russ asked. "Do we move back to the ridge here? Or do we go down the Indus gorge to meet the Khyber Rifles at Skardu or on the Karakoram Highway?"

"We come back to the ridge, Russ. Then the main body moves down into the bivouac leaving a holding force on the ridge: If we need a holding force, a rear guard, at that time. Depends on how badly we grease the people in Deosai," Curt fold him. "Once this is over and we're back at bivouac, we'll get Tim to start bringing in her Chippies to lift us back to the real world. Let the Khyber Rifles hack it themselves for all the help they've been thus far. They can have Deosai when we're finished with it."

"Yeah, sloppy seconds would serve them right!" Nick Gerard decided. "But how about evacking from the Deosai facility itself, Colonel? It would ·save having to fight our way over this ridge again what with the altitude problem and all. I figger we're going to be beat to the socks by the time we clobber Deosai."

"We'll decide that when the time comes."

"So, our withdrawal plan is pretty loosy-goosy, then?" Russ asked.

"Affirmative. Let's not make any detailed plans for the operation following the assault," Curt confided in them. "We've been through this before. Once the furball starts, it's going to take on a flow of its own."

"So, we'll do what we always do," Nick observed. "Play the cards as they're dealt and win anyway."

"I can live with that," Russ decided. "We've got a general idea of a general plan of operations following our assault. That's all we need for the moment."

"Experience tells me that all of you will fight this your own way. You always do. Makes being the regimental commander a real challenge," Curt told them.

"A force committed is out of the control of its commander," Kitsy observed.

"You've been reading military history again," Curt noticed.

"Yes, sir. You told me I should. Remember?"

"Okay, let's get ready to move out! Let's get down there, take care of this matter, and go home!" Curt told them in conclusion.

They all agreed to that.

And two hours later, they were all wondering why they'd been so gung-ho about it.

As they moved off the ridge and down into the Plains of Deosai, every Washington Grey was thinking what every soldier in every war thinks about before combat.

Will I live through this?

Will I be wounded? Injured? Maimed?

Will I let my comrades down?

Is this damned gun going to work right for a change?

What am I going to do when I piss in my pants?

They moved slowly across the three kilometers between the ridge and the Deosai facility perimeter. Each unit followed the edge of high-altitude meadowlands and kept to the cover of trees where possible.

They moved as quietly as they could. The Mary Anns and the Jeeps were running silent on their power packs. When the shooting began, they'd shift back to their turbines and recharge packs while fighting.

The sun was well down and twilight was deepening as Bravo Unit moved into position. Russ reported all Bravo Jeeps and Sierra Charlies were in defilade or camouflaged. Their positions overlooked the perimeter fence from the cover of trees and high grass about a hundred meters away.

"Grey Head, Mustang Leader here. Three Red Hammers in sight," Dyani reported quietly by hushed tacomm, the gain turned down to a whisper. "They're on patrol. They take about ten minutes to pass a given perimeter point again."

"This is Assassin Leader. Do you have the Red Hammer control centers in sight?"

"Affirmative. The towers on the corners. I see laser beams sending commands from the towers. Range three-three-nine from Bravo Leader beacon. Figure your own parallax distance."

"Mustang Leader, you must be right up against the perimeter fence to pick up the beam transmissions!" Curt said.

"Yes, sir, I am. And well hidden, I assure you. Just don't shoot at us if you see a beaconed target moving near the fence!"

"Grey Head, Alpha Leader is here," Kitsy reported in. "Alpha is in position. We have our initial targets ranged. No probing or sensor interrogations detected."

The Greys might have pulled off their slow, deliberate, stealthy deployment without detection, Curt thought jubilantly. But he checked it. "Grey Major, this is Grey Head. Do you detect any Deosai sensors painting us? Or you?"

Henry Kester's voice came back. "We're now being painted with pulse micrometer radar. And some infrared lidar beamed at the ridge. They know we're here. Hell, they ought to! We creamed their kids earlier today! Bastards! Sending boys to do adult work! Grey Head, I've hacked up a program that will confuse the shit out of them down there. I'm sending back multiple returns that will make them think the whole damned regiment is still up here!"

"Good show, Grey Major!" Edie Sampson popped in. "I knew you could do it! How's the arm?"

"Well, Grey Tech, you ain't the only good techie in the outfit! You're good, but you ain't exclusive," Henry fired back. "As for the arm, I'll survive. Grey Head, I'm seeing other sensors painting Deosai from orbit. Some friendly mono-pulse radar and some ultra-violet laser stuff. And some unknown stuff I think is Pakistani. Some ECM going on upstairs too. I think we can forget about that part of the fight, Grey Head. Leave that to the Aerospace Farce."

"Keep an eagle-type eyeball bonded to it, Grey Major," Curt told him. The Army field manuals stressed the maintenance of proper tacomm protocol and standard communications language. However, the Greys had read the manuals and put them back into the base library. They preferred to use familiar jargon and even slang. Maybe the enemy was proficient enough in American Army English to figure out what was being said. But it was certain that military commanders the world over had obtained and read the manuals. The enemy knew what standard comm language meant. So, jargon and slang became unofficial but effective code.

"Colonel, the Harriers are hovering in ground effect behind the ridge to the south," Russ reported directly to Curt. "Harrier Leader has four Harpies assigned to recce and the other four to tacair support. They can stay in hover for another forty-seven minutes. After that, they'll have to stage back twenty klicks for air refueling from one of the Chippies."

"Thank you, Russ. Do they pick up anything on their acquisition sensors?"

"Negatory. The sky is clear at the moment."

"Roger. Count us down to zero time," Curt told him.

"Roger. All Greys, four minutes to zero!"

After about a half minute of silence, Curt gave a "just in case I forgot earlier" order: "Alpha Leader, your initial targets should be the Red Hammer control towers."

"Roger, Grey head. Alpha Leader concurs. The Mary Anns will take them out first."

"Three minutes to zero!"

"Final reports, please!"

"Alpha Unit ready!"

"Bravo Unit ready."

"Grey Major ready!"

"Hellcat Leader ready!"

"Harrier Leader ready!"

Silence fell on the Plains of Deosai. It was too high for birds to fly and live comfortably, so no night calls echoed in the trees.

Curt checked the night-imaging equipment in his combat helmet. Everything was working properly. He could see the Deosai facility projected on his helmet visor as plainly as if he were viewing it by daylight.

"Two minutes to zero!"

"Grey Head, Harrier Leader reports a dozen inbound targets, bearing two-seven-two magnetic, range six-seven, angels six kay! Just popped up. Holding radar stealth but popping in and out of infrared stealth. Must be having propulsion problems caused by lousy maintenance. We have a passive laser lock on them, and we have them in the gate."

"Pakistani?" was the single-word question from Curt.

"Best guess is Pak. We saw some French *Vultur* aerodynes at Ghazi. They have a problem maintaining i-r stealth because of their engines. A heavy maintenance item. The 'dynes are coming in from the direction of Ghazi."

"Keep tracking. Report any unusual behavior," Curt told his tacair commander.

"Roger. We'll maintain track while scan. And we'll report anything heading in from the direction of India too."

"Affirmative that! If India is involved in this, I need to know ASAP!"

"Roger, sir!"

"I'd like to communicate with those inbound targets. I want to know the Pak intentions. But I've just about got a furious furball on my hands here. Paul, if you have a moment, give the Paks a call on the milicom freak and ask their intentions."

"Roger, sir, but we're spooling into max lift condition at the moment. And this Harpy isn't the easiest thing to fly manually!"

"One minute to zero!"

Curt made a final check of everything. He remembered Henry's admonition: "Don't fergit nothing!"

The first Saucy Cans round arrived twenty seconds early.

Larry Hall had probably miscalculated time-of-flight of the rounds in this rarified air.

They burst over the Deosai facility, the brilliant flashes lighting up the Plains of Deosai.

Then all hell broke loose.

The Battle of the Deosai Plains had begun.

Chapter Twenty-Five

"Mister President, you've *got* to relieve Carson of command!"

The President of the United States was a retired Army general. So was his National Security Advisor. That didn't mean a special bond existed between them. The Old Comrades Network extended only as far as the Outer Ring of the Pentagon. Insofar as the President was concerned, it didn't stretch across the Potomac and into the White House.

"That's a pretty strong recommendation, Jeff," the Commander in Chief told him. It was still early in the morning, but Washington was literally on the other side of the planet from Kashmir. The President had arisen at his usual early hour, gone through the Army fitness exercises as he had for more than thirty years, had breakfast, read the domestic and foreign situation reports, gone over the intelligence document, made a few telephone calls, and finally come down to the Oval Office. There, Jeff Pickens was waiting for him, having nabbed the first appointment slot of the day on the basis of an urgent national security matter.

"Yes, Mister President. Colonel Curt Carson has done some damned strong harm and caused grievous injury to the security of the United States of America!" Jeff Pickens was livid with rage. He'd just come from a long and difficult telephone conversation with the Secretary of State. The honorable lady had been unruffled even by Pickens's wrath. And Pickens had also gotten nowhere with the Secretary of Defense.

Pickens had finally found an excuse to get Carson. In the process, he'd settle things with General Wild Bill Bellamack as well. This would clear the decks of the men who had caused him the most embarrassment in his career. And also take care of the one remaining general who he feared might still implicate him in the Gulf arms scandal. Pickens was clean. But he knew that scandals never die in Washington. They just lie around waiting to be put to political use.

What Carson had done in Pakistan gave Pickens the opening he needed. Furthermore, he could sound properly incensed about it because he was angry. Carson had behaved improperly, Pickens believed. Carson had gotten out of line again. So, Pickens, in a fit of pique, had decided to deal Carson out of the game.

But Pickens was finding no support for his crusade to cashier Colonel Curt Carson. The current commander of the Washington Greys was a popular military hero. Carson could thank the attention of media personality Maggie MacPhereson for a lot of it. Pickens suspected that the two of them had had a fantastic "horizontal interview" on Sakhalin Island several years before. This made Pickens jealous as well as angry. Maggie MacPhereson had never paid any attention to Pickens! Len Spencer's Pulitzer-winning book about Operation Diamond Skeleton in Namibia had also painted Carson with a hero's brush. Spencer, a former Presidential Press Secretary, was still writing and talking about Carson, and Spencer had clout that radiated in all directions from the National Press Club.

On top of it all, the American public liked the legendary, quiet, private soldier who led his own life and didn't seek the spotlight.

So, Pickens tried to elicit Presidential support before making his last effort among the Old Comrades Network in the offices of the Joint Chiefs.

The President wasn't grabbing for the gold ring Pickens had presented. "I saw nothing unusual in the morning intelligence briefs that would lead me to that conclusion, Jeff," the President told him flatly. "As far as I know, Operation Hell Fire is proceeding according to plan."

"But it's not!"

The President had almost run out of patience with his security advisor. The retired general who had been politically forced on the President was highly opinionated. Some of his security advice in the past three months since the inauguration had turned out wrong. This had created additional work for the Commander in Chief and the Secretary of Defense. Now Pickens was making strong claims against a man the President knew and liked. These allegations could destroy Carson's career. If untrue, they could demolish Carson under the news media doctrine of "guilt by intimidation," the support of Maggie MacPhereson and Len Spencer notwithstanding. When the news media found a juicy and sensationalistic story, they went into a feeding frenzy in which they told the truth (some of it) and nothing but the truth. And they usually did it with loaded semantics that changed truth into fiction and vice versa.

The President knew Curt Carson very well. He thought highly of the man. He'd had Carson in his command, both in the Washington Greys as a raw lieutenant out of West Point and as a field officer in the 17th Iron Fist Division.

"All right, Jeff, I'll give you the benefit of the doubt to start with here. Maybe you know something I don't. Or that Al Murray's people didn't put into my breakfast briefing. If so, I should know about it. So, tell me. Start at the beginning and end at the end. And don't embellish it. If I want additional information, I'll ask for it. Time is short today."

The President had a lot of work to do. Several of his bills were before Congress. He had to prepare for the West World Economic Summit. And he'd promised he'd fly out to Fort Ord for the military reactivation of that historic base. The Kashmir matter held only passing interest for him at this point. He'd made the necessary decisions. He'd given the necessary orders. He trusted the people involved. He saw no reason to change anything yet. But maybe Pickens had a legitimate snivel. So, the President sat back in his chair and prepared to listen.

"Operation Hell Fire was to be a joint American-Pakistani mission," Pickens began, setting up his ducks in a row as best he could. "We had to accede to the Pakistani demand for joint control. Pakistan is far too important from a strategic standpoint. It's the Western bulwark against East World on the Asian continent. The East Worlders have had to bypass Pakistan and the other Islamic nations to extend their military and economic influence westward into Africa. So, we can't upset the Paks! If we do, we risk upsetting the

Middle East. The whole Islamic League is a powder keg! It has been for centuries. The disaffection of one member could lead to a collapse of Islamic support for West World!"

As Pickens paused for breath, the President put in, "Jeff, I've been there too. I don't think the Muslims are going to pull away from us in West World. Our religions are too similar. And that's the underpinning of the economic bonds that hold the West World alliance together against East World!"

"Religions be damned, Mister President! Those people can believe what they want, and that doesn't affect how they look at the world. They're on the bottom, and they want to be king of the hill again like they were when they damned near conquered Europe! So, this is a military matter! The Paks are the first buffer against East World aggression! Iran and the Gulf nations make up the secondary one. If they weren't willing to put their own soldiers into the field with our money, equipment, and training, we'd have to commit American lives to the security of the region," Pickens concluded, trying to explain his outlook on the matter. It was based on his many years of service in the Gulf region and his long association with leaders, politicians, businessmen, and soldiers of the Islamic League.

And it was biased.

Bigoted is probably the better word.

As a result of his long service in the Middle East, Pickens didn't like the Muslims. He didn't like their religion, which treated Jesus Christ as just another prophet. And he didn't like their classic underhanded way of doing business that depended upon the bribe or baksheesh. All relationships in the Muslim community were also nepotistic, and this bothered Pickens. He hadn't enjoyed having to deal with everyone's cousin in order to get anything done. He preferred the quiet favoritism of friends who could be changed as conditions required. His Old Boy Network based on favors and obligations worked and worked well. It was somewhat different from the Old Comrades Network that was based on personal trust and honor. Pickens didn't realize the similarity between his cadre and Muslim nepotism.

Basically, Pickens wasn't really a military leader. He was a military bureaucrat. He'd led troops early in his career. Then he'd discovered that the difficulties of scrambling up the greasy pole of promotion depended upon Army politics and massaging the bureaucracy. So, he'd slowly evolved into a bureaucrat.

"What has this got to do with Colonel Carson?" the President wanted to know.

"He was ordered to work with the Pakistanis," Pickens complained. "When the Paks wouldn't do what he wanted yesterday...last night...whenever. I can't keep the time straight because it's halfway around the world. At any rate, just before the operation was to start, Carson told their commander to go piss up a rope!"

"Jeff, I don't know if this office is still bugged or not, and I don't care. If it is, your vulgarity isn't going to look very good in the history books. Either way, the language of the recruit isn't acceptable here," the President warned him. "So, Carson told off someone he thought was an idiot? What's the big deal there? So, what else is new? I've known Carson to do that before!"

"So have I! He did it to me in Kurdistan! And Bill Bellamack backed him to the hilt!"

"And Carson won the campaign," the President pointed out. And Carson had won others too. The President remembered Zahedan, Trinidad, Namibia, Sonora, and the still-classified Kerguelen Island operation. One of the President's last operational commands as a general officer had been at Battle Mountain, Nevada. He remembered how Carson had almost disobeyed direct orders but had been ready to move within seconds once the orders were changed.

The President went on. "Hell, Jeff, the man has served under me! I taught Belinda Hettrick and she taught Carson. I encouraged initiative and independent thinking among my subordinates. I know how Carson operates. He listens to orders. He evaluates their exact wording against what he knows to be the tactical and strategic situation. And believe me, Carson understands the world a lot better than many of my staff people here! Then he figures out how he can follow those orders and win. As you well know, sometimes we can't give the sort of direct order we'd like to issue. We have to clothe it in the language of politics and diplomacy, so the politicians don't cut us to ribbons. I face that problem every day behind this desk. Sometimes I wish I were back commanding the Washington Greys. That was a far easier job to do!"

"Mister President, do I get the distinct impression that you're defending Carson here?"

"Yes, you do! And you're perfectly right to infer that!" The Commander in Chief realized he was getting angry at his National Security Advisor, so he calmed himself down. "Jeff, if Colonel Carson told off a Pakistani officer, he probably had more than ample justification to do so! Tell me, just what did Carson do that's got you so upset?"

"Operation Hell Fire started out as a perfect example of international military cooperation," Pickens explained. "The Paks were going to move their crack Fourth Khyber Rifles up the Karakoram Highway. The Greys were airlifted into the Deosai Plains two days ahead of time in order to become partly acclimated. The assault on Deosai was to be a classic two-jaw pincer movement. However, the Khyber Rifles were delayed eight hours. Their regimental commander requested that the assault, code Hell Mover, be postponed twenty-four hours. Carson told Colonel Khan of the Rifles that the Greys couldn't wait. Therefore, Carson decided to assault Deosai unilaterally. Carson is doing it as we speak, and the Paks are still hours away. Carson might go down to defeat! That may cause a lot of damage to our national security out in that part of the world."

"Why did Carson decline to delay the operation? Why did he decide to attack when he did? He doesn't do those things without good reason." The President knew there had to be something more to the story than Pickens had reported. He wanted to get the whole story out of his National Security Advisor. Otherwise, he'd get it from JCS, and Pickens might be greatly embarrassed as a result.

"Carson reported that the Greys came under attack by the Chinese equivalent of the Boy Scouts."

"Is that all? And is that the Chinese paramilitary youth organization?"

"Yes. The Red Scouts. Like the Soviet Young Pioneers. In a way, something like our high school ROTC."

The President had been briefed as a congressman concerning the Red Scouts. According to Al Murray, those boys weren't equivalent to either the Boy Scouts or high school ROTC. They were possible cannon fodder. Chinese plans called for them to be used in any battle as a last reserve. The Nazis had had a similar organization in the waning days of World War II. But this was the first time the President had heard that the Red Scouts had actually been used in combat.

"I know about the Red Scouts. What happened? Any damage? Any casualties to the Greys?"

"One Grey killed, three Greys wounded, and two vehicles destroyed. The Greys slaughtered nearly fifty Chinese boys."

"That's what I thought! Carson had justification for not wanting to delay. The man exhibits an exceptional concern for his personnel."

"And apparently damned little concern for the overall security posture of this nation!"

"So, he attacked to get the job done. Why do you think we sent the Washington Greys over there, Jeff? It wasn't to keep the Paks happy. It was to get into that NE facility, find out what it is, and get those Chinese scientists out of there!"

"But Mister President, in the process of doing that, he's got the whole Pakistani government damned upset with us!"

The President thought about this for a moment, then gave vent to one word that had become a part of Army parlance:

"*Scroom!*"

"Sir!"

"Sorry, Jeff, I disobeyed my own policy regarding vulgarisms in this office," the President said quietly. "Carson is doing what he was sent over there to do. I may not be able to give him a medal for doing it, but I'll figure out some way to reward him. As for making the Paks unhappy, I've got a whole State Department that worries about such things for me. Or is Fran Kellogg on your side in this?" The Chief Executive had a way of asking sudden and embarrassing questions.

"Uh, I talked with her, sir."

"I'm sure you did. What did she say, Jeff?"

"I don't understand her. She smiled. She said it would give her a real problem to tackle for a change."

It was the President's turn to smile. He'd chosen his Secretary of State with care. It was paying off.

"Tell me, Jeff, do you think we should pander to the Paks? Or anyone else in the world?"

"Sir, we must stay on good terms with them. Our national security requires it."

"So, you would rather base our national security on purchased friends rather than friends who respect us?"

"I said nothing about buying friends, sir."

"Jeff, money isn't the only thing of value that can be exchanged between people."

"Are you talking security umbrellas, sir?"

The President shook his head. "Not any more than the Police Commissioner of the District of Columbia talks about it. Or asks the citizens he protects for a pay-off. Citizens of this city or any visitors have the right to be secure in their persons. It wasn't always that way. It's the job of the police department to provide that security. They don't have to do it by bravado. Or by roughing up people, although the police carry nightsticks and know how to use them. Or even by shooting people, even though policemen carry loaded guns. They maintain order by their presence and the knowledge on the part of others that quick and positive action will be taken in case of trouble. So what's so different about the United States being the policeman in the world? You've heard me say it a hundred times:

The world may not like a policeman, but the world also knows that it's nice to have one around so everyone can go about their business without fear. It's only necessary that the policeman be respected, even if his presence is disliked. Especially by bullies. A necessary evil, if you will. But I'm preaching again."

The Chief Executive paused, then said, "East World is presently the group trying to bully the world. They're trying to do it militarily, economically, and psychologically. National security is a matter of keeping people of this nation safe everywhere in the world. That means we must keep the world itself safe. The world today is pretty small." He leaned forward and put his hands on the big desk top. That desk had been used by many people for over a century. Some were fondly remembered. Others had been crooks. Some had tried very hard but had been unable to live up to the responsibilities of the job. And some had merely sat behind the desk. "So now what do, you want me to do about Operation Hell Fire and Colonel Curt Carson?"

"I haven't changed my mind, Mister President. He's a loose cannon."

"Well, Jeff, Carson may be loose, but I know exactly where he's going to roll on the deck! He's reliable in his unreliability! So, what do you want to do with him?"

"I can only advise you, sir. And my advice is to move him out of the direct line of command."

The Chief Executive didn't say anything for a moment. Then he asked his National Security Advisor, "Jeff, how long has it been since you were in combat?"

It was Pickens's turn to hesitate. "Sir, I've been in command of units up to theater command, but you know I've never been in combat."

"I just wanted to make sure you remembered that, Jeff." The President had been shot at as commander of the Iron Fist Division. "As for removing Carson from command now, I can't and won't do it. One of my predecessors pulled the Iron Fist Division out of Yemen in the middle of a battle they were winning. It almost cost the Army four good regiments and all the people in them! So, I'll be damned if I'll joggle a man's elbow when he's fighting for his life with his friends and comrades, doing something he was told to do! Got any other suggestions?"

"All right, sir, when Operation Hell Fire is over and we have to pick up the pieces, take care of him then. Put him somewhere else if you don't want to get rid of him. Some nice base command somewhere. A faculty position in one of the service schools. In some advisory slot where he can't interact with foreign military officers and screw up this nation's security!" Pickens was adamant. The conversation with the Commander in Chief hadn't caused him to deviate one mil from his target.

Recently, Carson had embarrassed him once in Kurdistan. Then done it again in testimony before Congress following the Yemen debacle. And he would have damned near done so in Senegambia if Pickens hadn't been fast on his feet. Pickens hadn't forgotten for a moment. But he realized that maybe he'd blown his one big chance to get Carson. Pickens now knew he hadn't prepared his assault plan very well.

The President thought about Pickens's advice for a moment, then nodded. "Thank you, Jeff. I'll probably take your advice. I think I know just what I'm going to do with Colonel Carson when he gets back from Operation Hell Fire."

Maybe he'd won after all, Pickens thought as he left the Oval Office.

Chapter Twenty-Six

"Hellcat Leader, Black Hawk Four! First air burst salvo is twenty-five meters long!" One of Captain Dale Brown's Black Hawks from the birdbot unit was calling the shots from a Harpy assault aerodyne that suddenly swept into the Deosai facility area.

"Hellcat Leader, this is Scout Two! I'm on the ground and closer to the bursts. Make that twenty meters long!"

"Black Hawk Four and Scout Two, Hellcat Leader here! We're correcting! But you've got to admit that's pretty close at a range of seven thousand at a high angle over a ridge to boot!"

By the time the second Saucy Cans salvo arrived over the barracks targets, other action had started.

The fiery trails of 100mm M100A tube rockets, the multi-purpose Smart Farts, sliced the night darkness. Curt could see only two of them but knew the others were on their way. The missiles homed on the perimeter guard towers where the Red Hammer patrol warbots were controlled. Their smart guidance systems meant that they didn't miss. The 250-gram subnuclear non-radioactive warhead on the M100 was equivalent to a hundred times the same weight of Comp D high explosive. It could take out an armored vehicle with 300 millimeters of special armor. What such a warhead did to a steel guard tower was simple to describe: It obliterated it.

Most of the patrolling Red Hammers lurched to a halt. They didn't even swing their 53-millimeter cannons around to search for targets.

No one wasted Smart Farts against the patrolling Red Hammers unless the Chinese warbots looked like they were continuing to function. Those that appeared to remain working after the destruction of the control towers were promptly hit by other Smart Farts.

Rocketing the Red Hammers was overkill. But the Greys weren't taking chances on any new Chinese developments. The best G-2 and the latest information from McCarthy Proving Ground indicated the Red Hammers would be put out of action when their control centers were destroyed. But intelligence reports could be wrong, and a prudent warrior doesn't bet the farm on them.

East World war robots were a step above the crude Russian Silver Pilgrims. The Greys had encountered the *Syeryebro Palomneek* warbots on Sakhalin. They found them to be Russian copies of the old American Mark 60 Heavy Fire warbots, the obsolete Hairy Foxes. The Red Hammers were yet another duplication of the Mark 60, a literal Chinese copy. However, their command and control technology was as modern as shoes with laces. Only the American warbots were controlled by neuroelectronic linkage, the most highly classified military secret since the atom bomb.

"Grey Head, Mustang Leader! I confirm that the Red Hammers on the east perimeter are out of action! No sign of any laser command beams incoming to them. But they're swinging interrogation beams around trying to locate a new command center!"

"Are you in a position to take out their laser command pickups?" Curt wanted to know.

"Not at this time, Grey Head!" Dyani replied.

The second Saucy Cans salvo arrived on target. This salvo was mixed air burst and fused for ground targets. Four barracks erupted in the explosions of the ground burst rounds whose smart warheads found what they were looking for. The air bursts sprayed lethal shards of steel and high-density thermoplastic over the area. This was just in time to catch the first wave of human riflemen that erupted from the barracks.

The Mary Anns of Alpha Unit commenced firing, picking their targets as they emerged from the barracks.

"This is a goddamned fucking turkey shoot!" Russ Frazier yelled.

"Don't count on it! It just started!" Edie replied.

"But it's a Chinese fire drill in there! Look at them running around outside the barracks!" Russ persisted. "Just like a bunch of chickens when the tornado hits the coop!"

"Russ, we've done this before! You ought to know by now that when the attack is going well, we should be looking for the ambush!" Curt warned him. "Watch minus-x! *Always* watch minus-x!"

The regimental commander was pleased thus far. But he was also cautious. The assault had been too easy. Where were the other forty-plus Red Hammers? And possible boy soldiers who'd pulled the boring duty of night guards?

Reece reported no East Worlders outside the perimeter. But Curt wasn't sure. And he wasn't about to hang the whole operation on the verity of those reports. The Red Scouts had gotten right into their midst earlier in the day. Boys have a tendency to be very sneaky in the woods. They can move faster, present smaller targets, and be crawling up your back before you know they're there. He remembered his own boyhood days playing Capture the Flag, Hide-and-Seek, 40-Kilo Killer Gorillas, and other youthful versions of war. The Red Scouts didn't play such non-lethal games; they played for keeps.

"Alpha Leader and Bravo Leader, this is Grey Head! Watch your minus-x! I say again: Watch your minus-x! It's going too damned good!" Curt broadcast the warning via tacomm to his unit commanders.

"Alpha is looking! Negative on targets in our minus-x!"

"Bravo sees nothing in minus-x!"

"Black Hawk Leader, this is Grey Head! Do you see anything from up there that we ought to watch out for?" Curt asked his airborne scouts.

"Negatory, Grey Head, and we're looking. Not easy to shift from birdbot recce to doing the real thing with calibrated eyeballs!"

Another call came in from a Harpie overhead. "Grey Head, Black Hawk Two upstairs! I have a make on multiple Red Hammers emerging from the large shed north-east of the main building! They appear to be heading toward the south perimeter and Alpha Unit."

"I'll be go to hell! They don't know Bravo is here!" Russ exclaimed.

"Let's let them keep thinking that way, Russ," Curt told him. "Orders: Bravo cease fire and go to stealth! The new Red Hammers will probably pass between us and the barracks anyway."

He toggled his tacomm. "Alpha Leader, this is Grey Head. Do you have the make on the Red Hammers corning south on the right side of your front?"

"Ah, not, not yet...Okay, we have them! Affirmative, Grey Head! Just saw them! Okay, we've got good tac display data from Black Hawk on them!" Kitsy replied.

"Be prepared for a Red Hammer frontal assault on your unit," Curt warned her.

"Roger that! Can we get some tacair support? I'm going to need some heavy tacair against Red Hammers! Can Hellcat Leader move his barrage in about fifteen meters? That will lay the next salvo right on top of the Red Hammers! But I want to make sure! Alpha needs tacair. Alpha needs tacair *now!*"

"Harrier Leader, did you read Alpha Leader?" Curt asked.

"Affirmative! You want us to take out some Red Hammers?"

"Roger! Can you see them?"

"Put a laser designator on them for my Smart Farts to see!"

"Be careful! They could aim return fire on that designator!" Curt said in warning.

"I won't need it until after I fire tubes!" the Harpie pilot pointed out.

"Okay, Harrier Leader, let me know when you fire! Hellcat Leader, we need some SADARM rounds targeted for Red Hammers! Do you have their signatures in the data base?"

"Affirmative, Alpha Leader! Next salvo is going for the Red Hammers! SADARM heads! Here they come!"

The battle was now beginning to move on its own, taking its own flow and carving its own channel of action. The best that Curt could do was to watch this flow and try to direct his units to take advantage of openings.

"Black Hawk One reporting! More Red Hammers from the shed! They're heading west!" said another reconnaissance report from a Harpie overhead.

"Those Red Hammers must be controlled from somewhere! They're not artificially intelligent! And they're not being run in linkage with a Chinese warbot brainy. Anyone have a make on their control centers?" Curt wanted to know.

"Negatory! Nothing seen on the usual laser or micro-beam channels they use!"

"Grey Head, this is Grey Major!" came the call from Henry Kester up on the ridge. "I'm seeing something new on the spectrum sweeps from up here. It appears to be centered on the big building. Looks like something transmitting at several simultaneous frequencies in the electromagnetic spectrum. But I can't get a solid reading on it. Sort of like trying to pick up an FM radio signal with an AM receiver. It's there, but it isn't. Or like hearing a single sideband transmission without the carrier. Garbage. No pattern to it!"

"Any way to jam it, Henry?" Curt asked.

"Ask Edie."

"Edie?"

"Henry, try noise jamming one kilohertz on either side of what you're getting," Sampson told the regimental sergeant major, who'd been forced by a wound to stay out of the fight up on the ridge. "That might interfere with the main transmission. Otherwise, look at the phase between the electric and magnetic fields of the signals."

"Grey Tech, I don't see either one! I see a signal that's muddy but with no electric or magnetic field vectors!"

"What the hell?" Edie asked rhetorically. "What the hell kind of e-m transmission doesn't have field vectors?"

"Colonel, let's move Bravo in behind those Red Hammers," Russ suggested verbally to Curt. "Once they've gone past us to the south, we've got a clear shot at the main building! Then we can harass their ass."

"Edie, you and Henry stay on this weirdo radiation thing," Curt ordered. "Pick a chat freak and monitor the tac freak." He turned his attention to the tactical situation. "Russ, how many Red Hammers have been accounted for?"

"Wait one…The five on patrol were scrubbed. Eighteen came down the east side in front of us. Twenty-four are heading for the west side. Forty-seven total. Initial force estimates were forty-plus."

"Okay, that could be fifty or sixty too. I concur with your suggestion," Curt told him, then told his operations officer, "As soon as Bravo can work forward behind the Red Hammers to the main building, go for it! But watch minus-x! We could find another twenty Red Hammers harassing *our* ass!"

"Roger that!"

"Mustang Leader, Grey Head here! What sort of perimeter fence are they using? I haven't seen any wire."

"No wire, Colonel. Must be i-r or laser detector. Proximity barrier stuff," Dyani reported from somewhere out in the darkness in front of him.

"Okay, I want you to check it out before we send anyone through it," Curt told her.

"I've got four of us already through the perimeter security facilities," Dyani responded. "We're on the inside. No big deal. They depended on their Red Hammers to provide perimeter security."

As he checked his displays, Curt saw that in the melee he'd missed the fact that Dyani and three of her troopers were already "inside" the Deosai compound.

It was time to get in there and do their job. He turned to Pendleton and Taisha. "Are you ready to move? Ready to go?"

Pendleton checked the action of his Novia and nodded. "We're not getting our job done just standing around out here in the dark," he muttered. "I'm ready. I'll shoot at anyone who shoots at me. Or at Taisha."

Taisha didn't seem to be frightened of the possibility of being shot at. She calmly said, "Yes, Owen, let's do our job. The sooner we get Doctor Dongzhu and his colleagues out of the combat area, the better. We can't afford to lose him. He's one of the top neuroelectronic scientists in the world!"

"Will you know him when you see him?" Curt asked her.

She nodded. "I have never met him. But I have watched videotapes of his lectures. And seen him on interactive video conferences. He's never been out of China."

"Will he know *you?*"

"Of course not! But he will recognize American military uniforms."

"I hope so," Curt muttered. "I also hope he isn't spooked by this attack. If he's picked up a gun, he could be trigger-happy. I'd hate to have to shoot him in order to rescue him!"

"Colonel, it is my understanding that Doctor Dongzhu is a non-violent person, one who detests violence," Taisha told him forcefully. "That is why it did not surprise me when we received his message that he wished to be rescued from this weapons establishment!"

"We'll see," Curt muttered, knowing full well that many non-violent and pacifistic people could be very vicious and deadly when frightened or backed against the wall. He wasn't going to take any chances. "Owen, I want you and Taisha to stick to me like a composite welding compound. Getting Dongzhu out is only one of our objectives. You've got to make the scientific evaluation of this place. You'll need protection and support. I'm the one that provides it. If you get separated from me, toggle your beacon ident. Owen, you got your body armor on?"

"Damned right! Getting shot without it is sort of hazardous to the integrity of my mainframe!"

"Taisha?"

"I cannot wear that tight and restrictive garment."

"Goddammit! I told you to put it on!" Curt exploded. Then he went on with less anger. "Well, you didn't. I can't take time now while you do! If you get shot, you're going to have a hole put in you! So don't get shot!"

"I do not intend to. You are supposed to provide protection," Taisha pointed out.

"Taisha, I've got no control over wild shots," Curt advised her, then hitched his Novia up into carry position. "Bravo Leader, this is Grey Head! 'Charge for the guns!'"

Frazier recognized the quote from Tennyson's *The Charge of the Light Brigade*. "'Into the Valley of Death,'" he replied. "Bravo Unit all, this is Bravo Leader! Forward to the main building!"

To Curt, it was a strange advance. He had to depend on his night-vision sensors because everything beyond his helmet seemed to be shrouded in total darkness. All he could see was the scattered lighting of the Deosai facility. But through his sensors, he could see well. The main illumination for his i-r sensors was coming from orbit where an infrared beam was spearing down through the atmosphere on the Plains of Deosai. It was, in a sense, an artificial sun whose light could be seen only by those using the night-vision sensors such as Curt had on his combat helmet. Pendleton and Thisha didn't have night-vision sensors, so they were forced to follow him closely.

Not only was he short of breath because of the altitude, but he knew he was having a lot of trouble trying to think straight.

The high mountain meadow was covered with soft dirt and short grass. The area of the facility perimeter was more churned up than the meadow. Construction activities had disturbed it. Curt almost stumbled over the raw earth when he reached the perimeter road where the Red Hammer warbots had patrolled.

He checked his chronometer display on his helmet visor; it was too dark to see his watch on his wrist.

It was 2022. The Alpha assault had been on for only seven minutes.

Time had suddenly gone into slow motion, it seemed. Either that or the action was moving much faster than Curt anticipated.

"Alpha Leader, this is Grey Head! Bravo Unit has crossed the east perimeter!" Curt warned Kitsy. "Be careful not to fire into us!"

"We see your beacons, Grey Head and Bravo Leader!" Kitsy's voice came back on the tacomm brick. She was barely audible over the roar and crash of battle. "We're making lots of noise and nuisance on the south side! Hope that provides enough distraction for you!"

"How are you holding?"

"On tight!" was Kitsy's strained reply. She was under stress. "We can hold the Red Hammers! And we've taken out most of the adult soldiers. When we get a minute to look over their casualties, I think we'll find a mixed bag of Chinese and Hindus in this place. Got no trouble fighting them. But it's these kids that are giving us fits! They're so small and fast! And dammit, I don't like shooting boys who ought to be playing marbles! Can't shoot their balls off! They haven't got any yet!"

The compound was smaller than Curt imagined. Or they were making fast progress. He couldn't tell which. Bravo Unit got to the main building within minutes. Dyani and Sid Johnson were guarding a door they'd kicked open. Hassan and Steve Zugg deployed on either side of it, and their troopers were arrayed around the opening, most of them prone with their Novias aimed toward through the door.

"Anyone inside, Hassan?" Curt called.

"I don't know. I think so. My chem sensors get some readings. Mostly fear stink. Not unusual," the young officer replied. Then he asked cautiously, "Do we toss in a stun grenade? Or do we rush it? We've got no passive i-r illumination inside, so we've either got to break i-r stealth with helmet illuminators or use ambient light."

"No explosives! No shooting!" Taisha. yelled. "We don't know who's in there! And we don't know what equipment might be damaged!"

"I concur with Rosha!" Pendleton added over the roar of battle.

"Goddammit, that means we've got to punch in there and maybe take it in the shorts going through the door," Curt pointed out. He was unwilling to risk his people in such a vulnerable assault.

"Hassan, stand aside and let me go in there with Elliott!" Mickie Mikawa urged. "I'm so small they'll probably shoot over my head if they're shooting!"

Hassan yelled, "Okay, Mickie! Go! I'm right with you! Bobby Lee, are you up to it?"

"Shag ass and bypass, Captain!" came the call from Master Sergeant Robert Lee Garrison.

Before Curt could either object or agree, they'd done it. He would have let them anyway because they'd volunteered, done it on their own initiative.

Everyone was prepared for the rapid series of shots that followed immediately.

What they weren't prepared for was the call from Dyani. "Cease fire! It's Zeb Long and Deer Arrow! We came in through the roof ventilator!"

"Dyani! Did I hit you?" Mickie yelled.

"Yes! I'll have a welt for a week! Get in here! This place is a mad scientist's laboratory! You aren't going to believe this!" Dyani promised.

"Move it, Owen! In the door!" Curt urged. "Zugg, you and Joe Rose watch this door! Make sure-!"

He was almost thrown off his feet by the blast of an explosion.

"Dammit, Hellcat Leader, lift your fire on the main building!" Curt snapped into his tacomm as he staggered to maintain his balance.

"The Hellcats aren't firing on the main building!" Larry Hall's voice came back.

"Grey Head, Harrier Leader here! Take cover! Take cover! You're under tacair assault!"

"What the hell is going on?" Curt wanted to know.

"It's those *Vulturs* that were inbound! They went right past us without a twitch. They're Pakistani! They're laying ordnance on the main building!"

Chapter Twenty-Seven

"Pakistani *Vulturs?* Dammit, what the hell are they doing? Don't they know we're down here?" Russ Frazier exploded in anger. He heard something roar overhead. So, he pointed his Novia in that general direction and squeezed off a burst.

"Knock it off, Russ! You aren't going to create a Golden BB! Not if you haven't even got an i-r make on the target!" Curt yelled at his operations staffer.

"Yeah, I know, but it makes me feel better!" Russ fired back.

Curt knew he probably should take cover himself if the Pakistani *Vulturs* were laying ordnance. He didn't know whether the Paks had any smart people-seeking bombs. Or whether they were dropping dumb iron bombs just to flatten the area. He didn't know and didn't care. His first thought was to get those Pak aerodynes off the backs of the Greys.

He called up to his tacair support. "Harrier Leader, this is Grey Head! Knock off the recce! Go for those Pak 'dynes! Get them off our ass! Blow their shorts off!"

It was Colonel Cal Worsham's gravelly voice that replied. "Grey Head, this is Warhawk Leader! What the *hell* do you *think* we're doing? Sitting our *asses* up here burning up *fuel?* Christ, we let only *two* of them sneak through and drop *something* near you. What the hell, am I *never* going to hear the fucking *end* of it!"

"Worsham, you're supposed to be coordinating the exit airlift! What the hell are you doing up there in the furball?" Curt wanted to know.

He did know, and it was stupid of him to even ask. But he wasn't thinking quite straight at the moment. The altitude was indeed affecting his thinking processes, and he now knew it. He told himself he'd have to be extra careful and not pop off short when it came to decisions and orders. He also asked himself what the hell he was doing down on the ground right in the middle of the fight. The field manuals said that a regimental commander shouldn't be out in the FEBA. Curt usually ignored the books.

"What do you *think* I'm doing? *Playing* with this joystick? Damned *lousy* name for it, by the way." Under the stress of combat, Cal Worsham was even more vulgar and almost disrespectful.

Curt let it pass. The man was an outstanding air commander. The Army was lucky to have him. On the other hand, the Aerospace Force would have difficulty finding a slot for a pilot like Worsham.

Worsham went on. "The Chippies are either *inbound* per schedule and plan. Or they're *sitting* on the ground at Ghazi *ready* to spool up! I've got *my* part of this sheep screw working! I don't *know* about anyone *else!*...Ned, *look out!* Seven o'clock high! *On your tail!* I can get him if I jink!"

Another Pakistani bomb struck the barracks to the south of Curt's position. The explosion threw debris, rocks, boards, and pieces of people into the air. Some of this fell around Curt.

Saucy Cans fire continued to rain down on the barracks area, turning it into a lethal hell for unarmored foot soldiers.

Curt knew he shouldn't be out there where a stray bomb or a slightly over-ranged 75mm air-burst round might catch him. But he was having a lot of trouble thinking decisively at 5,600 meters altitude. The lack of oxygen was killing his night vision. It was also affecting his ability to think straight. He felt like he'd been tranquilized. Serious matters didn't seem to make much difference to him. As a result, he didn't move. He remained in the open running his hand-held tacomm and trying to get this latest sheep screw straightened out.

It took a conscious and definite effort of willpower for him to maintain command of himself and of the situation.

So, he snapped over the tacomm to Worsham, "You've got an air-to-air milicom freak. Get on it and tell the Paks to knock it off! I'm trying to get the word to the Paks at Ghazi or Islamabad so orders will get passed upward. Something screwed up!" Curt told his air boss.

"*Screw* talking to them!" Worsham yelled back, his coarse and loud voice almost overloading the audio circuits of every communication mode between his microphone and Curt's tacomm speaker. "They're *shooting* at me! And at *you!* I'm not standing *still* for that sort of shit! I'm busy as *hell* trying to shoot down twelve Pak *bastards* before they shoot down my eight Harpies! And before they plant *something* right on top of you!"

"Try talking to them on milicom, Cal," Curt urged him.

"Don't you *think* I tried milicom? *Shit,* the Paks aren't *talking!* They're *shooting!*" Worsham replied in haste and anger. It was obvious he was very busy flying an aerodyne manually, allowing the autopilot only to maintain some semblance of stability in the violent maneuvers. "Now shut the hell up! I've got to save *my* ass and *yours* too!" Worsham was under pressure. He was fighting for his life. The Harriers had only eight Harpy tacair aerodynes over Deosai; they were trying to handle a dozen enemy 'dynes.

A Harpy is a small aerodyne, but it isn't a full-fledged dogfighting airplane. It's intended for ground pounding, rock busting, gravel grinding, mud moving, and destroying enemy warbots from the air. Technically, it is *not* an air superiority fighter.

But no one had ever bothered to tell this to Cal Worsham or his tacair flight, Hands' Harriers. Or if they had, Cal and the Harriers hadn't listened. Like all pilots, they didn't always fly straight and level when they were upstairs. And they didn't just practice rolling-in attack runs when they were out flying training missions on the Goldwater Gunnery Range in southern Arizona.

Give any two pilots any two aircraft with any sort of maneuverability. Then put them out in an empty piece of sky. They will go one-on-one in a "friendly" dogfight. Sometimes, they will turn on the cameras just so they could see later who "shot down" who. The taped results often determine who buys the drinks. This tape rarely is seen by anyone other than the Warhawks.

Curt knew this. And he'd always managed to be doing something else when Worsham's people decided to play. He'd seen some of the videotapes. Although such activities were definitely non-reg, Curt was aware of two things. First, he knew he could issue all the orders in the world, but the orders couldn't stop it. And second, in a real combat situation someday, that fun-and-games practice might save the individual Warhawks and Harriers.

It was doing that right then.

The Harpies were outnumbered. But they had an advantage. They carried very effective night-combat equipment.

With this night-vision equipment, the Harpy pilots could see the *Vulturs* in the darkness. No matter that an aerodyne has engine exhausts that are naturally stealthed. The lift slots were still hotter than the rest of the aerodyne. The rapid expansion of the slot exhaust also cooled it quickly, but still not enough to drop it to ambient temperature. And the aerodyne airframe itself was usually either hotter or colder than its background.

On top of that, an aerodyne makes a good radar target even if it's covered with radar-absorbing material. Its slots, canopy, gun ports, weapon bay doors, or cargo doors break the low-observable features. Furthermore, the French *Vulturs* hadn't been sold with the best RAM on them. The French weren't about to sell all their top technology. And the Pakistanis didn't have the technical and repair know-how to maintain the stealth features. The Dzus fasteners used to hold the engine access doors in place, for example, provided enough radar return to make the *Vulturs* bloom on the Harpy's airborne radar.

And the French hadn't sold the Pakistanis those aerodynes with full night-sensor suites. So, the Pak pilots didn't know where the Harpies were.

Another factor was pertinent, Curt knew. The Harpies were well maintained. Their low-observable features were carefully inspected to make sure they were functional. Worsham's philosophy was simple: If his aerodynes were going to carry around all the additional weight of low-observable features., he believed those features should work. On the other hand, the Pakistanis, in common with people from other Muslim cultures in the Middle East, didn't like to do repair and maintenance work. It was considered to be beneath their manly dignity. They hired European or American mechanics and technicians instead.

As a result, the repair and maintenance often weren't done well. The mercenary technicians weren't the ones riding around in those *Vulturs* with their pink bods exposed. And if the 'dynes crashed out in the wild of Pakistan, chances are the Paks would never know why or never try to find out. The technicians didn't feel at risk for their jobs. So, the *Vulturs* might be working well, but probably were working only well enough to fly. That's all the Pakistanis really counted on: "Kick the tires and light the fires!"

Curt realized that Worsham had his hands full aloft. So, he decided to get directly to the Paks and have them knock off this nonsense. He switched tacomm channels. "Grey Major, Grey Head! Get me through to Khyber Head!"

"You've got it, Grey Head!"

"Khyber Head, Grey Head here! Acknowledge!"

It took twenty seconds of calling before the thick voice of Colonel Iskander Khan replied. "Khyber Head here. Go ahead, Grey Head!"

"What the hell are your aerodynes doing attacking Deosai?"

"The plan originally called for a night attack to soften up the defenses. We're stopped in bivouac for the night. You woke me up."

"Sorry as hell about that, Khan, but we don't fight nine-to-five battles! Now goddammit, knock off the tacair attack on Deosai! We're inside the Deosai perimeter! Those *Vulturs* are laying ordnance on us!"

"You were told to stay on the ridge and in bivouac."

"And I told you I couldn't because our presence had been discovered! The surprise element of our combined assault had been compromised! I told you I was commencing the assault after sundown! You *knew* we were here!" Curt snarled at the Pakistani commander. "Now you listen to me and listen up! Get on the hooter to Ghazi. Get those 'dynes the hell and gone out of here!"

"I'm in the Pakistani Army, Carson. I have no control over what the Pakistani Air Force does."

"The hell you don't! You got 'em here! You called for air strikes tonight. I thought you'd called off the airborne stuff when you couldn't hack the schedule. Now I think you forgot! So you get...them off our ass, or I will."

"Oh? How do you propose to do that?"

As Curt watched, the sky lit up with an explosion. A Pak *Vultur* had blown up in midair. He watched as it fell. When it hit the ground outside the perimeter, it made a huge fireball that lit up the Plains of Deosai. Curt waited until the shock wave of the explosion reached him. "Hear that, Khan? That's one of your *Vulturs* becoming a smoking hole in the ground! You just lost a couple of million dollars' worth of aircraft! Justify that to Islamabad! We're shooting your 'dynes out of the sky. What the hell, did you think we didn't have any anti-air capability? We'll continue to shoot them down until they get the hell out of here! My Harpy pilots are good, Khan! They've also got better night-fighting equipment."

"You'll have to account for your actions to my government, Carson!"

"Not if the records show we were attacked by your Air Force! Khan, in one minute I'm getting on the horn to Washington. And in ten minutes you won't be a colonel anymore."

Curt didn't know if he could pull off that one or not, but he knew he was acting with pretty high authority in the first place. He could certainly make life difficult for Khan when this was over. The Pakistani government knew where it stood between East World and West World. Curt didn't believe the Pakistanis wanted to jeopardize that position, especially by antagonizing the United States. Insofar as Curt was concerned, the Paks had done plenty of that anyway. He also knew that Pakistan preferred to side with West World. Otherwise, taking sides with East World would mean being overrun, occupied, and turned into a puppet satellite. The Americans, on the other hand, would give them military aid money, sell them weapons, and occasionally deploy a military unit to help the Paks get out of deep slime.

Curt figured he might be able to bluff this through Khan. He had to try. He recalled what General Belinda Hettrick had once told him: *"It's all a matter of bluff, Curt! Really it is!"*

Curt could play a mean hand of poker as well as hold his own in the Chinese game of Go. On the other hand, Khan had never had that kind of off-duty training.

"So get on the by-God horn to Ghazi, Khan! And get those 'dynes the hell and gone out of here! I haven't got time to snivel at you. And I'm not going to plead with you. I'm not going to fuck around! My people will finish shooting down those mothers in about four minutes. Then you're going to be in deep slime, believe me! Better start figuring out how you're going to explain to your Defense Minister the loss of twelve expensive French *Vulturs*. Especially when I've warned you what's happening! And told you what I'm doing about it to protect my unit! Grey Head out!"

He quickly toggled the tac frequency. "Alpha Leader, this is Grey Head! We're trying to get those Pak 'dynes off your ass!"

"Don't sweat it, Grey Head," Kitsy's voice came back. She sounded hassled but in control. He could tell that the altitude was getting to her too. She was breathing hard, almost gasping between words. "Nick just put a Smart Fart into one that came too close. From the looks of things here, the Harriers are having their own brand of fun up there. We've got this sheep screw about as much under control as we're going to at the moment! Go do your job. Get in there and get the hell out with what we came for!"

Another Saucy Cans salvo burst over the barracks area and the south perimeter where the fighting was going on.

Another fireball erupted in the sky.

"Got him! Got him! Got the sonofabitch!" came the cry from one of the Harrier pilots.

"Thank God! Then maybe you can knock off all this aerobatic crap," said one of the birdbot operators who was riding along to perform reconnaissance. "God-damned aircraft doesn't have any sick sacks..."

"Aw, sorry! Can't you take a few g's?"

"Head to toe, yeah. But not four ways at once! Pass the paper."

"Grey Head, this is Grey Major." Henry's voice alerted him on the tacomm.

"Go ahead, Henry," Curt replied quickly.

"Sir, I've noticed a little change in the modulation patterns I reported earlier," Henry reported. "I still don't know what the hell they are, but they're definitely there. And changing! Now it looks like voice patterns, but not quite."

"Record it, Henry."

"I am. I don't let nothing get by me if I can help it." Henry paused, then added, "Sir, you did the Greys proud by the way you told off Genghis Khan."

"Not everyone is like you, Henry. Not everyone listens to reason."

"Who says there's any reason in this at all?" the old master sergeant fired back. "I'm really beginning to think I'm getting too old for this crap...even in the rear and not busting my ass."

"Must be the altitude, Henry. I haven't noticed that you're any less mean than before."

"The milk of human kindness leaked out of me years ago, Colonel."

Curt knew that wasn't really true, but he had to get back to work. He decided that the situation was being handled well enough at the moment. The Greys weren't winning yet. But they weren't losing either. And they weren't taking heavy casualties or damage. Time to get with the main objective of the operation. So, he put his tacomm brick in beeper mode and slipped it into its position on his right hip. Then he headed toward the open door into the main Deosai facility.

The huge form of Master Sergeant Carol Head was waiting for him. He was standing just inside with his Jeep on the job as door guard. Without a word, he took Curt's arm in the dark and led him through the light curtain just inside the door. The curtain was part of a complex light lock that prevented the bright interior illumination from spilling outside.

"Colonel, the rest have gone ahead," Head advised him. "They sent me back to guide you in. Not to worry. No guards in here that we've found. This place must be cosmic top secret. No one gets in except those who are cleared and supposed to be here. No need to place guards for that. But you're not going to like what you see."

Curt couldn't figure out what the big Moravian master sergeant meant.

He soon discovered why he'd said that.

The brightly lit interior was like a set out of an old, low-budget science-fiction movie.

The interior of the main building at the Deosai facility was typical millennium high-tech architecture: strictly functional with no embellishment or ornamentation. It was like an industrial plant.

Head took him down a long, well-lit corridor. Their steps echoed off the hard walls.

The main building was perhaps fifteen meters tall. It looked like the inside of a chemical factory or a refinery. It also smacked of a prison.

The interior was split by long, high bays and corridors with two steel balconies or stoops above.

Some areas were filled with piping and large tanks. Curt saw other parts of the building that housed complex computers and other electronic equipment.

Head led him through a heavy fire door into a room that was less brightly lit than the rest of the building.

Curt didn't believe what he saw.

More than a dozen naked human forms lay on gurney-type tables at waist height. Pendleton and Taisha were hovering over one of these bodies.

The body of the man on the gurney was festooned with long

acupuncture needles that bad been inserted through its skin. Some of the needles had wires attached to them. The wires led to a complex computer array nearby. The man's head was covered with primitive EEG pickup electrodes, and his chest was arrayed with EKG pickups. A feeding tube entered his nose. Catheters had been inserted to remove urine and feces. Extensive vital-signs monitoring equipment was also nearby.

Every one of the still bodies in the room was similarly arrayed.

The man was breathing, but his breath was shallow.

"Good God in heaven, what's this?" Curt asked in both amazement and disgust.

"We don't yet know for sure," Pendleton told him.

"Well, let's find Doctor Dongzhu," Curt suggested. "This is supposed to be his."

Taisha looked up at Curt briefly and announced, "This is Doctor Wen Ling Dongzhu!"

Chapter Twenty-Eight

Curt had seen some revolting and disgusting things in his life. And he was no stranger to horrifying wounds on the battlefield. However, he was totally repulsed by what he saw on the gurney.

If it had been a man, it was probably barely alive at the moment in spite of the repetitive CRT traces on the vital-signs monitor.

"Good God Almighty!" he breathed. "They would do *this* to their top NE scientist?"

"I am not so sure that Doctor Dongzhu did not have this done voluntarily," Dr. Rosha Taisha remarked, carefully checking and noting the placement, depth, and voltage on each of the acupuncture needles that were all over the man's prostrate body. "He was a Stapp. He was a man who would not allow others to try something unless he had tried it first."

"But what the hell is all this?" Curt wanted to know, looking around. "A couple of dozen zombies wired up for God knows what."

"God may have nothing to do with it," Owen Pendleton observed. "This is something people did to people."

"Why?"

"I don't know," Owen admitted. This sort of thing was a little beyond his expertise. He was the top man in the country when it came to programming or mentoring artificial intelligence circuitry. He preferred to call it "synthetic intelligence" because he claimed the other term was an oxymoron. "Dongzhu and his colleagues were hot on the trail of something."

"Do you have any idea what it was?" Curt was dumbfounded by this building and the discovery that it seemed like a mad scientist's laboratory.

"Not yet," Owen admitted.

"Can you wake him up? Or, is he comatose?"

"We don't know."

"How long will it take to find out?"

"We don't know." Pendleton was being honest.

But his scientific honesty bothered Curt, the military commander who had to worry about getting out of here with Dongzhu within hours if possible. Curt didn't know whether or not the Chinese had reinforcements on the way. Or even if the Chinese might mount an air strike of their own.

Most of all, Curt worried about the sovereign state of India not more than twenty kilometers away on the other side of the old cease-fire line. India hadn't made a move in the Deosai matter thus far. If India and China were indeed the prime movers of East World, why hadn't India shown its hand?

But he could only fret about that. He had immediate concerns to worry about.

"How the hell are we going to get him out of here?" Curt asked. "Will he die if he's disconnected from all that equipment?"

"We don't know."

"I'm sending for Major Gydesen," Curt told them.

"Rosha is a doctor," Pendleton pointed out. "She can handle the physiology of this. She also knows a lot about neuroelectronics."

"Owen, that may be so. However, Ruth and her people are experts in applied neuroelectronics," Curt told them. "They've kept me and several of the Greys from going KIA."

"I think we can handle it, Curt."

"Dammit, Owen, the Washington Greys didn't come halfway around the world and fight their way into this place to bring home a piece of catatonic meat!" Curt objected. He picked his tacomm off his harness and keyed it.

"Grey Bio. this is Grey Head. How do you read?"

The voice of the chief regimental medical officer came back weak. "Barely readable, Grey Head."

"Stand by! Grey Major, this is Grey Head! Throw a relay patch so I can talk to Grey Bio!"

"Roger, Grey Head. It's done."

"How now, Grey Bio?"

"Much better! Do you have wounded?"

"Not that I know of! But we have a strange situation here that needs your expertise. I'd like to get you and your best KIA experts here ASAP!"

"Somebody gone KIA? How?"

"Not exactly. I'll explain when you get here. We may know more by that time. But bring with you all the KIA gear you think you'll need."

"Grey Head, might as well lift the whole Bio-tech Support Vehicle over there! We can't handle a KIA case with a pocket module!" Ruth Gydesen insisted.

"All right. Your Bio-tech van, then. Stand by to load it on a Chippie."

"Roger, Grey Head!"

"Warhawk Leader, Grey Head! Cal, when you get a break from your air defense mission, I need a Chippie to airlift the Bio-tech van over here from the bivouac," Curt broadcast to his air chief.

"You've *got* to be *kidding*, Grey Head!"

"I'll be damned if I am! What's the problem? Can't you hack it?"

"We may not be *able* to get it *off* the ground. *Altitude*, you know."

"Dammit, Cal, I don't want to know the gory details or listen to why you can't do it!" Curt exploded. He wasn't out of patience with his air boss. Curt was tired, weary, fatigued, short of breath, aching all over, and having to spend too much time concentrating on what to say and what to do next. "Bring it over in pieces if you have to!

Just get it here! And as quickly as you can! Make it so!"

"Roger, Grey Head! It's coming!" Worsham would bitch and snivel with the best of them. But when it came "right down to the lickin' log," as he'd say, he'd manage to come through and produce. This was one of those times. "I have two Chippies on the ground in bivouac. They're running light on fuel. We'll split the load between them. They may have to be refueled on the ground in Deosai, but we can arrange that too. Where do you want the Bio-tech van?"

"Let me know when you're inbound with the package. We'll have someone outside with a beacon for you."

Curt turned to Hassan and the rest of Bravo Unit who were in the room. "Okay, your job is to secure this building. I mean *secure!* I want a non-violent, squeaky-clean, and very warm-fuzzy environment for these scientific types to do the work we brought them here for. Keep your beepers activated. Don't mess with anything. If you find anyone, bring them in here…under armed guard!"

Hassan touched his right hand to his helmet visor in a quick salute. "Roger, Colonel! It's done! Assassins, let's go! We aren't needed here! We've got a job to do!"

"This place gives me the creeps! I'm not so sure I want to stay here anyway," Mickie Mikawa said with a shudder. This was an unusual statement from the petite officer who was in many ways a small samurai warrior. Several generations of her family living in Hawaii hadn't eliminated those genes from their bloodline.

Having established security and done what he could at the moment, Curt sat down. It felt good to sit down. He was breathing hard. His peripheral vision had a tendency to dim. Occasionally, someone would say something that sounded like gibberish to him. He knew the higher cognitive centers of his brain were suffering from lack of oxygen. He didn't care. The hypoxic condition was somewhat euphoric. It was almost like going on a binge without the gastric effects of excessive alcohol. But he forced himself to care. He recognized the insidious symptoms of hypoxia.

Besides, he wanted to stay close in to where the critical action of this mission was taking place. And that was here with Dongzhu. His orders were to get Dongzhu and his colleagues out of here. The orders didn't specify how or in what condition. Given Dongzhu's present condition, Curt decided that getting him out alive would be a suitable achievement.

It was Taisha who was now studying the acupuncture needle placement and the wiring that connected Dongzhu to the electronics of the room. Pendleton had shifted his attention to the electronics, computers, AI modules, and other wizardry of the system.

"Owen, I think I've discovered what they've done here!" Taisha said with excitement in her voice. She would be excited, Curt decided. He'd seen her excited by a scientific phenomenon many years ago. As a scientist, she got excited about such things. "The Chinese don't have good neuroelectronic capability. Even the de-rated American, European, and Japanese neuroelectronics isn't sufficient to run a warbot. The neural resolution isn't enough. And it isn't sharp enough."

"Tell me something I don't already know," Pendleton muttered. "I see some of the single-mode NE equipment here from Japan. Strictly industrial stuff, by the way. Not much AI involved at all. Primitive!"

"Some of these acupuncture needles are inserted directly into nerve ganglia!" Taisha exclaimed. There was a hint of horror in her voice. "It's as if they couldn't read out some neural signals through the skin. So instead it looks like they put the sensors right into the nerve trunks themselves! Same for the virtual reality transducers! I don't know which are which at the moment..."

"I may be able to work it through in a few minutes here," Owen said. "I'm backtracking from equipment to probes. I can tell from how the probes are terminated. The command probes run to inputs here. The virtual reality data comes through outputs," Owen continued in a distracted fashion. He was concentrating on tracing wires to plug panels and the attendant equipment. "Yeah, that's what it looks like! The Chinese didn't have the neural coding data that permits us to read neural output as commands and interpret sensor input as, virtual reality." He shook his head in disgust, dismay, and disbelief. "They went right into the man's brain in some cases! Real old evoked-potential stuff out of the last century! Ugh!"

Taisha paused, then straightened up and looked around. "Where are the attendants? I find it difficult to believe they'd leave all of these people including Doctor Dongzhu wired up like this without having someone on watch somewhere!"

Curt brightened at that. "Taisha, Owen, does this stuff look like it's being transmitted to a central control room? By hard wire, for example?"

"I haven't got that far yet," Owen admitted.

"Negatory! It's not!" Sergeant Major Edie Sampson spoke up for the first time since Curt had come into the room. "This is all self-contained here! I see some output cables from some Mitsubishi computers leading out through the walls in cable ducts. But I don't know where the cables go. However, all the vital-signs monitoring equipment is here..."

"Unless they've duplicated it somewhere else," Owen interjected.

"Not a chance! The monitoring equipment dead-ends in here at its displays! Only the computer outputs are linked to somewhere else. I think we ought to be looking for a LAN set up in this building," Edie remarked, "I say that because I've just discovered a keypad and monitor. It's hot and online. But just sitting here eating electricity and crapping waste heat."

Curt had a bright idea. That was highly unusual, considering the altitude and the stupid-dumb way everyone was acting. "Edie, do you think you could 'talk' to Dongzhu through that keypad? Or that he might be able to communicate back to us?" He knew that somewhere a communications link should exist between those wired-up brains and the outside world.

"Might be worth a try. What do I send? *'Come here, Mister Watson, I need you'*? Or maybe, *'What hath God wrought'*?"

"Send a question mark. An interrogation mark," Curt suggested.

"And follow that by the ASCII decimal 063, then 3FH in hex," Pendleton added. "The computer will then have a choice of what to respond to. All are ASCII codes for a question mark."

Edie sat down in front of the terminal, exhaled sharply, and hit the proper keys.

Nothing appeared on the screen.

But a little audio transducer somewhere in the rack gear suddenly squawked.

It sounded like gibberish. But it was a sound.

"Hit it again!" Curt urged Edie. Some of the sounds were familiar, but Curt wanted to listen carefully this time.

Edie re-entered 3FH on the keypad.

"Nin hau? Nin shi shei? Wo shi yi-sheng Dongzhu Wen Ling!"

"Dead nuts on, Edie!" Curt exclaimed. "Somehow we've made verbal contact with Dongzhu through this collection of chips and modules! I can talk to him! Owen! Taisha! Come here!"

"I can hear you now," the tinny loudspeaker voice spoke in English. "Why do you speak in English?"

"We're Americans," Curt explained, then added in Mandarin, *"Wo shi mei-go!"*

"My English is good. I can use it easier now. I do not have to make sounds with my throat and mouth. Only with my mind." There was no accent in the English words and phrases that came from the little loudspeaker. "Did you come because you received my message?"

"Yes, we did," Curt replied. It was strange that he was talking to a person this way. Yet it wasn't strange because he was used to communicating verbally with warbots and computers. In his days as a warbot brainy, he'd also spoken directly to the mind of another person through linkage. So, it was no big deal for him. "I am Colonel Curt Carson of the United States Army. I have other people here with me. Here is Doctor Owen Pendleton and Doctor Rosha Taisha."

"Ah, so! Doctor Pendleton, author of that excellent paper on cross-feed between different neuroelectronic sensory inputs. And Doctor Taisha, whose work I know from her recent monograph on neuroelectronic control enhancements in muscle feedback situations at the last meeting of the International Academy of Neuroelectronics." The voice was becoming more confident now. "Speak up, please. I can hear you perfectly well through the little audio transducer."

"Doctor Dongzhu, why did you let them do this to you?" Pendleton asked. "Or didn't you have a choice?"

"The voice is male. It must be Doctor Pendleton," Dongzhu's voice replied. It was flat, emotionless, without inflection. Perhaps, Curt thought, that was why Dongzhu preferred to use English. Chinese is a language of vocal inflection. The way a Chinese word is spoken can often change its meaning. English can be spoken without inflection and still be understood. Hundreds of local dialects of English around the world are proof of this. Apparently, vocal inflections were not possible through this strange system of direct connection neuroelectronics that the Operation Hell Mover people had discovered. "I was not forced to do this. I am known as a scientist who will not allow experiments with the nervous systems of others until I have also been a subject. That is the excuse I used for this. My real purpose in doing this was to communicate with you."

"We saw the modulation on the six-hertz Schuman pulse," Taisha remarked.

"And that voice must be Doctor Rosha Taisha's. I will meet you all in the flesh someday soon, I hope..."

"How do we get you out of Deosai, Doctor?" Curt wondered, looking at all the equipment that was apparently life support and neural support for Dongzhu and the others in the room.

"It will not be easy. We do not have the technology of American warbot neuroelectronics. We cannot quickly link and delink. I will need help."

"Doctor, my regimental medical officer, Doctor Gydesen, is on her way. She'll be accompanied by some of our specialists in rapid neuroelectronic delinkage. She has some of our first-level therapy equipment with her," Curt advised the bodiless computer voice. It was still strange knowing that the voice really wasn't a voice but only neural signals from a quiet body lying on a gurney nearby. Curt should have been used to it as a former warbot brainy before his years as a Sierra Charlie who interacted directly with people.

"Be careful," Dongzhu's voice warned. "Some people in Deosai would like to capture your American neuroelectronic equipment."

"We thought of that," Curt reassured him. "We don't have anything you can't find in any American hospital. It's the way we use it that counts."

"Again, be careful! The military forces here are very powerful."

"They once were. They aren't now," Curt advised him. "We've fought against Red Hammers before."

"But beware the Army's new secret weapon."

"What is that?"

"I have not been told."

"Whatever it is, we're ready for it," Curt promised. "How do we get you out of here without killing you?"

"Find my associate, Doctor Qian Xuesen. He knows what to do."

"Is he in the building?"

"Yes. He was here before he told me the attack had started. He put me into standby condition when he heard the first explosions."

"Does he speak English?"

"All of us at the Institute of Intelligent Machinery Development read, understand, and speak English. If we did not, we would not be able to keep up with the most advanced neuroelectronics in the world."

Curt reached for his tacomm. "Assassin Leader, this is Grey Head! Search this building for a Chinese scientist. His name is Qian Xuesen. Don't worry if you mispronounce his name. He'll answer.

Get him down here as soon as you find him."

"Grey Head, Assassin Leader here. We've got him, sir. Just found him in what appears to be the main transmitter room. I don't know if he was trying to turn off that transmitter because we finally got here or if he was attempting to sabotage it. We got him before he did anything." Hassan always did a thorough and professional job.

"He was supposed to tum it off," Dongzhu explained.

"Why?" Pendleton asked. "We want to study it."

"There is nothing to it but a transmitter."

"We want to see," Owen persisted. "We want to know how it could put out so much r-f power at such a low frequency without a major thermonuclear power plant nearby."

"That is simple," came the flat computer voice. "Terrestrial piezoelectricity."

"What?"

"Did you wonder why the facility is located where it is?"

"We determined it's here because Fort McCarthy was at a resonant point for any six-hertz signal originating here."

"I wish I could display body movements. That will be possible when Qian arrives. Doctor, we could have used any frequency other than six-hertz. We could have located this experimental facility anywhere. The strength of the Schuman pulse must only be enough to overcome the ambient flux. It is the modulation on the Schuman pulse that is the important element."

"We quickly discovered that," Taisha said. "It interferes with neuroelectronic robot control."

"Yes, which is why it was developed. China has put much work into it. The first transmitter was located here because it is an experiment. We needed large amounts of power. We could get it from the Earth itself," the voice explained. "We are at a point where two tectonic plates meet. The Indian plate is colliding with the Asian plate. This has formed the Himalaya Mountains. It also produces strain between rock strata. There is much quartz in this area, most of it deep. Quartz is piezoelectric. When subjected to the application of physical force, it produces an electric voltage. There is enough of it underground here to produce gigawatts of electric power if the proper machinery is used."

Curt jumped on part of that statement right away. "You said this is an experimental location. Does the PRC have others?"

"Yes. Many. They are under construction now. Some are nearly finished. The reason why I have taken risks here and communicated to you requesting asylum is simple. The new facilities of China and India will be capable of affecting all neuroelectronic equipment anywhere in the world. Since we in China use people instead of robots in our industrial and military activities, this will not greatly affect us. But NE robots of all types all over the world will become uncontrollable. The circuitry will feed deadly commands back into the human operators before they know it. I cannot condone the application of my expertise to a weapon that will indiscriminately kill millions and millions of innocent, peaceful people all over the world when they work with neuroelectronic technology!"

Chapter Twenty-Nine

"All neuroelectronic equipment? Everywhere in the world? How?" General Bill Bellamack's voice over the little satellite comm unit indicated both surprise and disbelief.

"I don't know," Colonel Curt Carson admitted. "But I don't have to be a robot scientist to know that this Chinese breakthrough means we'll be forced to change a lot of things!"

"That's putting it mildly!" Bellamack agreed. "And let me get this straight. Dongzhu told you that East World has several of these transmitters under construction or ready to go once the Deosai experiment works?"

"That's what he said."

"And, dammit, it did work! Does he know where these other facilities are?"

"He said he doesn't."

"Do you believe him?"

"I don't know. I was talking to a disembodied computer-generated voice," Curt explained. "No inflections. No body language. I can usually read those factors along with the words. They give me some indication of whether the person is lying or not. But I can't tell in this case."

"'*Any* informed or educated guess as to how they're doing this, Curt?" Bellamack pressed him.

"Only that somehow they've bypassed our neuroelectronic technology," Curt guessed, basing his speculation on the way Dongzhu and the others were wired up in that morguelike room inside. Curt was now standing outside so his little satcom unit would perform better. It was a wee-watter in the first place, and the metal structure of the building attenuated the signals too much when he tried to use it inside.

291

"How the hell did they do that?"

"We know their Red Hammer warbots use single-channel NE like sound or muscle command. That's pretty widespread technology. But they've never been able to crack the neural codes that allow us to run the full NE sensory and command suite. That was pretty obvious in-side the building here. What they've done is make an end run around our technology. They're using a lot of acupuncture technology. These guys look like pin cushions. Major Gydesen and her staff are inside now. They're working with one of Dongzhu's assistants, Doctor Qian Xuesen."

"Spell that for me. I'll get an intelligence check on him."

"I can't. Pinyin can have several spellings for a given sound, depending on the intonation," Curt advised him. "We're calling him Qian. We'd like to call him the Yellow Peril because he looks just like those evil Chinese scientists in some of the horror flicks. But I can't insult him. He's the only one who knows how to get Dongzhu out of that coma so we can airlift him."

"Curt, you've *got* to get Dongzhu out of there alive and sane!" Bellamack emphasized. "He's the key to this whole weapon system! Without him, we may be five years behind the power curve!"

"Maybe. Maybe not. Pendleton and Thisha know something about what's going on. At least, they act that way. Or they're learning damned fast." The two McCarthy Proving Ground warbotic and neuroelectronic scientists were deeply into the situation inside the building now. The way they were talking and the subjects they were discussing were now far beyond his know-how as a military officer. "Pendleton is handling the hardware and software side, and Taisha is coping as best she can with the jellyware, thanks to help from Ruth Gydesen. As for me, I'm no robot scientist..."

"What do you need? Could Pendleton use more help?"

"I don't think so. He hasn't asked for anything or complained about not having something. But I need something, General," Curt told the Army COS bluntly. "And I think you can arrange it there on JCS."

"Name it."

"Do whatever you can to keep East World out of here!"

"That's a tall order, Curt. Specifically, what are you worried about?"

"They could have reinforcements on the way right now. We can't hold up against any strong push to blast us out of here."

"What's the sit? Did you take many casualties in the assault? Did you lose warbots or equipment?" Bellamack asked with concern because he had once commanded the Washington Greys.

Once a Washington Grey, always a Washington Grey, Curt told himself. To put Bellamack at ease, he reported, "Some wounded. No firm report yet. Nothing too serious. No one killed. Major Gydesen has her hands full with that plus Dongzhu. We did okay against the Deosai garrison. We hit them with far more than they thought we would. And we did it sooner than they thought we would. We overwhelmed them and exploited the element of surprise. East World still doesn't understand the Sierra Charlie doctrines, and that's something in our favor. But General, we're only kilometers from India. And China is just over the mountains. If this experimental facility is as important to East World as I think it is, East World isn't going to stand by idly and let us get Dongzhu out."

"Providing they know he's asked for asylum. But let's assume they know. Okay, I repeat my question: What do you want me to do?"

"Let the Paks know what's going on here.," Curt suggested, thinking about the overall strategy and the consequences of this on the world situation. "Let them know how serious it is. Get them mobilized fast. Nothing like a threat to get East World's attention. Or anything that would convince them we caught them testing their new weapon. Some of the people in State are going to have to be real creative, General. They'll have to convince the various ambassadors in Washington that we know exactly what's going on here."

"We'll tell State that we do know. They won't know differently," Bellamack confided in him. "If it turns out later they discover we don't, we tell them that we were premature in our evaluation based on a rapid but incomplete survey of the facility. You let me handle that through General Palmer. As CJCS, he's very smooth. Dave Henshaw is also pretty savvy on these things; he's a good SecDef. What else?"

"Wouldn't hurt to scramble some Black Devils off Diego Garcia, then out of the ZI. East World won't know if they're recce or KE killer missions," Curt went on. He forced his oxygen-starved brain to recall the present defense posture and to decide which elements would be most usefully deployed to save their asses in Deosai. "Get the Navy off its security blanket and have them surface the *Cromwell* and the *Soucek* off India. Have them launch patrols but no attack 'dynes. Let East World know we're capable of hitting them where it hurts if India interferes in Deosai."

"Jesus, Curt, that's a major step up the wartime escalation ladder!" Bellamack pointed out. He didn't sound concerned about it. Curt believed Bellamack was just warning him about it.

"Hell, activating a weapon that will kill innocent neuroelectronic robot operators indiscriminately world-wide *isn't?* Or sending in the Washington Greys to hit this place wasn't?" Curt asked rhetorically, trying to ensure that this whole operation was kept in perspective.

"But the situation *is* escalating!"

"Not my worry, General. That's why people in Playland on the Potomac get paid the big bucks," Curt reminded him. "I'm here carrying out my orders. That's as far as I intend to go in this. You asked me what help I needed. Thank you for that. I told you. My response was made here in the heat of battle. We're in a situation where we could screw up and never get home."

Bellamack knew Carson extremely well, and he knew Curt wasn't being disrespectful or insubordinate. He was a regimental commander with all the awesome responsibilities for people the position entailed. Bellamack had been there too. "I didn't mean to infer I wanted a full-bore War College analysis, Curt."

"I know that, sir. One last item: Get the Paks to hold the Fourth Khyber Rifles in Skardu as a reserve. Let East World know they're there. The Rifles fought well in the last Indo-Pak skirmish. India respects that regiment. So does China. The Khyber Rifles' presence will act as a deterrent to India or China. They don't want this to blow up into a general war either. That's not in their long-term interests."

"That makes a lot of sense, Curt. What the hell are you doing out there running a regiment? Christ, with that sort of thinking, you ought to be on JCS staff!"

"If someone wants me there, I'll get orders and go, General. But I'm here right now." Curt paused for a moment. "Oh, yes, one final request: Just don't say anything about all this in the morning press briefing. If we do it right, it won't trigger a journalistic stampede. It might make the throwaway segment of the evening news. If anyone asks, it's just another exercise or two. And it definitely needs to be kept quiet until we can get our pink bods out of here! Otherwise, we're hostages to news stories, and the East Worlders will play it that way!"

"I concur! I'll do what I can! Keep it up, Curt! You're doing an outstanding job!" Bellamack told him.

If that compliment had come from just the Army Chief of Staff, it would have been enough. But it bad come from a former commander of the Washington Greys. Curt knew that anyone who commanded the Washington Greys demanded far more than satisfactory performance from everyone...and got it. Thus, the accolade was doubly meaningful.

Curt signed off and returned the satcom unit to his pouch as Kitsy came up to him.

The fight had ended. All was quiet over the Plains of Deosai now except for the roar and rumble of incoming Chippewa aerodynes ready to airlift the regiment out. Overhead, Curt could hear the muted rush of the four Harpies that remained on recce and patrol while the other four were air-refueling.

"Sir, we've got a hell of a lot of prisoners," she reported wearily. "And we're having trouble with them."

"What kind of trouble?"

"No trouble with the regular Chinese soldiers. They just sit down and wait. It's those kids who won't give up." Kitsy was very upset about the young Chinese boys she'd had to fight against.

"Feed them and tell the adult soldiers to maintain discipline," Curt suggested.

Kitsy shook her head slowly. When she was wearing her big combat helmet, it made her head look huge in comparison to her petite form. "The PLA soldiers won't have anything to do with the Red Scouts. In fact, they dislike them. I think they're afraid of them. Those boys are pretty damned violent, Colonel. Like they were taught all the nasty ways of killing people and all the ways to escape when captured. The ultimate juvenile delinquents. Juvenile killers! I hate to kill kids. But these little bastards have no redeeming characteristics at all. They're not civilized. They're just meaner than hell. The only thing I'll give them credit for is that they're tenacious. Never say die. We've shot three of them trying to get out and refusing to stop when challenged."

Curt sighed. "'*The Guard dies, but never surrenders!*' Used to be that way in European armies once too. Gallant and heroic, to be sure. But senseless. At least by our lights, Kitsy."

"Yeah, we're taught something else, I guess. Like each individual is unique and can be trained or educated for years of service to the person and the group. The Chinese seem to treat the Red Scouts like organic warbots."

Curt knew she'd stumbled on something there. He thought about that for a moment, then remarked, "Look at it this way, Kitsy. The Red Scouts are the East World's real warbots. They can be trained to follow orders because they're so young and the world is so new to them. they fight until they're destroyed because they're told they have nothing to live for anyway. They've got far more built-in AI than even our most advanced warbots. They're easily manufactured by relatively unskilled labor. And they're the one thing that East World has a lot of: people."

"Is this what we're going to be up against in confrontation with East

World?" Kitsy asked.

"Probably. Their Red Hammer warbots were just diversions. Those drew our tech-oriented attention from what they were really doing with counter-neuroelectronic technology and Red Scouts," Curt decided.

"I just hope we've caught on to what they're doing early enough that we can head it off," Kitsy remarked. "I don't like the idea of killing boys. I've killed my share of men with no regrets; they would have killed me otherwise. And I don't mind fighting warbots."

"Kitsy, I don't want to cook off on this," Curt said. He'd seen what was going on in Deosai, and was reluctant to admit it. "But at this point, I have a sneaking hunch that our warbots have become obsolete."

Kitsy sighed. Curt couldn't tell whether it was a sigh or just another deep breath. Oxygen was at a premium here at 5,600 meters altitude with everyone under stress and expending a lot of physical effort. "Well, I guess I can look at it in a positive way. If we'd been warbot brainies, this would have been a disaster. But because we're Sierra Charlies who operate against Red Hammers as well as Red Scouts, maybe we can brag that we saved the Free World again after all."

Curt grinned. Some of Kitsy's puckish sense of humor had peeked through the battle-weary facade. It helped Curt regain his own perspective on affairs too. "Hell, Major Clinton, that's our job! That's what we get paid for!"

"Colonel, I've got Alpha Unit pretty well situated," Kitsy went on as she nodded in agreement with Curt's observation. "I'd like to check up on the rest of my battalion. How do I get into this big car barn? And where's the action once I'm inside?"

Curt thought about what she'd see in there - the rows of silent bodies arrayed with acupuncture needles and festooned with electronic cables. "Uh, it's pretty grim in there, Major. Are you sure you want to see it?"

"Damned right! I came this far and fought this hard, so I want the full two bit tour! I'm entitled to it!"

Curt agreed that she was.

Besides, Kitsy usually had some interesting insights on things from her specific viewpoint of the world. He was interested in what she'd see that maybe everyone else had overlooked.

It turned out to be timely that Curt returned to "the morgue" when he did. He didn't have time to gauge Kitsy's reaction because Major Ruth Gydesen saw him come in and called him to come over.

The regimental medical officer was working over Dr. Dongzhu's body. She was assisted by Chief Nurse Helen Devlin, her chief internist Tom Alvin, and her unit's nurse specialist in cardiology, Bill Molde. A sallow Chinese - apparently Qian Xuesen - was working alongside her. So was Rosha Taisha. Owen Pendleton and Edie Sampson were handling the hardware side.

"This is the damnedest sheep screw of Western and Oriental medical techniques I've ever tangled with!" Ruth told Curt in exasperated tones. "Qian seems to know what's going on, but Taisha's Chinese is so rusty we can't really communicate. Curt, you know Mandarin. I need you as a translator!"

"What's the big problem?" Curt wanted to know.

"In non-medical terms, I've got to get this guy unplugged and conscious without killing him in the process," Ruth explained.

"And his heart isn't that good," Molde added.

"Hell, he doesn't look over forty-five!" Curt observed.

"His heart acts like it's seventy-five!" the special cardiac nurse said. "Old, irregular, probably full of fatty tissue, maybe even wearing out. And we don't have the facilities to do a heart transplant here!"

"Qian seems to know the acupuncture techniques used," Ruth went on. "But every time we try to do something with those needles, Dongzhu goes into cardiac fibrillation!"

"I know something about acupuncture!" Taisha insisted. "The needles are balancing his meridians. They are also eliminating the pain of the deep cranial insertions."

"I defer to the distinguished doctor from McCarthy Proving Ground," Ruth muttered. From the sound of her voice, she wasn't really happy about it. "I studied acupuncture only at the University of California under Doctor Han."

"Oh? Really? Excellent! Then it is not necessary that I explain it to you!" Taisha replied ingenuously in a distracted tone. Her attention was almost totally riveted on Dongzhu. "Then you realize that the insertions often have nothing whatsoever to do with what a European-trained physician would suspect."

"Indeed!" Ruth was also concentrating. "I sometimes use direct-current voltages on some insertions. But this is the first time I've seen waveforms being used. What do you make of some of the voltage waveforms being applied to some of the needles?"

"From the looks of the signals, he's being cardiac-paced."

"Doctor Qian, does Doctor Dongzhu show a history of heart disease?" Ruth asked the quiet Chinese doctor working alongside them.

"*Ta san nian qian faguo xinzang bing,*" Qian replied. He understood what Ruth and the others were saying in English, but he wasn't proficient enough to reply in the same language.

"Dongzhu had a heart attack three years ago," Curt translated. Qian had a Yunnan accent, but Curt could cut through it.

"Wonderful!" Ruth murmured. "I'm afraid that if we take him all the way off this procedure, he'll spend too much time trying to readjust his own heart condition."

"We could try open-heart massage if he goes into cardiac arrest," Molde suggested.

"Measure of last resort," Gydesen decided. "If we have to go into the thoracic cavity to keep him alive as we bring him out of this hard-linkage mess, we may not be able to keep him alive during air evac."

"We've got to get him out of here," Curt reminded her. "He knows more about this NE weapon than anyone. And this is only the test bed. The Chinese have built others."

"We may not be able to get him out," Ruth advised her commander.

"Then dammit, let me get back on the audio!" Curt snapped. "I want to get him to spill his brain about it while he can! Owen, let's go over with Edie at the voice box console. We're as useful as tits on a turret here!"

"Roger that," Pendleton quipped. "I've got a bunch of questions for him."

The first question Curt asked the comatose Dr. Dongzhu was straightforward. "Doctor, we're trying to get you out of hard linkage here. Doctor Qian isn't helping much. Can you give us step-by-step instructions about how to do it?"

"Yes," the tinny, flat voice came back. "Be wary of Doctor Qian. I do not trust him completely. I will tell you why soon. Do not disturb the acupuncture needles. Do not change the signal feeds. The delinking procedure is a long one. It will take at least four days."

"We haven't got four days, Doctor," Owen remarked. "We may be attacked again within hours. If the facility's electric power is interrupted, will that disturb the procedure?"

"You do not have four days? That is too bad," the emotionless voice replied. "However, if the electricity is disrupted, the emergency generator will take over. We must have a constant and reliable source of power for our procedure. Otherwise, rapid delinkage will cause deep catatonia culminating in death within three hours. Let us assume that the electric power is not interrupted. If that is the case, delinkage can be carried out in about six hours. Trauma will be extensive. However, I understand that you Americans have techniques permitting rehabilitation for people who have undergone such rapid delinkage."

"We do," Pendleton admitted. "It takes four to six months, but we can do it."

"Then we should proceed with the fast delinkage. I am willing to risk the consequences if you can rehabilitate me."

One thing for certain, Curt decided. Dr. Dongzhu had guts. He'd voluntarily put himself into this condition so he could send a clandestine message to America. Now he was willing to take the chance of going KIA in a new way. And trusting that the Americans would get him out of it.

However, Curt wanted to hedge the bets. "Doctor, American NE therapists were able to rehab Doctor Taisha from deep catatonia. But there's always the chance that we can't rehab you completely because of this unusual hard-wire linkage. I want to make sure we get as much information as possible before we try it. Owen, you've got your recorder?"

"Right here," Owen said, pulling the little enclosure out of his hip pouch. "Okay, it's running. We'll record for later use and perhaps to refresh your memory after therapeutic rehab. Doctor Dongzhu, would you explain this weapon and how it works?"

"Yes. Attend me!" The Chinese scientist began to lecture on his subject of expertise. "Because in China we do not have the capabilities as you do of handling multiplex nervous system signals in and out through the skin, we have used our Oriental mind-body techniques to accomplish similar results. These are not yet to the point of development as sophisticated as your non-intrusive neuroelectronics. However, we now possess the necessary means using acupuncture to insert probes directly into the nerve ganglia themselves and into specific portions of the brain. We have researched the field of event-evoked potentials in order to find this, and we have completely mapped the human brain in this regard."

"Do you understand this?" Curt whispered to Owen.

"Yes! You bet!"

"So, he's not making it up just to get out of here?"

"Not only no, but hell, no! This is fantastic! My God, what a weapon they've got here!" Owen whispered back.

Dongzhu continued speaking through the audio equipment. "We know the signals necessary to reach the deep brain and to disrupt normal neuroelectronic robot commands and feedback data. For use in neuroelectric countermeasures, we can generate the necessary disrupting neuroelectronic signals. These are used to modulate various types of scalar waves which do not behave in the same manner as electromagnetic waves although they propagate through the ether in the same manner. I do not approve of this application of our new expertise. However, it was strongly supported by the Ministry of Defense. I was forced to organize my department to perfect it. Doctor Qian Xuesen was placed in charge –"

The lights went out.

Chapter Thirty

It's always a shock to go instantly and unexpectedly from brightly lit surroundings into total darkness. This time was no exception.

But Curt was still wearing his combat helmet and had his infrared high-vision sensors on standby. Without thinking about it, he flipped down his helmet visor and switched to operational mode.

Owen Pendleton didn't have a combat helmet with a high-vision sensor suite. He was caught in the sudden blackness. "What the hell?" he yelled.

"Lights! Get some lights!" Ruth Gydesen shouted.

"Lights, hell! Get some power to this equipment!" was the cry from Bill Molde. "Dongzhu's heart! Check his heart! Check his breathing!"

"The acupuncture needles are in the way!" said the quiet, professional voice of Helen Devlin. "Okay, got it! Nothing. Nothing. His heart stopped! Molde, we need to pump him! Get up on the table over him!"

"I can't see a damned thing! I don't want to get jabbed by those needles!"

Kitsy Clinton turned on her helmet light. "This will have to do until I get my hand torch out!"

As quickly as her helmet light came on, there came a muffled *thwup!* The light went out. Someone had fired a small-caliber silenced weapon at it.

Curt had turned around in time to see Qian point a small Chinese Type 46 silenced 7.65mm pistol at Kitsy's helmet light. But by the time Curt could bring his Novia around from the sling carry position and shoot, a small form had brushed quickly past him. He saw and heard two bodies collide. When they went down, he heard a scream that was quickly drowned in a liquid gurgling sound.

Within seconds, flashlights and helmet lights came on.

Kitsy was on the floor shaking her head. Her helmet had been torn off by the impact of the bullet. As quickly as Ruth saw that, she was at Kitsy's side.

Edie Sampson rose from the floor. In her right hand was her assault knife. Its blade was dripping red goo. In her other hand was a Chinese Type 46 automatic pistol. "Goddamned sonofabitch won't shoot anyone else!" she growled.

When Curt flashed his hand lamp on the still form on the floor, he saw that Edie had neatly sliced the man's throat.

Taisha, Devlin, and Molde were frantically working on Doctor Dongzhu. The power failure had caused all the electronic equipment in the place to quit. Molde was now atop the man. Ignoring the acupuncture needles, he was pumping the Chinese scientist's chest. Helen had her stethoscope on Dongzhu's neck over the carotid artery. Taisha was trying to remove and reinsert some of the acupuncture needles.

"Kitsy? Are you okay?" was Curt's first question.

"No, but I'll live if I survive this headache," said a small voice from the little major.

"Stay put, Kitsy. You might have a concussion," Ruth told her. "You'll be okay there for a minute or two. If you start to pass out, yell! In the meantime, I've got to see about keeping Dongzhu alive."

"I'll be okay, I think, if I can catch my breath. Damned hard to breathe here…"

Curt heard the rasping, gasping sound of Cheyne-Stokes breathing coming from Dongzhu. It stopped with a rattle in the man's throat.

"Doctor, no pulse. No heartbeat. No pressure. Now no breathing," Helen reported. "If I can get my EEG powered up, I'll check brain activity. But I'm almost afraid it's a waste of time. He warned us about what might happen if he was suddenly disconnected."

"So? Keep it up! We can't let him die!" Ruth insisted. And she was immediately at the side of the prostrate Chinese scientist. "He may be comatose, but we can bring him back if he's not brain-dead."

There were other sounds in the room now. Other comatose bodies were twitching and jerking in spasms. Curt heard more Cheyne-Stokes breathing, more death rattles.

And he was forced to stand there. The Washington Greys couldn't save them.

The building echoed with an explosion.

Curt grabbed his tacomm from his harness. "This is Grey Head! Bravo Leader, report! What the hell is going on?"

"Bravo Leader here," said the calm voice of Hassan. "Got a small problem out by the power bay. Some of those Red Scouts must have got loose again! They must have grenades and explosives stashed away in all sorts of hidden places. We caught one of the little bastards just after he put a grenade right in the most critical part of the electric power input board. Took the emergency generator switch-over panel with it."

"Where is he now?" Curt wanted to know. If escaped boys continued to run around the facility dealing death at every occasion, this was a decidedly unhealthy place to stay, he decided.

"He's joined his honorable ancestors, if he had any," Hassan reported.

"Who's guarding the prisoner enclosure?" Curt called. "Alpha Unit officer in charge of prisoners, acknowledge!"

"Panther Leader here," came the response from Lieutenant Dan Power.

"Power, can't you keep those little bastards from escaping?"

"Only if we shoot them, sir," the officer reported. "And they've got it down to a science. A couple of them will create a diversion while another one goes over the hill in the commotion. I've had to put all the Jeeps on this detail. And keep our beacons hot so the Jeeps don't shoot at us instead of Red Scouts."

"We can't keep screwing around like this! How many Red Scouts left over there in the prisoner compound?"

"Ten."

"Stuff them in a Chippie under *heavy* guard, have the Chippie pilot haul them about ten klicks to the north, and dump them out on the ground," Curt ordered. "We can't screw around like this."

"They'll die out in the mountains in this environment," Power pointed out.

"They're tough as nails, Lieutenant. And they'll continue to kill if we keep them here," Curt pointed out. "Lieutenant, drain all the milk of human kindness out of your system. Otherwise, those little bastards will kill you too!"

"Yes, sir! It will be done, sir!"

Major Russ Frazier signaled to Curt and called out, "Colonel, I'll take charge of that detail. The milk of human kindness in me got curdled a long time ago. I'll make sure those little bastards don't bother us anymore while we're here!"

"Does Bravo have the building secure?"

"It does now! And I'm going to see to it that the place continues to be secure. This will take me about fifteen minutes," Russ promised.

"Can we get power back?"

"Hassan, Bravo Leader! How about power?" Russ asked.

"Coming, sir. Little hot-wiring job here will do it. Give us thirty seconds!"

"Okay, Russ go do it. Report back," Curt told him. Later, he regretted it.

Frazier disappeared out the door.

"Grey Head, Grey Major here. We've lost the Deosai carrier and all the other stuff emanating from down there," Henry Kester reported in.

"Yeah, Henry, we know that. We've lost power in the main building. And we lost the people we came to get when the signal went away," Curt replied sorrowfully. Curt had liked Dongzhu. The scientist had had real balls to do what he did. He'd taken a chance…and he'd lost. "When we get power back in a few minutes, we'll do our survey of the building and prepare to depart. So, haul your ass off that ridge and get down here for pickup. Looks like it's over. We'll be going home."

"Uh, not exactly, Grey Head," Henry advised. "I've got hypersonics that just bloomed over the northern horizon. Better take cover."

"Check their beacons, Henry. They're probably ours," Curt told him.

"Maybe. Maybe not. But I've got to give you warning about it," Henry reminded him, always aware of his responsibilities and a little pissed off that he hadn't been down in the thick of things. "Also, action over the cease-fire line in India. Looks like a squadron of something just scrambled off Srinagar."

"Get on the horn to Ghazi about it. And to Tiffany too."

"Colonel, I just don't want you to get caught with your bots down," Henry explained. "If I was you, I'd make sure a few Smart Farts were on a few shoulders and ready to be targeted."

"We'll do that, and thanks."

"And I'm going back down to the bivouac instead of beating through the hills to where you are. The road is in and it's better. I don't favor trying to make my own road in the dark in this miserable terrain. And I'm get-ting too old for all this screwing around in the wilderness at night," Henry declared. "I'll stand by for pickup there when the Chippies recover the Hellcats. Staying up here on the ridge makes me a real inviting target. I want to make sure I'm still around when you hand me that new Purple Heart. And you wouldn't want to lose all my expertise, would you, sir? On second thought, don't bother answering that. Grey Major out!"

"Grey Head, this is Mustang Leader!" Dyani reported in.

"Where are you, Mustang Leader?"

"Up to my usual tricks, Grey Head. We see a column of vehicles advancing cross-country at night with lights on and air cover over them. They're coming from the direction of Skardu."

"The Fourth Khyber Rifles," Curt remarked. "Khan wasn't about to let the glory of this operation go past him!"

"I hope it's the Rifles, Grey Head. I'll check it out." Dyani paused, then went on. "Grey Head, I hate to report we had to shoot four Red Scouts a few minutes ago. They were trying to mine the power plant building. We had better night vision sensors than they did. And they wouldn't surrender."

"You did right, Mustang Leader."

"Maybe so. But I wonder, Grey Head."

"Grey Major, Grey Head here! Henry, don't fold your tent yet. Patch me through to Khyber Head."

"Rats, I didn't act fast enough! And the OCV was cold and wouldn't start fast. Okay, you've got it, Grey Head!"

"Khyber Head, this is Grey Head! Report your position and intentions."

"Grey Head, Khyber Head is on the northwest edge of the Plains of Deosai," Colonel Iskander Khan's voice replied. "We will join you in the facility in about an hour."

"I thought you'd bivouacked for the night, Colonel." Curt could resist putting in that little barb. Not very long ago, Khan had been running a nine-to-five mission. Now that had apparently changed.

"Plans changed, Colonel. It was obvious that you needed our support sooner than tomorrow morning," was Khan's reply. The man's voice now sounded much friendlier and more polite. Apparently, the word had somehow gotten passed.

Curt stifled a guffaw. "Thank you, Khyber Head." *Noblesse oblige,* Curt thought, and went on. "Khyber Head, squawk your beacons so we can see you coming. I wouldn't want any problems to arise. If my people or warbots see unidentifieds approaching, they're sure as hell going to shoot first and interrogate afterward. We've been shot at a lot here tonight. We're a little bit spooked."

"Roger that, Grey Head. Judging from what the reports say you've accomplished already I don't think we want any problems either."

Khan might not like Curt or the Washington Greys. But the man now had respect. Under the circumstances, that was all that Curt could expect. That was enough.

In the dim light thrown by several hand lanterns, light sticks, and helmet lights, Ruth came up to him. She didn't look happy.

"Dongzhu didn't make it," she said sadly.

"I didn't think he would," Curt admitted. "Not after what he told us while he was still able to do so. It just makes our job a lot tougher. Let me put it another way: Pendleton and Thisha are going to have to work fast without knowing what they're looking for or at."

"If I can be of use, I'll help them. There isn't much else I can do here," Ruth said with dejection.

It seemed to Curt that she wanted to say something else and was having trouble saying it. Curt knew there was only one other bio-tech situation that had occurred in the room. So, he broke the ice. "What's wrong with Kitsy?"

"I don't know," Ruth admitted. "She's having trouble walking."

"Oh, my God!" Curt breathed. "Concussion?" Ruth shook her head. "No signs of it. But her neck got snapped pretty hard when that pistol bullet hit her helmet."

"Oh, oh!"

"She's having a little trouble maintaining her balance," Ruth admitted.

"Where is she?"

Ruth took him to where Kitsy was seated on one of the empty gurneys.

Kitsy's face was drawn with fatigue and effort. She braced herself firmly with her arms on the gurney. A slight smile flashed across her pixie face when she saw Curt. "Colonel, I'm probably going to have to go back to Walter Reed for some repairs," she told him. "When that round hit my helmet and jerked my head, something got pulled pretty bad back where they hot-wired my spinal column. Must have pulled something loose. Probably just a couple of wires.

Maybe a quick re-soldering job is all I need. Other than that, I'm fine."

"Ruth, what about that?"

"That sounds rational. Kitsy knows more about her internal wiring than I do. She's sort of a special mod in that regard, if you know what I mean." Ruth was trying to be lighthearted about it. She liked Kitsy. Everyone in the regiment did.

"We'll get you in for your thousand-hour inspection and checkup, Kitsy," Curt told her. "Take off your gear and relax. Who's your Number Two?"

"Lew Pagan."

"Really? Why?"

"He's from The Citadel, sir! The Citadel! The fountainhead of Southern military tradition!" Kitsy tried to smile, but she was tired.

He tried to grin. "I'll give you two weeks for maintenance, Kitsy! Then you be sure you either report back or tell me why. Understand?"

"Yes, sir!" Her eyes might be tired, but they sparkled for a moment. Then they grew somber. "The rest will give me a little time to do some thinking. I really didn't like having to fight the Red Scouts."

"Yeah, you mentioned that."

"I don't like the idea of killing children. That wasn't supposed to be part of the deal."

"Sometimes we have no choice of enemies, Kitsy."

"I know that. But I'd feel better if I didn't suspect the Chinese deliberately ran these kids in against us just because we're a mixed-gender military force," Kitsy commented. "If they were trying to catch me where it bothers me, they succeeded. So, I've got to figure out if the Red Scouts are just another weapon; if I can convince myself of that, I'll feel better about going for twenty-and-out."

Before Curt could think of a suitable answer, his tacomm beeped. "Grey Head, this is Panther Leader!" Dan Power's voice was shaken.

"Grey Head here! Go ahead, Panther Leader!"

"I think you'd better get over here, sir. We've had more than a little problem."

"With the prisoners?"

"Yes, sir. I need to discuss it with you when you get here." Power was reluctant to talk about it.

Curt called Lew Pagan. "Puma Leader, Grey Head here!"

"Puma leader is listening, Grey Head."

"Lew, Kitsy's injured. You're taking TACBATT temporarily. Make sure that Pendleton and Taisha aren't hassled while they continue - their inspection of this main building." Curt had snapped the orders. They included orders he didn't like to give.

"What about the Alpha and Bravo Units?"

"Revert to the T-O-and-E! Alpha and Bravo Teams are no longer needed as such!"

"Roger, sir!"

"And I'll be over at the prisoner compound if you need me. Problem there. Know anything about it?"

"No, sir. I'm at the power station. But I heard shots from that direction in the last few minutes."

"Shit!" Curt snarled to himself in disgust. He thought he knew what had happened. So, he started out the building toward that area.

He wasn't far from wrong.

Lieutenant Dan Power met him. The young officer was white and shaken.

"Looks like the PLA prisoners are still here, Lieutenant," Curt said as he checked the area in which the prisoners had been detained. It was surrounded by some of the razor wire Alpha Unit had found when they came into the area. It was also surrounded by four Jeeps as guards. Several dozen Chinese prisoners were still there. Most of them were asleep on the ground while others just sat and watched.

"Yes, sir, we still have the Chinese."

"We'll turn them over to the Paks so they can be exchanged," Curt observed. "Did Major Frazier load those kids on the Chippie and transport them out in the hills where they couldn't hassle us while we were here?"

"I don't think so, sir."

"What do you mean, you don't think so?"

"No Chippie showed up. The Major ordered me and my platoon to accompany him with the kids out into the darkness there. He ordered us to load and lock," Power explained in halting words. "He...he said he'd been ordered to take care of the little bastards permanently. I refused to obey his orders, Colonel. So, he took three Jeeps and went out there with the kids himself. That's when I called you."

"What happened?"

"We heard the Jeeps fire on automatic a few minutes before you got here, sir."

"Where's Major Frazier?"

"Still out there, sir."

Curt looked. Then he saw Frazier and three Jeeps come out of the woods beyond the perimeter. With a sinking feeling in the pit of his stomach, he waited until Russ got within earshot, then called, "Major Frazier, report to me at once!"

Frazier moved slowly in a wandering fashion toward Curt. The regimental commander recognized the walk of a man suffering from altitude sickness. Another of the syndromes was lack of judgment and inability to think coherently. Frazier finally stopped in front of him and saluted. He was panting hard. "Major Frazier reporting as ordered, sir!"

"Major, what did you just do with those boy prisoners?" Curt got right to the point.

"Took care of them, sir. They won't bother us now."

"I told you to take them about ten klicks away by Chippie and put them on the ground. They're hardy enough they could survive that. No Chippie was reported. What did you do?"

"I had the little bastards shot! Got two of them myself and administered the coup de grace to a third who was still kicking."

"You shot prisoners in cold blood?"

"You bet! They weren't soldiers! They were kids! And they'd do the same to us!"

"That's what I thought you did, but I wanted to hear you say it," Curt remarked, both angry and sorrowful at the same time. "Major Frazier, you have just admitted to a crime under the Geneva Convention and the Uniform Code of Military Justice. You have admitted this before witnesses. Give me your firearm and place yourself under arrest. You are hereby relieved of your duties!"

Chapter Thirty-One

"Well, let's tie up some loose ends here before most of you scat out on some well-earned leave," Colonel Curt Carson told his staff.

The conference room in the regimental headquarters building at Fort Huachuca had some empty seats around the table. It was Colonel Pappy Gratton's official job as regimental adjutant to give the report on that.

Pappy was glad he hadn't spent those days up in the western Himalayas of Kashmir. When the Greys of TACBATT and the operating staff had gotten back to Ghazi, they'd looked like death warmed over to him. The altitude or the combat stress had taken their toll. Maybe both. "The body of Lieutenant Harlan P. Saunders will be interred in Arlington in three weeks," Pappy reported. "Chief Master Sergeant Major Henry G. Kester is back on duty, as anyone can plainly see."

Henry was at his usual seat at the table. The blue and white ribbon of his Purple Heart now mounted an additional oak-leaf cluster. "Excuse me, sir, but once Major Gydesen's people patched me up, I was never off duty. But I was forced to sit on my ass on that ridge and do make-work while the rest of you got shot at. But I guess that was the best place for me to carry out my duties. Which are to keep all of you from making too many mistakes."

Only Henry Kester, the top NCO in the Washington Greys, could speak that freely. Not only was he the top man, but he was minus-T-and-counting on his retirement. He'd stretched it as long as he could. Forty-two years was a lifetime, but the Army had been Henry's life. Few people manage to stay in that long, even with the outstanding progress in biotechnology. Henry could afford to be more crusty than usual. He was getting out. Actually, he was being *forced* out because he'd used up all his excuses for re-upping. And the Army had run out of NCO ranks into which to promote him.

"Thank you for correcting me, Sergeant Major," Gratton said easily. Both men were almost the same age. But each had taken a different career track. Pappy was looking forward to getting out himself, but he believed he still had a lot of work to do in the Washington Greys. The Greys needed him. He wasn't about to let them down.

"Walter Reed Army Hospital reports that Major Clinton's injuries to her hot-wired neck have been repaired. I'm sure we're all happy to know she's been cleared for return to non-combat duty. However, she asked for extended medical and accumulated leave," Gratton reported.

Curt wasn't sure about Kitsy. The petite officer's reactions to the Red Scouts in Kashmir had been stronger than those of any other of the ladies of the Greys. Kitsy had sounded like she'd had enough fighting if she had to kill boys in the future. He wanted to talk to Dyani about that. The two women had once been bitter rivals but had become the closest of "big sister" friends.

"Our other wounded were returned to duty in the field, thanks to the outstanding work of Major Gydesen and her bio-tech teams," Gratton went on. "Therefore, we're short only in the officer ranks. We need a new lieutenant to fill Harlan's slot. We have a request in to division, Fort Benning, and DCSPERS. But no action yet. Knowing the lightning speed with which the system works, I am not holding my breath. And as the final item, the Colonel will have to decide who he wants as his Ess-three operations staff officer."

No one mentioned Russell B. Frazier, Lieutenant Colonel, AUS (Ret.). Curt hadn't pressed charges. In fact, he'd recommended promotion upon retirement. One does not dump on an old comrade just because of one indiscretion, in spite of a long-term personality defect. A regiment had to have some super-aggressive people. And Russ had been operating under tremendous stress both psychologically and physically. Curt knew the man had never been happy as a staffer; he was a combat officer. The physical stress of high altitude had pushed him over the edge. And he'd taken the honorable path of resignation. Russ might have been a "Kill-'em-all" type, but he was still an honorable man. He would be welcome anytime at the Club. *Once a Washington Grey, always a Washington*

Grey.

"Have you anyone in mind, Colonel?" Joan Ward asked.

Curt shook his head. "I want to wait until Kitsy reports back," Curt admitted to them. "I want her recommendations on top of those of all of you."

"That's your adjutant's report, Colonel. I'm happy we didn't lose a lot of people in Kashmir. We could have lost the whole tactical battalion."

"No, you're damned good," Curt told them all. "You don't give up. I can't foresee any situation where we could lose the whole regiment. Now we're going to have to do some more pioneering. We've got to learn how to operate so East World can't possibly use any neuroelectronics weapon against us. And that brings me to the next staff officer report. Ess-Two? Intelligence?"

Captain Dyani Motega's report was brief. "No new information about the East World neuroelectronics weapon. McCarthy Proving Ground is still trying to make sense out of what Colonel Pendleton and Doctor Thisha saw there. In the meantime, we're under orders not to use any NE linkage equipment. And we're to maintain careful scrutiny on all the warbots' AI equipment. I believe McCarthy will figure this one out." She paused, then said something that was very much Dyani Motega. "I would like to apologize to everyone because I've already apologized to Doctor Taisha. I didn't believe she could have changed deep down inside. But she did. She proved it. Maybe she also proved there's really something good in everyone, no matter how many demons they carry with them."

"We have no Ess-Three report," Curt observed. "That's okay. We don't have any operations at the moment. We're in a post-operation stand-down R&R mode. And we need it. Major Dearborn, how about Ess-Four, Logistics? Anything to report?"

"Yes, sir! I'm catching slime from higher headquarters. Mostly Quartermaster. I'm not exactly sure how I'm going to cover the loss of about fifty expensive and experimental new anti-infrared camouflage uniforms!" the supply officer remarked. "Why did everyone throw them away? Why didn't they just stuff them in a compartment somewhere and bring them back? Didn't they realize all the paperwork and justifications I'd have to deal with?"

"Expend them in combat," Curt told her. "I'll sign off on it."

"Sir, I tried that," Harriet replied. "I was told that if the uniforms were expended in combat, how come the people who were wearing them weren't?"

Curt thought about that for a moment, then said, "Yeah, I guess maybe they've got us on that one. Let me talk to Battleaxe about it. But it would help if I had a sample so I could show her how bad those damned things smelled."

"Colonel, I brought mine back."

Curt turned to Dyani. "You did? I didn't smell it around quarters!" He'd slipped on that. Everyone knew he and Dyani officially had separate quarters, but that was merely for administrative purposes. The two hadn't left one another's company since the return from Kashmir.

"Sealed in a plastic baggie, sir, of the sort we ladies carry along in the field for attire of many sorts that becomes highly aromatic," Dyani admitted. Harriet nodded. So did Edie Sampson. "May I express an opinion that some of the male side of the roster should start doing the same, please? We enjoy the fragrance of active men, but it often becomes a bit too much."

"Harriet, issue sealable plastic baggies to everyone," Curt snapped, cutting right through to the heart of the matter by issuing an order.

"Yes, sir, but where do I get them? They don't have a QM number!"

"Why, the same place you get yours, of course! And since it's a non-reg purchase, I think we have some discretionary funds around for that purpose. And especially since this is a matter of discretion!"

Harriet grinned. "Yes, sir!"

"Regimental Sergeant Major? Your input, please?"

Henry Kester merely replied, "Colonel, if any problems exist on my turf, you'll never hear about them until they aren't problems anymore. That's *my* job!"

"Technical?" Curt fired at Edie Sampson.

"We're monitoring for anti-NE signals," the chief tech NCO reported. "They come and they go. We've disabled all the NE linkage equipment. I don't want someone to decide it's okay to make a few tests and end up KIA."

"Can we fight without NE warbots?"

"Sir, we just did!"

She was right. A human warrior is less predictable than a warbot except that one can always predict that the human will be unpredictable. This characteristic had allowed the Third Herd to carry out its orders in Kashmir with a minimum of casualties and losses.

Curt turned to his chief of staff. "Joan, you've got the wrap-up slot as usual. Anything you need to add that the others didn't talk about?"

"You're not taking any leave, Colonel?" Joan Ward asked.

Curt shook his head. "Thanks, but I've been clean around the world lately. And up on the roof of the world as well. I'm sticking to Fort Hoochy-Coocha and boring administrative routine for a change."

"But you can't get any rest that way!" Joan objected.

"Leave equates to vacation, which equates to a change of scene or routine," Curt told her. "This is a change for me. I don't have to fight. I don't have to issue orders that could lead to death or injury."

He paused and sighed in resignation and frustration. "Besides, here on base I'm buffered against the news media by the divisional PAO. Outside that gate, I'm an official hero. But God knows why. We busted up, Deosai, but East World has other Deosai-like facilities. And we didn't rescue East World's top neuroelectronics scientists. I don't think Operation Hell Fire was very much of a success at all."

"We did our best," Joan reminded him.

"But we didn't win," Curt muttered.

"Sometimes we can't be the judge of that," Joan pointed out. "But I do understand your reluctance to face the news media and your adoring public."

"If you've been in one ticker-tape parade, you've seen them all," Curt said. "I'll leave that sort of stuff to the generals. As for the adoring news media, they can get all the information they want out of the unclassified operation report. They aren't going to get anything more than that out of me anyway. The classified report can damned well leak out of Fort Fumble. It's Washington's job to be the calibrated leak in the system, not mine. Anyway, the newshounds and newsharpies have no business revealing our threat analysis and suggested counter-moves to East World!"

"And you're not even going to take a few days off in Bisbee or Tucson?" Joan pressed.

"No. Not planned. We'd have to go incognito if we did. Which means we'll do it on the spur of the moment if we decide to."

No one in the room needed to ask why Curt used the plural pronoun. It wasn't the "imperial we."

"So J.I.C., who's Number Two if you bug out?" Joan needed to know the answers to pesky little questions such as that. It was her job to take care of such matters.

"You are," Curt said simply, knowing that it would be only temporary. Joan would never be a regimental commander; she had what it took to be an outstanding chief of staff, however. And Curt's long-term plans for training a successor had now been totally blown away.

Joan Ward didn't bat an eye. "Yes, sir."

"Anything else?" Curt looked around the table. No one said anything. They all looked tired.

Curt glanced up at the wall clock. "Well, eleven hundred hours! Nothing like putting in a full day's work! Meeting is adjourned. Uh, I guess I should say, 'Dismissed!'"

Curt went back to his office, saw that no messages were waiting, noticed that no urgent business awaited his attention, and punched out on the computer terminal.

Dyani met him in the hall. Together, they stepped out of the headquarters building. There was no question that the two of them would walk rather than take the regimental commander's vehicle parked in its reserved slot in the parking lot.

To Curt, it was a pleasure just to walk in the bright sunlight and the warm, dry air with the woman he loved.

The two of them said nothing for several minutes as they walked. Then it was Dyani who spoke. "Let's not go to the Club for lunch. We can have an off-base restaurant deliver to quarters."

"Good idea. Your quarters or mine?"

There was a twinkle in Dyani's eye. "Rumor Control has enough to fritter about. How would it look if the regimental commander went to a subordinate's quarters?"

"None of their damned business!"

"Yes, but it's a nice, warm afternoon. People will talk."

"Let them! It's only a matter of time before we decide to make it official."

"But it isn't time yet."

"I agree. It isn't time yet. With this new East World anti-warbot weapon, the Third Herd is the Number One Sierra Charlie outfit. We'll be called out to handle a lot of brushfires because we can fight without NE warbots," Curt observed.

"Well, no brushfires this afternoon except those we kindle," Dyani said.

"Superwoman!" Curt muttered under his breath.

"Super Colonel!" Dyani shot back softly.

The inevitable happened three hours later. The comm unit in Curt's quarters sounded off at the most inopportune time. This had become a given in their lives.

The screen flashed:

PRIORITY COMMUNICATION
This communication will be classified
TOP SECRET.
Enter scramble Code Alpha Three Tango.
Enter your password.

"Oh, my God! Don't tell me we have to go out and save the Free World again so soon!" Curt growled.

"Put on a shirt," Dyani suggested. "That code is one assigned to The Man Himself. Try to look military."

It was indeed the Commander in Chief.

"Good afternoon, Curt! Sorry I had to disturb you in quarters. I know you've come back from a difficult operation and deserve some R&R. But I need to talk with you."

The President's face and manner were very familiar to Curt. He'd served under the man. "Sir, I'm at your service at all times."

The President looked down at another terminal screen in the Oval Office desk. Behind him, the shadows of late afternoon showed that the Rose Garden was breaking out in the new life of springtime. "I've studied your reports. Both of them. Outstanding work!"

"Thank you, Mister President, but a great deal of the contents are the work of my staff," Curt explained.

"But not the parts in the classified report that deal with the grand strategic, operational, and theater impacts of this new East World development," the Chief Executive told him. "The threat analysis to our doctrines and our foreign policy are extremely insightful. Your security evaluation shows exceptional thinking and a lot of basic understanding of people in those different cultures."

"Thank you, sir. I'd like to say that I don't think I did anything unusual." Curt wasn't trying to be self-deprecating. He was trying to be honest. When one spoke with the President of the United States and one's Commander in Chief, one spoke the truth as one saw it and called the shots as they were. Besides, Curt had reported to this man before when the President was a two-star leading the

17th Iron Fist Division. He felt only a little more of a twinge of awe than he had when he was a second lieutenant and had made a briefing report to General Jacob O. Carlisle. "I just kept my eyes open. I've met people from a lot of different cultures. I've been there myself. I like to think I understand something about the way they think. And about how they look at the world."

"I think you do. And I agree with your assessment that we now face one of the major national security crises of this century. It's going to take the best brains we've got to guide us through it. That's, why I need your help, Curt."

"Whatever you ask, sir, I'll try to deliver one hundred per cent. But I'm no robot scientist, sir. I'm just a bird colonel commanding a combat regiment."

The President shook his head. "No, not if I can talk you into something else. I've got two matters to discuss with you Curt. One is immediate. The other can wait until you get to Washington."

"Sir?"

He looked down at a piece of paper on his desk and said the words that dropped a bombshell on Curt Carson. "Curt, I need you as my National Security Advisor. Will you accept?"

Curt didn't know what to say. Finally, he managed to ask, "Sir, will this take me out of the line of command? I'm a professional warrior, Mister President, not a brainy consultant. And I'm only a bird colonel!"

"It will not take you out of the line of command. This has been done before in history," the President pointed out. "And you won't be a bird colonel. If you agree, I'll sign this commission and Congress will confirm your promotion to major general within days. You've proven your value to the country by what you've accomplished in your career. I believe your experience and intellect are now needed by the nation in a larger role. Again, will you accept my offer?"

Curt turned his head and looked at Dyani. They didn't need to speak to one another. They communicated between themselves better without words.

Curt asked her the question, *Should I?*

Dyani replied, *Do it!*

Not without you!

We are as one!

Curt took a deep breath. It was good to be able to fill his lungs with oxygen again. But he felt giddy at the moment nonetheless. Then he said, "Yes, Mister President. I accept, sir!"

"I'm delighted! Can you come tomorrow? I'll have a hypersonic waiting for you at Libby at oh-eight-hundred tomorrow morning, your time." The President wasn't wasting time about this.

"Yes, sir! What was the other matter, sir?"

"We'll discuss that when you arrive," the President remarked, then added, "Please be sure that Captain Dyani Motega accompanies you. It will be a delight to see her again."

Curt was too stunned to ask why.

Chapter Thirty-Two

"Colonel Curt Carson reporting as ordered, sir!"

"Captain Dyani Motega reporting as ordered, sir!"

The two of them stood at the salute before the Commander in Chief's desk in the Oval Office.

It had been a whirlwind day. They'd left the openness of Arizona behind them and were now in standing at the center of power of the United States and perhaps the world.

Curt had never been in the Oval Office before. But he'd seen it so many times on television and in photographs that it seemed familiar. It was also comfortable because of the spartan surroundings in which the President liked to work.

Military people often carry emotional baggage with them in their movements around the world, but they don't carry much in the way of physical baggage. Thus, the decoration in the Oval Office was quite sparse in comparison with how other Chief Executives had projected their personal likes and lives through its furnishings. Many former Presidents had been naval officers, but there was now no question that the present occupant was a retired general of the Army of the United States.

Between the windows behind the President hung only two documents. One was the President's diploma from the United States Military Academy. The other was the document commissioning the President as a second lieutenant in the Army of the United States.

The huge carved-oak desk made from the timbers of the H.M.S. *Resolute*, a gift from Queen Victoria, was bare except for a green desk blotter and an ancient fountain-pen set. Several documents lay on the blotter.

The President nodded his head at his longtime aide, Kim Blythe, who quietly disappeared through a door. The Chief Executive then arose from behind his historic desk and returned their salutes with the comment, "Welcome to Washington! At ease! And you're General Carson and Colonel Motega now." He picked up two documents from the desk blotter. Instead of handing them across that broad desk, he walked around it and presented them directly to both officers.

"Thank you, sir!" Curt muttered. He couldn't think of anything else to say. Military courtesy and customs are supposed to tell an officer what to say and how to be-have on every occasion. But this one wasn't covered. So Curt was more than a bit surprised and shaken by this.

"And thank you. I certainly didn't expect this, Mister President," Dyani remarked. If she was surprised, she didn't show it. But that was Dyani.

"I know you didn't. And that's why it gives me so much pleasure to present these to both of you," the President told her. He'd aged a bit since they'd seen him last in person on Sakhalin. The job did have its unique stresses. But he appeared in excellent health and he was. Years of rigorous exercise and the sort of iron personal discipline required of a military commander in the twenty-first century ensured both physical and mental fitness.

He indicated the, facing sofas on the fireplace wall of the office. "Please sit down," he told them.

Three pictures relating to the Commander in Chief's background now hung there. Curt couldn't help but notice them. The center one showed the Color Guard at the United States Military Academy. On the right was the painting of General George Washington reviewing his ragged troops in the blowing snow at Valley Forge. On the left was the painting of General Grant receiving a dispatch in the Wilderness campaign. Curt realized these weren't prints or reproductions. They were the original paintings.

"And relax. The official and formal protocol can be reserved for others," the Commander in Chief went on. "It isn't often I get to meet and chat with two former Washington Greys like myself."

"Sir, you used the term former Washington Greys. Does that mean

I've been reassigned?" Dyani asked. This bothered her.

The President sat across from the two of them. "Yes. And please relax. It's not necessary to sit in a plebe brace! I know we're not back at Fort Huachuca and this isn't divisional headquarters. But you look uncomfortable, both of you."

"Sir, if we do, it's because we've suddenly been called to the most important office in the nation," Curt pointed out. "I know one reason we're here. I think we're both uncomfortable because neither of us know the other reason."

"Well, you're not going to be reprimanded, that's for certain!" the President said lightly, crossing his legs and leaning back. "Colonel Motega, you deserve, to know why I asked you to come and why you've been promoted. Since General Carson has accepted the position of National Security Advisor, it was only proper that you have a rank appropriate to your new assignment. The record clearly shows how well the two of you work together. In fact, you're a team. General, you're the planner and strategist. Colonel, you're the scout, the intelligence arm. National security needs both of you at this time."

Curt detected a note of concern in the President's voice. The remark indicated some difficulties with NIA, DIA, or the other alphabet spook agencies. The new general officer wasn't attuned to the political scene yet, and he was concerned he might be stepping in some political slime for asking about it. But Curt had never worried about asking questions of a superior in private. In fact, the President and General Hettrick had trained him that way. "Sir, if I'm going to be your National Security Advisor, I need to know something right at the start. This nation has a large intelligence community. Are we going to have trouble with them?"

The President waved his hand. "No, of course not! I have no reason to distrust anyone in our intelligence community," he explained. "But they do tend to be stealthy. My former security advisor destroyed a lot of trust with the intelligence community. He burned a lot of bridges. These will be desperately needed in the years to come. General Carson, Colonel Motega will be your scout as she's been in the past. General Murray thinks it's a good idea. So does

General Bellamack. In fact, my decision to assign you two to these positions has helped rebuild some of those burned bridges."

He noticed Dyani's impassive face. He couldn't tell if she liked what was happening. He didn't know that this was Dyani's standard, noncommittal expression. It was that of a scout who wants to discover as much as possible while revealing as little as possible.

"Don't you feel comfortable with this assignment, Colonel?"

"Sir, I follow orders. I go where I'm told to go. What I see and hear, I report truthfully," Dyani said simply.

"I know," the President remarked. "So be truthful with me."

Dyani smiled. "In this situation, sir, I gladly accept the assignment!"

"Outstanding! Please report for duty with the general as soon as you can arrange your affairs at Fort Huachuca."

"Sir, who will command the Washington Greys?" Curt wanted to know.

"You have a temporary regimental commander. She'll do well until we have the opportunity to talk about this with General Bellamack and General Hettrick."

Motioning for them to remain seated, the President got up, retrieved another folder from his desk, and returned. "Now for the second matter. You had a very illustrious ancestor, General Carson."

"Yes, sir. But we're separated by two hundred years."

"A grave injustice was done him," the President went on, looking at the papers in the folder. "When I learned of it many years ago, I vowed I'd do something about it someday when and if I had the power. Well, I have it now. And I've seen to the correction. How much do you know about your ancestor, General?"

Curt had tried to find out when he'd had the time available to do it. But the historic record was sparse. Before the days of computers and data bases, records tended to be neglected. Or people didn't keep them. "Sir, I read *Trailblazer*, his autobiography."

"Then you know that Christopher 'Kit' Carson was commissioned as a Lieutenant of Rifles by President James K. Polk."

"Yes, sir. But in those days the Senate had to confirm all commissions. For some reason they didn't confirm Kit Carson's, and he never did anything about it," Curt said.

"And the reason they didn't confirm the commission is reprehensible to us today," the Commander in Chief went on. "Politics was involved, of course. It took a bit of digging to discover that Kit Carson had an Indian wife then."

Dyani remained impassive, but she said in a quiet voice, "Yes, and she was Crow."

"I've reissued that commission, General," the President went on, "And yesterday the Senate passed a resolution of apology and confirmation of the reissued commission. Occasionally, we do something right. Sometimes it takes more time than necessary." He handed the folder of papers to Curt. "It gives me great pleasure to present this to his equally illustrious descendant."

One document inside was just that: a standard officer's commission. But it was subtly different. It was made out for Christopher Carson, back-dated to 7 June 1847, and personally signed by the current President.

Curt was almost totally overwhelmed by what had happened in the past few minutes. All his years of combat and command hadn't prepared him for this. He'd never tried to capitalize on his ancestor, and he'd never enjoyed the role of a combat hero. He'd had his job to do in a profession he'd selected because something inside him told him it was what he should do. He'd never questioned that voice deep down inside.

But this was a cusp in his life. No matter what had happened before, what lay ahead would be totally new and different.

He suddenly realized that his combat days were over.

So were Dyani's.

Curt looked at Dyani. "Well, is it time, Deer Arrow?"

"It's time, Kida. But ask me anyway."

Curt did.

"Yes," was Dyani's simple answer. "But it's unnecessary."

"Huh? Why?"

She paused before she answered. "We've been married by Crow tradition for years."

"What's this? What do you mean?" Curt was getting more confused by the moment. Things were happening too fast.

"When a brave and a maid wish to marry, they simply go off by themselves. When they come back, they announce it. And it's done," Dyani explained quietly, but she was radiant as she did so. She too knew that their lives had changed. Then she admitted without the slightest trace of contrition because Dyani had never carried guilt, "Perhaps I should have answered you completely once when you asked me about my nickname for you. But warriors who regularly face the realities of war are often reluctant to do the same when it comes to love. 'Kida' means more than 'manly' or 'protective.' It also means 'husband.'"

The President cleared his throat. He was beaming broadly. He knew these two people were in the right place at the right time to influence the future of America and the world. And he also saw they were facing their own future with the sort of honesty and integrity he wanted in the people around him. "I expected this might be a somewhat historic occasion," the President remarked. "But I didn't expect you'd be the first to propose to one another in the Oval Office. Let me take this a step further. Can I offer you the White House for the ceremony?"

"No, sir," Curt said staunchly. That scared the hell out of him. It would turn the ceremony into a media event. Both of them wanted it in a place that had great meaning and was full of great tradition for two warriors. "Thanks for the offer. But would you help me arrange for the Chapel at West Point, please?"

Appendix One
Order of Battle
Warbots #12

17th "Iron Fist" Robot Infantry Division, Major General Belinda J. Hettrick, commanding

Colonel Joanne Wilkinson, COS, 17th Iron Fist Division

Colonel James B. Ricketts, G-1, 17th Iron Fist Division

Lieutenant Colonel Eleanor S. Aarts, G-2, 17th Iron Fist Division

Lieutenant Colonel Hensley Atkinson, G-3, 17th Iron Fist Division

Lieutenant Colonel Adrian D. Kleperas, G-4, 17th Iron Fist Division

27th Robot Infantry (Special Combat) Regiment, "The Wolfhounds," Colonel Frederick H. Salley, commanding

Lieutenant Colonel Martin C. Kelly, operations officer (S-3)

7th Robot Infantry (Special Combat) Regiment, "The Cottonbalers," Colonel Maxine Frances Cashier, commanding

3rd Robot Infantry (Special Combat) Regiment, the "Washington Greys," Colonel Curt C. Carson, commanding

Headquarters Company (HEADCO) ("Carson's Companions")

Lieutenant Colonel Joan G. Ward, chief of staff

Lieutenant Colonel Patrick Gillis Gratton, regimental adjutant (S-1)

Major Russell B. Frazier, operations (S-3)

Captain Nelson A. Crile, regimental chaplain

Chief Master Sergeant Major Henry G. Kester, regimental sergeant major

Sergeant Major Edwina A. Sampson, regimental technical sergeant

Tactical Battalion (TACBATT) ("Clinton's Cougars")

Major Kathleen B. Clinton

Battalion Sergeant Major Nicholas P. Gerard

Reconnaissance Company (RECONCO) ("Motega's Mustangs")

Captain Dyani Motega (S-2)

First Sergeant Tracy C. Dillon

Bio-tech Sergeant Allan J. Williams, P.N.

Scouting Platoon (SCOUT) ("Saunders' Scouts")

1st Lieutenant Harlan P. Saunders

Platoon Sergeant Sidney Albert Johnson Sergeant Zebulon P. Long

Sergeant Clara P. Lewis

Birdbot Platoon (BIRD) ("Brown's Black Hawks")

Captain Dale B. Brown

Platoon Sergeant Emma Crawford Sergeant William J. Hull

Sergeant Jacob F. Kent

Sergeant Christine Burgess

Sergeant Jennifer M. Volker

Assault Company A (ASSAULTCO Alpha) ("Pagan's Pumas")

Captain Lewis C. Pagan

Master Sergeant First Class Carol J. Head

Bio-tech Sergeant Virginia Bowles, P.N.

First Platoon: ("Stone's Stingers")

2nd Lieutenant Willard G. Stone

Platoon Sergeant Charles P. Koslowski

Sergeant Paul T. Tullis

Sergeant Christa Jenkens

Second Platoon: ("Power's Panthers")

1st Lieutenant Dan G. Power

Platoon Sergeant Betty Jo Trumble

Sergeant Dennis W. Dent

Sergeant Lloya Ann Monte

Assault Company B (ASSAULTCO Bravo) ("Hassan's Assassins")

Captain Hassan Ben Mahmud

Master Sergeant Robert Lee Garrison

Bio-tech Sergeant Maria M. Metford, P.N.

First Platoon: ("Steve's Strikemasters")

2nd Lieutenant Steven M. Zugg

Platoon Sergeant Isadore Beau Greenwald

Sergeant Maria Lunalillo

Sergeant Joseph James Rose

Second Platoon: ("Mikawa's Marauders")

1st Lieutenant Matsu Mikawa

Platoon Sergeant James P. Elliott

Sergeant A. W. Guilford

Sergeant Anita Svensen

Gunnery Company (GUNCO) ("Hall's Hellcats")

Captain Lawrence W. Hall

First Sergeant Forest L. Barnes

Bio-tech Sergeant Shelley C. Hale, P.N.

First Platoon: ("Taire's Terrors")

1st Lieutenant Jerome "Jay" Taire

Platoon Sergeant Andrea Carrington

Sergeant Howard J. Coon

Sergeant Marjorie Stanford

Second Platoon: ("Kyger's Killers")

1st Lieutenant Theodore "Tiger" Kyger

Platoon Sergeant Victor Joulinan

Sergeant Elisa Monahan

Sergeant Honoria Jean Wilkins

Air Battalion (AIRBATT) ("Worsham's Warhawks")

Lieutenant Colonel Calvin J. Worsham

Battalion Sergeant Major John Adam

Tactical Air Support Company (TACAIRCO) ("Hands' Harriers")

Major Paul Hands

1st Sergeant Clancy Thomas

1st Lieutenant Gabe Neatherly

1st Lieutenant Bruce Mark

1st Lieutenant Stacy Honey

1st Lieutenant Jay Kennedy

1st Lieutenant Richard Cooke

Flight Sergeant Zeke Braswell

Flight Sergeant Larry Myers

Flight Sergeant Adam Nieswader

Flight Sergeant Grant Brown

Flight Sergeant Sharon Spence

Airlift Company (AIRLIFTCO) ("Timm's Tigers")

Major Timothea Timm

First Sergeant Carl Bagwell

1st Lieutenant Ned Phillips

1st Lieutenant Mike Hart

1st Lieutenant Dorothy Peterson

1st Lieutenant Nancy Roberts

1st Lieutenant Larry Rosenberg

1st Lieutenant Jess S. Switzer

Flight Sergeant Kevin Hubbard

Flight Sergeant Jeffrey O'Connell

Flight Sergeant Barry Morris

Flight Sergeant Ann Shepherd

Flight Sergeant Robert Pritchard

Flight Sergeant Harley Earll

Flight Sergeant Sergio Tomasio

Flight Sergeant Joseph Kalakava

Service Battalion (SERVBATT)

Lieutenant Colonel Wade W. Hampton

Battalion Sergeant Major Joan J. Stark Vehicle Technical Company (VETECO)

Major Frederick W. Benteen

First Sergeant Raymond G. Wolf

Technical Sergeant Kenneth M. Hawkins

Technical Sergeant Charles B. Slocum

Warbot Technical Company (BOTECO)

Major Elwood S. Otis

First Sergeant Bailey Ann Miles

Technical Sergeant Gerald W. Mora

Technical Sergeant Loretta A. Carruthers

Technical Sergeant Charles Lemming

Air Maintenance Company (AIRMAINCO)

Major Ron Knight

First Sergeant Rebecca Campbell

Technical Sergeant Joel Pruitt

Technical Sergeant Richard N. Germain

Technical Sergeant Douglas Bell

Technical Sergeant Pam Gordon

Technical Sergeant Clete McCoy

Technical Sergeant Carol Jensen

Logistics Company (LOGCO)

Major Harriet F. Dearborn (S-4)

Chief Supply Sergeant Manuel P. Sanchez

Supply Sergeant Marriette W. Ireland

Supply Sergeant Jamie G. Casner

Supply Sergeant Leroy P. Betts

Bio-tech Company (BIOTECO)

Major Ruth Gydesen, M.D.

Captain Denise G. Logan, M.D.

Captain Thomas E. Alvin, M.D.

Captain Larry C. McHenry, M.D.

Captain Helen Devlin, R.N.

1st Lieutenant Clifford B. Braxton, R.N.

1st Lieutenant Laurie S. Cornell, R.N.

1st Lieutenant Ely Brandon, R.N.

1st Lieutenant William O. Molde, R.N.

Bio-tech Sergeant Marcela V. Jolton, P.N.

Bio-tech Sergeant Nellie A. Miles, P.N.

Bio-tech Sergeant George O. Howard, P.N.

Bio-tech Sergeant Wallace W. Izard, P.N.

OTHERS

The Hon. Jacob O. Carlisle, the President of the United States of America.

The Hon. Walter Van Tilberg Hopkins, Vice President, United States of America.

The Hon. Frances B. Kellogg, Secretary of State.

General Albert W. Murray, USAF (Ret.), Director, National Intelligence Agency.

General Jeffrey G. Pickens, AUS (Ret.), National Security Advisor.

The Hon. David P. Henshaw, Secretary of Defense.

General Charles D. Palmer, AUS, Chairman, Joint Chief's of Staff.

General William O. Bellamack, JCS, COS, AUS.

Admiral Thomas A. Weaver, JCS, CNO, U.S. Navy.

General Roger Wilcox, JCS, COS USAF.

Lieutenant General Oliver G. Hayward, JCS, Commandant USMC.

Colonel Owen Pendleton, Chief of Warbotics Development, McCarthy Proving Ground, Nevada.

Dr. Willa Lovell, Director of Advanced Warbotics, McCarthy Proving Ground, Nevada.

Dr. Rosha Taisha, Chief Neuroelectronic Scientist, Warbotics Development Branch, McCarthy Proving Ground, Nevada.

Colonel Iskander Ghulan Khan, commanding officer, 4th Khyber Rifles, Army of the Islamic Republic of Pakistan.

Dr. Wen Ling Dongzhu, Director, People's Institute of Intelligent Machinery Development, Beijing, People's Republic of China; Chief Scientist, Deosai Research Establishment.

Dr. Qian Xuesen, research scientist, People's Institute of Intelligent Machinery Development, Beijing, People's Republic of China; Assistant, Deosai Research Establishment.

Appendix Two
Trailblazing

Curtis Christopher Carson is directly descended from Christopher "Kit" Carson (1809-1868) and is the eighth generation of his family to serve with honor and distinction in the United States Army.

From 1882 until 1967, the genealogy was lost to the family. Kit Carson's descendants were unaware of their relationship to the "Boone of the West" until a search was made through the genealogical archives of the Church of Jesus Christ of Latter-day Saints (the "Mormon Church") in Salt Lake City.

Curt Carson's illustrious ancestor was married in February 1843 to Josepha Jaramillo of Taos, New Mexico. She was the daughter of Don Francisco Jaramillo, who was prominent in Southwestern history in the nineteenth century. The branch of the Carson family line through this marriage is still lost to history.

However, it was little known - although revealed by Kit Carson himself in his autobiography, *Trailblazer* - that the frontiersman had two Indian wives who bore children by him.

One was a Cheyenne woman. Little is known about the children of this union.

The other wife was thought to be Sioux, until research disclosed she had been taken as war booty by the Sioux from the Crow tribe. Genealogical research revealed that this Crow maid was a daughter of the Crow chief White Man Runs Him, the father of Straight Arrow, who was in turn the founder of the Motega family. Subsequent generations of the Motega family served in the United States Army with valor, honor, and distinction.

The present Carson family of Curtis Christopher Carson is descended from the union of Kit Carson and his Crow/Sioux Indian wife. The mixed ancestry of the family was kept private for several generations because of social intolerances.

The marriage of Curtis Christopher and Dyani Motega thus unified the two family lines of American warriors and scouts separated by two hundred years.

Appendix Three
Glossary of Robotic Infantry Terms and Slang

ACV-Airportable Command Vehicle M660.

Aerodyne: A saucer-shaped flying machine that obtains its lift from the exhaust of one or more turbine fanjet engines blowing outward over the curved upper surface of the craft from an annular segmented slot near the center of the up-per surface. The aerodyne was invented by Dr. Henri M. Coanda after World War II but was not perfected until decades later because of the predominance of the rotary-winged helicopter.

ALO: Active Level of Operation readiness.

AOG: Aircraft on the ground.

AP: Anti-personnel.

APV: Armored Personnel Vehicle.

Artificial Intelligence or *AI:* Very fast computer modules with large memories which can simulate some functions of human thought and decision-making processes by bringing together many apparently disconnected pieces of data, making simple evaluations of the priority of each, and making simple decisions concerning what to do, how to do it, when to do it, and what to report to the human being in control.

ASAP: As soon as possible.

AT: Anti-tank.

Beanie: A West Point term for a plebe or first-year man.

Beanette: A female beanie.

Birdbot: The M20 Aeroreconnaissance Neuroelectronic Bird Warbot used for aerial recce. Comes in shapes and sizes to resemble indigenous birds.

Bio-tech: A biological technologist once known in the twentieth century Army as a "medic."

Black Maria: The M44A Assault Shotgun, the Sierra Charlie's 18.52-millimeter friend in close quarter combat.

Blue U: The United States Aerospace Force Academy.

Bohemian Brigade: War correspondents or a news media television crew.

Bot: Generalized generic slang term for "robot" which takes many forms, as warbot, reconbot, etc. See "Robot" below.

Bot flush: Since robots have no natural excrement, this term is a reference to what comes out of a highly mechanical warbot when its lubricants are changed during routine maintenance. Used by soldiers as a slang term referring to anything of a detestable nature.

Cee-Pee or *CP:* Slang for "Command Post."

CG: Commanding general.

Check minus-x: Look behind you. In terms of coordinates, plus-x is ahead, minus-x is behind, plus-y is to the right, minus-y is left, plus-z is up, and minus-z is down.

CINC: Commander In Chief.

Chippie: The UCA-21C Chippewa tactical airlift aerodyne.

CIC: Combat Information Center. May be different from a command post.

CJSC: The Chairman of the Joint Chiefs of Staff.

Class 6 supplies: Alcoholic beverages of high ethanol content procured through non-regulation channels; officially, only five classes of supplies exist.

CNO: The Chief of Naval Operations.

CO: The commanding officer.

Column of ducks: A convoy proceeding through terrain where they are likely to draw fire.

CRAF: Civil Reserve Air Fleet.

Creamed: Greased, beaten, conquered, overwhelmed.

CTAF: Common Traffic Advisory Frequency.

CYA: Cover Your Ass. In polite company, "Cover Your Anatomy."

DCSOPS: The Army's Deputy Chief of Staff for Operations.

DCSPERS: The Army's Deputy Chief of Staff for Personnel.

D-M: Davis-Monthan Aerospace Force Base, Tucson, Arizona.

Downlink: A remote command or data channel from a warbot to a soldier.

ECM: Electronic Counter Measures.

FAM: The French arms maker, Fusil Automatique Mitrailleur.

FCC: The Federal Communications Commission.

FEBA: Forward Edge of the Battle Area.

FIDO: Acronym for "Fuck it; drive on!" Overcome your obstacle or problem and get on with the operation.

FIG: Foreign Internal Guardian mission, the sort of assignment Army units draw to protect American interests in selected locations around the world. Great for RI units but not within the intended mission profiles of Sierra Charlie regiments.

Fort Fumble: Any headquarters but especially the Pentagon when not otherwise specified.

Furball: A complex, confused fight, battle, or operation.

G-1, G-2, G-3, G-4: Elements of a general's staff; G-1 = Personnel; G-2 = Intelligence services; G-3 = Operations; G-4 = Logistics and supplies. In a regiment, these are known as S-1, S-2, S-3, and S-4 because they aren't part of a general officer's staff.

GA: "Go ahead!"

General Ducrot: Any incompetent, lazy, fucked-up, incompetent officer who doesn't know or won't admit those short-comings. May have other commissioned officer rank to more closely describe the individual.

Go physical: To lapse into idiot mode, to operate in a combat or recon environment without neuroelectronic warbots; what the Special Combat units do all the time. See "Idiot mode" below.

Golden BB: A small caliber bullet that hits and thus creates large problems.

Greased: Beaten, conquered, overwhelmed, creamed.

Harpy: The AD-40C tactical air assault aerodyne which the Aerospace Force originally developed in the A version; the Navy flies the B version. The Office In Charge Of Stupid Names tried to get everyone to call it the "Thunder Devil" but the Harpy name stuck with the drivers and troops. The compound term "newsharpy" is also used to refer to a hyperthyroid, ego-blasted, over-achieving female news personality or reporter.

Headquarters happy: Any denizen of headquarters, regimental or higher.

Humper: Any device whose proper name a soldier can't recall at the moment.

ID or *i-d:* Identification.

Idiot mode: Operating in the combat environment without neuroelectronic warbots, especially operating without the benefit of computers and artificial intelligence to relieve battle load. What the warbot brainies think the Sierra Charlies do all the time. See "*Go physical*" above.

IG: The inspector general.

Intelligence: Generally considered to exist in four categories: animal, human, machine, and military.

Intelligence amplifier or *IA:* A very fast computer with a very large memory which, when linked to a human nervous system by non-intrusive neuroelectronic pickups and electrodes, serves as a very fast extension of the human brain allowing the brain to function faster, recall more data, store more data, and thus "amplify" a human being's "intelligence." (Does not imply that the Army knows what "human intelligence" really is.)

JCS: Joint Chief of Staff.

Jeep: Word coined from the initials "GP" standing for "General Purpose." Once applied to an Army quarter-ton vehicle but subsequently used to refer to the Mark 33A2 General Purpose Warbot.

J.I.C.: Just In Case.

KE: Kinetic energy as applied to KE kill weapons.

KIA: "Killed in action." A warbot brainy term used to describe the situation where a warbot soldier's neuroelectronic data and sensory inputs from one or more warbots is suddenly cut off, leaving the human being in a state of mental limbo. A very debilitating and mentally disturbing situation. (Different from being physically killed in action, a situation with which only Sierra Charlies find themselves threatened.)

LAMVA: The M473 Light Artillery Maneuvering Vehicle, Airportable, a robotic armored vehicle mounting a 75-millimeter Saucy Cans gun used for light artillery support of a Sierra Charlie regiment.

Linkage: The remote connection or link between a human being and one or more neuroelectronically controlled warbots. This link channel may be by means of wires, radio, laser, or optics. The actual technology of linkage is highly classified. The robot/computer sends its data directly to the human soldier's nervous system through small nonintrusive electrodes positioned on the soldier's skin. This data is coded in such a way that the soldier perceives the signals as sight, sound, feeling, or position of the robot's parts. The robot/computer also picks up commands from the soldier's nervous system that are merely "thought" by the soldier, translates them into commands a robot can understand, and monitors the robot's accomplishment of the commanded action.

Log bird: A logistics or supply aircraft.

Mary Ann: The M60A Airborne Mobile Assault Warbot which mounts a single M300 25-millimeter automatic cannon with variable fire-rate. Accompanies Sierra Charlie troops in the field and provides fire support.

Mad minute: The first intense, chaotic, wild, frenzied period of a fire fight when it seems every gun in the world is being shot at you.

Mike-mike: Soldier's shorthand for "millimeter."

MRE: Officially, Meal Ready to Eat; Soldiers claim it means "Meal Rarely Edible."

NCO: Non-commissioned officer.

NE: Neuroelectronic (see same below).

Neuroelectronics or *NE:* The synthesis of electronics and computer technologies that permit a computer to detect and recognize signals from the human nervous system by means of nonintrusive skin-mounted sensors as well as to stimulate the human nervous system with computer-generated electronic signals through similar skin-mounted electrodes for the purpose of creating sensory signals in the human mind. See *"Linkage"* above.

NIA: National Intelligence Agency, supposedly the reorganized Central Intelligence Agency except that the NIA doesn't officially exist. Ask anyone.

Novia: The 7.62-millimeter M33A3 "Ranger" Assault Rifle designed in Mexico as the M3 Novia. The Sierra Charlies still call it the Novia or "sweetheart."

NSC: The National Security Council.

OCV: Operational Command Vehicle, the command version of the M660 ACV.

Orgasmic!: A slang term that grew out of the observation, "Outstanding!" It means the same thing. Usually but not always.

Oscar briefing: An orders briefing.

Papa briefing: A planning briefing.

POSSOH: "Person of Opposite Sex Sharing Off-duty Hours"

POW: Prisoner of war.

PTV: Personal Transport Vehicle or "Trike," a three-wheeled unarmored vehicle similar to an old sidecar motorcycle capable of carrying two Sierra Charlies or one Sierra Charlie and a Jeep.

Pucker factor: The detrimental effect on the human body that results from being in an extremely hazardous situation such as being shot at.

RI: The Robot Infantry combat branch of the United States Army.

Robot: From the Czech word robota meaning work, especially drudgery. A device with humanlike actions directed either by a computer or by a human being through a computer and a two-way command-sensor circuit. See *"Linkage"* and *"Neuroelectronics"* above.

Robot Infantry or RI: A combat branch of the United States Army which grew from the regular infantry with the introduction of robots and linkage to warfare. Replaced the regular infantry in the early twenty-first century.

RPV: Remotely Piloted Vehicle, an early form of birdbot.

RTV: Robot Transport Vehicle, now the M662 Airport-able Robot Transport Vehicle (ARTV) but still called an RTV by Sierra Charlies.

Rule Ten: Slang reference to Army Regulation 601-10 which prohibits physical contact between male and female personnel when on duty except for that required in the conduct of official business.

Rules of Engagement or ROE: Official restrictions on the freedom of action of a commander or soldier in his confrontation with an opponent that act to increase the probability that said commander or soldier will lose the combat, all other things being equal.

SADARM: Search and destroy armor, a type of warhead. Saucy Cans: An American Army corruption of the French designation for the 75-millimeter "soixantequintze" weapon mounted on the LAMVA.

SC: Sierra Charlie. (see below).

Scroom!: Abbreviation for "Screw 'em!"

SECDEF: The Secretary of Defense.

Sheep screw: A disorganized, embarrassing, graceless chaotic fuck-up.

Sierra Charlie: Phonetic alphabet derivative of the initials "SC" meaning "Special Combat." Soldiers trained to engage in personal field combat supported and accompanied by artificially intelligent warbots that are voice-commanded rather than run by linkage. The ultimate weapon of World War IV.

Sierra Hotel: What warbot brainies say when they can't say, "Shit hot!"

Simulator or *sim:* A device that can simulate the sensations perceived by a human being and the results of the human's responses. A simple toy computer or video game simulating the flight of an aircraft or the driving of a race car is an example of a primitive simulator.

Sit-guess: Slang for "estimate of the situation," an educated guess about your predicament.

Sit-rep: Short for "situation report" to notify your superior officer about the sheep screw you're in at the moment.

Smart Fart: The M100A (FG/IM-190) Anti-tank/Anti-aircraft tube-launched rocket capable of being launched off the shoulder of a Sierra Charlie. So-called because of its self-guided "smart" warhead and the sound it makes when fired.

Snake pit: Slang for the highly computerized briefing center located in most caserns and other Army posts.

Snivel: To complain about the injustice being done you.

Spasm mode: Slang for killed in action (KIA).

Spook: Slang term for either a spy or a military intelligence specialist. Also used as a verb relating to reconnaissance.

Staff stooge: Derogatory term referring to a staff officer. Also "staff weenie."

TAB-V: Theater Air Base Vulnerability shelter.

TACAMO!: "Take Charge And Move Out!"

Tacomm: A portable frequency-hopping communications transceiver system once used by rear-echelon warbot brainy troops and now generally used in very advanced and rugged versions by the Sierra Charlies.

Tango Sierra: Tough shit.

Tech-weenie: The derogatory term applied by combat soldiers to the scientists, engineers, and technicians who complicate life by insisting that the soldier have gadgetry that is the newest, fastest, most powerful, most accurate, and usually the most unreliable products of their fertile techie imaginations.

Third Herd, the: The 3rd Robot Infantry Regiment (Special Combat), the Washington Greys (but you'd better be a Grey to use that term).

Tiger error: What happens when an eager soldier tries too hard.

TO&E: Table of Organization and Equipment.

TRACON: Terminal Radar Control facility at an airport.

Umpteen hundred: Some time in the distant, undetermined future.

Up link: The remote command link or channel from the warbot brainy to the warbot.

VLF: Very Low Frequency radio wavelength.

Warbot: Abbreviation for "war robot," a mechanical device that is operated by or commanded by a soldier to fight in the field.

Warbot brainy: The human soldier who operates warbots through linkage, implying that the soldier is basically the brains of the warbot. Sierra Charlies remind everyone that they are definitely not warbot brainies whom they consider to be grown-up children operating destructive video games.

ZI: Zone of the Interior, the continental United States.